DIM SUM, DEAD SOME

A Josie Tucker Mystery

EM KAPLAN

Cover design by the author

BLACK
CROW
BOOKS

For Mom

CONTENTS

SPECIAL THANKS TO

Amy Bush

Katherine Cruz

Esther Kaplan

JD Kaplan

Elizabeth Snively

Lee Turner

and

Melissa Manes, who is a wonderful beta reader.

You can contact her at scriptionis@gmail.com.

i

PART 1: THE RECIPE

Across the crowded pages of a glossy magazine, you spot a recipe. Coyly, it glances back at you from underneath its parsley lashes….What is a recipe other than a proposition? It's a business plan, a pick-up line, a marriage proposal. It's a sales pitch that says, "Check me out, babe. Here is what you get if you take me home with you, if you *voulez-vous coucher avec moi.*"

If a recipe is heavy with cream and butter and Kobe beef, you may expect 4000 thread-count sheets. If a recipe flaunts a trendy ingredient like *moghrabieh* or quinoa, it says with a charming smile and bobbing eyebrows, "I'm new in town, kitten. Give me a test drive." If you're seduced by mouth-watering, high-resolution photos, but your results require a hazmat team and antibiotics, then you, my friend, have been duped. More than one of us has taken the walk of shame after a bad selection off the evening's menu.

Josie Tucker, *Will Blog for Food*

CHAPTER 1

"I need you to talk me down from a ledge." Holding her cell phone to her ear, Josie stood on the sidewalk on Beach Street with her back to the San Francisco wharf. Above her, the bright Ghirardelli lights winked at her in the dusky twilight, seducing her. The sign beckoned to her like a lover, a lactose lothario, a casein casanova.

She shivered even though the temperature was nearly twenty degrees warmer than at home in Boston. Here, the sun was just now setting, night cloaking the bay in darkness, the lights shining on the water. She could hear the occasional squawk from an ocean bird, the low bellow of a boat horn on the bay. The air smelled like ocean and fish, and Italian food. She wasn't far from North Beach, and the wind was blowing the aroma of garlic straight to her nose. She sniffed again. Maybe someone nearby was simmering clams in white wine—San Francisco was an olfactory paradise for a food critic. Especially one who couldn't eat.

Josie's hooded sweater and denim jacket were doing a good job of keeping out the wind and helping her to blend in with the smattering of tourists trying to be hipsters with their hands in the holes of their sweaters, just like the song. She was seeing a whole lot of funky, knitted caps and ferocious "statement" beards walking around the wharf this evening as she stood blinking at the Ghirardelli sign. She shivered again, not from the cold, but from the fact that she was about to do something very, very bad to her stomach.

On the other end of her phone, her boyfriend Drew said, "Are you anywhere near the Golden Gate Bridge?" His boyfriend status was a recent development for them. They had been long-time friends, college buddies who had recently discovered that they were better off dating.

Much, much better off, she thought, her insides doing an unnatural happy wiggle from top to toe. Grouchiness was her natural state, but Josie and Drew were two flavors that perfectly complemented each other. Peaches and cream. Peanut butter and lemon grass. Bacon and beetroot. Bacon and, well, anything.

"Noooo," she said, not able to keep the rise out of her voice, which made it sound like a question. She noted with amusement that he didn't sound too worried. He didn't believe for a second that she would intentionally harm herself. Should she be worried that he wasn't worried? Maybe it was better not to overthink that one.

"You're not by the Bay Bridge?" he continued, "Or any other body of water or tall building—nothing you could fall off? Coit Tower? You're not cutting in line at the deli counter at Whole Foods? Nowhere you could get hurt?" Although he was joking, he knew about her propensity for getting into bad situations, ones in which she ended up with fractured bones.

She let out a long breath, which lifted the hair on her forehead. "I'm standing in front of Ghirardelli Square," she said with false bravado. The part about getting hurt was debatable if she wanted to include further injury to her testy gut. She was struggling to sort out her recent food intolerance issues. Not a good thing for a food critic. Not at all.

The phone rattled as Drew switched ears. She could suddenly hear him better, as if he'd left the noisy cafeteria of Brigham and Women's Hospital in Boston where he was doing doctor's rounds and had entered an office or a janitorial closet or something. "Don't do it, Josie," he said, crystal-clear and serious. He was inordinately concerned about the well-being of her stomach. Which was understandable, considering he was her physician as well as her *boyfriend;* she could barely even think the word without smiling like a dope.

She elaborated, throwing in a little extra drama to push her point. "Ghirardelli is an internationally famous ice cream shop and chocolatier. They're known world-wide. As in, *around the entire globe.* There's probably someone far away, in some place like Bora Bora, who is thinking about Ghirardelli chocolate right this very minute," she said. "I'm standing here, within touching distance. Yesterday, I was in Boston,

4

three thousand miles away from this temptation and now here I am. Standing in front of it. I mean, right in front of it." She deliberately blinked a couple of times to make the sign wink at her in a flirtatious manner.

"Okay, listen to me, Josie," Drew said, his deep voice sounding a little hassled, all scratchy and irritable, which made her insides warm up. She wished she could touch him, especially that soft patch of skin right below his ear that... He interrupted her thoughts, admonishing her. "Don't think of The Now, think of The Later. If you eat that stuff, you're going to be in a world of pain." His unspoken meaning was that he wouldn't be nearby to help her with the aftermath as he had been before on occasion.

He had a fair point. They were on opposite sides of the country this week. She needed to behave responsibly. Not only would she be alone, moaning on the bathroom floor in the middle of the night with him thousands of miles away, but her entire career as a food critic relied on her stomach's well-being. She needed to let it heal, to baby it, to treat it right. Who knew how lenient Julieanne, her boss at the Daily News, would be if she ever discovered the current extent of Josie's diet limitations. Josie could no longer eat dairy. Spicy foods and gluten were on the chopping block next if her gastric problems didn't clear up soon. She could fool her editor only so long without feeling like the world's biggest phony, the most massive liar on the planet, especially after Julieanne had agreed to convert her column to blog format and to keep her on the payroll even though print subscriptions were dwindling more and more each day. True, the ad sales from Josie's blog alone were keeping their department afloat, but Josie didn't like being dishonest. At least about the little things.

Telling Julieanne she'd felt great hadn't been a lie the last time Josie had spoken with her. Right after the adventure in Arizona that led to Josie's broken ribs and concussion, her stomach had been as good as new. Back home in Boston, she'd been able to eat whatever she'd wanted. Creamy New England clam chowder. Cheese-filled blintzes. Pizzeria Uno and Due—she would have eaten Tre, too, if that existed. Take that, mysterious malaise. *Sayonara*, stomach upset. *Adios*, anxiety.

But now in March, a few months later—so recent from her last tussle with bad guys that she was still afraid to sneeze for fear of hurting her ribs—her stomach was acting up again. Yes, her digestion was a cruel, capricious mistress.

"Talk to me, Josie, what are you thinking?" Drew demanded, still on the line while she'd been wool-gathering. She liked this bossy side of him; it gave her something to rebel against. Plus…it was kind of hot.

"You're absolutely right," she told him. "I'll fight it. I'll be in control. I'll be responsible."

"That's right, babe," he said. "Stay strong. You don't need it. Resist that triple chocolate ice cream soda."

She fell silent, drool suddenly pooling in her mouth.

"I shouldn't have mentioned that last part," he said, sighing. She could almost see him running a hand through his dark, thick hair. Torturing his scalp was his go-to frustration move, and she saw it often.

"I'll call you later," she said, and touched the red button on her phone's screen, still hearing his parting groan of frustration. She stared at the tiny photo of Drew's handsome face on her phone's screen. She wanted to touch the thumbnail, as if she were petting him, but putting her fingertip on it would call him back. So she refrained.

Then with a certain, self-aware fatalism, she stepped toward the bright, sparkly Ghirardelli lights.

⌘

A week earlier, Josie had been sitting on the ratty couch in her apartment in Boston not too far from the Green Monster at Fenway, proofreading her latest blog entry aloud to her dog Bert, when her cell phone vibrated. It took her several seconds to identify the buzzing sound—her cell phone was a recent acquisition due to the trouble she'd had out in Arizona—and then it took another couple of seconds to figure out which button to press to answer the call. There it was. The green one. *Duh.* Tech expert, she could never claim to be.

Her caller ID failed her. The phone screen said only "Private

Caller," but she recognized Greta Williams's steely voice immediately by its cool greeting, which was just one word: "Josie."

Josie patted Bert's broad, bony head—part Labrador, part army tank—and countered with, "I'm a little disturbed by the Svengali role you've assumed with me." Was Greta Williams a Svengali, the evil person who dominated and controlled her, yet mesmerized her at the same time? *Yeah, kinda.* Maybe Josie's delivery had been a little rude, but it was the truth. Of course, she meant it. Josie always meant what she said. It wasn't her fault that other people refused to believe she wasn't a people person. They always thought her grumpiness was cute...as if she would joke about a thing like that.

Greta wasn't fazed by Josie's bluntness. Instead, she said, "I have another business proposition for you."

Words Josie both dreaded and craved. How sick was that? It was because of Greta and her horrible offspring that Josie had nearly bitten the dust—literally—in Arizona just a few months ago in autumn. It was because of the Williams family that Josie had bad dreams about weddings, wedding dresses, wedding shoes, and matching handbags. Being "almost-killed" changed a person's outlook on life—it had made Josie less prone to wasting time, more likely to cut right to the point. In the past couple of months, she had taken stock of the most important things in her life: friends, family, and food. The three Fs. True, she'd done a lot of philosophizing from the comfort—and safety—of her couch, but she had decided that if she saw something she wanted in life, she was going to speak up about it. At least, that was the plan.

Yet, she had missed hearing from Greta Williams, the old battle-axe, during the last few weeks. They'd come to a certain *understanding* and while they weren't kindred spirits necessarily, they had a healthy respect for each other. All Josie's medical bills had been paid in full and, because of her brush with evil, her friends were more precious to her now than ever. So, no harm done, right? Except Greta, it appeared, had Josie's new unlisted cell phone number. On speed dial, no doubt.

"What can I do for you?" Josie had said, compulsively saving her work to her navy blue mini flash drive with its broken lanyard loop. She pushed aside her feeble laptop with her latest blog entry because she needed her full attention for this chat with Greta, and if her laptop fell asleep, there was no guarantee it would wake up. After all their time together, her Dell deserved to die peacefully in its sleep, so Josie was trying to mentally and emotionally prepare herself for that day. And to remember to back up her work as compulsively as an OCD person reaching for antibacterial hand soap.

What could Greta Williams want now? Chances were, Josie would be able to do a quick errand for her Beacon Hill benefactor and possibly earn enough cash for a new laptop and a new piece of costume jewelry for her mother who had dementia—something shiny for Mama to look at since she was in a nursing home. Josie hadn't gotten very good interaction during their visits in the past few months, but her mother had cooed over the crystal light catcher Josie had hung in her window the last time. So yes, Josie was a little mercenary when it came to running other people's errands, but her heart was in the right place. That should count for something, right?

With her patented formality, ever a testament to her Boston blue blood, Greta said, "I would like you to go to San Francisco for me."

Well. So much for a quick errand.

"And why is that?" Josie asked, making bug-eyes at Bert. He had as much of a chance of guessing Greta's agenda as Josie did. Her dog—part pony, possibly—thumped his tail a couple times, and then heaved his big brown body onto Josie's slipper, jabbing her on the top of the foot with his bony elbow. Did dogs even have elbows? His knee-bow or whatever...

"I'm interested in investing a second round of funding into a small start-up software business that is based in the Bay Area. The company is called Applied Apps." Greta paused while that salient bit of information traveled the input pipe to Josie's brain.

Applied Apps? Despite being a generic and altogether forgettable moniker for any company with aspirations, the name was ringing a bell. A faint little chime that got louder and louder. Josie wracked her brain. Did she know any small businesses like that? Why would a little start-up software company in Northern California sound so familiar? Josie had only ever been as far north as Santa Cruz that one time in high school she'd stolen her uncle's Chevy truck and…Aha. Susan's boyfriend. Of course.

Josie's best friend Susan had a Silicon Valley sweetheart named James whom she had been dating long-distance for almost a year. Which was bizarre, because Susan was so Golden-Age-of-Hollywood beautiful, so Veronica Lake lovely with her porcelain skin, loose blonde curls, high cheekbones and natural elegance, it was almost impossible to think of any guy dating her and not wanting to see her, to be near her daily. When Susan walked into a coffee shop, people of both genders dropped their cups. Crumbs fell out of open mouths. Throats gulped. Next to her, Josie always felt like Kato—the Green Hornet's Asian sidekick, only female and crazy—though she would never admit it out loud. This modern couple, however, Skyped and Face-Timed often, so maybe seeing pixelated versions of each other over broadband was enough for them.

Josie, obviously, still didn't get it. When she was with Drew, she liked holding his hand, seeing his little frown of concentration when he was reading a book or a medical journal, and feeling the warmth of his leg when he sat close to her on the sofa—the little wordless moments between them. The internet was great and all, but skin-to-skin contact with the person she wanted to be with, the guy she had the hots for, was the best thing ever. *Dopey smile alert. Again.*

Susan and James had met online many years ago. They had met posting on a message board, so they had a long-term virtual friendship that had started even before internet dating was a legitimate thing. It was before all that matesforlife.com, datemydog.com, and whatnot. Another mental shrug from Josie, because how could James have seen how gorgeous Susan was from just a little profile picture? Or maybe that was the point for Susan—with James, she would always know he had chosen her for her personality and not her looks. *Hmm. That was one to ponder.*

Josie had learned that by day, James Yu worked for a very large and established operating system company in Cupertino—not Apple, but one of its many robust, long-lived competitors that was probably not even a blip on the Apple radar. Nevertheless, James's company employed thousands of people and had been in operation for several decades, one of those staples of the software industry that kept plodding along, dot-com bust or not. His day-job company was probably buoyed up by government contracts or, even better, the banking industry...which in turn was bailed out by the government. Josie pictured the whole cycle as a modern-day fiscal Ouroborous, that mythical creature that grew only because it ate its own tail.

Outside the nine-to-five, James and a fellow-coworker named Ivan had started a business venture on their own, making...Josie had no clue. Something else *software-y*. Here was where her brain fuzzed out whenever Susan went into details. It was definitely something to do with the internet, and that was about as specific as Josie could get. From what Greta Williams was telling her now, maybe she should have paid more attention.

"...I invested twenty thousand dollars with them three months ago," Greta was saying. "And another twenty upon delivery."

"Let me get this straight," Josie said as her brain plugged back into the conversation. She'd missed the first figure Greta had mentioned, but the rest added up to forty thousand. Even to a woman with pockets as deep as Greta's, losing that much had to be irritating. She wouldn't quite be reduced to parking the Bentley on the corner lot with a For Sale sign taped inside the windshield, but the loss had to smart. Especially the hit on her ego. Greta had a large one, which Josie admired and held in awe, more so than if it were a eight-carat diamond on a starlet's finger. She figured she could never have too many role models.

Josie continued, "You gave James and Ivan a round of funding based on their proof of concept for their...project." Here, she fudged, obviously, because she had no clue what their company did. "And now you want a demonstration of their product or a show of progress before you give them the final round?"

"Correct," Greta said.

"And you know that my friend Susan is dating James?"

"Yes," Greta confirmed.

"And you want me to go out there to surreptitiously observe and determine whether you're making a sound investment?"

"Yes," Greta said again.

Josie said it again, just to be clear and maybe to press a few of Greta's buttons, "You want to know if you have given a lot of cash to a couple of irresponsible bozos and you want me to snoop around and see if you'll ever see your money again?"

After a pause and a little click, which might have been Greta's teeth snapping together, the older woman said, "Precisely."

Josie thought for a minute. Obviously, this was no coincidence. Greta was extended her far-reaching tentacles not only into Josie's life, but into her friends' lives. Rather than feeling outraged or ready to launch into a lecture on boundaries and personal space, Josie felt...warm inside? Someone cared for her enough to snoop into her life.

In addition, here was a chance to scope out James on someone else's dime. Susan was one of only a small handful of people on this little green marble called earth for whom Josie cared, deeply, and it mattered to Josie very much whether James was worthy of her friend. Susan's parents were disengaged, self-absorbed with their retiree lifestyle in Savannah. Who else was there to look out for her, to have her back? Who other than Josie had been with Susan loyally these last ten years? Josie barely had to think about it.

"All right. When do I leave?"

CHAPTER 2

Sitting at a bentwood chair at a table inside Ghirardelli's, the din of the supper crowd around her, Josie fiddled with her menu and drummed her fingers with their gnawed-back nails on the tabletop. The truth was, she had lost her taste for ice cream. Constant, repeated pain from eating something could do that to a person. *So there. Negative behavioral conditioning did work, Professor Pavlov.* Seriously, how many times did a person have to suffer in order to learn her lesson? Josie was still teachable, for Pete's sake. So, forget the ice cream. However, the chocolate was calling her name with a megaphone. Waving pom-poms and doing backflips.

A server in a black polo shirt walked by hoisting a triple-layered ice cream soda that looked about a foot tall. Frothy mounds of whipped cream, sprinkles, cherry, and a chocolate wafer nestled right on the top. Josie averted her eyes, sweating like a...what was that inappropriate saying?..."a whore in church." Okay, screw that part about losing her taste for ice cream—her dairy lust was still alive and kicking her common sense's butt. Pavlov was right after all. She was salivating like a dog. That was the thing about desserts—so many of them looked better than they tasted. It was all about the show, the looks, the pretty façade. Kind of like a beauty queen contestant who had no real life skills other than competing in pageants.

Right? Yeah, she would keep trying to convince herself of that. With a slightly self-disgusted sigh, she pushed back her thick, dark hair, which was behaving itself today by some miracle. Instead of getting the silkiness of her Thai mother's hair, she'd inherited the Tucker coarseness. Their Germanic stubbornness was so pervasive, it came out through the very roots of their hair. She'd looked it up once—in old Dutch, the word *tuch* meant "to tug sharply." She pictured her ancestors yanking on their hair in frustration, anger, and in general railing at the gods. Over the centuries, Tucker hair had to be tough to survive their temperament. So good hair days like this were a gift not to be taken lightly. The same went for good behavior days.

Earlier in the day, James, in his little blue Nissan Leaf electric car blasting aneurysm-inducing dubstep music, had dropped Josie off at Union Square while he and Susan ran errands, and Josie had hoofed it up and down the blustery streets all the way to the wharf. The walk was only about two miles, but the concrete hills had almost killed her. By the time she got to Telegraph Hill, her "dogs were barking," as her Aunt Ruth liked to say, meaning her feet were throbbing like nobody's business. And possibly, she was going to need physical therapy for shin splints. So even if she weren't going to tax her stomach with dairy—and she *definitely was not,* she reminded herself—it felt dreamy just to sit in one of the Ghirardelli chairs and to *imagine living with no regrets.*

As it had turned out, the timing of Josie's trip had been perfect. Which made her wonder exactly how much interest Greta Williams had taken in her daily life...Was she going to have to sweep her apartment for electronic bugs later? Susan had already been planning to come to San Francisco to see James. Even though this visit was only the second time the two internet sweethearts had gotten together in person, James had very kindly offered Josie a place to stay—a spare room and a Wi-Fi password—which was perfect for her staying incognito. Staying in a ritzy hotel room on Greta's dime would have been lovely, yet a dead giveaway of Josie's ulterior agenda. Instead, she was sleeping in James's guest room-slash-office in his upper-story apartment on an unsurprisingly slanted street not too far from The Haight. They thought she was here on a mini vacation, gathering notes for her blog.

"Sorry for the, like, dismal place," James had said. "I'm saving up for a house in San Jose. I'm looking at a little three-bedroom house off the freeway for 750 thousand. It's kind of a fixer-upper." Josie waited for him to laugh, but there was no punchline to his sad sky-high-priced Northern California real estate joke. *Ouch.*

To reach James's current front door, they climbed up a precariously mounted, retro-fitted steel fire escape...thingy. Basically, it was pieces of mesh and rebar, twist-tied together, that vibrated like a Jamaican steel drum with every step she took. One of Drew's nephews could have built a sturdier structure out of Legos and chewing gum. The first time going up, James had run up it nimble as a mountain goat on his long, wiry legs, leaving them to follow, clutching the railing as if their lives depended on it, which didn't seem too much of a stretch. Each subsequent time they had to clomp up or down those steel steps, all Josie could think about was the horrific 1906 earthquake and how this was possibly her last moment alive, clinging to a wobbly metal toothpick in the San Francisco skyline.

Needless to say, it had been a relief to walk around the city by herself for a while on solid, albeit severely angled, ground. Still...up and down, up and down. She was on an ant hill teeming with bugs in Burberry coats and thrift store sweaters. Sure, this particular hill had amazing an bay view when the fog burned off, and even better cuisine, but it was overrun with dour, salaried youngsters, whom she could only observe with fascination.

"What can I get for you?" The Ghirardelli's server was a young blonde woman, who surprisingly had no tattoos, extraneous piercings, or dreadlocks. Josie gazed at the menu, more than a little dazzled, rainbow-colored sprinkles in her eyes, so to speak. The whole left side of the menu listed multi-scoop confections, described in loving, gluttonous detail. She would bet every dollar she had that *here was a menu that did not make false promises, by George.* She scanned it again, from left to right. Somewhere in the middle was a dairy-free sorbet with crystalized ginger that waved a white flag, begging her to be a responsible twenty-seven year-old adult, but Josie ignored it, and ordered a brownie. Simple and safe, right? Just a brownie...

Covered in dark chocolate fudge. With whipped cream and sprinkles. And a cherry.

While Josie waited for her doom-on-a-plate to arrive, she took out her smartphone. She logged onto the free Ghirardelli Wi-Fi to do a Google search for James and his fledgling company, which was called...she floundered for a few seconds before she came up with the name Applied Apps. Again, with the boring, almost meaningless name. Would they at least have a decent webpage?

And they did.

Wow, Josie was impressed. Their webpage had moving thingies and buttons and other things she had no idea could be done on a site—and all of it looked pretty good on her three-inch phone screen. They had an enthusiastic mission statement full of buzz words and business jargon. A blue corporate logo of a globe spun in the upper left corner. Their main product was called Shasta. Although she still had no idea what it did. Something for businesses that fast-tracked…something. She tried reading the mission statement again. The company was "founded with the vision of producing innovative and affordable solutions to enable businesses to explore and develop through practical and profitable steps…"

Ugh. Josie was ready to throw in the towel from the jargon alone. She cleared her throat and looked up at all the other restaurant customers around her who were staring at their phone screens… techno zombies like her.

Frowning again at the website, she had never thought she had just average intelligence—or lower-than-average smarts either—until now. She spent the next few minutes reading the rest of the Applied Apps page, which was packed full of three-letter acronyms—which were called TLAs? *Really?* She skimmed on about their multi-tiered customer support packages that could be purchased with the Shasta product, until her head was ready to explode. Or maybe it was from squinting at her tiny phone screen—funny how her eyesight worsened with her lack of comprehension. Irritated, she couldn't tell if Shasta was a legitimate product or if she was resentful because she didn't understand exactly what the heck it was.

Praise the cocoa gods, her server returned with her brownie…no, not a brownie. What arrived on a plate was a work of art, a darned chocolate composition with depth and character and history. It was the Ansel Adams of brownies—grayscale gradients of black and white, full of meaning and expression, topped with a florid Maraschino cherry. Josie gaped at the swirls of fudge, whipped cream, and chocolate jimmies, and said a little prayer.

She was in so much trouble.

The server said, "I know, right?" She glanced at Josie's face, which was probably a grotesque and blatant expression of food lust. What a thoughtful and discreet panderer of dairy transgressions the girl was. She set down some extra napkins next to Josie, eyed her again with a wry, knowing smile and said, "Yeah, I'll just leave the two of you alone."

⌘

That night, Josie sat on the pulled-out futon in James's cluttered guest room. She'd popped some anti-lactose tablets, but they were doing nothing for the Triassic-like growls and gurgles coming from her midsection that spelled certain volcanic activity in her near future. So when James and Susan said they were going out to dinner, Josie was happy to opt out with a wave and a hidden side cramp. Yes, she had been incredibly dumb this afternoon with the whipped cream. *Fine, with all of it.* At least she hadn't eaten the whole thing—because there had been that one streak of chocolate left on the spoon...*I was such an idiot.* So much for living in the moment and grabbing life by its lactose-filled horns.

Groaning at her willful stupidity, she opened her ancient laptop to log into work and see what interesting tidbits her email inbox had for her. She plugged in her mouse and put aside her flash drive—she carried it with her everywhere. She now saved her work compulsively. Anyway, it would be a lot easier to search for information about James's start-up company on a bigger screen. She browsed for a while. She answered a friendly message-slash-grandbaby-announcement from her email pal sillydaisygirl16, whom she'd once met on a connecting flight home. Then she sent a brief reassurance to Drew that she was still alive, at least until it was time to pay the porcelain piper. Email communication with Drew was good for now. She'd call him later, after she knew for sure whether or not she was going to die from her dessert. In a sappy fit of homesickness, she changed Drew's contact name in her phone to *The Boyfriend.* After her phone saved the change, she gave it a loving pat, although it was a poor substitute for being near Drew. She even missed, with an addictive ferocity, the clean way he smelled, like a soap, laundry detergent, good old pheromones, and possibly some oregano…maybe fresh rosemary. He was from a large, Italian family. She had always loved Italian food.

In the meantime, looking around James's office, she thought she would, well…snoop. She set her laptop aside—shutting it down because the fan inside of it sounded like it was going to launch a space shuttle. She sidled over to James's less-than-new particle board desk. A messy stack of loose photos caught her eye first. She studied each one. Most of them were of James and an older guy Josie assumed was Ivan. The older possibly-Ivan man was a few inches taller than James, rotund in the belly, and twinkly in the eye. His eyes themselves were crystal blue and full of mirth and mischief. His hair swooped back from his forehead in a thick, blond wave. The three of them would be meeting him for breakfast tomorrow, so she could confirm it was him later—there weren't any photos of either James or Ivan on their company website, so she didn't know for sure.

James was twenty-two, an almost cringe-worthy number of years younger than Susan. Five years, but it felt like more at this age. Maybe it wouldn't be a big deal if they were in their thirties. Right now, it meant he'd been in middle school working on his Pokemon card collection while she and Susan had been moving into their freshman dorm rooms. While they'd been deciding their majors, he'd been obsessed with Pikachu.

Josie knew about James from what little Susan had told her. She knew that, as his official day job, he worked for the mega software company, called PPS, which was another of those meaningless computer industry acronyms. No one she asked knew what the initials stood for, and it wasn't explained on their website. So, who knew? James didn't know when Josie had asked him. He had started there when he was a junior in college, when they still had internships. Since the dot-com bubble burst, companies had cut back drastically on their perks, like in-house dry cleaning, daycare, free sodas, and, apparently, internships. Back in the high tech salad days, he'd had a paid internship as well as tuition for the rest of his college credits, which he completed at San Jose State. He had graduated quickly and was obviously bright.

But very, very messy, Josie thought, looking around. A dusty guitar languished in the corner, not on its stand but next to it. She saw piles of thick computer programming books—and holy cow, one of them had James's name on the spine as author. She spied a badge from San Diego Comic-Con from two years ago; a skateboard festooned with cartoon skulls; several empty Red Bull cans; and a once-neatly mounted rack of martial arts belts of various colors up to red now hanging crooked on the wall by only one of its two pegs. Under the piles of papers and laptops—she counted at least four, with their Gordian knot of cables and cords—on the desk against the wall, there was a broken…lightsaber handle? And several action figures, including Natasha and Boris figurines from *The Rocky and Bullwinkle Show*. Apparently, she had checked into Bachelor Nerd Hotel.

Josie was intimately acquainted with messy—*she* was messy, for Pete's sake—but this place made her one-bedroom walk-up by the Big Green Monster in Boston look like a Martha Stewart magazine layout. Unable to stop herself, she peeked in the accordion-doored closet in her room. Two empty hangers on the clothes bar and a jumble of papers, bent-cornered notebooks, and…were those vinyl records? She examined one album which was "Sinner's World" by an eighties punk metal band called Fall From Grace. From inside the sleeve, a black and white flyer slipped out, showing a picture of a long-haired, sweaty punk belting out a song at a mic. Josie could have sworn they were an old band from her hometown of Tucson; she looked around for a turntable but didn't find one anywhere in the rest of the apartment. Maybe the LPs were left over from a previous tenant. At this rate, she wouldn't be surprised to find the remains of the previous tenant under this junk.

Off the room James and Susan were sharing, Josie peeked into the microscopic bathroom, which seemed to have been cleaned with a fastidious hand. Susan's cosmetics bag was by the edge of the sink—yep, there was her this year's patterned Vera Bradley case with some bareMinerals cosmetics poking out. Josie's eyes wandered around the small bathroom, which was salmon pink, thanks to the aforementioned possibly-deceased previous owner. It looked as if James had even cleaned the base of the toilet, which had to mean that he probably really liked Susan, right? She averted her eyes from the rest of the bedroom, not wanting to know whether her best friend and her boyfriend were getting frisky under a Yoda sheet set.

In the tiny kitchen, she found almost no food, just two cases of Red Bull along with some Dr. Pepper and an out-of-place block of expensive knives that were probably used only to spear the plastic wrap off frozen pizza. Opening a sagging cabinet door over the sink, she hit on the motherlode of breakfast cereals. She found every type of crappy, sugary, tooth-melting variety Josie's dad had refused to buy her when she was little: Choco-Sugar Bombz, Lucky Clovers, Honey Crispies, and Fruitycombs So many varieties. The breakfast of champions seemed also to be the breakfast, lunch, and dinner of programmers. No wonder he didn't have any food in here, she thought, looking around at the peeling linoleum and dated appliances; this kitchen did not inspire culinary greatness. Josie wondered if James were taking his vitamins because he seemed to be lacking some variety in his diet—anything natural, pretty much. She hoped he was mature enough to take care of himself and didn't need her friend to mother him. *Because if so, poor Susan.*

Just as her stomach gave a pitiful moan and lurched from one side to the other, like the *Alien* movie—the first one with Lance Henriksen, that attractively robotic and creepy older guy—she spied a shiny, newer laptop under a pile of newspapers on the counter. As she sucked in a breath on the backside of a stomach cramp, she debated whether to open the laptop. Scoping out her friend's boyfriend to see if he was a good match for her friend was one thing, but was Josie ready to cross the line into being Greta Williams's paid informant, her hired help? Was she ready to take the next step? Had she morally cashed that check already? Josie eyed the Dell for about sixty seconds before edging the newsprint *Chronicle* with its pink Entertainment section away with her finger. Maybe she'd just see what happened if she lifted the computer's lid. Surely, the laptop would be locked, so her moral dilemma would be moot, right?

A couple of days ago, Greta Williams had sent Josie, by same-day courier, a credit card for business expenses with a spending limit higher than the sum total of all credit cards she'd ever had. Also in the courier's envelope was a private investigator's license issued by the Commonwealth of Massachusetts for Josette M. Tucker—a P.I. license *for which Josie had never applied* nor had ever even considered applying. Yet, she had accepted it without question—the paper was now folded up in her wallet—but now she wondered what a P.I. license actually meant. Was she entitled to open her host's computer so she could dig through his files? Doubtful. Would she be betraying Susan's trust as well?

Okay, she told herself. Judging by the escalating noises and pressure in her midsection, she was on a Mission Impossible stopwatch. Seriously, a Tom Cruise hanging-from-the-ceiling, clock's a'ticking countdown. She would allow herself five minutes of peeking. So, with a deep breath, she lifted the laptop's lid.

And found it unlocked.

Yeesh. Seriously? What computer guy left his laptop unsecured? This fact alone made Josie wonder whether Greta Williams should have given him a single cent of her Beacon Hill blue blood money. James should have had some kind of encryption or at least a password, for crying out loud. Even Josie, technical troglodyte, locked her laptop. Sure, her password was *potsticker*. And maybe it was on a sticky note right above her desk. However, all she was protecting were blog entries and dog-shaming pictures of her pooch, Bert. He liked to snooze on her pile of dirty laundry and occasionally eat her socks—not in pairs, of course, just single socks. Still, even she knew better than to leave her computer open and free as a bird.

And worse, he had a veritable stranger staying with him in his apartment—*her*. Yes, Josie was the best friend of his girlfriend, but he shouldn't go around just trusting people like that. She could've been a malicious person or a thief. She could've been...well, herself. And look at her now.

Josie poked the touchpad a couple times to see what screens James had open. Most of them were browser windows—none of them contained inappropriate *hentai*, thankfully—and she was not going into his browser bookmarks for love or money. She had her limits, after all.

Many of his browser screens were, no surprise, comic book-related. One was a message board—possibly the one on which he and Susan had met. In the back of the desktop were some black and green screens, obviously some kind of program running because the nonsensical text was scrolling by faster than Josie could read. No problem—she had no idea what it was anyway, but it looked *programm-y* and real. Like in the movie, *The Matrix*, with all those weird symbols zipping up and down. Minus the creepy biomechanics plug for the back of the neck.

She ripped off a tiny corner of *The Chronicle* to jot down the message board address. After carefully layering the windows on the screen the way they had been before, she closed the laptop, and then finally retreated into the bathroom to address the ticking time-bomb detonating in her stomach.

CHAPTER 3

The next morning when she woke up on the lumpy futon that smelled a little like seaweed crackers and hay, Josie's food hangover and midsection soreness was minimal, thankfully. She was up for round two of her San Francisco food adventure by the time Susan and James were awake and dressed. The plan for brunch was to meet Ivan at a place called Yeppa on Divisadero Street. Eggs, Josie could handle. As long as they were milk-free, they were one of her go-to foods when all else failed.

She stood in James's tiny kitchen on the peeling linoleum floor under the twitching fluorescent light as they got ready to leave. "Is this Ivan?" she asked as she pointed to a photo stuck to his fridge. She squinted at the photo more closely. In the shot, James and Ivan were at a big company function at a round dinner table for about ten. White tablecloths, lots of wine glasses and heavy silverware. Ivan was pictured mid-laugh, his mouth open wide, his blue eyes jolly. For a heavy guy, he photographed well. In the picture, James's face was flushed and shiny—typical Asian red cheeks from drinking. Though she was Thai and not Chinese, Josie had that same alcohol enzyme problem, a legacy from their shared ancestors. Meaning that she was even more prone to making bad decisions under the influence. She needed far less liquid courage than the average person to get to that point.

"Yeah," James said, distracted. He was punching buttons on his phone, not bothering to look up. She was becoming well-acquainted with the top of his shiny black head, thanks to the amount of time he spent staring at his device, avoiding actual human eyeball-to-eyeball exposure. It was weird trying to talk to someone who rarely made eye contact—she was never sure he was actually listening to them, Susan included. James said in slowly halting words as he tried to multitask, "I'm just texting Ivan again to see if he made reservations. For some reason, he's not hitting me back."

He glanced at the photo briefly—her finger was still on the corner of it. "Oh yeah, that was the PPS company holiday party a couple years ago when they still did parties at Christmas. That was a huge event. Open bar. Cash prizes all night long. They even gave away a trip to Hawaii. Crazy, right? That photo is totally embarrassing. I was wasted, but Ivan's wife likes to take pictures." Which explained all the other photos of the two of them she had seen on his desk.

"Wife? Ivan has a wife? Are you serious?" Susan said, her delicate eyebrows shooting upward. "I had no idea Ivan is married. He never talks about his wife online. I thought he had a girlfriend once, but I didn't know she was his wife. I mean, in all the years I've known you guys, I never knew it." Susan was leaning against the countertop, looking like she stepped off the page of a women's magazine—except unPhotoshopped. She had real, human proportions and was gorgeous as ever in her casual khaki pants with a wraparound knit shirt and cashmere cardigan. Josie was in her usual jeans and t-shirt. Susan had managed to tie her scarf around her neck in a complicated knot that looked natural. Josie always felt like scarves were choking her, both physically and emotionally because of their pretentiousness. On Susan, they looked great.

"Yeah, they've been together as long as I've known him—since before they came to the United States. He's old, in his forties. I think they went to MIT together in the 80s." Josie didn't think of that as old. Old was a state of mind. However, the way James was Nintendo-ing his phone buttons, typing with his thumbs at hyper-speed—now that was making her feel old.

"Ivan is from your message board, too?" Josie asked. She knew what an online message board was. She'd visited quite a few, especially online forums where people talked about food allergies, the recent bane of her existence as they would be for any self-respecting food critic. She was a sprinter who had been hamstringed, a race car driver who had lost her best mechanic, a teenager who had been banned from texting. She was temporarily handicapped in a way that could spell the end of her fledgling career if anyone ever caught wind of it. So for now, it was her little secret. She could deny its existence to her heart's content.

Susan, who was a graphic designer, had told her a few times about this message board they used for chatting with each other because they were spread geographically. Susan made a decent living doing freelance graphic design work, creating covers for books, CDs, and most recently, some print ads for magazines. For all Josie knew, Susan had probably created a magazine spread for fifteen ways to tie a scarf. She also had a large following on Pinterest, one of those websites Josie kept meaning to check out. Some online stuff was a little foreign to her, but she was getting better, thanks to her blog and fan comments. She made it a point to research the comments she didn't understand—more to prevent herself from looking like a dummy than out of personal interest. Although that didn't always work out.

"Yeah," Susan said while James was still pecking at his phone. "Ivan's been on it for years, too. We all met playing this...online game." A faint flush crept up Susan's normally porcelain neck and cheeks. Josie's eyebrow shot up. Game? She had heard of things like this. Orcs, pandas, warriors, and spell-casters. Apparently, even movie stars like Josie's friend Patrick were playing those games, too. He had told her he enjoyed the anonymity, the break from screaming teenage fangirls— though if that were true, he should have rethought taking that last shirtless werewolf role. And, hmmm...actors drawn to role playing games? Kind of made sense.

"Were you...*an elf?*" she teased Susan, trying and failing to dial down the snarky tone. Josie had never seen any evidence of cosplay, or costume play, at Susan's brightly colored apartment in Boston. No embarrassing Princess Leia metal bikini or Sailor Moon skirt. Was this a whole new side of her friend that she'd known nothing about all these years? It was like finding out your uncle was secretly into wearing women's undergarments. Nothing too terrible, but unexpected and...incredibly nerdy and out of character, for someone she was supposed to have known for such a long time.

"Maybe I was," Susan said sticking out her tongue, and then blew her off abruptly by turning to James. "Time to go?"

"I don't know. I can't get Ivan to answer me. I don't know if we even have a reservation. If we don't have one, we might have to share a big table with random people. I'm completely flipping out. Ivan always has his phone on him. I mean, always. Even when we were in Vegas at the...swimming pool, he kept checking it and playing Candy Crater and stuff. The guy is married to that thing."

Josie wasn't always the fastest on the uptake, but she had caught James's hesitation in talking about Vegas, as well as his shifty eyes. Something had happened in Vegas that was apparently staying in Vegas. Girls? Gambling? Those were the usual Vegas transgressions, she thought. She glanced at Susan, but her friend hadn't noticed.

James ran a hand through his jet-black hair. He was of average height and lean-limbed. Not out of shape, though, which was good, considering he was a computer geek. Maybe it was the martial arts. She remembered the different colored karate belts she'd seen in his guest room. He was wearing skinny-legged jeans—he was trying too hard to be trendy, maybe to impress Susan—a nice sweater with the tails of his shirt showing under the waist, and really great shoes. Josie was impressed by the square-toed leather tie-ups. She normally didn't notice stuff like that, but Susan had been slowly trying to educate her. James and Susan made a pretty good pair with his dark coloring and her light skin. They both had an elegance to them that belied their underlying nerdiness. This was a whole new side of Susan that Josie had never really known, but somehow, it made sense. Why else would Susan have chosen Josie for a friend, had they both not been misfits of some kind or other?

Instead of delving more into the Vegas thing—of all people, Josie was familiar with the dumb things people did in Las Vegas—she said, wanting to get the show on the road, "Should we see if he's waiting there for us? Maybe he has his phone, but it died?" Otherwise, they would probably hang around his depressing little kitchen for hours while he waffled about whether they should just head to the restaurant without having heard back from Ivan. As Josie understood it, this was the modern state of socializing. First, he'd talk to his friend online about meeting up. Then, he texted to confirm the date of the meet-up. Next, he texted before he left. Finally, they met in person. And discovered they had nothing to talk about, so they'd pull out their devices and ignore each other.

"Sure. Okay," James agreed, trying to hide his anxiety. But Josie knew all too well about nervousness, too. He was clearly unsettled by his friend's absence.

Josie didn't want to admit it, but she had hoped that Ivan, as the older, possibly more charismatic person in their partnership, would be more responsible than James. The twosome's disorganization was another strike against the stability of their start-up company. Were they worthy of the thousands of dollars that Greta Williams was considering throwing their way? Their credibility was doubtful right now, Josie had to admit. If she had to vote right now, she'd be giving a thumbs down to their startup company.

⌘

Back home in Boston, Josie and Susan were two parts of a quartet of friends who had been hanging out together since college. Drew, Josie's *boyfriend*, was the third. Benjy was the fourth, and Josie felt like she was betraying him as she watched Susan and James hold hands at brunch. Benjy had been in love with Susan since almost Day One, or rather, Night One, when they had met him at a frat party at college. Nothing good had come from the party—which was a terrible story for another time—except for their true and abiding friendship.

Benjy was the social and emotional equivalent of a toddler. He was cute with his shaggy hair and bright blue eyes, extremely loyal, guilelessness, and...possibly ADHD. No—that was mean-spirited of Josie. She had no right to criticize him for not having found his path in life yet; she of all people knew that fate tossed them wherever it wanted. She was a food critic who couldn't eat. Who was she to judge him?

She was always sticking her foot in her mouth when it came to Benjy. He certainly never did anything to earn her cutting remarks, usually made under the inhibition-erasing influence of alcohol, yet another reason for Josie to avoid drinking. No matter what she said, he always forgave her later. According to about 60 percent of ancient Chinese philosophers and one very Christian one, that made him far superior to her. She needed to exercise patience and understanding, to support him while he floundered from one cockamamie scheme to the next trying to find his way in the world. Currently, Benjy had a line on some mall carts, those kiosks that sold sunglasses, embroidered caps, or braided bamboo plants.

Yeah, that wasn't shouting "responsible" to her.

She sighed. If Benjy wanted to win Susan's attention, he was going to have to step up his game, and fast. Josie would be willing to bet that James, as young as he was, would be buying a ring within the next few months—and she didn't mean a friendship ring. Any ring from James would pretty much be the *lord* of the rings, the one ring to bind them.

⌘

Even by the time the three of them had finished brunch a couple hours later, Ivan still had not shown up. For once, Josie hadn't concentrated much on her food, despite the pillowy-soft scrambled eggs with sautéed mushrooms and caramelized leeks, a little kosher salt and just the right amount of pepper. The tension rolling off James was palpable, and it messed with her culinary experience. Under the table, his knee jiggled like he'd gone over the legal limit with his Red Bulls that morning and was heading into AFib territory—atrial fibrillation, as she knew from Drew. James had given up texting Ivan and had actually left him a voicemail, which was a desperate gesture for a message board inhabitant—*actual* spoken words for another person *actually* to hear. *Shiver. Horrors.*

James was in such a state of panic that he was considering calling Ivan's wife, Olga. As they stood outside of the restaurant on the split street planted with scraggly stick-like trees down the center, he explained that he had Olga's cell phone number in case of emergencies, like an earthquake. The Big One, as Californians sometimes called that mythical doomsday event always looming on the horizon. Though Josie noticed none of the alarmists had any desire to move out of the area.

James also had Olga's number in case a computer server crashed and needed to be restarted in the middle of the night. James told them, jamming his phone into his back pocket, that Ivan could be an extremely deep sleeper, thanks to a sleep aid he took regularly. He'd sometimes slept with his head on his desk, snoring like a bullfrog, when they pulled overnight coding sessions.

"How did you guys start a company on the side?" Josie asked, trying to distract him. As much as she also wanted to know where Ivan was, James's anxiety was making a knot in her already-taxed stomach. If she could get him to focus on something else for a few minutes, she might actually be able to digest what she'd eaten instead of feeling like there was a lump in her belly.

"It happened pretty quickly. We liked each other right off the bat. We met at PPS," he said, breaking out into a grin, which made him look about twelve years old. "We're officemates now, but back when I first started, I had a desk that was in a storage closet. I would come in after my school day ended and just sit there trying to find something to do. Seriously. They didn't even know where to put me. People would come in and out to get pens and notepads and stuff. They thought I was the retarded—sorry, Down's Syndrome—mailroom guy or something." Here, he glanced at Susan apologetically, though Josie grimaced. Her own cousin, Libby, was developmentally slow, but had never been labeled anything other than *beloved*. "Ivan was assigned to train me on his project. I was a lowly high school intern, but I ended up showing him a lot of stuff about C++ because I had already published a book on it—we were using C++ way back then, if you can believe it, which is total ancient history." He was clearly enamored with his own narrative.

Josie nodded, faking comprehension. She glanced at Susan, who was listening to him avidly, looking a little bemused, a little indulgent. Josie wondered, suddenly, if this truly spelled the end of her group of four friends from school. If Susan decided to be closer to James, she'd probably move out here. Totally depressing. Instead of Susan Skyping James, Josie would be Skyping Susan.

Was it normal to be this possessive of her friend's time? *Yes,* she decided. It was normal for her—a person who didn't have that many people in her life she could call close friends. She would hold on to her friends with everything she had. Because when something as rare as a best friend was in her possession, it was more valuable than precious gems or the perfect soufflé recipe.

"So you two decided to start a company up on your own?" Josie prompted him. She didn't really resent James's presence in Susan's life. She just thought that he hadn't proven himself worthy of Susan yet. Josie was willing to admit that she had set the standard high for him to meet. She may possibly have been setting him up for failure.

"It wasn't anything official at first. It was just a bunch of side jobs. Because, I mean," he floundered for a minute, "having our side company is totally illegal in terms of PPS. They could take everything we've developed so far, so we've been keeping it off the radar. On the down-low, if you know what I'm saying." He grinned at Susan, looking sly and proud of himself.

Josie had to work to keep the expression of disbelief off her face, so she turned away and pretended to watch a passing car. Shady business practices? Red flag for an investor like Greta Williams. No investor wanted to hear that ownership of James and Ivan's entire project could be claimed by PPS. Luckily, James wasn't looking at her, as engrossed in his own words as he was.

"A friend of a friend needed this chatroom for..." James's face turned pink despite his golden-brown complexion. He was definitely telling her a partial truth, she could tell. First Vegas, now this. She made a mental note to find out more about this chatroom project. Her gut instinct was telling her it was something shady, like a porn site. "Well, anyway, he needed this chat program for a website. So, he contracted the work out to us to be done in six months. We built it, like, in one weekend. And it was pretty sweet. Really fast. With a webcam option. And you have to understand, this was all about ten years ago, so this technology was pretty new still. And we smoked it. We killed it. We did the whole thing and earned, like, ten thousand dollars each. It was fantastic. Totally sick. I don't even think Ivan told his wife about the project or his share of the money." James flicked his eyes toward Susan and smiled apologetically. "I bought my car."

"I remember you telling me about it. Then you guys went to Las Vegas right afterward," Susan said. "You said you won a bunch of money at the craps tables." Josie could believe that. Craps tables and not poker—James did not have a poker face. His face was as transparent as hers, like Bahamian water on a clear day.

"Yep. And no pictures that weekend, if you know what I mean." He gestured for them to follow him as he started off down the street where he'd parked his car. They had about three minutes left on the parking meter, by Josie's estimate, and about ten minutes' worth of walking, but James didn't seem worried. Maybe he was the same as Susan in that respect. Blessed by the traffic gods—never a red light at a bad time, never a parking ticket even if well-deserved.

What exactly does he mean? Josie wondered, narrowing her eyes. James laughed then, which grated on her nerves. He had a weird, high-pitched explosive laugh. Josie gawked at him, but Susan just smiled, stepping over a splotch of gum on the sidewalk as if she were gliding down a catwalk. Josie watched her best friend with a sharp eye, but couldn't detect any cracks in her foundation, cosmetic or emotional. *Why is Susan selling herself short?* Josie watched her profile as they walked down the street feeling as if it might be her duty to save Susan from making a serious mistake. James laughed again. Fifty years of that laugh, and Josie would want to smother him with a pillow. She cleared her throat. Yeah, she was annoyed by him and resentful of him, no doubt about it. He was a kid, for crying out loud. Did Susan want to spend the rest of her life with him? Or even the next few months?

Deep breath, she told herself. *You are a smooth stone on the beach, not a prickly cactus.* She repeated this mantra in her mind three times until she felt less like...herself. Screw it. She was a cactus, through and through.

What if Susan tied herself to James permanently before seeing who he would truly become? Josie didn't want her friend to make a mistake while in the throes of a temporary infatuation. Decisions made under the influence of early love could have incredibly long-reaching consequences. A quickie Vegas wedding was the stuff nightmares were made of.

"So, you're a kind of a big deal. A famous food critic, right?" James said, surprising Josie out of her thoughts. Of course, Susan had to have mentioned Josie, since Josie knew about James. It went both ways, she supposed.

"I don't know about famous," Josie said. "But I have a blog." She was a little embarrassed, still unsure of the legitimacy of the new direction her career had taken.

"She has a massive following," Susan bragged, elbowing her gently. "I set up her Facebook page and her Twitter account. Her blog entries get cross-posted to her page automatically. She has almost 43,000 followers last I checked."

"Cool," James said, seeming to reassess Josie. "Do you have an RSS feed or a podcast for a subscriber base? Have you been to South By?"

Josie frowned and tried to answer the one question she understood. "South By Southwest, the music festival in Austin?" Even Josie had heard of that, mostly due to Susan's connections in the music industry creating artwork for CDs and liner notes. Lady Gaga had been to the South By Southwest musical festival, forcing music purists to vacillate between nausea and fits of rage. Supposedly, it was a small festival that had grown out of proportion into a massive, commercial enterprise. Maybe Josie would go down there and check it out someday...maybe go on a barbecue tour of the Texas hill country. Now *that* was more her style.

He shook his head. "I meant South by Southwest Interactive, the technology part of it. Tons of bloggers go there. Like, really famous people. Like The Oatmeal. You should look into it."

Josie smiled and nodded, again faking it. Oatmeal? Was that a code word for something? This kid was speaking a whole different language from the one she'd been taught growing up. He was probably fluent in tax code, too. Or Ikea instruction booklet. That was definitely a foreign language that would be useful to know. Yes, she was relatively new to blogging, but she didn't want to admit to *him* how little she knew. She was trying to gain his trust, not his pity or his condescension. He was already making her doubt her own intelligence. She didn't need to give herself any other reasons to feel inferior.

"Hey, while you're here, you totally need to come eat at my parents' restaurant—an old school dim sum parlor. It's super famous. It's been there forever, almost thirty years—way before I was born. I'll take you guys there tomorrow, if you want. Maybe I can get Ivan to meet us there." A worried frown flitted across his face as they reached his car. The meter was blinking, but his windshield was free of tickets.

"Sure, that sounds great," Josie said. Dim sum, she could handle. No dairy there. Just a lot of grease, pork, and shrimp. Mountains of it. Dim sum sounded good.

Hopefully Ivan would show up and save both the funding for their fledgling company and James's future with Susan, which were inexorably tied together in Josie's mind.

CHAPTER 4

James and Susan went out again later that night. He was taking her to a blues club, which was a remarkably sophisticated move on his part. Score one for James—Susan liked both blues and live music. Josie marked a point in his favor on her invisible tally sheet. It was such as grown-up thing to do. Maybe the kid had some skills after all. If he racked up enough credit, Josie might even stop thinking of him as "the kid."

While she was alone in his apartment listening to the strange creaks and thumps of the building, Josie worked on her next blog entry about the Ghirardelli empire, menus, and truth in advertising, and made a couple of calls. She dialed Greta Williams first, since that was the easier call to make. As the number rang, she opened her laptop intending to go to the website of the message board she had seen on James's computer.

"Josie," Greta's voice said after only two rings. Josie could almost see Greta sitting at her Queen Anne desk. Greta's couches and chairs looked stately but were a pain in the butt—literally—to sit in. Josie would never understand that style of furniture. She figured life was too short for uncomfortable chairs.

Without any preamble, because Greta favored the direct approach, Josie said, "James's partner Ivan seems to be AWOL." Using a military term was cheesy, but she couldn't stop herself. Josie's dad had been in the military, and old habits die hard, especially now that her dad was gone. The lingo was a piece of him that popped up unexpectedly now and then, so she never wanted to squelch it. Greta's husband had been a military man at some point before making her a widow, so maybe the old battle-axe didn't mind.

"How long has Ivan Sorokin been missing?" Greta asked. She didn't sound the least bit surprised. Either Greta already knew, or else she expected bad things to happen—hard to tell which was true, especially with Greta's past.

"Since yesterday morning, I think. Not long enough to file a missing person's report," Josie said. That amount of time a person was missing, she knew, had to be 48 hours. Anyone knew that from watching TV. Though, as she spoke, she pulled up another browser tab on her laptop and discovered, to her chagrin, there was actually *no waiting period* for filing a missing person's report in the state of California. *Crap.* Stupid misleading TV. "Scratch that," Josie amended out loud. "I think we might need to report it. After we check with Ivan's wife."

"I'll send you a text message with the name of a contact in the San Francisco Police Department, a Detective Maxwell Lopez. After you speak with Ivan's wife tomorrow, please make an appointment with the detective."

Josie was silent for a minute. "Why do I get the feeling I'm not the only one on your payroll."

It was Greta's turn to be silent, pretty much confirmation to Josie's mind. *All righty, then. Conversation over.*

The truth was, Josie was not only on Greta's payroll, but she was also a Visa card-carrying employee with a spending account. Greta had included the credit card in Josie's pre-flight package, along with the freaky P.I. license now in her battered leather wallet. Whether that made her more culpable in whatever schemes Greta had planned, Josie didn't know. She didn't want to spend too much time dwelling on it either. She just needed to focus on the task at hand and keep moving forward.

After Josie had hung up with Greta, she dialed Drew while she stood at James's window staring at the foot traffic down in the street. It was only March and the annual Gay Pride Parade wasn't until the end of June, but Josie was seeing a whole lot of pride going on tonight—same-sex hand holding, tender cheek-kissing, plenty of PDAs that made her miss her sweetheart back home in Boston.

"Hello, boyfriend," she said cheerfully when Drew answered his phone. She could picture his dark hair, his unshaven face, and his lop-sided grin. So GQ, except more low-brow, more middle-class, more *hers*.

"Hey Josie, I'm glad to hear you're not dead. You stood strong against the chocolate temptation, I take it?" He was huffing and puffing—either taking the stairs at work or using the barbells they kept at her apartment. He had nice, muscular legs. His arms weren't bad either, so picturing him on the stairs or with barbells was no hardship for her. Usually on the weekends, they worked out together in her apartment. Since her Arizona trip, she'd been more focused on building strength in her arms and legs. There was no telling when she might need to lay the smackdown on someone. She'd been thinking about signing up for a self-defense class, too, as soon as she stopped feeling phantom pains in her ribs. The Arizona trip had done a number on both her body and her self-confidence.

"Mmm-hmm," she said, which was mostly a lie because in the face of chocolate temptation, she had rolled over and shown her belly. So, her response to his question would have been a lie if it had been actual words. But as a sound, it was just a...*nonverbal* lie. Okay, it was still a lie. She was going to need to perform some serious moral reparation for this entire trip, or else the universe was going to kick her in the seat of the pants. She wasn't sure what she believed in terms of the afterlife and judgment by a higher power, but she did believe in karma because she'd witnessed it in action more than once in her life. Seeing was believing in her book.

"So, listen," Drew said. "I have something important to say. I know why you're out there in San Francisco. You went there with a specific agenda. As usual, you had a mission in mind. You're playing it close to your chest, keeping your own counsel, not exactly telling me about it. I want you to know I respect you for it, and I totally trust your judgment."

"You...do?" Josie asked, stepping away from the window, scratching her head. She, in fact, had not mentioned anything about Greta sending her to research James and his start-up company. Drew didn't like Greta, to put it mildly. He blamed her for the Arizona incident, a decent reason to distrust her. Josie had almost been killed. So, she had neglected to tell Drew about Greta's agenda, her interest in investing in the company, and the fact that Josie had flown out on Greta's dollar.

"Absolutely," Drew said. There was a *clang* in the background, and Drew's breathing changed. He'd set down a weight, which meant that he was in her apartment; this made her smile. Her plants would be watered, her dog would be fat and happy, and someone would be waiting for her at home. He was getting sweaty in her living room. She missed him. A lot. But she was emotionally stunted just enough not to blurt it out loud.

Drew went on, "You're vetting James for us. You're trying to see if he's good enough for Susan, since none of us has met him yet. I think that's terrific and I'm glad you're there."

Crap. Caught in another half-lie. The rate at which these were stacking up wasn't good for her digestion either. "Right," she said, "and so far, the jury's still out, but I need to tell you that what I'm really doing is—"

"Oh, man," he said as she heard a tinny ringtone in the background. "I'm so sorry. I'm getting a call from work on my other phone. I gotta take it. But I swear to you, when you and I each have some free time after you get back, we are going to have a talk, okay?"

That sounded ominous.

"A serious talk?" she asked. She could hear him speaking into his other phone to a nurse about dosages and treatment plans. He was talking in his even, low doctor voice. The solemn, controlled one that usually meant something serious was happening and an elderly patient, possibly, could be dying.

He came back on the line. "I have to go in, but when you get back, we're talking. I have...something important I have to ask you. It's a question, an important question, something I want...to propose."

Her heart stuttered. "Waitaminute. What?" she said. "We're having THAT talk?" *Impossible.* It was way too early for a proposal. She wasn't ready. This could not be happening. Her heart started to pound, but not for the right reasons. Darn it, she was so not ready for this—not that she had cold feet—but she *legally* was not ready to marry Drew. Emotionally, yes, after she stopped lying to everyone and avoiding old problems instead of addressing them and banishing them. If it came to that, she was going to have some problems getting a marriage license.

He laughed, clearly pleased with her reaction, but he didn't say anything else to enlighten her or to allay her anxiety.

"We've been going out for only a few months," she said, stalling.

"Come on, Josie," he said, laughing again. "We've been together for way longer than that. Years. We met when we were eighteen. Well, I was eighteen. You were a little younger, Ms. Smarty Pants getting into college early. Still, that was ten years ago. Ten years, I've been waiting for you."

"Yeah, but we didn't know we were seeing each other, in *that way*. You know what I mean. Like, in a *kissing* kind of way."

"Hmmm...I did," he said.

"No, you did not." She paused. She'd harbored feelings for him for so long, she had never considered the idea that he had as well, for her. "You did?"

He laughed again, though she did not. "I gotta go. We're continuing this conversation, I promise. I definitely won't forget."

And she let him hang up because, well, he had to go help someone. It was a matter of someone's life or death. He was a great doctor and he was pretty much her hero.

Crap. This was not good.

⌘

The fact was, Josie had some unfinished business with an ex-boyfriend back home in Boston, if she could even call Joe Armstrong that. A *way, way, way* ex-boyfriend. She still cringed at the thought of having once been all lovey-dovey with the creep. They had been together for a couple of months of weekend dates, including a so-called romantic getaway of which she remembered only parts, thanks to some strong alcohol. As soon as he had realized that she didn't have his social drive, his desire to be featured in the Boston who's who column along with the likes of the Shriver-Kennedy clan, he'd dropped her faster than yesterday's news. Talk about ego-bruising.

She dreaded having to contact Joe, to coerce him into giving her what she needed—namely, his signature on some papers, which was a simple thing to ask of a person—but there was no getting around it. The situation had gone on far too long and had to be dealt with. However, it could be...postponed ever so slightly. Just a teeny while longer while she dealt with this James issue.

Actively putting it out of her mind for the time being—because she was an expert-level procrastinator—Josie used her own laptop to check out the message board that James, Ivan, and Susan all frequented. She typed in the web address from memory into the bar at the top of her browser. A banner at the top of the screen designed to look like the cover of a fantasy novel, complete with a fire-breathing dragon, said "Lounge Lizards of Doom." Whatever that meant. Things on the internet were about 85% absurd to her, but she was trying to embrace it, sort of like watching a Dr. Who episode. She couldn't quite get into that program. Her TV-addicted buddy Benjy was into the show, and for him, she'd tried watching it. To her, it was a real head-scratcher. Speaking of accessible, the Lounge Lizard message board was open to the public—she didn't need a username or password to read the conversations.

The threading topics ranged from the latest superhero movie that had opened over spring break, to the newest video games, to things Josie couldn't pretend to understand...some things called Torrent, reddit, and Wildstream? She clicked on that last link and discovered it was a discount outlet for computer games—not so helpful to her and not particularly relevant to her interests. A couple of the conversations talked about sports, some were about TV shows, and others were intensely personal, like dating, divorce, and etiquette when going to watch strippers at a club, of all things. Most of it was random, daily conversation, water cooler chatter in an office building.

Scrolling down the screen, she found that each person's name was made-up. WackadooSamurai, nPawn, Sarchasm, and maybe 40-50 other distinct ones that she could tell. As Josie read downward, trying to identify James and Susan, she stumbled across a post from early morning of the previous day:

Zenmaster: Anyone heard from Ivanovich?

Xav: What's up? Don't you guys, like, live together in your mom's basement?

Zenmaster: Haha. No, that was last year. And only for a few months after his wife locked him out. Tho' I still see him every day. Just not lately. I'm going through withdrawal.

Xav: I think there's a cream for that.

nPawn: Nope. Haven't seen him in game. Message me if you need to. Always here to help.

Zenmaster: K. Thanks.

So it seemed that James, using the screen name Zenmaster, had been looking for Ivan—called Ivanovich—online here on this…lounge of snarky, doomed lizards. His message was probably the equivalent of sending out an APB, an all-points bulletin, for someone like James who was married to his computer screen and engrossed in this online world. Josie wondered, briefly, what Susan's screen name was. She read for awhile but didn't see any likely candidate pseudonyms for her friend. What would she call herself? PradaBaby for her love of fashion? DesignGrrl for her skills? Who knew.

Josie kept scrolling down until she found the last message posted by Ivanovich. She found a message dated early Saturday morning, the day before they were supposed to meet for brunch at Yeppa's. He'd asked someone about installing a more heavy-duty fan in his wife's—actually, he called it "his girl's"—computer. The comment sounded completely mundane. Well, fairly geeky, but still, nothing that rang any alarms. Nothing that screamed, *I can't take the daily grind anymore and I'm stealing the startup capital and moving to Tahiti.* She scrolled down some more, but didn't find any other conversations that included him after that. On the whole, the message board had not been helpful in finding the missing programmer. She sighed and stood up, setting aside her laptop.

At James's chipboard desk, she flipped through the photos of them one more time. She saw pictures of James and Ivan skiing and looking sunburned. Drinking Red Bulls on a beach looking sunburned. Outside a movie theater for the opening showing of yet another superhero movie looking…not sunburned, but pink-faced and possibly drunk. Josie stood in the middle of James's guest room, the shrine to his disorganized mind, her hands on her hips. Nothing was setting off any bells. Nothing was out of the ordinary. Where was Ivan, the no-show startup company wheeler-dealer? Didn't he realize that thousands of dollars were slipping through his fingers?

CHAPTER 5

"It's Tuesday. Do you need to go to work, James, or are you taking the day off?" Josie asked the next morning as they crowded around James's tiny breakfast table waiting for the water to boil. Susan was trying to make a cup of instant coffee, the only kind James had, which was gross, even to a tea-drinker like Josie. She was no coffee snob, *but come on*. Even she wouldn't stoop to use granulated coffee to soak ladyfingers in for a church potluck tiramisu. Even if she were using Cool Whip instead of mascarpone. She had her limits, after all. James was chugging a Red Bull for breakfast, his Adam's apple bobbing in his lanky neck above his shirt collar. Josie had decided to pass on any breakfast that came out of his kitchen because they were headed to Chinatown for dim sum in a few minutes.

Finally, finally, James had broken down and called Ivan's wife, Olga. Unfortunately, she had not answered her phone, and he'd had to leave a hastily spoken, stuttering message—so, no word on that front yet. They would have to wait for a return call to help settle their anxiety. At least Josie hadn't had to call Ivan's wife herself—cross that item off her to-do list. Now, she just needed to contact Detective Lopez at the number that Greta Williams had given her, which she planned to do right after lunch.

"I *am* at work," James said, his facing lighting up with a self-satisfied grin. He gestured to his laptop, which was open and scrolling that green text on a black screen, exactly how it had looked when she'd been playing James Bond and snooping yesterday. He explained, "I'm logged in from here. Running stuff right now. If someone sends me an instant message, I'll get it on my phone. Pretty sick, right?" He appeared pleased with himself. He definitely loved taking the easy route with his shortcuts, his "life hacks," as the bloggers were calling it. She had to applaud him for not conforming to the old nine-to-five standard—in that, they were of similar minds. Josie hated the thought of working at a desk all day long. However, this was interesting—no one actually knew James wasn't physically at work. Did Ivan do this, too? Before she could ask, James answered her unspoken question, gesturing to his computer screen as if it were a person.

"That's how I know Ivan is *somewhere*, and we just can't find him. He's been logged into the machine running processes and compiling stuff, adding his changes to our build non-stop since Friday. I don't get why he isn't calling me back. And he's not logged into instant messaging."

Josie frowned. "Are you saying he's at work right now?" She tried not to be pushy or to press her point too persistently, but she felt she had a right to ask. She was acting on Greta's behalf after all, even if James didn't know that. As for reining in her temper, that was in deference to her friend.

She and Susan stepped closer to James, where he was pointing to his laptop's screen. "Well, yeah. See, that's Ivan right there. This is our PPS project. I mean, our legitimate day job that's in Cupertino, not our side company." He pointed to a nonsensical stream of characters. The symbols were flowing by on the screen, but she could see them occasionally pause, be erased, then re-entered. Someone was typing—and typo-ing—right as they watched. It was like voyeuristic programming. Viewing this was like watching a really, really boring version of a computer hacker movie, except with no special effects and no hunky leading man. Wow, she knew what to do if she ever had trouble sleeping in the future.

"If you say so," Josie said, pushing back her hair, still not sure that what she was seeing was proof of a human being on the other end. She grimaced at Susan, who shrugged her cashmere-clad shoulders, a non-participatory Daphne to Josie's Thelma, if they were part of the Scooby gang. Susan was along for the ride, but not as intrigued as Josie was by the whole situation. Apparently, Josie had been overly blessed by the stick-your-nose-where-it-doesn't-belong gene. "Where is Ivan physically? Can you tell if he is at the PPS office in Cupertino?" Josie was dumbfounded at how hard it could be to find a person in this digital age of super-connectivity. Everyone was plugged in, totally connected, but a person could still be unreachable?

James scratched his head with indecision. "I guess he could be. I should be able to tell what IP he's logging in from, but it's giving back the one from PPS. I mean, I could call the PPS switchboard and see if he'll answer his desk phone, but I doubt it. Ivan never answers that thing—it has too many buttons and this obnoxious old-school ring like there's a real, actual bell in it. I think he turned off the ringer anyway. If we were talking about his cell phone, that thing is glued to his hand. He should be answering it. I mean, if it's not out of battery. Maybe it's not charged, you know?"

"Well, don't you want to go to PPS and actually check to see if he's there?" Josie asked, her usual tart edge slipping into her voice. She should have been controlling it a better, but she was itching to kick James in the seat of his pants—not just metaphorically. While she wanted to see Ivan's desk and work area, she didn't understand why James was so reluctant to go search for Ivan. How much goading would it take to set this guy in motion? Was he that much opposed to doing something to find his friend and partner? Maybe there was more at work here than laziness. She gestured at Susan to help encourage him behind his back, but Susan merely shrugged. James, whose company's future was on the line, should have been more willing to do something. His attitude had Josie scratching her head.

"We *kind of* have to get going if we're going to meet my parents in Chinatown," James said, in his typically hesitant, almost passive-aggressive way. "After lunch, *I guess* we can drive down south and see if Ivan is in the office. I mean, it's *kind of* a long drive. And we *might* hit rush hour at some point. I guess *we could* do it. That okay with you, Susan?" James cleared his throat and flicked his dark eyes to Susan.

At the prospect of meeting James's parents, unflappable Susan finally looked a little nervous. She nodded and said, "It's good with me."

Josie clamped her lips together, suppressing the desire to shove them all out the door and get moving. Daylight was wasting. Any mystery, big or small, got under her skin until she ferreted out the truth. While she sympathized with her friend's anxiety, behind her back she may have cracked her knuckles.

⌘

James needed to deliver a computer that he'd fixed for his parents. Before they left his apartment, he put all of the parts—tower, monitor, keyboard, speakers, and cords—in the front seat of his little electric car. Susan and Josie ended up sitting in the backseat together—and if that wasn't a metaphor for what Susan's future life would be with him, Josie didn't know what else to call it. *Big clue, sister,* she tried to tell her friend by ESP, but the message attempt did not go through no matter how hard she squinted at Susan, no matter how hard she thought. The connection failed, so to speak.

She wanted to take Susan by the hand, look her directly in the eyes, and ask her, "Are you really sure about this guy? Is he worth your time? Aren't you better than this?" But riding smashed in the backseat of James's car like a sardine marinated in second-hand energy drink fumes wasn't the best time or place for a conversation of that nature. A chat that required massive quantities of chocolate and possibly adult beverages. More than one of each. Possibly mixed together. She'd yet to try a chocolate martini, but she'd sacrifice her dignity for a good cause. Heck, she'd done that for less.

While they were strapped into the back of his tin can deathmobile, James turned on his radio, again cranking up the volume on his favored dubstep music. "Oh my gawd, what is that noise?" Josie said, clutching her head. "It sounds like robots fighting. I think my ears are bleeding." He laughed and turned the sound down one measly notch. *Wow, thanks for staving off my brain damage,* she thought, eyeing the placid expression on his face in the rear view mirror. She wondered if the electronic popping and warbling screeches of music directly reflected the chaotic state of James's mind. His generation had been bottle-fed on Super Mario Brothers' MIDI music. Maybe this was a natural progression...*unnatural* progression was more apt. Josie was learning to accept her boyfriend Drew's love of 70s rock and his awkward mancrush on Steve Perry from Journey, but this dubstep stuff...it was exploding her brain cells like little plasma firecrackers. And she probably didn't have any extra to spare.

Casting a sideways glance at Susan, Josie could tell from the tightening around her usually smooth mouth that meeting James's parents was a big deal for her—it wasn't the ear-shattering music tensing her up. Susan's blue eyes were opened too widely, and she was biting her peach-colored upper lip. True, meeting a boyfriend online wasn't as unusual as it used to be, but meeting his parents was daunting no matter what the circumstances were. Except for when Josie had met Drew's mom Natalie, she thought. Warm fuzzies at first sight, pretty much for both of them, Josie and his mom. Drew's father had died while they were in college, sadly—and strangely, although that was a story for another time—so she knew only his mom. Natalie was all about making food, and Josie was all about enjoying it. What more was there to say? Plus, they were both enamored with Drew, so there was also that they had in common. Josie was absolutely sure that James's parents would be impressed by Susan. She made a good living, was beautiful and well-spoken—and nerdy enough to appreciate their son. All good things in Josie's book. It was James who needed to make sure he was up to par now.

She was worried about Susan's state of mind. Enough so that it made her inner smart aleck emerge.

She leaned toward her friend and whispered, "So, if you play online role-playing games, does that mean you go to Renaissance fairs, too?" Though she would admit it only under duress, Josie had been to a RenFaire once in her high school years—not in costume, thank you very much—and she knew all about the Society for Creative Anachronism, those people who loved costume play and celebrating medieval times with the benefits of modern-day inventions, like sunblock and serviceable Port-o-Potties within range of their jousting matches.

"Shut up," Susan said, elbowing her hard. The girl had a sharp elbow. Clearly, she'd been putting her elbow-jabbing training hours in at Macy's and Filene's Basement, because *ow*.

Josie returned a verbal jab, "Not that there's anything wrong with being so, you know, into something, so enthusiastically. I just didn't know you were like that."

"I'm not." Susan was trying to fight her smile.

"Not into the corsets and petticoats, then?" Josie prodded again. "Merry widows and feathered hats? Pints of mead and turkey legs?" Actually, Josie had enjoyed petting baby goats at the petting zoo, at the RenFaire she'd visited. And she still had a Celtic knot charm on a leather cord somewhere in her apartment—a souvenir from that day.

"Come on. No." A flush crept up Susan's neck.

"So, you haven't entirely embraced your true inner nerdy goddess, yet?"

"Will you stop, please?" Susan said, though she didn't look all that upset, just embarrassed. Of course Josie would have stopped if she thought she were actually bothering Susan. Josie was just trying to take her mind off the situation.

Josie found it interesting that Susan was putting up with a large amount of geekiness for James's sake. But maybe there was a limit to Susan's involvement in the nerd scene. For as long as Josie had known her, Susan was much more into high fashion than Medieval fashion. Prada, Manolos, and Tim Gunn—not tankards of ale, excessive cleavage, studded leather, and weaponry. Josie tried to suss out the disconnect, but came up empty.

James dodged a blue Smart Car with a silver racing stripe and then took a pedestrian-crowded corner on two wheels, making Josie yelp. He zipped through a red light and turned the corner without using a signal. Josie scrambled for something to hold on to, but ended up gripping Susan's knee. She gave it a reassuring pat and let go, though she was the one who may have needed reassurance more. As they righted themselves around the corner, he came to a hard stop about two inches away from the back bumper of a taxi cab.

"I don't mean to point out a stereotype here," Josie told him, "but you are one scary-ass driver." People always jokingly told her that Asians were terrible drivers. Yeah, that was a super funny joke even after the first twenty times she'd heard it...*not*. In addition to the million or so times she'd heard criticism about Boston drivers—those nutjobs took traffic laws, like red lights, as *mere suggestions*—she was an Arizonan at heart and felt she should be exempt from comments about Boston drivers. It seemed James and Susan were both insane drivers—at least they had that in common. The couple who saw accidents in their rear-view mirror together, stayed together? James laughed that weird, high-pitched burst of heh-heh-hehs, but didn't say anything else. He just drove on, with them captive in the back.

Maybe I should have made out a will, Josie thought. *Who will take care of my dog Bert when I'm gone? Who will be at Greta Williams's beck and call if I'm not there?* She had the momentary uncomfortable thought that she was completely replaceable because her dog loved her boyfriend more than her. And Greta had a list of minions as long as Santa's naughty list.

On a throb of music, James brought them out onto Jackson Street with a sharp turn that left Josie's lower intestines on the street behind them. He had taken them on a straight shot through Chinatown on a one-way street. Because the day was clear, Josie could see the Bay Bridge ahead of them. Red, yellow, and the occasional green business signs in Chinese lined the sides of the street. Josie had taken a couple years of Mandarin in college to meet the requirements for her East Asian Studies minor, but characters flew by so quickly, she had no idea what they said. Not that she remembered much written Chinese—spoken was much easier for her to understand. She was still pretty good at ordering food and finding a bathroom—her essentials for survival.

James zipped past a perfectly respectable parking garage, turned down an alley, and ground to a halt in a tiny unmarked space. Josie could almost feel her brain-matter sloshing around inside her head. She definitely felt her stomach, although that was a given in its recent fragile state. Thank the Lord, they had made it without dying. They parked behind a dumpster, a really smelly one, Josie realized with a gasp, as they pried themselves out of the back of his tiny car and wobbled to the greasy pavement. The morning fog had burned off, and the sky was so crystal blue, it felt like she had a straight line of vision into outer space, which made her dizzy as heck.

So far, everything about this trip was throwing Josie off balance—the slanted streets, scaling the side of the building to get into the apartment where they were staying, the pell-mell driving from place to place and dodging tiny, eco-friendly clown cars. What next, an earthquake? She looked around for some wood to knock, but came up empty.

"Can you just carry this?" James was asking her, an impatient edge to his voice. Josie turned around from looking for wood to ward off bad karma to find Susan already loaded down with computer parts. She stepped closer and James handed her a keyboard with a cord, the end of which promptly uncoiled and tried to plunge into an oily, rainbow-colored puddle. As she balanced the keyboard and grabbed the cord with the other hand, he loaded the heavy computer tower on top of her stack.

"Whoa." She narrowed her eyes at him. He didn't notice.

"You got it?" he asked without looking at her. "You seem pretty strong, right? I think you can take it."

"Yep. Got it." The metal box was heavy and slippery, but she was too stubborn to say so. She was so going to kick him in the shin. After she set all this crap down. And made sure she wasn't bleeding anywhere. She wondered briefly about her tetanus booster status...Truly, James was like the little brother she'd never wanted to have.

He heaved up an old-school box-shaped monitor into his own arms, and got Susan to shut the car door and lock the car with his key fob. He took off down the alley without waiting to see if they were following. Chivalry was dead in this younger generation, not that Josie expected it or always appreciated it. But, still, a little consideration for them as people he wanted to impress would have been nice. Granted, his arms were fuller than theirs...but for some reason, it suddenly felt as if they had left America, as if her voter registration card had suddenly evaporated and she was expected to haul the day's water on her back as well. Was this equality or bad manners? She had no idea.

⌘

"Ma, Ba," James said in Chinese. "This is Josie." He gestured at her in an off-handed kind of way. His entire posture, his demeanor had changed since they'd entered Chinatown. He seemed thinner, more hunched over, and more furtive, and his previous minimal amount of eye-contact was now pretty much down to zero. His size had deflated with his self-esteem.

To get to the restaurant, he had led Josie and Susan down the alley, through a banged-up metal door, and inside a dingy hallway. Josie gathered from looking around at the yellowed posters that they were standing in the back offices of his parents' restaurant. They were downstairs from the main dining room, which explained all the loud voices and metal banging sounds coming from overhead. She eyed the ceiling, wondering about its structural integrity. She would never understand why people had built this city on such shaky ground. Yes, it was the Golden Mountain, the frontier city that had prospered during the Gold Rush, but layer after layer of denizens had lived here since, perched on their slanted foundations like ticks grabbing hold of the skin of a dog, though the itchy plates under the earth were trying to shake them off. Give her the vast sky of Tucson and the Sonoran desert where she had grown up any day. Even Boston, where she currently lived, didn't give her the same tilt-a-whirl feeling as this place. She suddenly appreciated the Hitchcock movie *Vertigo* in a whole new way. So far, she found the entire Bay Area to be dizzying. So far, by a fine margin, she was finding that she liked the people of the Bay Area more than the natural land itself. Usually it was the other way around. In general, people got on her nerves and made her crave wide open, unpopulated spaces.

While Josie nodded at James's parents and grimaced under the weight and sharp edges of the computer she carried, James took the parts from Susan's arms and arranged them on the cluttered desk. He pushed aside folders, a large calculator, and one of those deadly spikes used for taming and impaling unruly receipts. Never in a million years would Josie have one of those things at her own place—one clumsy trip over her dog and she'd be staked faster than a vampire on *Buffy*. She'd recently binge-watched all seven seasons of that show.

Josie's eyes adjusted to the dimly lit office as she glanced away from the memo spike to the middle-aged Chinese couple. They were staring at her as if she were a bug impaled on that very spike. The man stood with his arms hanging straight by his sides; the woman had crossed her arms over her chest. They had streaks of gray in their hair, though hers was permed in curls all over her head, and both wore wire-framed glasses that perched on the tips of their noses in an identically gravity-defying manner.

"Josie, these are my parents, Howard and Cynthia." He took the computer tower from her and scooted it across the top of the battered metal desk.

"It's nice to meet you," Josie said, proud of herself for pulling out manners that didn't get a whole lot of use. Finally free of the heavy load, which had left parallel red marks on her forearms, she stepped forward and held out her hand. Which neither Mr. or Mrs. Yu took.

All righty then. Josie stepped back so James could introduce Susan, who was the guest of honor on this trip. Josie didn't mind being brushed off in favor of her friend. James, however, had dropped to his knees on the grubby gray carpet and had crawled under the desk to plug computer cords in a hidden electrical outlet. *What the heck?* Wasn't he going to introduce Susan, his girlfriend, the woman who had traveled thousands of miles to be here?

Josie looked at Susan and mouthed, "Awkward," while James's parents stared at them both with stony, unmoving expressions. She couldn't get a read on his parents at all and had no idea what they were thinking. She herself had more than once been accused of being the "inscrutable East," that placid unreadable face that evoked stereotypes like Charlie Chan, the great fictional detective. Which was totally ridiculous because Josie had the worst poker face of all time. She usually came away broke from game night with her friends. James's parents, however, could probably give Charlie Chan a run for his money.

"And this is Susan," Josie said, not able to stand it anymore. Sure, she wasn't the best at etiquette—she was no Emily Post—but she was better than nothing. The Yus hadn't met their son's girlfriend before. This was supposed to be a milestone day for them. Something special. She glanced down at the bottoms of James's shoes. He still hadn't emerged from under the desk. Honestly, how long did it take to plug in two cables? She gave his leg a surreptitious tap with her foot. More of a kick. He pulled away from her and kept working.

The older couple looked at Susan, but neither said anything. Maybe they didn't speak English.

If not, this was going to be a fun lunch.

CHAPTER 6

Josie was in heaven. For people who had never eaten dim sum, or Chinese brunch, the meal—the whole experience—could be a greasy pig-out fest. Tiny dishes flew by on carts, fast and furiously. A million types of dumplings with who-knew-what was inside of them were stacked in metal tins. Buns and tarts, gelatinous cakes—things that looked sweet but tasted savory, and vice versa. Eating and pointing at new dishes could happen simultaneously and at a break-neck pace as hot food arrived on wheeled carts right at the table faster than a person could humanly consume it.

At her peak eating capacity, Josie had once been able to clear six small plates of dumplings in under fifteen minutes. A gross display of gluttony, she knew, especially since she was now experiencing the karmic equivalent of comeuppance in her diet.

It wasn't supposed to be a slam-bam Kobayashi—the hot dog champ—competitive eating event. Some people, scholars included, theorized that dim sum was actually created by an ancient Chinese emperor for his lover. Since Josie had stopped eating for quantity and had started to focus more on the experience itself, she had come to love the idea of a leisurely repast of little dishes, tiny delicacies to be eaten slowly, morsel by morsel, perhaps even lifted bit by bit to a lover's lips, like a hummingbird sipping from the stamen of a honeysuckle flower. The words *dim sum* could be translated as "heart's delight." Which was rather beautiful, if taken that way. If a person nibbled sweetly at a savory golden triangle filled with only the most delicately seasoned meats, and if such morsels were proffered on the tips of exquisitely lacquered *kuàizi*, or chopsticks, by a lover late in the morning while reclining on silken cushions...well then, that was seduction.

In the din of laughter, the fussiness of toddlers who could use chopsticks better than Josie, and the clang of metal lids coming off steaming towers of cylindrical dishes, Josie took in the sights and sounds of the massive room. The restaurant was more banquet hall than diner. Industrial, high-traffic carpet covered the entire place, but failed to dim the noise level much. Josie counted at least 20 round ten-person tables and spied additional private rooms off to the side. Most of the tables were filled with families that included babies in highchairs, elderly white-hairs who needed walkers, and every age group in between. Some families were so large they spilled across several of the round tables, but for the most part, people kept to their own little orbits of activity.

Probably three-quarters of the clientele were Asian of some kind, the rest folks who didn't give a rat's ass about crossing cultural boundaries—Josie's kind of people. In truth, now that she looked closer, she saw more than a handful of mixed-race families. Always curious about racial dynamic, she observed all customers being treated with deference, at least outwardly. Whatever the servers thought, they were polite to everyone.

Aggressive Cantonese was the dominant language, and Josie couldn't understand a word of it other than the names of the dishes, which she had long ago committed to gastric muscle memory. *Because the stomach got what the stomach wanted, even if it involved memorizing the nuances of a tortuously tonal foreign language.* Bored-looking teenagers pushed rolling metal carts piled high with stacks of tins and dishes. Josie spied steaming *hagow*, the glassy rice-wrapper purses stuffed with minced shrimp and garlic. With those always came *shumai*, more dumplings, but this time upright, like savory tide pool anemones, stand-up pouches filled with pork and garlic, each with two or three tiny bits of carrot on top for color. Her nose and salivary glands were working overtime, and her stomach gave an impatient yowl.

Others of her favorites sped by. *Bao*, or buns, stuffed with all different kinds of filling—sweet barbecue, tangy pork, or red bean paste—either steamed pale white like moons clipped by flour-dusted scissors into a pucker on top or baked with a golden-brown egg gloss. She whiplashed back and forth trying to get a glimpse at each cart, but refrained from ordering—sticking her hand up in the air and making eye contact would have been her *modus operandi*. The Yus were the elders at their white-tablecloth-covered table; they were the hosts for today's lunch, so she took her cues from James and deferred to them.

To the chagrin of her salivary glands, they ordered nothing from the carts. In fact, they ignored them and waited for a server to approach with a pot of fresh loose-leaf tea. Josie sniffed the tea that was handed to her. The glossy white teacup smelled not of the jasmine some of the trendier restaurants served, but of strong brown *oolong*. Harsh to the unindoctrinated, oolong tea, popular with southern Chinese, was the perfect flavor to offset the rich dishes that would soon be filling their white-clothed table top. This variety tasted woody and thick, evocative of its *black dragon* name—she'd done a blog entry on tea not too long ago. While Mr. Yu seemed content to sit quietly with his arms folded over his chest, Mrs. Yu spoke in rapid Cantonese to the server, who interrupted her. They were barely taking turns, talking over each other. The server nodded, left, and returned with a plain, printer paper menu that Josie strained to see.

Aha.

How they were ordering now was what Josie thought of as "advancing to the next level". The tea-stained paper didn't look like much, but it was the secret menu for regulars and people in the know; in this case, people who knew how to read traditional Chinese. Usually, they were hand-written and duplicated on a spotty copy machine, probably in the same back office where they had set up the computer.

Like an empress, Mrs. Yu looked down her nose through her glasses at the spotted menu and seemed to berate the server. Then again, all Cantonese sounded like squabbling to Josie, some kinds more than others. Josie watched in awe, squinting and cocking her head as if that would help her comprehend a dialect wholly foreign to her—she'd studied some Mandarin in college, but it was no help here.

Josie suddenly figured out Mrs. Yu was confirming which was the best vegetable of the day because the server, a young man in his twenties, suddenly said in English, "Right. Benny picked it fresh, just this morning in Gilroy." At that, Mrs. Yu finished ordering with a regal nod and then stared around the room, avoiding eye contact with the rest of them.

⌘

Josie swiveled around on her butt to watch the server's retreating back as he reentered the swinging kitchen doors.

"What I wouldn't give to see the inside of that kitchen," she couldn't stop herself from saying out loud. She craned her neck, but glanced back at her hosts hopefully. A kitchen like this at the peak of brunch time traffic would be amazing. The flash of pans, charred woks, angry Cantonese between sizzling bursts of steam and smoke. Nothing in the world could replicate the raw energy of a kitchen in full swing. Nothing even came close.

Mr. Yu remained silent while his wife made a *pshaw* noise that Josie had thought happened only in books. "You are not interested in that," Mrs. Yu proclaimed, crossing her arms as if her word was the final say. Clearly, she didn't know with whom she was dealing.

"Seriously, that place must be a beehive of activity." Josie raised her eyebrows, trying to goad them into answering. Her words kept coming out, though she wished someone else were saying them—she knew she was starting to sound like an idiot. James remained silent, and Susan's jaw was clamped shut as well, though she was shooting daggers at her erstwhile internet white knight in pixels.

Josie rambled on. "How many cooks do you have back there? Or is it the same as a bakery, where they come in at 4:00 a.m. to make all the dumplings ahead of the brunch rush? Or," she continued speculating aloud, "is everything pre-made and frozen raw and then cooked according to how many tables are being seated?"

Mrs. Yu rolled her eyes and pushed up the sleeve of her shirt, displaying a wrap on her arm. "The kitchen is very dangerous. Things are always being prepared no matter what time of day it is. I cook, too. That's how I got this injury. And that's how I lost this finger nine years ago." Above the new bandage on her wrist, she showed them the long-ago injury of a missing finger, down to the first knuckle, where her index finger should have been. She pushed up the other sleeve to show an immense burn scar that ran across her inner arm. The skin was healed now, a silvery-white and shiny melting riverbed down her flesh.

"Whoa," Josie said, impressed, her eyes bugging out. Susan coughed delicately into her napkin and looked away, turned off by the unappetizing view of Mrs. Yu's finger stump. Josie didn't mind it—it wasn't like she'd found the missing fingertip in a dumpling or anything. "All veteran chefs have scars. It's a badge of honor. Like a battle scar."

Mrs. Yu's mouth curved into a smile, but Susan didn't really warm up to the idea. "Whatever," she said, and mouthed, "So gross," at Josie across the soy sauce and chili sauce bottles.

Josie tried to explain the machismo to Susan. "Scars are as important to chefs as...their personal set of knives. Those things are sacred in the culinary world."

"I know, right?" Mrs. Yu said, suddenly sounding super Americanized. She smiled at Josie, but then abruptly frowned. "But you still don't go into my kitchen. I don't have enough insurance for that."

She folded her arms across her chest, and that was that. The kitchen, so to speak, was closed for discussion.

CHAPTER 7

"I've never been to San Francisco before this week," Josie tried again to start a conversation some minutes later while they waited for food. She drummed her fingertips on the tablecloth, not able to take the silence. Two small children chased each other around their table, and she smiled at them. She found her patience was being pushed beyond its limit by the Yu family, both James and his parents, more than once this morning. "I've been to Santa Cruz, but this is my first time in the Bay Area. But Susan has been here before." She nodded at Susan, trying not so subtly to drag her into the conversation. Susan's eyes bugged out at Josie. "Susan is a graphic designer, so she uses a lot of technology," Josie added lamely, as if technology were a tangible thing that could be purchased in a packet, like baking soda or MSG. She was getting desperate. James stared at the tablecloth.

"You're not Chinese," Mrs. Yu said to Josie. Her comment sounded like an accusation. She had, of yet, still not directly acknowledged Susan at all. Yes, James's mother was behaving like a dragon lady. And as usual, Josie found herself trying to please her, just as she felt with Greta Williams. Chalk it up to Josie's own mother being...unavailable because of her dementia.

"My mother is Thai," Josie said, nodding, matter-of-fact. Her father had been an American G.I. while her mother, who was in a convalescent home for dementia patients, was fully Thai. Even after all these years in the United States, her mother's English was still a little broken...and getting worse now as the dementia increased. Josie would probably have to invest in a Thai language course online soon if she wanted to talk with her mother at all. Her parents' multicultural union made Josie an American-born mix, as many people were. Thai people generally had round faces, but her father's contribution to her gene pool erased some of that attribute. Some people could still see her ethnic roots in the shape of her face, while others had no idea. Still others guessed incorrectly with sometimes humorous results. Mexican. Indonesian. Indian, of both flavors. Josie didn't mind because she often used other people's confusion to her advantage.

"Thailand," Mrs. Yu said. "That's close to China. I've never been to Thailand, but I hear they have a lot of drugs there. And prostitution. Maybe even a *coup d'état* in the last couple of years. They have a king and a big military. Have you ever been there?" she wanted to know. Mrs. Yu appeared to be evaluating Josie far more than was suitable for her being just a visiting friend of a friend of a son. She felt like she was being sized up as a potential mate. Josie glanced at James, who was picking his fingernails. *As if.*

"No, I haven't ever been there," Josie said. "I was born in Massachusetts." She actually wasn't sure if she ever wanted to go to Thailand. Not that she'd have any trouble staying away from the social and humanitarian ills that Mrs. Yu had mentioned, but sitting on a long international flight with a testy stomach didn't appeal to her in the slightest. One day, maybe, if she ever got a handle on her digestive issues, she could add a food tour of Southeast Asia to her bucket list. She could call it "Girl Versus Stomach."

Mrs. Yu nodded. "I haven't been there either. Just Hong Kong and here. I have a sister in Boston, but I have never been there. She comes here to see me because she's the younger sister. I have lived in San Francisco for thirty-five years. I used to own the dance studio across the street before we opened this restaurant. I had to sell my studio because we could not afford to run both places." Here, she shot a scowl at Mr. Yu, who sat impassively, his arms still folded across his chest. Josie wondered if he were a practitioner of mediation, yoga, or tai chi. Or if he just held a black belt in ignoring his ornery wife. Not that Josie minded Mrs. Yu's brusqueness. Josie liked strong, uppity women. Women with vertebrae made of steel. Like Greta Williams. They made excellent role models. Strong women who didn't back down from challenges. A lady who couldn't be put in her so-called place. *Rarrr.* Josie was drawn to them like Susan was to an artful Macy's window display.

Mrs. Yu said, "With my dance studio, I have been here and Las Vegas. And then I used to go to Anaheim every year for the dance competition with my girls. Once we took a Les Mis theme show all the way to Nationals." Mrs. Yu had a gleam in her eye that bordered on fanaticism—long after the time it should have faded into sentimentality. A bit alarming, but hey, who was Josie to mock someone else's dream. True, she was having trouble reconciling the plump, dowdy woman in front of her with the image of a stage mother or dance coach. The sequins and costumes and choreography. Staying up all night planning the next routine. Draining the retirement fund to pay for travel and competition fees. But who was Josie to judge? People had been trapped in the web of worse addictions. Like playing video games. Or gambling. Or eating fried pork rinds.

"Do you have a daughter?" Josie suddenly asked. She didn't know if James had any siblings. She'd put her money on him being an only child—he had that privileged, entitled attitude that came not from money, but from being flat-out indulged—but she wasn't totally sure. Plus, she didn't know where the Yus stood in the socio-political one-child-per-household area.

Mrs. Yu confirmed, "No, James is our only child. But he used to dance. So beautiful. So graceful. He won many, many trophies. He might have been a top dancer at the professional level." Josie's head whipped toward him just as Susan's did. He was a dancer? She'd bet a million bucks that little bit of trivia had not gone into his high school yearbook caption. James's eyes stayed glued to the tabletop. He cleared his throat, a sudden redness traveling across his cheeks and the tops of his ears.

"Are you a dancer?" Mrs. Yu asked Josie, again completely ignoring Susan—Josie knew for a fact Susan had done tap, ballet, jazz, and modern dance from *en utero* through college. As a toddler, Josie had been dragged to ballet by her mother—one of the last activities Josie remembered clearly in which her mother had actively participated—and during her final public performance, had torn off her pink tutu on stage and had stomped on it to tune of Vivaldi's *Four Seasons—Spring*. She had been *une petite tempête*, a little summer thunderstorm in the middle of eight perfectly-behaved cotton-candy clouds. Josie's dark-haired mother, sitting in the front row of the audience, had laughed raucously, perhaps already exhibiting signs of her impending dementia. Or maybe, just a part of her true nature, which Josie shared.

"No, not me. Two left feet, but—" Josie intended to bring Susan into the conversation, but she didn't get a chance.

"You write for a newspaper?" Mr. Yu interrupted, clearly dismissing the subject of dance. Josie could feel her eyebrows shoot up again. Why so much interest in her? How did they know about her blog? Her blog had a large subscription pool, but the demographics had most of the readers pegged as East Coast denizens. She had only recently made some headway in the national scene, thanks to word-of-mouth and shared links on Facebook and other sites. Lord help her, she'd also started Tweeting recently. She was hoping a larger site like *The Huffington Post* might pick her up as a guest sometime, but they hadn't so far. She looked at James, who was staring off into middle-distance. Susan was shooting invisible daggers at him.

"Yessss, I do. I write for *The Daily News*, which is a mostly-online publication now although they have a small print circulation. I have a weekly blog. It comes out on Wednesdays." Which was tomorrow, she reminded herself. *Yikes.* Even though she was here messing around in California, she couldn't neglect her actual day-to-day paying job. She needed to keep her dog happy in biscuits and Greenies after all. Baby needed a new pair of booties for his paws on the winter sidewalk next year—he'd hated the last pair so much, he'd hidden them in the back of the closet. She knew it was cruel and unusual punishment to put shoes on a dog, but the sidewalk had been frigid last winter…and it was kind of hilarious. She was a bit, but not enough to attract the attention of the Animal Cruelty people.

"Your column is about food. Is that right?" Mr. Yu said, pushing his glasses up. He peered at her with his head slightly tilted. He had a nice face, a very scholarly face. Like his wife, he had unusually stiff posture. They were both sitting stick-straight, as if they'd taken lessons from Greta Williams. Their faces were almost entirely placid. She was beginning to figure out where they were coming from, metaphorically. If she were correct, James was due for another kick in his scrawny shin.

"Yes, I write a food column." It was pretty much about food, between the paragraphs of pointless yammering, so that wasn't a total exaggeration. Her stomach didn't squeeze, so that was how she knew, because after all, her gut was her moral compass.

Mrs. Yu turned her curly head toward her husband and said sharply, "She's much more philosophical than that. I have read much of what she has said. She writes about food, but also about love and life. About disappointment and things not being what you expect them to be. It's very, very deep." She suddenly smiled at Josie, which transformed her owlish expression into a charming, funny face. Josie couldn't help but smile back. "Maybe you could write an article about our restaurant." Then she shrugged, "But nobody could read it unless you put it in the Chinese newspaper."

Whoa. Mrs. Yu was one of her readers? The idea of this bespectacled harridan squinting at Josie's words on the web gave her pause. *Did I say anything offensive in the last post?* She wondered, backtracking through her mental edits.

"So you know how to cook?" Mr. Yu asked. His face was solemn. She imagined him wearing the tunic of an ancient Chinese scholar, probably green, and sporting one of those wispy Fu Manchu beards with an equally wispy soul patch. He was cool and aloof. Probably not the type of dad to hug or high-five his kid.

"Of course she does," Mrs. Yu said, rolling her eyes behind her wire-framed glasses. "She writes about it, doesn't she? She can't write about it if she doesn't know anything about it."

"I know how to make a small number of dishes well," Josie said, which was the honest truth. She didn't experiment as much as she used to because of her stomach situation, but she still loved it. Food was imbued with all kinds of meaning: memory, hope, and expectation. And, of course, culture. From sauerkraut to lutefisk, from crêpes to samosas.

Mrs. Yu jabbed her husband in the arm with her elbow. "See how smart she is? We are glad to meet you. It's nice that you could come all this way to spend time with James. And also bring your friend, Susan."

Here, finally, she afforded a forced, fakey smile in Susan's direction.

Susan was still frowning at James—shooting death lasers from her pupils, to be more precise. Clearly, Mr. and Mrs. Yu had been led to believe that their son was dating Josie, *not Susan*. And who had misled them in such a manner? And whose job was it to enlighten them as to the truth of the matter?

Josie waited a millisecond before blurting, "I'm glad Susan was already out here visiting James before I decided to come. That way, they could both show me around a little."

Behind the lenses of her glasses, Mrs. Yu flicked her eyes at her son, but said nothing. *So, she was going to play it that way, was she?*

Josie pressed the issue. "I had been looking forward to meeting James for a long time. Susan has told me so much about him. I felt like I already knew him from everything she's said. They have known each other for so long, it's not surprising that they finally started *dating*."

Mr. and Mrs. Yu avoided all eye contact—so that's where their son got it. Josie had just about enough of this farce. She wadded up her cloth napkin and was prepared to toss it on the table top, ready to grab James by the elbow and haul him off somewhere to have a little talk, as her Aunt Ruth liked to say, a "Come to Jesus Meeting" full of reckoning the likes of which he could expect to experience again only standing outside the pearly gates of heaven.

Then, the meal arrived and, Lord help her, Josie was weak. She became distracted...completely overwhelmed by the culinary prowess of the kitchen. She fell back into her chair stunned. Yes, she could be bought—by fresh vegetables, perfectly steamed or sautéed, bright green but tender and sweet. Tender, new bok choy, baby broccoli, long beans, each on a separate platter. A bird's nest basket of deep fried noodles overflowing with seafood. Crispy roasted duck cut into perfect rectangles, reassembled into their original duck form. A couple dishes of fresh dumplings and *bao*, because they probably had seen her eyeballing the carts.

Everyone had her price, and Josie's was food. Yes, she could be bought. Her irritation at James momentarily forgotten, she picked up her chopsticks and tucked in. Yes, she was weak. *So very, very weak.*

She took a bite of a delightfully chewy bun, the seasoned bits of barbecued meat in a purse of sweet sauce inside bursting with flavor in her mouth. She may have moaned. Mrs. Yu smiled at her, looking self-satisfied.

If they fed her this way, she might have to rethink her whole stance on James, even if he was a wussy who couldn't tell his parents who he was dating. She glanced at Mrs. Yu again across the steaming tins of dumplings. The woman was fierce and protective of her son, Josie realized with envy. Some people had all the luck. Maybe she could just get them to *adopt her.*

CHAPTER 8

"How could you do that to me?" Susan sat in the passenger seat of James's electric car—now vacant of computer parts—a perfect position for whacking him on the shoulder. Which she did repeatedly. James flinched with each smack but kept his eyes on the traffic.

Yeah, you tell him, girl. Although Josie felt enough guilt to cringe as well.

Josie blinked, staring lazily out the window in a rice gluten coma from lunch. She *loved* James's parents. By the end of their early brunch, she had gotten a firm handshake from Mrs. Yu, a nod from Mr. Yu, and an extracted promise that she would stop by again before she went back to Boston. Too bad she wasn't Susan. Yes, she had totally abandoned her friend for the food—Josie had not come to Susan's rescue either—but it had been a matter of survival; there had been nothing they could do about the awkward situation sitting at the lunch table. Josie had not wanted to humiliate Susan any further. True, Josie had a few choice words for James, but she was letting Susan lay into him, as was her most-likely-soon-to-be-ex girlfriend's right.

"You gave your parents a picture of *Josie* instead of me? You told them about her instead of me?" Susan fumed, her cheeks bright pink now. Josie had never seen her this upset. Ever. "Are you ashamed that I'm not Chinese? I was an East Asian studies major for heaven's sake. I'm not a total *da bizi*." Josie's command of Chinese was poor, and Susan's was probably just as bad, but apparently, they both still remembered what that meant—"big nose" or essentially, foreigner, or white person.

"It's not like that," he tried to say.

"Well, what is it like then?" A strand of Susan's blonde hair fell over her forehead—the only thing out of place on her entire swan-like person.

"It's not me, it's *them*. I'm sorry. I just couldn't tell them about you. I was trying to work up to it. I mean, I was going to tell them, but I just didn't find the right time."

"You're...chickenshit," Susan said, her cursing completely out of character. And slightly redneck, shockingly. Josie brimmed with pride.

"It's them," James insisted in a weak, apologetic way. "They're kind of...racist."

Silence fell over the car. True silence, because the car's electricity-powered engine didn't even block out road noise—or the honking of the car that James cut off as he veered into the HOV, high-occupancy vehicle lane. They were on the 101 headed south, with San Mateo and Redwood City flying by on the left side of the car as they headed to PPS in Cupertino. They were leaving the hip-and-trendy, revitalized urban hills for the tech sprawl of San Jose and the South Bay area.

"What do you mean, 'kind of racist'?" Susan finally said. She'd flung her hand out in questioning disbelief, her palm up, the universal symbol for *WTF? What the ever-loving f-bomb?*

James flinched, thinking she was going to smack him again. "They've lived in Chinatown almost their whole lives. The only place they travel is back to Hong Kong to see family. You heard them. They read Chinese newspapers. They watch Chinese TV. They don't even vote in the presidential elections. Why do you think? Because they don't like white people." Josie was baffled at this announcement.

Susan asked, "Don't they serve all kinds of people in their restaurant, even tourists?"

"Well, yeah, but those are paying customers. So that's different."

"But..." Susan seemed to run out of steam. Josie knew what she was trying to say. *How could they hate me?* She'd been on that side of the fence before. Been there, done that. With a *whack* for emphasis, Susan said, "I thought you were my boyfriend. Aren't you supposed to stick up for me?" And that, Josie thought, was the bottom line.

However, James didn't capitulate. Instead, he only shrugged and said, "Yeah, I guess. I mean, kinda. They're *my parents*, you know."

"This isn't the Ming dynasty. This isn't Confucian China," Susan argued with another *thwack* to his arm. "You can speak up for the woman you're dating if she's being treated badly by your parents. You left me out on a limb back there. You totally...didn't come to my rescue." Susan slumped in the passenger seat.

Josie picked at her perpetually ragged cuticles in the uncomfortable silence. In the front seat, tropical depression Susan was brewing. In all their years of friendship, Josie had never seen Susan treated this poorly by a guy she was dating. Even the fourth friend of their group, poor rudderless Benjy at home, though he might have had to borrow money to take Susan to the movies, would have treated her like a precious gift. The men she dated typically showered her with attention, with high-ticket gifts, with the equivalent of frankincense and myrrh in the code of dating clichés—earrings, scarves, gift certificates because they knew she loved to shop. They were on time to pick her up for the theater. They were courtly in their manners. They were moneyed, either by serious employment or by family connections. And they were never disappointed by her company. Who could be? She never asked for any of the gifts. She never acted bitchy or snobbish. She was who she was. Kind of a marvel, a modern-day miracle—a woman who was as beautiful on the inside as on the outside. Josie would never even try to assign herself to that group.

As of this very moment, no further vetting would be necessary for James. Susan would be jettisoning his cowardly butt out of her life all by herself.

If you pick a child for a boyfriend, you should expect childish behavior, Josie reasoned.

⌘

Josie felt an enormous amount of guilt—she'd more or less betrayed Susan. Because after lunch, Mrs. Yu had changed her mind and taken Josie on a tour of the kitchen after all; and now Josie felt chummy with the little Chinese firecracker of a woman. So with a full belly, Josie had been led through the swinging white dented doors into the den of iniquity that was a dim sum factory in full-swing.

Great billowing clouds of steam shrouded the workers. Their shadowy forms slipped back and forth behind towers of stacked bamboo and metal steamers. Oddly, the place smelled more like a sweatshop than a kitchen—wet wood from round bins, moist heat, wet dough, and bodies packed closely together. Yes, Josie detected a whiff of garlic and seafood, too, but the predominant odor was *industry*.

Josie knew that many of the smaller, mom-and-pop dim sum places like some of the ones in Tucson usually recruited relatives to work the kitchen and work the carts. She'd once peeked into the kitchen of Gen's Garden, Tucson's main dim sum parlor, when she was a teenager. Grannies, aunties, and uncles made the dumplings by hand. Some of them pushed the squeaky-wheeled carts and told you what dishes you needed to try, despite what you picked out. *Chicken feet are very good for your health. You try one. And turnip cake is fresh right now. Take one of these.* More than once, Josie had choked down an extra black bean *pai guat* sparerib when she thought she couldn't eat another bite, so she wouldn't insult a sweet, but pushy Chinese grandma.

This place was no mom-and-pop joint, Josie realized as she looked around. James's parents were running a massive-scale operation, employing droves of workers. To one side, two middle-aged women in matching t-shirts, hairnets, and gloves stood at opposite sides of a metal table that was laid out with banana leaves in an overlapping pattern like fish scales—or a massive dragon hide. Fast as a wink, one of the women put a mound of flavored sticky rice in the center of a single leaf and wrapped it up as if it were a birthday present. Then the fastened bundles went into clean steamers, ready to be heated.

A handful of men worked the large industrial steamers. Their long-handled metal tongs lifted and replaced the round bins with the repetitive motion of automatons. They exchanged an occasional glance, but for the most part kept quiet. The main source of the human noise came from Mrs. Yu herself. As soon as they hit the interior of the kitchen, she went on an awesome rampage, haranguing the cooks, poking at dishes about to leave the kitchen, and in general, making the staff quake in their shoes. Josie saw the whites of eyes as they watched her without drawing attention to themselves.

"This is cold," she yelled at a waitress. "What are you waiting for, a written invitation?" The rest of her verbal volley was in Cantonese, but Josie was open-mouthed with wonder. James's mother was a modern-day General Mao; her little red book was composed of the sharp commands issuing from her mouth. Josie bowed down to her.

The activity in the kitchen increased by half. Dumplings flew from countertop to steamer baskets and into the heat. The carts started flowing from the kitchen in double-time. The waiters straightened their shirts and waistbands, stiffening their spines. Josie's jaw snapped shut and she smiled. A well-run kitchen was a thing of beauty.

In the end, Susan had to grab hold of her sleeve and drag her out of the restaurant.

CHAPTER 9

After about forty minutes of a white-knuckled car ride south after lunch, Josie climbed out of the back seat of what she was coming to think of as James's Eco Death Trap of Doom. She stood for a minute with shaky knees, marveling at how quickly the euphoria from her heavenly brunch had worn off.

The PPS company campus in Cupertino reminded Josie of a small college, with its mature trees and clean but not fussy landscaping. Large agapanthus grass with their purple puffs of stalked flowers lined the drive—Josie's Aunt Ruth had called them "society garlic," which made Josie laugh. As if garlic could be polite. In Josie's experience, garlic took no prisoners. She couldn't help how her mouth quirked up in a half-smile as she passed them. James took them past three large buildings, and then walked them to the side entrance of the fourth. Susan had stopped speaking to him, so they silently trailed James up the steps where a door was propped open with a rock. A wall-mounted camera hung overhead, and Josie eyed it. But James walked right into the building without giving it a second thought.

"Do we need to check in or get a visitor's pass? I thought there would be a lot of security in a place like this." Josie looked around, feeling a tad nervous. Didn't corporate secrets and computer viruses and...uh, theft of office supplies happen here?

James led them down a beige-carpeted hallway. Josie frowned, running her hand down the wall—even the walls were carpeted in a weird, matching beige fabric. Maybe it was for sound-proofing. Or for posting notices. Or for keeping the inmates from hurting themselves. Whatever the purpose, it was odd. They passed a supply closet where she saw stacks of neon-colored sticky notes, highlighter markers, and other office supplies in great quantities—the bounty of a well-established company, fat with decades of profit. They walked by a break room that had a fridge and three or four vending machines filled with computer industry manna, junk food. Doritos, Ruffles, Twinkies, Zingers, and oh Lord, even Bugles, those cone-shaped corn snacks that fit on the tips of her fingers like evil snack food Press-On Nails. The white but scuffed fridge had a multitude of hand-written messages taped to the door, including one in big letters that said, "Whoever has been eating my tikka masala every day this week, I'll find you. And I will flog you."

Nice attitude. Although, if someone stole Josie's lunch on a daily basis…Yes, she could totally get behind the violence in this case.

"We could sign in at the front desk, I guess," James admitted, "but nobody does it. It's lunchtime, so people are always coming in and out anyway. They won't notice. Besides, we're just going in for a few minutes to see Ivan and find out what's going on. Maybe he heard from our investor and started the next phase of Shasta." For a minute there, his baby face looked hopeful. Josie cleared her throat and nodded though she knew it wasn't a possibility. She had the inside track on whether Greta was going to come through with the rest of their start-up funding. Josie more or less *was the inside track.*

The three of them walked farther down another hallway of closed office doors. No cubicles anywhere, which was a surprise to Josie. When she tried to picture a startup company, the first thing that came to mind was a cubicle farm—even *The Daily News*, where Josie's editor still had a desk, had downsized from a traditional office to just a small hive of cubes in a rented facility. But then James turned the corner and she saw that the center of the floor on this level was all cubicles. They'd simply come down a hall that was lined with offices for what were probably more respected workers, or people who needed privacy for their projects.

James stopped at the end of a hall and pulled out a key, which he used to unlock an office—apparently, they were valued employees. Josie stood outside the doorway and slid her finger across the magnetic nameplates next to the door frame. One sign said *Ivan Sorokin* and the other *James Yu*. Her finger hit the edge of Ivan's nameplate and, by accident, moved it off-center a few millimeters. She tapped the other side and realigned it. Inside the office, the lights came on automatically; they were motion-activated, which meant no one inside the office had moved in a while. In fact, the office was empty.

While she was standing half-in and half-out of the office, a little man—shorter than Josie, which meant extremely short for a man—passed by her in the hall with a mug. "Thank goodness, it's lunchtime," he said gesturing with his soup mug. He went into the break room they had just walked past. She gave him a slight smile, enjoying his clipped British accent.

"What the...?" From inside the office, James exclaimed loudly, drawing Josie in. He was saying, "What is this? I don't understand."

⌘

James stood over Ivan's desk, peering at the computer screen. All Josie could see over his shoulder were Star Wars action figures lining the shelf above the computer monitor. A mini Han Solo and a Luke Skywalker on his furry kangaroo thing peered at Susan and her as they crowded behind James. "What's going on?" Josie asked. They squinted at Ivan's screen where they saw the same scrolling program, the lines of code they had seen from James's laptop. "What does that mean?"

"I'm not sure. I mean, it's his project here, obviously," James said though it wasn't remotely obvious to either Susan or her. "It looks like Ivan is working, but he's not here either. I mean, of course he's not right here." He gestured to Ivan's empty chair, waving his hand through the space that Ivan would have occupied had he been there. James leaned over the desk and moved the computer's mouse, which took control over the screen. The typing and scrolling abruptly stopped. The three of them glanced at each other uncertainly.

Then, two small video windows popped open. They all leaned closer, but only James's face—the closest one to the webcam—appeared in the outgoing video screen. A face appeared in the incoming window.

"That's not Ivan," James said frowning, clicking the keyboard to adjust the volume. "Hello? Who's there? Who are you?" With the mouse, he clicked the corner of the incoming video window and dragged it so it was bigger. The three of them stared at the face of a young Chinese man.

"Hello?" James said again.

"Hello?" the man echoed in thickly accented English. He was sitting in a stark, white office. But even from the simple construction of the room, the stark furnishings, and the man's simple clothes, Josie got the feeling he wasn't in an office at PPS. Maybe not even in California. He said, "Hello. This is Jun. Where is Ivan?" Then, seeing that James was Chinese, the man switched to Mandarin.

Josie was surprised to hear James reply in Mandarin. His parents had used Cantonese at lunch, but apparently, James knew more than one dialect. She herself knew only the basics from college classes, so she quickly lost the gist of the conversation after both men introduced themselves and admitted neither knew where Ivan was.

"I don't believe this," James said in English to Susan and her. He spoke with Jun a few minutes longer. Then the two men said goodbye, and James closed the video window. "This is totally crazy," he said, "This guy is doing Ivan's work. Ivan subcontracted out his PPS project to this guy—he's a Chinese citizen. *In China.* Like, the entire project—it's a confidential project. I mean, it's not NSA-level stuff, but it is banking. Ivan hasn't been writing any of this code. *None* of it. The whole project— that's weeks of work. All the work has been written and checked in by this guy." He gestured to the computer behind him, and then whispered. "I'm pretty sure that's illegal. Ivan could get in serious trouble, I mean with Homeland Security—probably, I don't know. He gave this guy his security clearance for our company. Oh my God, we're going to be put on the watch list."

Susan stood straighter and said, "Should we tell someone? Who do we call, your HR department? Do you have a number?" Like Josie, Susan was a freelance worker, a contractor who worked from home. Neither of them had any experience with a situation like this.

James ignored her while he stood there, staring into space, clearly stunned and still trying to process it.

"So, where's Ivan then?" Josie asked, looking around. The light on the office phone was blinking, but James himself had called that phone number earlier and left a message, so it could have been from him. The whiteboard by the desk was clean. A blank sticky note pad and pen sat on the desk. Other than the Star Wars figurines, there was nothing else there, as if Ivan hadn't been there in a while.

"I have no idea. Where would he be?" he asked himself.

"Where does he live?" Josie asked. She looked around. The small British man gave her a nod and a scrutinizing glance as he walked back by the door, this time going the other direction. He abruptly stopped and came back. His pressed long-sleeved plaid shirt was neatly tucked into the waist of his blue jeans, as if he couldn't quite pull off the casual workday look.

"Hullo," he said, bushy gray eyebrows popping upward. "New starts?"

James stood up quickly, stepping in front of Ivan's computer screen to block it. "Oh, hey, Colin. Yeah. New…uh…tech writers going through orientation. Not really sure what they'll be working on yet. I was just going to introduce them to Ivan. I didn't realize he was working from home today."

"Fantastic. I guess it means our hiring freeze is over. We'll be back to getting our Christmas bonuses before long," the little man said with a solemn expression and a wink for Susan, "As for Ivan, I haven't seen him in weeks, not in person at least. Just the same as this one here," he nodded at James, "he always calls into the project meetings, except when it's something silly, for instance when we have birthday cake. Usually he comes in for cake. No one passes that up. Had a birthday in our group just today, but he missed it. Not like him at all. I mean, cake. Am I right? Who would miss that?" He looked at Josie, who was able to nod in genuine agreement. Because, *cake*.

"But he's…not late with any of his deadlines, right?" James said. Josie knew the three of them were thinking of the Chinese man secretly tapping away on a keyboard halfway around the world, pretending to be Ivan.

"Not at all. He's checking in his code faster than he ever has before, actually. And I'm hardly opening any bugs against it. It's as if he took a course in coding over his last holiday, his stuff is so much cleaner than before. You can tell him I said so next time you see him." Colin looked pleased. He was cute in an inappropriate uncle way.

"Uh, sure," James said, rubbing the back of his neck, his shiny hair rumpled and standing up straight from his stressful afternoon.

"Well, nice to meet you ladies," Colin said with a hopeful smile aimed especially at Susan. Aaaand there went the suggestive eyebrows again. "Maybe I'll get the chance to work closely with you in the future. I always *adore* tech writers." He walked away with a whistle.

James muttered, "Move along, Colin, before you have to take HR sexual harassment training. Again."

Josie waited to make sure the man was out of earshot, then asked again, "Where is Ivan's house?"

"Down farther south in Santa Cruz. Near the beach. We used to have bonfires there. His wife usually telecommutes from their house, too. She should be there today."

"Let's go find him then." She wasn't going to take his usual hemming or hawing for an answer.

⌘

Josie had been to Santa Cruz once before when she was in high school. To say she'd been having a rough time was an understatement. Her dad had just died of a heart attack. Her mom had been placed in a nursing home that cared for dementia patients. Josie had been sent to live in southern Arizona with her Aunt Ruth and Uncle Jack, who were actually her dad's aunt and uncle and a good deal older than Josie. She'd been a young punk kid with a massive chip on her shoulder, apt to get into fistfights with some of the Spanish-speaking girl gangbangers after school. She'd thought that she could pull one over on her aunt and uncle, that they were too old and feeble to either understand her troubles or to keep a handle on her.

Rodeo Vacation week in February of her senior year, she'd told them she was going camping on Mt. Lemmon with a friend. Instead, she'd taken her uncle's 1988 Chevy V8 truck and left Arizona with no intention of ever returning. She headed north on I-10 into California, driving up through Phoenix, LA, and Bakersfield for almost twelve hours straight. She made it as far north as Santa Cruz where she parked near the beach not too far from the famous Boardwalk where tourists, surf rats, and so-called lost boys hung out. She had been hungry, tired, almost out money, and almost out of anger—at the world, at herself, at her dad for abandoning her, at whoever she could think of. Her feistiness had slowly dissipated. She'd sat on the beach all day, ignoring the people who tried to talk to her—missionaries who tried to save her, tourists who tossed coins into her half-full soda cup—and for the most part, she had been invisible.

She'd stayed at the beach until she got cold. When it grew dark, she climbed up into her uncle's truck and drove back to Arizona. Her Uncle Jack, though he was a car enthusiast and took meticulous care of all of his cars and trucks, never questioned her about the added mileage. She'd always loved him more for that.

CHAPTER 10

Needless to say, Josie felt strange going back to Santa Cruz, even after all this time. Ten years had passed since she'd last been here. This time, she was riding into town from the north instead of the south and she was crammed into the back of a little electric car instead of driving her uncle's stolen pickup. James was using his car's GPS navigation system to find Ivan's house—he'd been there before, he just couldn't remember exactly where it was—and she was doing her best to fight carsickness. She'd read on the internet that carsickness is caused by feeling of not being in control. External forces—the rocking motions caused by James's foot on the gas and brake as he avoided his opponents on the road, like in the old video game Frogger—worked on her body. She got the feeling that for James, life in general was a video game. She only hoped that he was aware that he didn't have multiples lives, and when they were all squashed on the highway, the game *was over*.

They had driven down Highway 17 in the bright, mid-day sunshine and were now circling around a neighborhood north of Highway 1, more inland than toward the ocean. The houses were cute bungalows, most of them single story with a lot of landscaping, both mature plants and quirky garden design, packed into just a few square feet of front yard. Cookie cutter houses that had grown into their individuality with a vengeance over the last few decades—what she saw was more than just a cute garden gnome here or there...more along the lines of a full oversized gazebo including entire arrangements of outdoor furniture plopped right in the front yards. Overhead power lines criss-crossed the street, confirming that this was an older neighborhood that had been retrofitted into the age of internet, Wi-Fi, and digital TV.

James parked in the street in front of a white picket fence that corralled a yard overflowing with pink and white roses mixed with spiny century plants. Wedged crazily in the center of the front yard was a red-bricked patio surrounded by raised garden beds, with a picnic table and numerous Adirondack chairs—far more furnishings than the yard had space for. Just a car-length away to either side was a neighbor's house. To the left was a multi-tiered garden design of blue grasses and red lava rock. To the right was a lush, waving Japanese hedge in front of a miniature red maple. The helter-skelter variety, compacted into such close proximity, made Josie dizzy. Or maybe it was the car ride. Or both.

James led them up the cracked cement drive, where an older model, slightly rusty Toyota sat on nearly-bald tires. Josie's Uncle Jack would have had a minor stroke from the car's condition—he'd always expounded the moral fortitude that proper car maintenance demonstrated. A clean-living person kept a car in good shape, both inside and out. He wasn't merely a car enthusiast. For him it was a philosophy and a way of life. The poor old Corolla in the drive clearly needed a foster family. James rang the bell of the tiny house, and the door opened with a gust of cigarette odor and floral perfume after just a couple of seconds, as if someone had been standing right behind it.

Ivan's wife was a tall, muscular woman—taller than James, which meant about 5'9" or so—with a heavily-lined face and dyed red hair. She was in yellow shorts, flip flops, and a flowery blouse that came to her thick, white wrists, which were adorned with about ten bangles each. Her toenails and fingernails were painted matching deep red, darker than her lipstick, which lined her mouth. Smoker's lines fanned out from her lips. With so much height and makeup, Josie's eyes wandered to her neck to check for an Adam's Apple—which wasn't there. Olga was on her cordless house phone. She frowned when she recognized James and held up one thick, grub-like finger while she finished talking, which explained why she had been standing by the door. Clearly, she was a compulsive pacer while on the phone.

They stood on the scrap of a front porch until Olga finished her phone conversation and hung up her cordless house phone with a beep. She said to James, "What do you want?" Her tone wasn't hostile, just unpolished and abrupt, her voice deepened from smoking. She had a slight accent that Josie guessed was Russian, though she wasn't good at pinpointing the origin of Eastern European accents. People who sound like Boris and Natasha were from that vague, militaristic cold region that consumed a lot of vodka and harbored former American spies.

"Is Ivan here?" James asked her. He had that weaselly, hunched over posture again—Josie was quickly beginning to identify it as a signal that he was anxious or insecure, usually in the face of a woman who scared him.

Olga frowned and turned on her flip-flopped heel, revealing a blurry, blueish-green butterfly tattoo on her ankle. They followed her into the house, which could have been cute inside if not for the décor. Josie peered around. The inside was tiny, but completely decorated in a beach motif—shell-encrusted lamps, rattan and wicker indoor-outdoor chairs and couches with palm-leaf upholstery in the small sitting room, and a parrot-shaped clock ticking on the wall, its red, green, and blue tail feathers swinging away the seconds. Josie liked the so-called "bones" of the little house, but the sheer amount of stuff inside made her intensely claustrophobic. No matter where Olga had come from, she had embraced the beach lifestyle fully, kitschy fabrics and all. Josie figured, with some airing out from the ocean breezes and a couple of dumpsters to haul away the contents, the house would be lovely. In Tucson, it probably would have been worth a couple hundred thousand bucks. Here, it could have been closer to a million.

Olga set the phone upright on its cradle and put her hands on her hips. Her voice was a strange mixture of lazy and irritated, definitely condescending toward James. But maybe it was the accent. Whatever the case, she clearly hadn't checked her messages. "What do you mean, where is he? Ivan is with you. He said he was staying in the city this weekend so you could work on your other *leetle* project, whatever it is. That thing that you spend all your time on that's going to make you rich, the Shasta thing." She said it with an exaggerated grimace of her dark lips. She was a hand-talker, flinging out her red nails with each statement, her wrist bangles jangling with each shake. It made Josie want to back far away so she wouldn't get scraped or impaled by the woman's blood-colored fingertips, but the wall behind her didn't leave much room to retreat. She was forced to stand her ground.

Now she had more important things to worry about than getting scratched by this Russian bodybuilder disguised as a California work-from-home techie, mermaid wannabe. Josie dug into her jeans pocket for her cell phone because based on this new information, it was time to call Detective Lopez.

Ivan wasn't at work. He wasn't at home. His business partner thought he was with his wife. His wife thought he was with his business partner. All these tidbits added up to a big fat zero.

Ivan truly was missing.

⌘

As she dialed the police, James and Susan quizzed Olga more. Josie kept one ear on their conversation and the other pressed to her phone.

"When was the last time you actually saw Ivan?" James asked. He was still not making eye contact, Josie noted. Instead, he was staring at the ticking tropical bird clock behind Olga. Not a parrot, maybe a macaw, although who really knew the difference. Weren't they both types of birds that outlived their owners? That always gave her the shivers—that a pet could be eyeing her, waiting for her to die first so it could take over her rent-controlled apartment in walking distance of the Fenway. Speaking of questionable motives, Josie couldn't tell if James was hiding something or if he was genuinely confused. Or, possibly, both.

Josie saw Olga shrug and frown. "What are you telling me? You don't know where he is? How come he's not with you? He said he was going to work with you all weekend. He told me this on Friday." The tall woman was waving her hands as she spoke, barely taking a breath between thoughts, an ability which Josie had always secretly admired. "Last time I saw him, he was packing an overnight bag to stay in his place in the city. He has that apartment in Chinatown. I don't know where it is. It's disgusting is all I know. Very cheap, dirty, and smells like garbage. I am from Omsk in Russia. I grew up incredibly poor, but I went to school and got a good job. Then I came here. I don't need dirty, smelly things in my life. His apartment...that I think smells of rotten vegetable and garlic. He tells me this after he gets it. I don't care as long as he pays for it out of his own money. We have separate checking accounts, so I always know how much I have. I don't let him spend my hard-earned paycheck on strippers and drinks. He can do whatever he wants with his own money though. And I don't care. I am the one he's married to. He always comes back home to me. We have been together for nineteen years. We will get through the problems, whatever they are." Olga paused for a breath. She was just getting started in her rant, and Josie was already worn out from it. As few as two sentences could have Josie panting—clearly she needed to work on her ranting and raving skills. Olga was world-class.

Mentally, Josie backed up in the conversation and quirked an eyebrow on hearing about Ivan's apartment. He had a separate place back in Chinatown where they had been driving around and eating lunch? James could have mentioned that while they were there. They might have saved themselves a trip.

Next to her ear, her call had finally started ringing at the other end. Apparently, Greta Williams had given her Detective Lopez's direct number and not a main switchboard connection, because he picked up right away. She turned away from the others. "Detective," she said mindful of the people talking behind her, "My name is Josie Tucker—"

"Right," he said. He sounded young, but even for a stranger and an officer of the law, he sounded terse and on edge to her. "I've been expecting your call. Where are you?"

"I'm in Santa Cruz right now," she said, confused, but trying to play it cool. She pretended she knew what the heck she was going to say to him and how she was going to explain what was going on.

"You're at the Sorokin residence?"

"Yeah..." She dragged out the syllables. "How did you know that?" She fought the urge to look over her shoulder, but couldn't stop her eyes from looking side to side.

He didn't answer, but she could hear him taking a deep breath before he spoke. "A neighbor found Ivan Sorokin's body in his

Chinatown apartment. Multiple stab wounds. It's a real horror show, to put it mildly. It's probably the worst I've ever had. I almost lost it, if you know what I mean, and that type of thing doesn't usually bother me. We have a team processing the scene. Please don't disclose any information to his wife. My partner is headed to you now—she's almost there. She should be there in ten to fifteen."

"Oh—," Josie said, the blood draining from her head, "—kay."

Ivan was dead? Missing, she could handle, but dead…she felt a weird sense of déjà vu. The last time she'd gotten involved in a quest for answers surrounding a death, she'd ended up almost, well, dead herself.

Lopez's voice was soothing now. He sounded more human…and faraway, as Josie's vision swam a bit. "I want you to grab a ride back with my partner after she's done interviewing Mrs. Sorokin. My partner's name is Sarah Dicarlo. She knows who you are, that you're a corporate P.I. hired by a private investor. You have I.D.?"

"Uh…yes," Josie was able to say though she felt faint. In all the scenarios she'd imagined—Ivan running off with the startup's seed money from Greta Williams; Ivan in Las Vegas gambling with strippers; Ivan on a tropical island with SPF 85 on his cherry-red cheeks; Ivan in South America in a wide-brimmed hat looking out over the majesty of Machu Picchu—her imagination had never constructed a violent end. His vibrant, jovial face from the photo on James's fridge floated through her mind.

"All right, good." His tone started to loosen up, to sound more easy-going. He'd been all business at first, but she'd caught him at the exact wrong moment. Her first impression of him was skewed. "Dicarlo may ask to see your identification, so that's good. She doesn't know anything else about you. I vouched for you, but she knows me, so that doesn't always work. She may not trust you right off. If that happens, just keep the rest of our connection and Greta Williams to yourself. You can hang with me once you get back up here. We'll dig up some leads while we wait for the lab to process the evidence from the scene. Due to the nature of the crime, all that blood, it's top priority with the lab and the M.E. so I think we won't have to wait that long. The media is going to be all over this one. It's ugly. Exactly the kind of gruesomeness they like on prime time."

"Sure..." While she was surprised by Lopez's level of trust and familiarity with her, the sand-colored rug with the shell border on the entryway floor in Olga's house swam in and out of Josie's vision. A dried starfish mounted on the wall waved its arms at her. Upholstered palm fronds closed in on her. She gulped a couple of breaths when she realized she had stopped taking them regularly.

"Good. I'll see you in a while then. Greta had nothing but high praise for you. My family owes her a lot, so I'm fully trusting her on this. She said to give you full access to what I know. We'll get back on the same page on this one. Hopefully, we'll get this bad guy quick." Then he hung up. Josie didn't know what page Detective Lopez was on, but it had to be a better one than she was on right now. Frankly, the page *she* was on was making her nauseated.

"Are you all right?" Susan asked, looking at her closely, not missing a thing. James and Olga paused in their conversation, too, and watched her. Josie avoided making eye contact with any of them. The wooziness was coming over her in ocean-like waves—she could almost hear it pounding against the shore in her ears. An all-consuming *shwoosh* as her blood pushed in, then drained out of her head. She was about to lose it. Her cool. Her cookies. Her marbles.

Because here she was again, involved with another death.

"Do you mind if I...use your restroom?" she asked Olga.

PART 2: THE INGREDIENTS

Pet peeve #12,284: complex ingredients that make you go to the ends of the earth to find them. Quail eggs. Puffball mushrooms. Milk-fed *poulardes*. Why would you go to all the trouble to find unusual ingredients if the outcome is terribly risky? Isn't it better to put together common ingredients in interesting combinations for that surprise chemistry you would never expect? Unusual pairings of things you already have might just be the magic missing from your life. Sauerkraut cupcakes with beer frosting might be your Sonny and Cher. Lavender glaze for your lemon cake might be the Cary Grant in your comedy. Bacon in your dark sacred chocolate truffle might be...well, let's not take things too far.

Josie Tucker, *Will Blog for Food*

CHAPTER 11

Slightly less green around the gills now—no thanks to Olga Sorokin's mermaid-themed bathroom and decorative clamshell soaps—Josie stood aside in the Sorokins' beachy sitting room while Detective Dicarlo, Lopez's diminutive partner, broke the news to Olga that her husband had been murdered. While Josie herself knew that Ivan had suffered multiple stab wounds, she was intrigued to hear that the detective didn't disclose the horrid details to Ivan's wife.

Dicarlo was short in stature, even shorter than Josie's five feet almost-three inches, with blond hair in a tight, low ponytail and bright green eyes. She was wearing utilitarian black pants and a white button-down, and her badge was clipped to her waistband. Based on her direct, but not hostile stare, and her sensible black leather shoes, Josie decided that she liked her. Dicarlo had a definite Harriet the Spy vibe about her, if the girl detective had added a PG-13 vocabulary and a couple more decades of sleuthing under her belt. Dicarlo peered up at the much taller Olga after introducing herself as a member of the SFPD.

"Mrs. Sorokin, I'm sorry to inform you that your husband has been found dead." Dicarlo didn't seem sorry, actually, although she had pulled her eyebrows down in a semblance of somber empathy. Maybe she'd had to be a deliverer of this type of news before. Maybe years of police work had worn down any true ability to empathize. On the other hand, Josie admired her straightforwardness. The detective had probably chosen the most appropriate delivery possible, given the circumstances.

Olga was silent, but James turned pale and exclaimed, "Oh my God." He looked at Susan, then Josie, and then back at Dicarlo. His mouth opened and closed like a fish as he tried to process the information—truth be told, Josie had only a fifteen-to-ten minute start on him in hearing the news, so she wasn't doing much better. "What do you mean? Like...dead?"

Still wordless, Olga had gone still, her open mouth covered by the red-tipped fingers of her hands. She sank down on her shell-upholstered sofa. Then she stood back up to her nearly six feet and said, "It was that bitch, wasn't it?"

But James interrupted her, saying, "Are you sure it's him? I mean, it's really him, right?"

Dicarlo turned to him, angling her body between him and Olga. "I'm sorry, who are you?"

"I'm Ivan's partner," James said. After Dicarlo's eyebrows rose in surprise as she flicked her eyes toward Olga, he added, "His business partner. We have a company called Applied Apps."

"App Apps?" the detective said, shortening it in a way James appeared not to have considered. She took out a tiny spiral notebook and jotted the name down.

"Well, yeah, I guess." James frowned, his long-fingered hands fluttering. "But where is he? Did he get hit by a car? He's always texting while he walks. Or, like a heart attack? Because he's totally out of shape. His BMI is like, 33 or something. I was always telling him to try to lose weight. Where was he?"

"He was found in Chinatown," Dicarlo said. "At an apartment rented in his name."

"Yes, he has an apartment there—a dirty, stinking, filthy apartment. He was with that stripper, wasn't he? That *child*? Oh God, I just know it. All these years I gave him, and he was with her," Olga said. Everyone stared at her, but she just shook her head, shifting her cloud of coarse, red hair. "I can't believe this. Why would he do this to me? Why would he leave me like this?"

"This stripper—who would that be?" Dicarlo said. She was poised to write it down in her miniature notebook. Her pen was pink and said Hello Kitty, which made Josie mentally scratch her head.

Olga's eyes narrowed. Her lips pressed together tightly. She sat on the edge of the couch looking as if she had somewhere to go. Her eyes moved around the room like a bird trying to find somewhere to alight. "Ivan was obsessed with a stripper at some club in San Jose. A burlesque club called the Pony Palace, Pony Pagoda, or something like that. I don't know the girl's name—I don't know which one she was. Of course, I don't go to strip clubs. I only know because he went there often. I found receipts for his bar tab once—that's why we keep our money separate. I didn't think he was actually sleeping with her. I only thought...He had a crush, you know? He wouldn't betray me." She started to cry, her thick makeup running, and Josie had the overwhelming urge to flee the room. She took a deep breath. Olga's grief and discomfort were tangible, a big, wet wall of humidity.

James, too, was highly agitated—though he didn't seem too surprised at the news of the stripper, Josie noted. He kept running a hand through his hair. Susan put her hand on his arm to try to soothe him, but he brushed her off. "I just don't understand," he said to the detective. "How do you know it's him? Don't we need to go up there and identify him for sure? I mean, it could still be someone else, right?"

"The medical examiner is going to take care of him now," Dicarlo said, with an admirable kindness and patience. The little detective patted him on the arm, and unlike with Susan, he allowed it, which was annoying to Josie. "They have some work to do, but yes, it is your friend, I'm sorry to say. The neighbor identified him for us. Also, he had his I.D. and wallet still. So, you need to hang tight. I'm sure we'll get some more information for you soon."

Although according to the big exposé Josie had read recently online, there was about a three month lead time in most cases going through the Coroner's office. They were short-staffed, down a pathologist, and in danger of losing their Medical Examiner due to an investigation into his misuse of funds. The backlog of cases in a department that handled almost 1,500 homicides, accidents, and deaths that needed explaining meant that there was no guarantee whatsoever that Ivan's case wouldn't simply be thrown into the heap and forgotten. Josie kept all that to herself, of course, but she wasn't going to put a lot of hope in a quick turnaround from that department.

As the news started to sink in, James sat down heavily on the other end of the couch from Ivan's widow. He ran a hand through his hair. "Well, damn. Now what do I do?" he said to no one in particular.

⌘

Dicarlo skillfully arranged it so that Susan and James rode back to the city on their own. Josie had thought James might need the comfort in privacy. It didn't look as if he were feeling talkative anyway. The news had hit him hard, so it was Susan who was driving his tiny car back to the city as they pulled away. James stared blankly out the front window. Josie watched his pale, frozen profile as they left.

The detective had a few questions she needed to ask Olga Sorokin, and she wanted to do so without an audience. For whatever reason, she'd decided to let Josie stay, which made Josie wonder exactly what Detective Lopez had told Dicarlo about Greta Williams and their connection. She wondered how far the influence of Greta's money extended in this string of tenuous relationships, this linked chain of favors exchanged for favors. She visualized it as a mob-like version of pay-it-forward, and wondered if she, too, would be required to perform favors for others if she were ever asked.

"Mrs. Sorokin, I need to ask you a few questions so that we can figure out where your husband was during his last hours and what he was doing."

Olga Sorokin sat on her couch. She hadn't cried yet or yelled more, but she had asked for a glass of water from her kitchen and to light a cigarette. When Josie offered to get it for her, Olga said, "Use one of the shell glasses from the cabinet." *A shell glass. Of course.*

Josie wandered into the kitchen, her eyes watering from the scented candle on the counter—labeled *Ocean Breeze.* Dazed, she scanned the countertops and starfish-stenciled cabinets. For gawd's sake, even the knife block was adorned with shells, which was a heresy against Henckels. Where was Ivan's mark, his presence in this little fishbowl?

When Josie returned with the water, Olga was blowing her nose into a tissue and explaining, "The last time I saw Ivan was on Friday afternoon. He was here packing a bag. He told me he was going to stay in the city so he and James could finish an important part of their project. He was excited because he was sure they would get another round of funding from their investors soon. Of course, their main goal was to make a company and sell the entire thing to a bigger company, such as IBM or Google or something. They would be millionaires in that case, not just earning small peanuts here and there."

"Here's some water," Josie said, handing it to her. Olga's long flowing sleeve slid back as she took the glass from Josie. She had a lit cigarette in the other hand, which she left burning but unsmoked. Whatever Dicarlo had asked Olga while Josie had been out of the room had caused Josie to fall into the "good cop" role, which was awkward to say the least, considering Josie's habitually relativistic moral code. She would have much rather been asking questions by herself than playing a partnership role, but since she was a hanger-on here, she would take what she was offered and keep her mouth shut about it. At least about the important stuff. Because staying quiet wasn't her strong suit.

"I love your bracelets," Josie said gesturing to the many bangles. "Do you mind if I take a closer look?" When Olga frowned and held out her arm, Josie put her hand under it, supporting it, letting the sleeve fall back farther. The gold bangles were numerous, each significant in weight. Josie released Olga's arm and craned her neck toward the other arm so that Olga complied and held her other arm out to Josie, who repeated the same careful inspection. She counted the bangles, dragging the gold bands across Olga's smooth, white, and unmarked skin. "Fifteen. That's a lot."

"I had so much gold jewelry from a long time ago," she said. "Back when it was not so expensive. All kinds of single earrings where I had lost one of a pair. A ring from a guy I used to date. Trinkets and tokens. Things that didn't have any meaning for me anymore. I'm not sentimental. I had it all melted down and turned into these bracelets. I wear them every day."

Josie nodded, trying to show some enthusiasm, but had a shiver-inducing vision of Nazis harvesting and melting down the gold from their prisoners' teeth. "Great idea." She released Olga's other arm, allowing the sleeve to drop back down to her wrist. The gold bands jangled noisily.

"So, you were asking where I was this weekend," Olga said, considerably calmer. She tossed her bunched up tissue on the driftwood coffee table and folded her thick-fingered hands in her lap. "I was here both Saturday and Sunday working. I was trying to complete some work that had to be finished by Monday morning. I can show you my work logs to prove it. The only time I was not logged in was Friday night because I was at my girlfriend's bridal shower. She lives in Aptos. I'm sure you can ask her. I was there the whole time."

Aptos was the next little town over from Santa Cruz, fifteen minutes away, tops. Josie listened thoughtfully as Dicarlo took down the bridal shower friend's name, address, and telephone number in her notebook.

The simple facts as Josie saw them were that Olga Sorokin had an alibi, which could be easily corroborated depending on the actual time of death, and that her arms were free of any wounds that might have resulted if she had stabbed her husband multiple times. However, she had a strong motive—jealousy, based on her accusation that Ivan had been infatuated with a stripper—and she had the physical strength. So while Olga was temporarily on the back burner of Josie's list of suspects, she was by no means cleared.

CHAPTER 12

Olga Sorokin had called one of her friends nearby to come and stay with her for a few days so she wouldn't be alone in her new state of widowhood. Josie and Dicarlo left her sitting on her seashell couch in pretty much the same position she'd been right after she heard the news of her husband's death—hand over her mouth, staring off into space. Her situation was unimaginable to Josie. Even as removed from the victim as Josie was, she was still feeling the emotional shockwave of Ivan's death.

As she climbed into Dicarlo's black Chevy Tahoe, both of them having to use the side runners to boost their vertically-challenged—short like Disney dwarves—frames up into the high SUV, Dicarlo said, "Lopez says you're some kind of a corporate P.I. checking out Sorokin's startup company...damn, what's it called?" Dicarlo patted her coat pocket for her notepad. For a second, Josie thought Dicarlo was going to take notes about her, but it turned out she was just reassuring herself that she hadn't dropped it somewhere. Like a security blanket.

"Applied Apps," Josie said, somewhat numb still but surprised she was able to recall the name easily for once.

"That's right. What do they do again?" Dicarlo was hunched over the steering wheel despite her tiny stature. She had cranked the seat all the way forward so she could reach the gas pedal.

"No frickin' clue," Josie admitted, which was the honest truth.

Dicarlo barked out a laugh, her green eyes crinkling in the corners. Josie wasn't feeling smiley, herself, so she gave a token grimace. "I've been working this area for almost ten years now as a detective, and I still can't do much else other than check my email or make a PowerPoint presentation."

Josie nodded. "I'm a technical troglodyte, too. Although I run a blog." Then she froze up, internally, because, should she have kept that a secret? Her identities were starting to trip her up and she hadn't even been doing this kind of work for long, less than a year. Luckily, Dicarlo let it pass with another laugh.

"Nice job with the jewelry, by the way. No wounds on her arms, right? I like how you worked that." Then Dicarlo cleared her throat in a business-like manner. "Okay, so forgive my ass for being sort of out there, but you're super pretty. Like, model-pretty, and I don't mean that in a Kate Moss bag-of-bones way, but in a J-Lo way, but smaller and Oriental. Kind of ethnic and natural. It's just that your skin flippin' glows. Are you single?"

Josie, who had been staring out the window, whipped her head around to stare at her small companion. "Uh...No, not single. I'm seeing someone. I have a...someone." The word *boyfriend* suddenly stumbled on its way out of her mouth. It was a sweet joke when she said it to Drew, but a cheesy defense saying it now.

Dicarlo shrugged. "Bummer for me. And a word of advice, I don't know how well you know him—he said you were a friend of a friend—but look out for Lopez. He's a total player. We always hit on the same women. He goes for the shorties, too. And I don't mean 'shawty' as the kids say. I mean short women. It works out well if he's my wingman and the girl turns out to be gay. But you know, in this day and age, I shouldn't be afraid to give it a try, right? Nothing gained, nothing lost or something—unless some religious wing nut bludgeons me with a Bible in a dark alley."

"Hopefully, that's less of a problem here in the Bay Area," Josie said.

Dicarlo continued "The problem with me, is I really need to find a nice conservative girl from some place like Nebraska to settle down with me. We'd get the whole American dream—the white picket fence, a couple of labradoodles—and vote Republican for the rest of our lives happily ever after. They just don't have that type of girl in a liberal town like this one. I just want to hunt and fish and live off the land. Clean my gun at night in front of the TV while I have a Bud Light. But I can't have the best of both worlds, so I gotta settle for the one that's going to keep my rent paid and my lifestyle judgment-free, if you know what I mean. You know, you're really easy to talk to. I don't usually put all that out there in the first five minutes I meet a woman. Sorry I hit on you, by the way." As if Josie fit Dicarlo's pipe-dream profile in the slightest.

"Don't worry about it." Josie coughed, uncomfortable. She wasn't bothered by being hit on by a woman, or even by Dicarlo specifically. Josie was having trouble shifting gears from thinking about dead Ivan to dating. Dicarlo didn't seem to be having any problems with it. Everything about this trip was spinning Josie around. Ups and downs, like the streets of the city. Thoughts buzzing around like those compact electric cars she saw everywhere, and she wasn't enjoying it much. She needed some open space to sit and think for a minute, to process everything going on. Because, frankly, this whole trip was a visit to crazytown.

"Anyhoo," Dicarlo said, smacking her tiny hand against the Tahoe's steering wheel and flooring the gas pedal. "We need to track down this stripper. We can probably get a visual description on her from the landlord if Sorokin was taking her to his apartment in Chinatown. We'll go pick up Lopez, touch base to see if there was anything left in the apartment that would point to her. We'll grab something to eat because, man, I'm starving. I could eat the leather off my shoes. Then, maybe you'll be my wingman at the Pony Pagoda. Damn, I always wanted to see the inside of that place."

"Sounds...great," Josie said.

Oh, boy.

CHAPTER 13

"We got a partial footprint," Detective Maxwell Lopez said by way of introduction.

He tossed down some color photos next to the sushi menu on the table between Josie and Dicarlo. They had arranged to meet at a hole-in-the-wall sushi place not too far from Golden Gate Park. Josie, surprisingly, had found that despite the emotionally turbulent day, she had an appetite. It was somewhere after four o'clock, so she didn't know whether it was late lunch or early dinner—but found she didn't care, so she decided to go with it. The *shamisen* music plucking gently in the background soothed her. Lopez fanned out the crime scene photos on the table, and Josie was subjected to a full-color array of the crime scene. She saw a cracked black and white tile floor in one photo. In another, the back of a bloodied hand in a puddle of...holy geeze, that was a lot of blood. Annnnd, there went her appetite.

"For crying out loud, Max," Dicarlo complained. "We're eating here."

"Not yet, you aren't." He went around to the other side of the table, then held his hand out to Josie. He was tall, *really tall*—over six feet—looked as if he spent all his free-time in a gym, and, oddly, was Chinese. He caught her confused look and smiled a big, white-toothed grin. He had one of those perfectly smooth, almost elastic faces that moved easily through a range of emotions, like an actor or comedian. "You're wondering about my last name, aren't you? Half of my family is from Mexico City. The other half is from China. It makes for interesting holidays. Tamales and pork fried rice. Except both sides of the family love tripe." He shivered his broad shoulders for effect.

"I'm Josie," she said, taking his proffered hand with its long, smooth fingers. He held hers slightly too long, and for a minute, she thought he was going to lay a big, sloppy, inappropriate kiss on the back of it. She tugged her arm back until he released his grip with a shrug that said *win some, lose some*. Or maybe, judging from the twinkle in his eye, *lose some, try again later*.

"I told you he was a player," Dicarlo grumbled. She crossed her arms and huffed, making her blonde hair rise off her forehead. Her freckled nose wrinkled in...jealousy?

"I'm totally wounded," Lopez said clutching his shirtfront. He grinned in a lop-sided way that Josie liked, and which also caused the nearby pretty Japanese waitress with the eyebrow piercing to turn bright pink. "If it makes you feel any better, I only recognized you because I got a picture of you. Your last name is a fooler, too. Josie M. Tucker—that ain't Asian and clearly, you are a lovely Cambodian or Thai lady, as I can tell by the shape of your face. And don't worry, I didn't make your photo my phone wallpaper. Yet. But I might now that I've seen you in real life. After you agree to be my girl."

"Stalker alert," Dicarlo said coughing into her fist like a frat boy—a five-foot tall, white-blonde female frat boy. "Smooth, real smooth, Max. She's taken." Josie wasn't really keen on having a stalker, but if the detective had discovered what her middle initial stood for, she'd happily *off him* the first chance she got—no one learned her middle name and lived to tell.

Lopez shrugged. "I don't see any ring on her finger. Like Beyoncé says. No ring means she's fair game." He dropped into the chair on the other side of the table and smiled up at the waitress, who dropped her pen and sank to the floor to retrieve it. He tilted his head at Josie in a way that said he was sure of his charm. "Did you already order?" he asked them all. "Because Josie really needs a Rooster Roll."

"Jesus. She doesn't need a Rooster Roll." Dicarlo was rolling her eyes.

Josie glanced at the paper sushi menu on the table in between her hands. A Rooster Roll didn't look too bad, just the standard cucumber, avocado, king crab, and *masago*, those tiny delightfully salty-sweet bright-orange fish eggs—no cream cheese to cause havoc with her stomach, at least, so she'd be all right. "Sure. It sounds fine to me." In fact, it sounded less adventurous than her usual order, but she wasn't feeling up to anything rubbery today. Not with the whole kick in the seat of her pants by The Grim Reaper. Nothing like a gruesome reminder of mortality to make her belly beg for comfort food. With that in mind, she ordered a bowl of miso soup to go with her Rooster Roll.

"You're an ass, Max," Dicarlo said, which Josie didn't understand but let drop. Dicarlo ordered teriyaki chicken, straight-up cooked and sweet-sauced, totally unadventurous with white rice, and a salad with no Japanese sesame dressing. Josie could appreciate simplicity—especially now that she was supposed to be restricting her diet—though unadventurous food wasn't the kind of lifestyle choice she would make for herself. She enjoyed pushing the boundaries whenever she was able. But maybe some people were just made to eat plain food. Born that way, so to speak.

"So anyway," Lopez said after he was done flustering the waitress with his order—though it had more to do with his personality than his meal choice—"the footprint we got is a smallish-sized woman's boot. A size six or a seven work boot, like Doc Martens, something with a thick sole. We got the lab working on ID-ing the exact size and type of boot. They have access to a shoe print database, if you can believe that. Millions of shoe prints registered by maker and model. Totally helpful. I think we're going to have the results soon."

"If the prints belong to the killer, I don't think we're looking at his wife then," Dicarlo said, wrinkling her freckled nose. She turned to Josie. "Did you get a look at that Amazon's clodhoppers? Eff me if she was anything less than an eleven. Sorry," she said, and explained. "I've been spending time with my nieces, two year-old twins who repeat every effing thing you say, and I'm not allowed to curse around them. But as far as suspects go, we always look at the spouse first."

"Sure," Josie said, "That's what they always say on TV shows." Though she was more partial to cooking shows, she'd occasionally wandered off course into the other jurisdictions in the realm of reality TV, like *Forensic Freaks* and *Cold Case Calamities*. They both looked at her blankly. *Oops*, she thought fiddling with her chopsticks, *my greenhorn status is showing.* She was feeling out of her league with these detectives who were in the middle of a *murder investigation.* Good Lord, what was she even doing here? She had a sudden flashback of sneaking around an Arizona resort against her better judgment and all common sense. She shook her head silently at herself.

"So, the print was made in the blood when it was fresh, correct?" Dicarlo asked. "Don't show us the G.D. photos again right now. You hear me? Some of us have delicate stomachs." She rubbed a tiny hand across her shirt's midsection.

"Yeah. Wuss," Lopez muttered without any venom. Josie knew his teasing was mostly for show—she had heard real tension in his voice when she'd first introduced herself to him earlier on the phone. His voice had been clipped and entirely professional. She suddenly realized that he must have been standing in Ivan's Chinatown apartment right about then, possibly looking at Ivan, or what was left of him, while speaking with her. "Ivan Sorokin has been dead for a while. Maybe a few days. Don't know when the last someone saw him was."

"He posted something on a message board he frequented Saturday morning at about 9:30 a.m. I mean, if it was truly him posting. The entry was time-stamped," Josie offered. She got the same blank stare as before from the two detectives.

Dicarlo shrugged, as if adjusting her previous assessment of Josie. She got out her little notebook and Hello Kitty pen and said matter-of-factly, "I'll just put that on the timeline then."

Josie cleared her throat. "Also, there's some weird stuff going on at Ivan's job, the one at PPS. If you have someone who's good with computers, you might want to send them over there. Apparently, Ivan farmed out his work to some guy in China who was probably working for peanuts, probably just a fraction of Ivan's salary, I'm guessing."

"Are you serious?" Lopez said. "That probably breaks all kinds of laws I don't even know about. Definitely gotta contact PPS and shut that action down ASAP." He said it like "a-sap." And then he added, "Crap, we might need the FBI. I hate those guys." He sighed, loudly and dramatically.

"And how the frick did you find that out about his computer and this guy in China?" Dicarlo wanted to know.

"I…uh…was at PPS the other day. You know, as a visitor hanging out with Ivan's business partner, James." Josie had no idea if that was something she should have mentioned, but frankly, she wasn't quick enough on her feet to make up a lie about that one. Her lies were piling up faster than she could sort them out, so she was trying to minimize the new, smaller ones. Her brain could stretch only so far trying to keep track of them all before she'd have a cerebral meltdown.

"Ah, yes. That kid from the widow's house. James Yu. What do you know about him?" Dicarlo asked. Josie could tell she was about to jot something else down in her microscopic notebook. Her manner wasn't threatening in any way, but still, Josie felt as if she were under a spotlight.

"I don't know how I feel about him yet," Josie admitted, fighting the urge to run a finger around her t-shirt collar, which suddenly felt too tight. "I'm staying at his apartment actually—his girlfriend is my college friend. He doesn't know I'm here with the two of you. And he doesn't know why I'm actually here in California—I'm taking a closer look at his startup company and his business practices." She didn't bring up Greta Williams's name—that part, she kept to herself. Lopez was familiar with her benefactor, for sure, but she had no idea about the extent of Dicarlo's involvement.

Lopez made a noise. "You're living at his house? I don't really like that idea. That's kind of weird. *Totally* weird. You might want to think about getting out of there and getting a place to stay separate from him. Distance yourself from that guy…because you never know." His concern for her was genuine, and not the least bit smarmy for once, which made her rethink her inertia in finding a hotel room and putting some distance between them. Maybe she'd better take care of that as soon as she got back and spoke with Susan.

"Not that he's dangerous or anything," Dicarlo added, probably because she had met James and had seen his reaction to the the news of

107

Ivan's death. She pointed her Hello Kitty pen at Josie to emphasize her point. "But he's a person of interest right now. As you know *from TV*, the strongest motives for murder are love or money."

Josie nodded, having pretty much made up her mind to move herself out of the place as soon as she could. And if she were getting a hotel room, she was taking Susan with her. There was no way she was leaving her best friend there if James's innocence was in question. So, as soon as she got back to James's place from her little foray with the detectives, she would try to convince Susan to leave. But if Susan decided to stay at James's, then Josie would stay with her.

Josie tilted her head. "I have to admit, I've had some extra insight being in such close proximity to James. But I don't know if I'm seeing him at his worst with his guard down, or his best." She thought about his subservience to his parents, his strange combination of intelligence and newborn-calf helplessness. Did he have anything to do with Ivan's death? Could he have committed such a violent, passionate, intimate crime? She remembered Olga's outburst and said, "What about the stripper?"

"Ah, yeah. Her. Definitely a person of interest. She could also have smaller feet than Mrs. Amazon Clodhoppers," Dicarlo said, flipping through her notebook. "Mrs. Sorokin said the stripper works in San Jose at the Pony Pagoda. You know, the place with all the lights out front. Pretty hard to miss. Lopez, you got any one dollar bills? After lunch, we're going on a field trip."

"Awesome. Welcome to San Francisco," Lopez said, toasting Josie with his water glass.

At that moment, the waitress brought a massive platter of sushi to their table, beautifully plated, an array of orange, pink, and green. In the center of the plate was Josie's Rooster Roll. Fluffy rice pieces were bespeckled with sesame seeds, meticulously arranged to suggest male private parts—the "cock," in Rooster, she realized, with a mental forehead slap as she felt her face grow warm—with a florid spray of bright orange *masago* eggs spurting out of the tip.

⌘

"So, tell me about your family," Josie said to Lopez. She was done playing her impromptu role of sushi urologist. She had gingerly dismantled and consumed her meal with as much dignity as possible. Namely, very little dignity.

Dicarlo had gone to the restroom to wash up. Although the petite detective had eschewed the chopsticks and used a fork, she had still managed to drip teriyaki sauce on her white shirt. Left alone at the table with chatty Lopez, Josie figured she would rather hear him talk about himself than flirt with her. Although he was attractive, with his long legs crossed casually under the table, taking more than their fair share of space, she found his aggressive flirting exhausting and indecorous, considering the circumstances—after all, a guy was dead. It was creepy to be flirting over crime scene photos. More importantly, he wasn't Drew.

"Your family immigrated from China?" she said, prompting him.

"Oh yeah," he said. "The fam came over from China about three generations ago. Real *Deadwood* kind of people, if you ever watched that show. I *loved* that show—it was five kinds of awesome. I always wanted to be a gunslinger, an 'I'm your Huckleberry' kind of badass." He mimicked the line from the movie *Tombstone.*

"That is, without a doubt, the worst southern accent I have ever heard," Josie told him, which made him laugh. "I was just thinking you'd do well in Hollywood until you did that." She shook her head in mock disgust. She had been kind of thinking about giving him the secret contact information for her friend Patrick who was an actor in L.A.— Lopez would be great in an action movie, and he definitely packed charisma. Eh, maybe she'd think more about that later. Her friend Patrick was still begging her to move to California—as if *that* would ever happen. He sent her weekly emails trying to recruit her to be his personal assistant, so maybe she'd send Lopez his direction as a distraction. Maybe the distraction technique worked equally well with Hollywood actors as it did with toddlers.

"I'd love to be in a movie. Hook me up. *Aw yeah*, I could totally be a buddy movie sidekick. Do you think they're making another *Hangover* movie?" he said. He laughed as he pondered his future career in film. Then he went on, "So, anyway, my great-greats were, like Confucian Chinese. You know about Confucius, right? All that honor your parents, follow the rules, and be cool to one another—the original *Bill and Ted*, you know? They left China before all that Cultural Revolution and communism stuff. All those crazy regulations and the police state. So this whole 'one child per family' is a totally foreign concept to my family." His face was animated, and—Josie had to admit—handsome. Not that she was comparing him to Drew, whose company she was missing right now. She was merely enjoying Lopez's company for the time being. Today. Now. Lunch only.

"You have a big family then?" Josie had been hoping to get Lopez to weigh in on James's co-dependent situation with his parents, but she wasn't sure if he'd be able to provide any more insight. Lopez was even more of a contrast to James than Josie was.

"Enormous. We're all over the place," Lopez confirmed, rocking back in his chair, his long legs brushing hers under the table. "Plus, we're Catholic. We converted for the Mexican half. For added *flavor*," he said with a gangsta street emphasis, which again, was awful. "You should meet my cousin Juan Pablo. Dude wears a belt buckle the size of my head. Boots, western shirts with the snaps, and Wranglers. The whole bit. He owns a restaurant in San Antonio called *El Chino*. Most awesome *mole* you could imagine." He sighed and rubbed his full—and flat—abdomen.

"Sounds great," Josie said. She hadn't attempted to eat *mole*, that stewed savory blend of Mexican cocoa and chiles, in a long, long time. It was still on the TBD list—to be determined if she could still handle it. But she wasn't ready to give up hope yet. She would live to eat another *mole*.

"Hey, you write a food column. You could go there and review it, right?"

She shrugged, which was her best go-to noncommittal move.

"That would be *so* awesome," he said, his large, white teeth shining like white squares of Chiclets gum in his smooth, tanned face. "You ever been to Texas?"

Josie shook her head. "No, but I've been told I need to go to Austin for some of the festivals."

"I'd love to take you there. You and me at the Driskill Hotel. I guarantee you'd forget your boyfriend in three days—no, two days," he pushed further, leaning forward to rest his chin on his hand with that lop-sided grin he favored. She could imagine he had a high success rate with his pick-up lines.

Josie ignored him. His flirtation wasn't really harassment, but more of an irritant. Like too much lime in her guacamole, trying to take over and ruin the balance of flavors. Maybe his behavior had led to his departmental pairing with a lesbian partner who was clearly not the target for his scattershot flirting. "James Yu said I need to check out South By Southwest Interactive." She didn't want to talk about the tech conference as much as she wanted to discuss James some more.

"Oh yeah," Lopez frowned, a wrinkle appearing between his dark eyes. "What does the kid know about it?"

"He's a really smart guy, but kind of...dumb, if you know what I mean." At Lopez's confused look, she clarified, "No street smarts. No common sense. If there were a fire, he'd be more likely to pull the smoke detector off the wall than get out of the house. I'd trust him to save the world if we needed to calculate the trajectory of an incoming meteor about to hit the earth or whatever. But I don't think I'd trust him to babysit my dog." Josie could imagine her dog shaking his bony head in disgust at James, wondering if the ridiculous human would ever feed him or take him for a walk. James would probably sit at his computer for days until Bert yanked the computer charger out of the wall socket, which was saying a lot for a dog who would rather sleep in the sunshine than chase after squirrels.

"Huh," Lopez said. "What about giving him a whole pile of seed money? Would you trust James with that?"

Throughout the whole lunch with Dicarlo, neither Josie nor Lopez had broached the topic of Greta Williams or their joint connection with her. Josie had followed his lead and hadn't brought it up on her own. She had missed her opportunity to quiz him about it while Dicarlo had absented herself to the restroom—she was on her way back now—and Josie could see her making her way across the restaurant. Clearly, he was talking about Greta Williams's money now, and Josie simply didn't know the answer to that one.

CHAPTER 14

After lunch, Josie had to sit in the backseat of Dicarlo's Tahoe because Lopez was riding shotgun with his long legs. She used her cell phone to check on Susan.

"I was about to text you, but I didn't know if you were out doing official business, detective-y things with that policewoman," Susan said. She sounded like she had a stuffed up nose. Little did she know, nothing Josie did was ever officially sanctioned by anyone. She was rebel like that—authority chafed like a pair of damp jeans on a hot day.

"Are you okay? Have you been crying?" Josie asked with an intense pang of guilt since she'd more or less abandoned her friend. Josie wasn't exactly a fountain of nurturing, maternal supportiveness, but when she chose her friends, she stuck by them. At least, she always intended to. *Major cringe. Bad, Josie.*

"Well, yes, I have been crying. You know I'm a stress-crier." Susan considerately held the phone away while she blew her nose.

When she came back, Josie said, "I do know that about you. Are you feeling any better?"

Susan sighed. "It's such a horrible mess. I don't know what to do."

"I know. It's a tough situation," Josie answered vaguely and waited for Susan to go on because she had a feeling more was coming.

"Honestly, Josie," and here, Susan started to whisper, "I finally decided to break up with James. I was going to do it at the end of this trip. That thing with his parents was the straw that broke the camel's back—I think I just called myself a camel, but you know what I mean—and seeing him for what he actually is...which is, a little boy, basically. I decided I was done with this whole thing. But now, I don't think I can. It wouldn't be right with his friend dead. With Ivan dead." Susan's voice broke when she said Ivan's name.

Relief swept through Josie. Thank the good Lord above for small favors. She wouldn't have to tell Susan how she was dating a self-centered dim-bulb. Sure, James would probably be a millionaire someday, but still, Josie didn't think it was worth the aggravation. "I'm sorry to hear it, but I know what you mean. You're kind of stuck with him for a while, aren't you?" It would be super bad timing to break up with a guy when his best friend had just been murdered, even if he wasn't the killer himself.

"You're not one bit sorry and you know it," Susan chided. "But I still love you for it. How long are you going to be out today? I could use some commiseration. And maybe some ice cream, if we can find you that coconut milk kind without dairy. James left me here without a car."

Josie's eyebrows shot up. Susan was by herself? "James left you there alone and went out," she said slowly, having a hard time believing that even Mr. Thoughtless would ditch his supposed girlfriend at a time like this. "Where did he go?" She noticed the two detectives in the front seat tune into her conversation.

"He was extremely upset about Ivan. I mean, you can't blame him. But where do you think he went?...To his parents' place, of course. I guess they live right near the restaurant in Chinatown. So he went home to his mama. Probably not even that far from where they discovered Ivan in his apartment." Josie found that odd. If her business partner had been found gruesomely murdered in Chinatown, that would be the last place she'd want to go, parents there or not. Maybe James wasn't afraid of encountering the killer himself?...Because maybe he knew who the killer was?

Josie said, "Yeah. That's strange...Well, I'm taking a short trip to San Jose to check out a...bar to track down a lead," she fudged, because Susan didn't need to be thinking about strippers mixed up with her almost-ex-boyfriend. "But I'll be back later. We can walk down the street together and grab something to eat. And Susan, if you want to get out of there, I'll get us a room at a hotel. Don't worry about it. It'll be on me." Actually, it would be on Greta Williams's credit card, but Josie didn't mention that. In the front seat, Lopez flipped his thumb up in approval.

"Yeah, I do want to get out of here. I don't know how to do it—how to tell him that I'm leaving."

"We'll figure something out together." Josie had no clue what to do either. The idea that someone was relying on her in a tricky social situation was laughable.

Nevertheless, Susan gave one last sniffle and then said, in an entirely new, energized tone of voice, "All right. I'll go pack up our clothes."

Josie mentally applauded her friend. When Susan made up her mind to do something, *that was that.* Susan had a lot of beauty supplies and changes of clothes, but she would probably be repacked and ready to mobilize in a half-hour's time. In contrast, Josie's belongings, including her laptop, were a scattered mess in the guest room of James's apartment—she wasn't kidding about being a slob herself—but she didn't mention that at the moment. They'd have plenty of time to gather her stuff up when she got back later.

Yeah, right after she was done at the strip club.

⌘

Call her inexperienced, but Josie had never been to a bar of this nature, a so-called gentleman's club, though she had yet to see anyone who qualified as a gentlemen loitering outside in the parking area. In truth, there weren't a lot of loiterers. The place looked fairly upstanding, and she had a feeling from the start that the Pony Pagoda wasn't a typical nudie bar. For one thing, its sprawling parking lot, the immense size of which was possible only this far south of San Francisco, had valet parking—which Dicarlo ignored with a derisive snort.

The sign for the club was made with old-fashioned incandescent lights, and called to mind a movie marquee. Not a single tacky, flashing neon in sight. The sign was a beautiful retro blast from the past, the likes of which could have graced the Las Vegas strip during its nascent, glamorous days—a massive row of overlapping block slanted letters that spelled out "Burlesque" and then underneath, a double P with smaller letters spelling out the rest of the club name. Offset to one side was an animated prancing pony with a tasseled cowboy hat. The sign was classy, in a tacky kind of way that definitely reminded Josie of the famous Nevada strip.

"So, let us do the talking," Lopez cautioned her. "You're simply here to observe and see what you can see that we don't see." There he went, talking in circles again.

"Yeah, you're not exactly official, so just let us take lead here," Dicarlo said.

Josie was glad just to be included, so she nodded, wholeheartedly agreeing with them. She would be their good little sidekick, no matter how much it chafed. She would keep her mouth shut and watch them go to work.

"Good," Lopez said. Then the two detectives, a modern-day Mutt and Jeff, flashed their badges at the doorman before Josie even thought to reach for her wallet for the cover charge. Honestly, she hadn't even thought about using her newly-minted P.I. license—it hadn't even crossed her mind. Lopez put his big hand in the small of her back while she was still hesitating and said in a very cop-like manner, "She's with us," and she was escorted in with a little bit of pressure, suddenly feeling not so much a law-abiding citizen as a suspect.

The interior of the Pony Pagoda was chilly and dark, smelled of canned air and cigarette smoke. Though smoking inside public places had been banned for years now, a ghost of the stench remained. Josie felt transported back in time to the 1950s. Reflective paths lit up the black-carpeted floor and pointed the way to an up-lit stage framed by baby blue velvet curtains which gaped open at them. The main floor was dotted by intimate tables with two close to the stage and four larger groups in the back where a black-topped bar with a lit-up edge ran the length of the wall. To the far right, a live, three-piece jazz band—piano, sax, and percussion—wailed a sultry, grinding tune more fit for a noir film than suburbia at 5:00 p.m. on a Tuesday. Josie fully expected Sam Spade to start narrating the scene in voiceover or for Sammy Davis Jr. to toddle on stage, crystal highball in hand. He, of course, wasn't on stage.

Instead, as a painted, lit placard that was lowered from the ceiling announced, Lady Lily was.

"Holy Baby Jesus in a buggy," Dicarlo said. The three of them stood mesmerized.

Lady Lily was a dead-ringer for Rita Hayworth or possibly Jessica Rabbit. In her red sequined, full-length dress, she stepped and turned, posed in pin-up fashion, then smiled with a wink. As she sashayed across the stage, she made her bountiful curves bounce in a way that Josie had never considered possible for a normal human female. In time with the music, Lady Lily *ba-doom ba-doomed* across the stage on her sparkly red heels and swiveled, earning catcalls and applause that made Josie frown and examine the audience, which was made up of maybe two dozen people at the most because it was still too early for the happy hour crowd. As expected, most of the clientele were men, some whose faces were lit by the glow of laptops, which may have explained their presence during business hours. A sign to the lower right of the stage announced free Wi-Fi in incongruously hand-painted 1950s lettering.

While Lopez and Dicarlo stared at the dancer, Josie twisted to the side and spied a hand-written chalkboard done up stylishly in more retro lettering surrounded by hand-drawn sparkles and sputniks that made her think of *The Jetsons* and *Bewitched*, which she had watched on the rerun channel when she was a kid. The board announced which women were performing that afternoon and into the night. Pin-up photos of the women hung along the wall. Some of the performers held fans, feathers, or some other theme, like Western theme, Polynesian, or— Josie squinted—Perriot the mime, *which was disturbing. The stuff of nightmares,* Josie thought. Also heavily represented were bullet-breasted bustiers à la Madonna in her Blond Ambition phase, dark lipstick, and dramatically sculpted eyebrows that would have put *Mommie Dearest* Joan Crawford to shame. The women's names appeared, painted in cursive lettering on the scrolled signs below their photos. Josie read across the wall and halted abruptly at one in particular. She turned back and scanned the chalkboard with this evening's line-up.

Then, a man in a gray plaid vest with rolled-up shirt sleeves approached them. His boot-polish black mustache looked entirely fake to

Josie, and his unlit cigar was equally for show. This guy clearly took his role as proprietor to heart—he looked and dressed as if he were in character. "Can I help you, detectives?" he said. "I'm the manager, Marty Glen. Jake, our doorman, let me know you were here, so I thought I'd offer to show you around, if you want. We usually run a 'boys in blue'—or ladies in blue, as the case may be—special on Tuesday." He nodded at Dicarlo, who looked intrigued.

Lopez, craning his neck, spied a woman entering a side door to go backstage. "We need to speak with some of your dancers. We're looking for one of them who might have witnessed something at an apartment in Chinatown over the weekend and who might have information for us."

"All right," Marty Glen said, in what Josie thought was an overly-helpful tone. His carnival barker voice which made her mind wander toward circus oddities from the past, like JoJo the Dog-Faced Boy. Marty interrupted her errant musings about whether there had ever been a bearded-lady in the history of burlesque. "Any person in particular? You want whoever is here right now? We have a fairly large roster. Lots of girls paying for college and saving for mortgage down payments these days. More than a few single moms, too. We'd probably make a decent profit if we opened a daycare out back. But if you have a particular girl you want to talk with—"

Lopez tried to bluster his way in. "We're not—"

Josie pointed to the chalkboard of the evening's performers and blurted out, "Her. We'll talk to her."

The board said *Shasta*.

CHAPTER 15

Maybe it was pure chance that a dancer at the Pony Pagoda had the same name as Ivan and James's side project. While Josie was constantly fighting to dig the company name out of her brain, she had no problem recalling the name of the product. This was California, after all. Josie had assumed their project had been named after Shasta Mountain up at the end of the Cascades mountain range, the gorgeous craggy peaks that run from Canada down through Seattle and into Northern California. However, it was apparent now that their software had been named after a distinctly more female set of mountain peaks—ones made of flesh and packed into a tightly laced corset. Josie didn't know for sure, but she wasn't going to ignore the coincidence.

As Marty the manager gamely led the three of them backstage, Josie peeked into each room they passed. Most of the small dressing areas were storage rooms that had been converted into rooms for two or three women each. The dressing room doors were all uniformly open with standing, old-fashioned screens that the women stood behind while they changed into their costumes. The cigarette-girl costumes and the music from the main stage gave even the backstage area a retro feel. A dancer in fishnets, a bullet bra, a corset, and not much else passed them in the tight hallway. Lopez held up his mitts in a "hands off" gesture and stepped against the wall with a big grin.

Straight out of a gangster noir movie, Marty the Mustache was saying, "Like I told you, Shasta's been performing here for a month shy of a year. She's not as popular as some of our other dancers, but she has a small but loyal fanbase. Some of our other ladies have been doing this since they were hardly more than kids—transitioned right from ballet classes to pom-poms to this. They're good enough to compete in the burlesque competitions. You may have heard of Viva Las Vegas, the one they got going on every April. I try to support them and help pay for their airfare, room and board. The owner of this place actually lives in Vegas full-time, so he's into it. And I figure whatever we can do to push burlesque as a legitimate art form only adds to our business and notoriety, you know?"

He led them down the hall and pointed into an open door. The dressing room was empty of people, though it was packed with pieces of frippery—feathers, wigs, headdresses, and shoes. "This is Shasta's space. Her trademark number is a jungle-themed deal," he explained, pointing to a leopard-print cloak hanging from a hook on the wall. "Her fans love the whip and the wild cat stuff. With her dark black hair and her hairstyle, she's a real Bettie Page, except more, you know, stacked." He cupped his hands in front of his chest. "Because everybody requests 'em larger in this day and age. As we all know, if you want to be successful in any business, it's supply and demand, basic economics. The customer is always right, if you know what I'm saying. She's not here yet, but she's due to come in soon—in about an hour." He checked his watch.

Dicarlo scribbled in her notebook again. Lopez was standing back, his hands in his pockets, looking as comfortable hanging around a place littered with women's undergarments as he would if he were at a hardware store. He picked up a leopard-print 4-inch pump from beside the dressing table. After checking the size, he nodded to Dicarlo and Josie, confirming they had a possible size match for the bloody boot print. The three of them simultaneously scanned the room as if they might find the bloody work boots lying out in the open. Unsurprisingly, they did not.

"Was Shasta at work on Saturday?" Dicarlo asked.

"I'd have to check the timecards to be sure, but I think she was," Marty mumbled, though the slight hesitation in his words was enough to set off a bell in Josie's head. She suspected he didn't want to go through his records on their account and was hoping they wouldn't ask him to do it. "She's usually the warm-up act for the more popular girls. I mean, she's a newer act, so it's not an insult or anything. It's the way things work, same as everywhere. Pecking order, you know. It means she goes on at about six o'clock when she's here—not the main act, but still, not the lunch hour. While you're waiting for her to come in, I'll go look for a copy of her timecard. Sound good?" His too-loud voice made Josie's neck prickle, but there was no way she was going to get him to relax and tell her something interesting with Lopez and Dicarlo nearby. Plus, Marty was pretty slick—he wouldn't be tricked into saying anything that might put himself or the club in jeopardy. He was "hard as a nut," her Aunt Ruth would say. There would be no cracking this guy's shell without some major pressure—and a warrant.

"Do you mind if I wander around the place?" Josie asked, careful to put an innocent look on her face. In truth, she was a third wheel in their detective troupe. Josie preferred being invisible, but it had to be on her terms. Otherwise, her skin got itchy and her temper flared, the same with situations that weren't under her control. Marty Glen looked her over, up and down. Apparently, he didn't find anything threatening or interesting—she certainly was no curvaceous bombshell compared to the women he employed. He said, "Sure. Knock yourself out, kid." With that, she was dismissed.

Nice.

Champing down a snarky comment—because, in truth, she'd gotten what she wanted—she retraced their steps back to the main room and squinted around in the dim light. She counted seating for over a hundred patrons in the theater area. It was about a quarter full. She wandered over to the bar where the bartender was pulling a draft beer for a waiting server. The bartender was an older guy, maybe in his fifties, with a salt-and-pepper pompadour and impressive sideburns.

"You old enough to be in here?" he asked her with a half-smile on his bristly face. She wished she could whip out an important-looking badge, but her wallet was still wedged in the back pocket of her jeans. Her flimsy paper P.I. license wasn't that impressive looking. While it had the seal of the Massachusetts Commonwealth on it, it still looked as if she could have gotten a high schooler to print it out at the local library. The whole idea of her carrying a license was so...cheesy. She was a food critic, for crying out loud.

Instead, Josie just shrugged, her hands in her pockets as she leaned against the bar. "I'm with the police detectives, the ones who went backstage." Man, that felt goofy to say. The bartender's eyebrows shot up in surprise and he leaned over the bar after handing the beer to the waitress.

"I thought you were applying for a job," he confessed with a slight grin. To his credit, he didn't look below her neck. She wondered if it were possible for a hetero man to become inured to cleavage. Perhaps working in a place like this made boobs boring.

"Marty didn't seem to think I'd fit in well here." She tipped her head toward the retreating waitress, whose short skirt twitched in a manner designed to drum up the biggest tips.

"Eh," he said dismissing that idea. "You could be up on stage easy. You could do Lucy Liu number like the dominatrix one she did in that Charlie's Angels movie. That was classy." She watched his face. He was serious. He was avuncular—not in a creepy uncle way—and he was honestly assessing her for employment at the Pony Pagoda. His lack of excitement over things that many people would find sexy struck Josie as kind of sad.

Thank the Good Lord for her blog and her boss Julieanne at *The Daily News* for making it so she didn't have to rely on shaking her...assets for rent money. Not that this place was as seedy as she thought it would be—it had that nighttime feel, that façade of legitimacy that existed only by the grace of darkness. All the wrinkles and stains showed up during daylight. While Josie wished she could lurk in the shadows, the outskirts of acceptable society, she preferred no one else co-exist in them with her.

"I'm more interested in what goes on behind the scenes," she said. "I want to see what keeps this place running."

He chuckled, restocking the bar with steaming hot glasses that a busboy delivered from the kitchen. "Nothing but drama some nights. We're a family similar to any other business that's been running for a long time. We got our Crazy Aunt Lulu just like any other family. My pop's sister. Never married. Never forgets a single birthday, anniversary, or holiday—always sends me a card and a one-dollar bill."

"Does she have about fifteen cats, too?" Josie didn't have a crazy aunt. Crazy was a different flavor in her family. Being "not right in the head" was a real ailment that evoked images of adult diapers, confusion, and feeling abandoned. Not much to laugh about. Although sometimes, the more it hurt, the better it was to make a joke, to prove that circumstances weren't getting the best of her.

"Nah, but she feeds all the strays in her neighborhood. Spends hundreds of dollars on canned food for feral cats. Meanwhile, she's on disability and living off the government." He shook his head and filled another drink order for a brunette waitress who had just come up and was eyeing Josie with suspicion.

When he came back, she asked him, "So who's the equivalent of your Crazy Aunt Lulu here at the club?"

"Is one of our people in trouble?" he asked, suddenly serious, his dark eyebrows shooting up near his pompadour. He kept his voice low and private though most sounds in the bar barely carried over the jazzy live music. "Which girl is it?"

"I don't know," Josie said truthfully. She didn't go into any of the details because she wasn't sure what she was allowed to disclose. She leaned on the bar closer to him. "Have you had trouble with the police here before?"

"Not really," he said. "Most of our people are clean. We're not the same as other clubs. Even our bouncers are clean. Marty doesn't hire anyone with a record, and we probably got a higher percentage of vegans and PETA members here than most yoga studios. All right, so that's a slight exaggeration, but I've worked at other strip clubs, and there's a big difference with these girls—they're all athletic, for the most part. You know, they take care of their bodies. They're always in training. Last year, we had a girl whose boyfriend got totally lit on New Year's Eve. He was a real lightweight, had about three beers. He crashed his motorcycle into a light post in the parking lot. No damage to the post, but he trashed his bike. Lucky he didn't wind up dead. Too bad you can't arrest someone for being a dumbass. That's the extent of the trouble here."

"No problems with customers getting too clingy or anything?" She, of course, was wondering about Ivan. Had he become possessive of Shasta?

"Nothing out of the ordinary," he said. "Guys and girls coming in for a nice show and a tasty dinner special."

She reached into her pocket and pulled out a picture of Ivan and James that she had filched from James's guest room—she guessed there was an advantage to staying there after all. She put her finger under Ivan's face and showed the bartender the photo. "Have you ever seen this guy here?"

"Oh yeah, Ivan is a regular. He's real fond of Shasta. I think he's got her schedule memorized. Or maybe typed into that computer he's always working on while he waits for her show. And that other guy, too. He's a regular."

Josie froze and flipped the picture around as if it would suddenly show a different face next to Ivan's other than James Yu's. Just to be sure, she put her finger on his chin in the photo and said, "This guy?"

"Yeah, him too. I never got his name. I wouldn't say he was a particular fan of Shasta's or anything. He didn't try to talk with her or bring her things as guys sometimes do, but he's in here almost as much as that other guy. I think they're work buddies or something. Always chatting and typing. Chatting and typing." The bartender mimicked picking out keys on an air keyboard with his broad fingers. "I figured they were working together, and that the scenery was better here than at the office."

Not good. According to this guy, it looked like James had some explaining to do, the twerp, hanging out in a nudie bar—well, an almost-nudie bar. The Pony Pagoda had standards, it seemed, as Josie flicked her eyes at the stage. The current performer, as relatively athletic and professional as she was, had stripped down to her pasties already. Josie clenched her teeth on behalf of her friend. She relaxed. Susan was a big girl—she had already made up her own mind. Even before this latest development.

"Boyfriend of yours?" the bartender said, taking a look at her face. Yep, Josie was definitely not playing poker anytime soon.

"Not mine, thankfully, but the boyfriend of a good friend. She's going to be pretty ticked off to hear about this."

"Hey," he shrugged his doughy shoulders. "Maybe he was just here for the lunch specials. You never know. Gotta give him the benefit of the doubt."

Josie smiled slowly. "So the specials are good? How's your kitchen?"

"Pretty damn good. We got a seared lamb chop tonight. A New York strip. Or a grilled Portobello mushroom vegetarian option," he said. He lowered his voice in a conspiratorial manner, "What do you know about commercial-grade kitchens?"

She leaned forward and narrowed her eyes, "I know my way around a kitchen. I've been in a few before."

"You want to take a look at ours? It's an unusual setup. I think you're going to be surprised at what you find back there. I always show my friends. Also it's a Tuesday night, so we're not too busy. You don't have to worry about being in the way or anything. Head through that door."

CHAPTER 16

Josie felt the tension in her shoulders begin to dissipate as soon as she pushed through the swinging metal door, admiring the sparkling shine of the stainless steel. Only an obsessive-compulsive staff could keep a steel door fingerprint-free. She stepped in far enough that she wouldn't be hit by anyone coming or going. The clock ahead of her read 5:30, so the staff was prepping for dinner. She looked around, wondering what made this kitchen so different from a typical setup that the bartender had insisted she come in.

"What the...?"

To the left of her were the ovens, stoves, vents, sink, stainless steel counters, and warming lamps. Straight ahead were walk-in storage, freezers, and coolers. All pretty standard equipment for a commercial kitchen. Off to the right, however, was a huge, undeveloped space, a sprawling and vast concrete area that had been something once. She felt as if she were looking at a classroom diorama of a kitchen inside of...*what the heck was this place?* Another reminder that outward appearances could be misleading.

She stared, trying to see the bigger picture—what the space used to be based on the leftover holes and marks in the cement. Was this kitchen even up to code? A large table and chairs had been set up by the door. Two of the club's burlesque performers were eating what looked to be dinner sitting in their bathrobes at a makeshift table, a picnic table that had been dragged indoors.

"You're wondering what this place is, right?" one of the performers said, wiping her mouth with a paper towel. She was bleached blonde, with a Marilyn Monroe hairdo—loose, mid-length curls that framed her face. Josie went toward them.

"Yeah, it's so..."

"Huge?" the woman offered.

"Weird? More than meets the eye?" her companion said. The second woman was a redhead with so much green eye makeup that Josie figured she had just finished a show or was about to leave for a circus gig with the Shriners. They were both so candid and so casual that Josie felt as if she'd stumbled across a restricted area with no public access. A private moment, as if she'd spied clowns smoking ciggies on break behind the Barnum and Bailey big top.

The blonde woman explained, "This whole building used to be a double theater back in the day. Two large movie screens. The owner was going to convert all this side into offices and private rooms in addition to the kitchen, but he temporarily ran low on funds. Now that we're profitable, maybe they'll consider it again."

"I doubt it," the redhead said. "They'd need people lining up outside behind a velvet rope to get the money for that. I don't see that happening anytime soon. I mean, business gets good when people are depressed. You should have seen how packed this place was right after the Bubble burst. Not that I was around then. I'm not *that* old. But I hear stories." She was, of course, talking about the Dot Com bubble bursting, when tech stocks and companies had taken a nosedive. Josie wasn't sure if she was lying about her age. Underneath all that makeup, the woman could have been hiding anything. "Things are going pretty good for tech geeks right now, so that means our business takes a hit."

"Are you a friend of Marty's? You don't have a clipboard, so I'm guessing you're not an inspector—also, no one is freaking out that you're back here. Usually, we get some kind of warning if someone's coming and we all make like we're invisible. You don't look like you're a dancer. No offense, but most of us are into the bling and accessorizing and the elective surgeries. Whereas you look *au natural*. Oh my God, the cost of beauty products. If you could only see my monthly bill." The blonde was looking at Josie's generic jeans, her makeup-free face, and her unenhanced bust line.

Josie introduced herself by her name only—no role, no official capacity. "I'm here with some people who are looking for a dancer named Shasta."

"Sasha Peters," the blonde woman said. "That's her name. Her stage name is Shasta. She called in sick today. She was sick yesterday." She looked down at her plate and picked at the last pieces of her dinner.

"And frankly, you think she's going to call in sick tomorrow?" Josie prodded gently.

Neither of the other women responded.

"Does Sasha do this often or is this a new development in her work ethic?" Josie asked.

The women looked at each other. Finally, the blonde woman said, "I don't think she's coming back here at all. We think she got a new job— we don't know where. Not as a dancer, I don't think. I mean, I've seen some girls lose it. They leave here and go somewhere worse, one of those places with the one-way mirror. You know, where you want to go home at night and scrub yourself really hard with Dial soap. Yuck. Sasha was talking to Lily a couple of days ago about making more money doing something else with better hours and in a better work environment. Someplace where she's more in control, but she wasn't super friendly with the rest of us. I mean, we didn't get a chance to bond or anything."

"She was smart," the redhead offered. Josie couldn't tell if the woman meant high intelligence was something that would separate Sasha from the other women or if it was a liability.

Josie's pulse picked up. She watched both of their faces closely, without seeming too anxious. "Did something happen to her?"

Again, both women kept silent. Maybe they were done talking.

Josie tried again, "What about a boyfriend or husband?"

"Yeah, she was seeing someone," the blonde said. "She was complaining about his apartment. Said it was pit, a real dump, up in Chinatown, which was a pain in the ass for her to get to since she lives here in San Jose."

Josie nodded. "Well, I noticed her belongings are still in her dressing room. She should come back and get them, especially the personal things. If she comes back for them, will you let me know? I can give you my cell phone number. All you have to do is send me a text or something."

"Sure," said the blonde, though Josie wasn't at all sure if she would. Still, it was worth trying. The woman dug in her bathrobe pocket for her phone and took Josie's cell phone number, or at least pretended to.

"Do you mind giving me your number in case I need to reach you?" When the woman shrugged, Josie handed over her cell phone for her to program in her number. "Thanks. Please, call me—either of you—if you see her. We need to talk with her." Josie glanced down at her new contact in her phone. It said, "Merrylin Monroe."

Of course it did.

⌘

"That girl Shasta isn't coming to work. She's twenty minutes late for her shift," Dicarlo was saying to Lopez as Josie walked up to them. They were both leaning against the bar, checking their watches intermittently. The show was over for now, so the house lights were up. Several of the servers in their short skirts and tight tees were taking orders for the early dinner crowd, taking the time to flirt while the room was lit.

"Shasta called in sick," Josie informed them. "Her real name is Sasha Peters. They said she lives in San Jose but that she's been seeing some guy with a crummy apartment in Chinatown."

"Well, shi—oot," Dicarlo said with a dumbfounded expression. "You learned all that in fifteen minutes? Hell, Lopez. At least we got her shoe size. Even Marty the manager came up empty on her timecards and employee info—I think we'd need extra motivation for that guy, if you know what I'm saying. He's not coughing up anything without a warrant, I'd bet. He's not as helpful as he wants us to think he is." Josie wasn't the least bit surprised to hear that about Marty. He'd rubbed her the wrong way, too, with his too-dark mustachios, like a silent picture villain.

Josie shrugged. "So what's the plan?" Lopez was rubbing his chin, which was devoid of a five o'clock shadow despite the late hour. She watched them closely, trying to pick up some investigation pointers, but she was starting to feel like one of the Three Stooges—not that Lopez and Dicarlo were incompetent. Far from it. But they weren't as willing as she was to cut corners and dig into the cracks. Of course, there was that whole upholding the law thing that they'd sworn to do when they'd agreed to carry the badge. She didn't have that issue.

Lopez finally said, "Since we're already down here, I'll go get Sasha's address from Marty Glen—even if I have to twist his arm—and we'll pay her a visit. Then, as much as I'll regret losing the pleasure of your lovely company, Josie, we'll drop you back by James's place in the city. After that, we gotta go check back with the M.E. about the autopsy results, try to push the toxicology results through, and also see if we got any latents or other unidentified DNA from the crime scene."

Good luck with that, Josie thought, remembering the M.E. office's three-month waiting period she'd read about in *The Chronicle.* The average mom was having to wait longer than that for a death certificate when her son was gunned down in the street. Josie didn't see the ruling on Ivan's cause of death getting back to them any time soon.

"I'm going to see what I can find out about Ivan's financials," Dicarlo said. "But first, let's hit Sasha Peters's address. For love or money, right?"

CHAPTER 17

Sasha Peters lived in a rental house in a neighborhood of 1950's single-storied cookie-cutter boxes directly off the highway in south San Jose, probably one of those three-quarter million dollar dumps that James had been saving up for. With Josie in the backseat once again, they passed a ratty-looking strip mall with a shipping and packaging store, a liquor place, and a paycheck advance payment counter.

From behind the steering wheel, Dicarlo peered over in a speculative way, "Huh. We know this place, don't we, Lopez?"

Lopez grunted his assent and turned around to explain to Josie, "A few years ago, we had a murder right over there. A security guard got shot in the parking lot. The bad guy did a string of robberies up and down this freeway. He'd hop on, hop off, and just about disappear. We had no idea how far up or down he was going, or where he were getting off. He was a magician, a comic book villain with an invisibility cloak. Dr. Evil, Highway Robber. It drove us crazy for almost four years. Which is why I don't like our local FBI liaison. Total dragon lady."

Dicarlo eyed him, "Lopez has a hard-on for her—excuse my language—a crush on her. That's why he says he hates the FBI. Where, in this case, hate actually means love."

"Shut up, Dicarlo." Lopez folded his arms and pouted. Josie could see the impetus behind incurable flirting might be an unattainable love. Heck, she'd lusted after her boyfriend Drew for almost a decade before they'd realized the feeling was mutual. Meanwhile, she'd gotten hitched to a moron while trying to distract herself from constant disappointment.

Josie looked at the strip mall where a woman in hot pink yoga pants was pushing a jogging stroller down the sidewalk completely unaware of the area's deadly history. Josie could almost imagine it. Actually, she could imagine a heck of a lot of nefarious things happening here, it was so run down. Newspapers blowing around in the lot. Potholes the size of small children—James's electric car would probably be swallowed up whole. The woman jogged by, adjusting an earbud that had fallen out. She barely paused as she crossed the street in front of them.

"So, how'd you finally get the guy?" Josie asked.

Dicarlo whipped the SUV into a side street without signaling. She gave a little shrug. "His girlfriend turned him in. Boy, was she mad. Good thing for us. Otherwise who knows if we ever would have caught him. She wanted half of his haul. He wasn't giving it to her, so she blabbed, lucky for us."

"Aha." Josie absorbed this, thinking about the girlfriend angle. She fiddled with the door lock while she wondered exactly how close Ivan was with Sasha Peters. From her picture at the Pagoda, she looked to be in her early twenties, about half Ivan's age, if that didn't fit every cliché out there of a sweet young thing. Because James hung out in the Pagoda with Ivan, he must have been aware of their relationship. The guy was oblivious, but not that oblivious, right? The more Josie learned, the more she realized James was keeping things to himself.

Because it was almost rush hour, the traffic peeling off the major roads into the neighborhoods was thickening—and becoming more aggressive as people saw their workplaces quickly disappearing in their rearview mirrors. Dicarlo's attempts to curb her cursing were crumbling the same way Josie's intentions disintegrated in the face of a forbidden food. Dicarlo swore a blue streak when the car behind them laid on the horn as they decelerated to turn into Sasha Peters's street.

"You think I'm slowing down to look at you, buddy?" she shouted at her mirror, her small hands gripping the Tahoe's steering wheel. "Yeah, that's right. I got a *badge and a gun*. Maybe you should *think twice* about who you're honking at. Maybe you should *think twice* about who's keeping the streets safe at night so you can go to your little nine-to-five, huh? Maybe *you should think about* who's running on five hours of sleep and twelve cups of coffee. Yeah, that's right. *I'm looking at you, you pantywaist*."

"Easy, Dicarlo," Lopez said. But Josie noticed he avoided touching the little detective and in fact, leaned his lanky frame away from her. They rolled to a stop in front of Sasha Peters's house, Dicarlo turned off the engine. Josie and Lopez eyed her while she took a couple of deep breaths until her small frame stopped quivering with fury.

"I'm good. It's okay." She looked at them. "I got it. I've been doing yoga these days. A little meditation. Some deep breathing. I'm gathering my *chi*. I'm much better now." She was panting like she was about to give birth, puffing out *hoo-hoo* and *hee-hee* until Josie was breathing along with her.

"You're good?" Lopez said. He looked doubtful, his eyebrows up near his hairline.

Dicarlo rolled her neck from side to side, and then nodded at her partner. "Yeah, I'm good." She took a couple more breaths, then said, "Okay, ready."

⌘

Lopez rang the doorbell a couple of times and knocked some more with no answer. Josie was pretty sure no one was home, but they heard footsteps approach the other side of the door. The steps paused. During the subsequent silence, Lopez held his badge up to the peephole. When the door remained closed after that, Lopez sighed.

"We know you're standing right there. Open up, please," he said, though he said the *please* in the same tone Josie's Aunt Ruth used right before she opened a can of whoop-ass.

Only after that did they hear a chain being scraped aside and a deadbolt turn. The door swung open, revealing a...vision.

"Whoa," Dicarlo barked. And although Josie didn't say it out loud, her expression probably said the same thing. Lack of poker face and all.

Sasha Peters was in full burlesque costume. Her Bettie Page leopard print halter dress fit her enhanced bust like a second skin. Her shiny, blue-black hair was long with a slight wave and a thick fringe in the front cut straight across her forehead. The only modern addition to the

1950s pin-up look were nearly-full tattoo sleeves extending from her collarbones all the way down to points on the backs of her hands. She was holding a riding crop, and her dark, sculpted eyebrow arched high as she looked at the three investigators on her front stoop.

"What can I do for you ladies...and gentleman?" she asked. Wonder of wonders, she had the same Russian accent as Olga Sorokin, though less pronounced. Josie could tell by Sasha's sultry pout that she was in character. Hopefully. Whatever Sasha was up to, she wasn't having a sweatpants-on-the-couch kind of day. Josie glanced at Sasha's feet, which were in black peep-toe stilettos, the size of which were roughly the same as Josie's feet, which would have been around a size seven. However, still no tell-tale blood-spattered work boots. *Too bad this sleuthing business couldn't be a tad easier,* Josie thought with sarcasm.

"We're looking for information about a friend of yours—Ivan Sorokin," Dicarlo said.

Josie, who was watching Sasha's face closely, saw the slightest hesitation before she said, "Sorry. I don't know anyone by that name." Pink crept into Sasha's fair-skinned throat, a telltale sign of a fib.

"That's strange because he told us we could find you here," Lopez said, surprising Josie with how smoothly he lied. Did everyone lie? *And why were they all better at it than she was?* "Can we come in and talk to you for just a minute? You look like you're on your way to work at the Pony Pagoda, so we don't want to make you late. We just need a minute of your time."

Sasha frowned. "I'm not late. I work from home. I don't work at that place anymore." She stepped back, and that was all Lopez and Dicarlo needed as invitation, as they purposefully stepped forward with more attitude than Josie ever could have managed. Maybe they taught that intimidator walk at cop school. The coursework could be called *Posturing 101 for the Po-Po.*

"Your boss Marty seems to think you're still coming in to work tonight," Dicarlo told her as she stepped inside. Josie followed them with an apologetic shrug at Sasha, who ushered them in with a haughty resignation and closed the door behind them, rolling her eyes.

"Well he's wrong. I gave him my notice yesterday. I left a message on his phone. I don't need that job any more. I'm making way more money at my new job. It's safer, and has much better hours." She strolled past them on her stilettos into her small front room. The area had formerly been a sitting room, but was now something *entirely different,* as if it had been revamped by...Martha Seedy. No mass-produced, mollifying artwork on the walls. No furnishings. No tchotchkes. In the center of the room was a backless wooden stool, a plain kitchen stool with rungs. Behind it, a drape of black velvet hung from the ceiling and covered the picture window. Facing this setup was a tripod and a camera, which was attached to a laptop.

"Annnd...what's this new job of yours?" Dicarlo asked, putting a single fingertip on the top of the camera.

Josie didn't want to know. She *really* didn't want to know.

Sasha said, "Don't touch that. It's very expensive and I'm borrowing it from a...friend. It's not mine until I can save up enough money to pay him back. If I break it, then I will have to save for two cameras. And that will make me very mad." The expression on her heavily painted face made Josie want to take a couple steps back, but Lopez wasn't the least bit intimidated.

"And would that friend be Ivan Sorokin?" he asked Sasha.

"I still don't know who that is. Even ten minutes later. And I'm still not going to know who that is ten minutes from now," she said. Her imperious attitude didn't fool Josie for a second. Sasha's hand fluttered a little as she put it on her animal-print-covered hip.

"Look, Sasha," Dicarlo said, "We have you at the club. We have Ivan Sorokin at the club. We have a landlord who can identify you as the person he has seen coming out of Ivan's apartment in Chinatown. We need to know if you were there over the weekend. We just need you to tell us how well you knew him. If you were using him for the money, we understand. A young girl like you has a lot to offer a guy like Ivan with the right financial incentive."

"Are you saying I'm a prostitute?" Sasha's jet black eyebrows shot up and her upper lip curled into a snarl. With her whip in hand, she made quite a picture.

The detectives had effectively put Sasha on the defensive, tag-teaming her in a way that made Josie cringe. When Josie looked at her, for some reason, she didn't see a murder suspect in a jealous lover's rage. She saw a barely-legal girl who was hiding her fear behind a massive wall of attitude and ink. Josie knew she could get Sasha to talk to her—and her alone. However, she didn't see the detectives agreeing to wait for her outside in the car while she talked with the girl. *Yeah, not happening.*

CHAPTER 18

After another twenty minutes of fruitless questioning by the detectives, Sasha's phone rang. Josie looked around but couldn't locate a phone. She realized Sasha's laptop was ringing, not an actual telephone.

"I have a call I need to take for work," Sasha said, pointedly looking at the front door. And while Josie took a step toward it, neither detective made a move of any kind—another useful cop posturing tip for Josie if she could ever master it. Sasha chuffed, clearly frustrated and out of patience with them. "Fine. Sit. Stay. Do not make a sound. Not a single noise. Am I clear?" She was good with the commands. Josie might have more luck imitating Ms. Pin-up Bossy Pants than trying to copy Lopez.

After seeing them ensconced on her couch, Sasha stomped over to her wooden stool, struck a pose with her hip jutted out, her whip gripped in one hand, and then pressed a wireless remote that had been concealed in the palm of her other hand. The light on her camera turned on, and she glared into the lens. So far, Sasha had been in nothing but a constant state of pissed-offedness since they had arrived. Josie pitied whoever was about to receive the brunt of her wrath now.

On the laptop's screen, a video chat window opened showing a young man in a football jersey sitting in what looked to be his bedroom, judging by the matching NFL paraphernalia posted on the wall behind him. Joe Montana, Steve Young, Colin Kaepernick, in order from squeaky-clean to tattooed—with the young man's head and thick neck blocking out everything between Young and Kaepernick. Josie, who wasn't much of a sports fan, had no idea who might even be between those players.

"Stuart, you are late," Sasha snarled in a tone that made Josie's eyebrows shoot up. "I told you to call me nine minutes ago."

"Yeah," he said. "Sorry. Football practice ran late. I told coach that—"

"Enough." She whacked the stool with her whip and turned her back to him, showing him what was probably a tantalizing view. The two detectives beside Josie were certainly enraptured. Lopez's jaw was hanging, slack. "Did you bring everything with you this time? I will not stand for the same ill-preparedness that you demonstrated last time."

"Yes, yes. Sorry," Stuart—Mr. Football—said. He reached for a backpack on the bed behind him. "I have it here. I'm all set."

She waited a half-second for him to settle himself, and then said, "Fine. I'll allow you the one transgression from last time, but never let it happen again. You know how I feel about insubordination." *Wow, good word,* Josie thought.

"Yes. Thank you," he said.

"Thank you what?"

"Thank you, mistress."

"Very well. Get out your tools. Equip yourself. Then we will begin."

Josie cringed, dreading what kind of *equipment* that entailed.

"Yes, mistress," Stuart said. He shuffled around on the desk in front of him, and then opened a large book.

"We review first. And then I will test you to make sure you have properly absorbed my lessons and committed them to memory. Now, you may begin."

"Yes, mistress." He read aloud, "'The Pythagorean theorem states that the square of the hypotenuse is equal to the sum of the squares of the other two sides. The theorem can be written as an equation, $a^2 + b^2 = c^2$.'"

Wow, this is sick, Josie thought. Of course fascinating, but still kind of sick. She couldn't decide if it was better or worse than she thought it might be.

"Stop right there," Sasha said. "Show me the proof that you must complete."

Hapless Stuart held up the book to his webcam, and Sasha squinted at it as it took a few seconds to come into focus on her laptop screen. "Fine. Now show me how you have begun. What is your approach?"

He hemmed and hawed and stalled.

"Stuart!" she shouted, smacking her whip on her stool loud enough to cause Lopez to jump. Dicarlo snorted at him, earning herself a scowl from *Mistress* Sasha. "How can you expect to pass Geometry and graduate high school if you do not apply yourself?"

He grinned a lop-sided grin in her laptop screen. "That's what my dad says, but it sounds waaaay better coming from you."

"Thank you," she purred, running her whip up her tattooed arm. "Now, begin your proof. Do you want to live with your parents for the rest of your life?"

"Hell, no," he said with enthusiasm, banging his meaty fist on his book.

"That's what I thought." She stroked her whip along her thigh while he scurried to put his sharpened pencil to paper.

⌘

"She made three thousand dollars last month as an S&M math tutor?" Lopez tapped his hand on the inside of the Tahoe's door as they made their way back into the city. "Clearly, I'm in the wrong line of work."

"Stuart the Defensive Lineman has pulled his failing grade up to a B-minus," Josie added from the backseat. "He's thinking about being an education major when he gets to college. Since he's been so inspired by his teacher."

"*If* he gets to college," Dicarlo corrected.

"*When* he gets a football scholarship and takes Sasha the Tutor with him to college, graduates with honors and retires his football jersey number, he'll end up running for public office," Josie said, causing Dicarlo to snort again.

The sky was getting dark, and Josie had just gotten a text from Susan, who had been cooped up all day in the apartment, as equally unable to go out without a car as she was unable to dump James. He had still not returned from seeing his parents in Chinatown.

"So, we have a definite suspect in Sasha Peters," Lopez said. "She didn't admit to having a pair of work boots, but with her wild wardrobe, some leather lace-ups would fit right in." He was thumbing through his email messages on his phone. "Here's the initial report back about the boot print from Jake at the lab. It's a women's size seven Danner work boot—I don't know that brand. I guess they're pretty popular." He was clicking on images and passed the phone over his shoulder to Josie. She saw a calf-high black leather boot with orange-yellow laces and GORE-TEX waterproof lining that cost well over $325 retail.

"Wow," she said. "Pricey." What she didn't say out loud was that she wouldn't have minded a pair of them in her own closet. Almost $350—that could be a car payment on a Lexus if you had good credit and if Chairman of the Fed, Ben Bernanke, were still around sitting on interest rates. But who spent that much on a pair of work boots when there was no actual physical work involved that would require them?

A woman who was *really* into costumes, that was who.

⌘

Before they reached the city, Josie asked the detectives, "So, tell me why we didn't let Sasha know that Ivan Sorokin is dead? Wouldn't that have been a trump card for us?" Josie felt strange saying *us*, but she was trying to accept her role as a tag-along Barney Fife in blue jeans.

Lopez shrugged and twisted in his seat to look at her, his eyebrows going up and down with his spoken thoughts as wildly as the ups and downs of the San Francisco streets. "Either she killed him and she already knows he's dead. Or, she did it, and we don't want her to know *we* know. Or she *didn't* do it and we need to string her along a little more until we find out exactly *what* she knows. In any case, we don't want her freaking out and making a run for it." Josie's head spun a little, but she caught that last part about not wanting to spook Sasha. Of all the people who were harboring secrets around here, Josie would put her money on Sasha to be holding the key pieces to this whole puzzle.

"She doesn't seem the type who would run from anything," Dicarlo said, banging her tiny fist on the steering wheel. "But you never can tell. She's just a kid, and kids these days—well, who knows what they're capable of. The internet, readily available weaponry, drugs of all kinds. Horrible music. Vine videos. Snapchat. Pranksters and morals in the crapper. Who knows."

"Tell us how you really feel, Dicarlo," Lopez said and laughed when his partner flipped him the bird.

"So, we're all in agreement that she and Ivan were seeing each other?" Josie asked, though staring at Ivan's face in the now-creased photo in her hand, she was having a hard time picturing them together. Sasha was so vastly different from Ivan's wife Olga that it was jarring— but maybe it was the differences that had drawn him to Sasha. Opposites attract, the same way contrasting flavors unexpectedly blend well together. Strange pairings that turn into something else entirely, as with food, a chemical reaction that can be combustible or magical.

"Oh yeah, definitely some hanky-panky there," Lopez said with a certainty that Josie didn't share. "And you can bet she wasn't tutoring him in math."

CHAPTER 19

By the time Josie winced her way up the rickety metal stairs of James's apartment, the sky was dark, and she was starving. Also apparently, Susan was ready to open up about her fizzled relationship with James. Over take-out cartons—one of which contained an intriguing avocado and pickled carrot spring roll in a delicately crisped rice wrapper that Josie was going to re-create later—Susan vented, "How am I supposed to break up with him when he's not here?" The sour expression looked out-of-place on her lovely, porcelain face.

"So you've made up your mind to break up with him for sure?" Josie said, trying to keep her opinion to herself. Knowing how transparent her own face was, she stuffed an entire spring roll into her mouth.

"Yes, pretty much. You were right. *You were right.* He's too young. Too irresponsible. Too self-absorbed. Too under his parents' thumb."

Josie chewed as fast as she could, but still managed to have a big mouthful left as she objected, "Waitaminute. I didn't say any of those things."

Susan gave her a look. "Right. Of course you didn't." She used one finger to draw a circle in the air in front of her own face indicating Josie's problem with her tell-all expressions.

Josie swallowed. "Sorry."

"When you're right, you're right." Susan shrugged. "And it's not as if he's fantastic in bed or anything. I mean, we haven't even…you know."

"Hm," Josie said, uncomfortable with the direction the conversation was headed.

"Nah," Susan said turning pink. "Not for lack of trying—on my part. I'm pretty adept at seduction. I'm not a nun, and he's fine. I mean, physically. All his parts, you know, work."

"Okay," Josie said. Even though it was not okay.

Josie didn't want to know more. Yes, she and Susan had always been close, but not that kind of close. Not the chit-chat about bodily functions kind of close. Although if she'd ever been the type of person to have a girlfriend, a girls' night out kind of girlfriend, then Susan was the closest candidate for that honor. Or dishonor. Whatever. Josie just wasn't that way naturally. Maybe it had to do with her mother, who had not been able to help Josie during her teen years. No giggling or gossiping. Or any so-called normal behavior. Until age 16, Josie had lived with her father, a career military man. After he had died, Josie found herself in southern Arizona, in the care of her great-aunt and uncle. So, no, not a typical upbringing, if such a thing did exist outside of advertisements and women's television networks. Having a *Cosmo* magazine talk with a girlfriend made Josie wish she were elsewhere.

"James just didn't want to sleep together. I guess he isn't all that experienced. I mean, how could he be if he wouldn't even sleep with me? He said he was saving himself for...marriage, I guess. Or the right girl. Which, as it turns out, isn't me."

"*Okay.*" Would Josie be expected to contribute in a meaningful way to this discussion about why James and Susan had never had sex? Would she then have to volunteer information about what she and Drew did in the bedroom. Or living room, bathroom, or kitchen? Josie felt horribly inadequate. She needed a *Dummy's Guide to Being a Girlfriend.*

"Yeah," said Susan. "So there was nothing going on *in there.*" She hooked a thumb over her shoulder at the bedroom behind her.

Please stop right there, Josie pleaded silently.

"Plus, he has a light saber nightlight," Susan said. "And he wears Donkey Kong underwear. Hard to stay in the mood when you're cringing and all. So I guess it's time to end it."

Josie whimpered.

"Do you know how hard it is to sleep with someone you're not intimate with? I mean, he's a good cuddler, but I think I saw more action as a kid at summer camp. Yeah. We're done. So done."

"His parents will be happy to hear that," Josie said—the first thing she could think of. She cleared her throat, wondering if her face was as red as it felt. "So when are you going to break up with him?"

The night was drawing to a close—it was almost midnight. Josie had made plans for the following afternoon to catch up with Detectives Lopez and Dicarlo, although she was thinking about blowing them off. She took out Greta Williams's credit card and ran her finger around the edge of it while she considered renting a car, maybe one of those daily Zipcar rental thingies. She needed her own wheels because she was quickly learning that she wasn't exactly a team player. In fact, hanging around with the two of them—as much as she didn't mind them personally—was getting on her nerves and making her feel trapped and claustrophobic. Likewise, while they were obligated to stick to laws and procedure, she was not. Nor was she particularly interested in doing so.

She had a natural distrust of authority. She might as well have been born with a *Question Authority* tattoo on her little golden behind.

"I thought I would do it tonight," Susan said. "I mean, at least initiate a conversation about going our separate ways. But he seems to be avoiding me. So, I guess it'll have to wait until tomorrow. The big B-Day. For breaking up." She brushed an errant strand of blond hair back from her face and grimaced.

"Or D-Day for dumping his butt. You could do it by text. Or on your message board." Josie couldn't stop the snarkiness from coming out. Yeah, right, as if Susan would end a relationship on a public forum. Josie regretted having said it—right up until Susan laughed.

"I know you're just trying to make me feel better." Susan then said, suddenly stricken. "Oh no. Do I have to leave the message board? Does he get it if we break up? He's been on it longer than I have. And he's met more of the other people who post there in person—face-to-face—than I have. Last month, a bunch of them went to Vegas to see if they could get banned from a casino for counting cards. I think they got kicked out of the Flamingo hotel. They've bonded—how could you not bond after that? If we split, does he get custody of them?"

"I think it's too soon to tell," Josie said with as straight a face as she could manage. She rubbed her forehead to help hide her expression, which was probably one of mockery because she couldn't stop herself from feeling that way. "You should let some time go by before you decide something that important."

⌘

Early the next morning with still no appearance from James, Josie went on the internet to check the Lounge Lizards to see what the denizens of the message board had been up to lately. She had already left a voicemail message for Greta Williams and was waiting for a return call. Josie had also made a reservation at a car rental place near the SFO airport, so she needed to go pick up her wheels later in the afternoon.

She brought up the web address and blinked in surprise. The message board had been incredibly active overnight. Josie scrolled down and read through several conversations that didn't make sense. Many of the messages had been deleted by the posters, so only responses remained. She saw a random "That's inappropriate here" and "Take it off-line, you two" without the messages to which they were in response. Clearly, there had been a spat between two users—Zenmaster, who was James as she had learned, and another user named Deeva, who obviously was Susan, the fashionista. Josie read through the online spat a couple of times, trying to fill in the blanks.

Josie scooted off the pulled-out couch and peeked into the room where Susan was sleeping face-down, passed out on...yes, Star Wars sheets. Floating Yodas and lightsabers which were glowing greenly in the still-black dark of the early morning. *Glow-in-the-dark. Classic.* Josie glanced back at her laptop. She read the board one more time and gathered that in the wee hours of the night, Susan had taken Josie's sarcastic comment to heart and had broken up with James publicly, *on the message board*, which was probably the social equivalent of tossing a drink in his face at a crowded party. Now, Susan was sleeping the sleep of the dead on those Industrial Light & Magic sheets either at peace with her act of public shaming or simply exhausted.

"Huh." Josie looked at the front door of the apartment and wondered if James would barge in any minute now to kick them out of his apartment. She paused and waited, but nothing happened. The morning was completely silent other than an occasional hungover, walk-of-shamer passing on the street below. She looked at the apartment door again and realized James would never bust in with verbal guns blazing. She was coming to realize that their computer goober *non grata* was a nonconfrontationalist, almost to an extreme. Who knew to what lengths he would go to avoid addressing a problem head-on. Lucky for her, because she was still in her jammies and didn't want to be kicked to the curb until she had her favorite jeans on.

Look at the evidence, the facts, she told herself. James hadn't told his parents about Susan. He hadn't had the *cojones* to tell his mother and father that he was dating a non-Chinese woman. Instead, he'd lied and misrepresented the truth. He hadn't told anyone that he frequented a burlesque club with his business partner. So, what other problems in his life was he avoiding? What other secrets was he keeping? Had he in some way cheated, scammed, or duped Ivan?

Josie went back to her computer and sat cross-legged on the sofa with it in her lap. She stared at the Lizard message board with her finger hovering over the mousepad, then she clicked the button on the site that said *Create a New User Account.* After a couple seconds of filling out the account form and submitting it, she went back to the board and posted her first message. Within minutes, she had responses.

Josie: Hi. I'm a friend of Deeva's.

Xav: Fresh meat. Are you a girl in real life?

Josie: Yes. I'm sorry to hear about your friend Ivan.

Xav: He was a good guy. If I were still drinking, I would raise a toast in his honor.

nPawn: Welcome. We'll try to keep it friendly.

Josie: I appreciate that, but it's not necessary.

Zenmaster: What are you doing on here? Get off.

Josie was startled to read the response from Zenmaster, who she already knew was James. He was online *at this very moment,* which shouldn't have been surprising. In real life, he was as unavailable in person as he was *available* online. Not a shocker.

Xav: Take it easy, man. You had a long night.

Josie: What am I doing here? I'm looking for you.

Zenmaster: You can stay where you are. I don't give a rat's ass. I won't be coming back. I'm staying with my parents till you're both gone. And tell that bitch I want my comics back. My first editions.

Whoa. Josie's temper flared, and her cheeks grew warm. She glanced again at Susan's sleeping form, but no one was awake to calm her down. James was either beating his virtual chest in front of his friends because he'd been dumped in public or he was just naturally more aggressive and rude online—Josie had witnessed this same behavior in other people before. For some reason, the internet made people more likely to be rude. Maybe because there was the whole delusion that a person on the internet was safe from physical violence, and therefore not culpable for inflammatory or aggressive words. One thing was certain—this online James persona was not the same James she had met in person. But if he thought she was going to take that kind of attitude from him, he clearly didn't know her either.

Josie: Sure, I'll tell your ex who dumped you to leave your comics on top of your Star Wars blankie next to your Pac-Man panties.

Xav: I love you.

nPawn: Ouch. I think Zen is going to need some ice for that burn.

She waited a while, but there were no further replies from James. She did, however, receive two marriage proposals from other random posters who had been following their argument. In truth, she had no idea if James was angry and stewing, cowed, or had logged off without seeing her comment. She would have to wait and see about that. However, one thing was certain—there was no way she could stay here at his apartment any longer, having just thrown down the Pac-Man panties gauntlet.

CHAPTER 20

Greta Williams called back right after Josie had arranged for a taxi to take her to the car rental agency. She walked down the rickety metal steps outside James's apartment, white-knuckling the rail with one hand while she talked with Greta with the other. After Susan woke up, the two of them definitely needed to find a hotel room on solid ground. One little tremor from the temperamental crust under this city and she'd be flung to the concrete ground below and probably squashed under thousands of bricks, to be mourned only by her dog Bert for about five minutes before Drew gave him another illicit table scrap...That was a little morbid, but the stupid stairs gave her the willies, big time.

"What news do you have for me?" her Beacon Hill benefactor sounded unusually chatty. Josie wondered for a minute if the woman had been looking forward to Josie's check-in call, but that was too weird to contemplate. Greta had millions, if not billions, of dollars. There was no way on God's green earth that the woman could be waiting for Josie to call while sitting home alone with nothing to do and no one to talk with. On her soft, soft cushions made of money. If that were loneliness, Josie was willing to try it herself for a month or two.

"One half of the start-up company that you invested in seems to be, unfortunately, deceased. Murdered, actually," Josie said without any preamble other than a clearing of her throat. Bad news was never easy to deliver, whatever the magnitude of impact.

Greta was silent for a couple of beats. "Ivan Sorokin, I presume," she finally said.

"Yes. Sorry about your initial investment. At the moment, it's not looking probable that you will see any return on those funds. I think you can kiss your dough bye-bye." Josie knew it sounded callous—a man's life had been lost—but she had a feeling Greta would want the information imparted as it affected her directly.

"What does Maxwell Lopez say?" Greta wanted to know.

"Detective Lopez and his partner have very kindly been including me in some of their interviews as they track down some initial leads." Josie wasn't sure exactly how much detail Greta wanted to know about their lack of progress so far—the boot print, the burlesque club, or Olga's anger at Sasha a.k.a. Shasta. Frankly, Josie didn't feel confident with the amount of evidence or the importance of anything they'd learned so far. In fact, she felt she could be doing better than she'd been doing—she just needed to try harder. By herself.

"What are your plans?" Greta asked.

Josie thought about it as she stood on the street corner watching for her cab, trying not to annoy passers-by with her phone conversation. A man in ripped blue jeans and a ripped suit coat walked by talking much louder than she was, and she felt better until she realized he didn't even have a phone or earpiece—he was just talking to the voices in his head, presumably. Josie pondered so long about how to respond to Greta's question that any other normal person on the other end of the line probably would have thought the cellular connection had been lost. Instead, Greta simply waited.

Of course, Josie wanted to stay—she wanted to remain in California for a few more days to find out what she could. She didn't know how to justify her desire or the cost to Greta. Most likely, Susan would return to Boston now that she and James had broken up—there was no reason for Susan to stay longer. In fact, she now had incentive to leave as quickly as possible, thanks to the midnight message board debacle. For Josie, that same niggling curiosity that had reared its head with the events in Arizona this past autumn was now getting under her skin. The itch was crawling up and down her spine like a shiver up and down the San Andreas Fault. She'd tumbled headlong into yet another sticky mess and again, possibly didn't have enough common sense to leave before she got dragged under.

"If I stay here in California," Josie began, the same moment her cab pulled up to the curb. She told the driver where she wanted to go and climbed into the backseat. She started again, "If I stay, I can pay for the rest of my days here on my own." She wasn't entirely sure how, but she did have a credit card of her own that could stand a little temporary abuse without giving up the ghost.

"You've hardly incurred any expenses as of yet," Greta said, which made Josie feel as if cameras were capturing her every move. Which was ridiculous, but as they passed a traffic camera at an intersection, Josie looked up at it and waved. A man in the white VW Beetle next to them smiled and blew her a kiss in return. As he pulled ahead of them, she off-handedly read his rainbow bumper sticker, which said, "Closets are for clothes."

All the half-secrets and untold parts of Josie's life, the people she kept things from, the people—her mother, for one—who weren't able to comprehend the things she told them, all of these things were suddenly a great and terrible burden. She was inexplicably tired of it all, tired of hiding what she was feeling and tired of having to feel as if she needed to provide a reason or a motive for what she felt.

"I want to stay here until I find out what happened to Ivan Sorokin," she told Greta more firmly. "And I'm going to need to spend some money to find the truth."

And then, she waited. It was now or never. As soon as she committed to getting her own transportation here in this city, she was in for good. She'd be mobile and free to do as she wished. Now she was laying her cards on the table, so to speak. She was saying aloud exactly what she wanted—giving her demands and expecting them to be met. Well, *hoping* they would be accepted.

"Very well," Greta said, her approval cool and unreadable.

Josie was staying. It was done.

CHAPTER 21

The ringing of Josie's cell phone saved her from the monotony of waiting in line for customer service at the airport car rental agency—although the people-watching was superb at this particular spot.

"Josie," Dicarlo said, "I have some information about Sorokin's finances that might be of interest to you. Hang on, let me get outside more away from the door." Some street noise and some rustling wind noises came over the phone. Josie marveled for a minute that she'd heard more nature via electronic devices this trip than she'd actually heard outdoors, *in nature*. Which was kind of a shame, considering she wasn't that far from Napa Valley, Tahoe, or the Sierra Nevadas. She shuffled up a couple of steps in the rental line, slouching like the rest of the brain-dead people around her who were staring at their handheld devices. She fought the urge to drag one foot and moan in zombie fashion. Only a few more people ahead of her to go. She snapped her mind back to Dicarlo, who was saying, "Normally, we wouldn't share them with an outside P.I. such as yourself—obviously—so I don't want to send them by email or anything. In fact, I went for a walk so I could make this call. No sense in raising any flags at work."

"I appreciate it," Josie said. "I don't know what Lopez has told you about our arrangement..." or the fact that they pretty much didn't have *any kind of arrangement*..."but I want to assure you that you can absolutely trust me to keep anything you tell me confidential. And if I find anything that I think would interest you, I'll tell you immediately." *Within reason*, Josie added to herself. But she had felt obligated to offer some kind of verbal disclosure aloud.

"Of course, of course. Guess we should have gotten that little formality taken care of right off the bat. But frankly, I was a little flippin' distracted by things. So many things. I'm not just talking about strippers. This whole case has things going on all over the place. Listen to what I'm about to tell you."

"Go ahead. I'm all ears," Josie told the detective.

"First of all, Ivan Petrovich Sorokin hardly had any life insurance. Like a piddly 75 grand that wouldn't even cover the balance on his mortgage on the house in Santa Cruz." The phone rustled on the other end of the line as Dicarlo switched ears.

"Wow, that sucks for Olga. I wonder if she's going to have to move out of her Little Mermaid dream house," Josie thought out loud.

"But listen to this," Dicarlo went on after a short, harsh laugh. "He didn't need life insurance. Ivan Sorokin was a fricking millionaire. I mean, millions of dollars. He had more money than I could spend in a couple of lifetimes if I was trying hard. We've got leads on his money all over the place. Off-shore accounts. Cash in safety deposit boxes. Gold bars in there, too. He definitely had a money-under-the-mattress mentality, a little old lady hoarding pennies. Except we're talking *way more* than pennies. We don't even know how much it's going to add up to once we track it all down. I'm guessing at least over fifty mil."

Josie blinked a couple of times before she said, "Wow, I guess Olga won't mind about the life insurance policy then." She mulled this over with a frown. If Ivan were that stinking wealthy, why was he working a normal nine-to-five job? Why was he living the average Joe life and struggling to finance his start-up company with a broke, unworldly kid like James Yu? Maybe it was money he couldn't touch for one reason or another—it wasn't his, he couldn't draw attention to himself, or…what?

A light came on in her mind. "Their start-up company, was that a front?" Granted, it was a virtual company to begin with. Basically, it was just two guys and a website. Maybe it was a way to move money from investors—Greta Williams, for one—into his own accounts.

"We're looking at that," Dicarlo said. "From everything we've seen so far, Applied Apps is totally legitimate and all by the books. The initial investment money is all untouched. They've made good on their initial product drops and proof-of-concept to their clients. Although I still for the love of God don't know what they do any more than you do, Josie."

Well, that was a bit of good news, Josie thought. Greta Williams's money was safe and sound. At least for now. But it was also bad news for figuring out where all the money had come from.

"Well, I gotta go," Dicarlo said abruptly, giving Josie the impression that someone else had either caught Dicarlo's attention, or had given her a little too much attention—discussing a case with Josie couldn't have been standard procedure. "Keep plugging along. Let us know if you find anything."

"Will do," Josie said, her mind abuzz with this new information.

⌘

Still thinking about poor Ivan's millions—because what good was the money to a dead man?—Josie made it back to James's apartment by the good grace of the GPS gods, and then by some other miracle, found a small parking space only a block away, which she maneuvered into with shocking gracelessness. But hey, she was out of practice driving—she'd only recently renewed her expired driver's license back home in Massachusetts. Retaking that test had been a major pain in the backside. She pressed the silent key fob lock to her rented, acid-green Kia Soul—she'd asked for a compact car, but they had rented their last one on hand, so they had automatically upgraded her to the next size—and wondered, briefly, if she would be towed or ticketed overnight. Hopefully, she could make it one night unscathed by the parking police, and tomorrow, she and Susan would check into a hotel.

"Honey, I'm home," she said opening the door to James's apartment. Susan came out of the bedroom looking fresh as a daisy...and wheeling her suitcase, a blonde Marlo Thomas from the opening sequence of *That Girl*, one of the shows Josie used to watch on the rerun channel late at night sandwiched between *Unsolved Mysteries* and *The Benny Hill Show*.

"Great timing," Susan said, adjusting her shoulder bag. "I just called a cab."

"But I rented a car," Josie said, confused.

Susan gave her a hug. "I'm headed home, lady. I've had enough of this business. I have reached my limit. *Seriously* reached my limit. This is where I draw the line. I mean, I know you're a tough cookie, but I'm not. I prefer to know where I stand on things. I can't simply hang out here in this limbo state. I have a life—and hearing about the end of Ivan's life makes me realize that I don't have to stay here where I'm not wanted. Enough's enough."

Josie completely understood. Frankly, she had expected Susan to depart ASAP after the online blowup with James. Josie returned her friend's hug, her slender body suddenly feeling fragile, and said, "But you don't need to take a cab. I can drive you now that I have a car. I have GPS. I won't even get lost. Too much."

Susan laughed, although her smile stopped short of her eyes. She pushed back a strand of her blonde hair, letting go of her smile. Her face fell momentarily before she appeared to straighten herself back up. "I know. Thanks. I'll be fine. I'm taking a red-eye flight back. Benjy is picking me up at Logan in the morning. I'll be so glad to get out of here...and on to the next screw-up."

Josie sighed and helped her friend pull her bag out of the apartment door onto the rickety walkway. "Don't be so hard on yourself. He looked good on paper...or pixels, I guess. I'm sorry it didn't work out. Because you know, you, of all people, deserve to find Mr. Right."

"That mythical creature," Susan added.

Then, they both paused a minute to look down the rickety, annoying flight of metal stairs.

"If I didn't love my Gucci luggage, I would give it a big push and let gravity take it down," Susan said with a sniffle. She laughed again, but for real this time, so Josie figured she'd be all right even if it took some time.

CHAPTER 22

After seeing Susan snugly tucked into her cab, Josie went back up the Scary Stairs of Doom to James's ratty apartment to pack her own bag. Staying another night here was out of the question, especially now that Susan had departed. Josie could admit it: she was going to be lonely without her friend, which was a strange predicament for a non-people-person like Josie. In essence, she liked to be alone, but not *lonely*, if that made any sense at all. Besides, being in this crumbly old building in what might possibly be the apartment of a killer was creepy. At this point, everyone was a suspect in Josie's mind.

Back in the guest room, Josie jammed her t-shirts into her army surplus duffel, thinking how Susan would cringe at her abuse of her garments. Josie's dad had taught her how to roll-pack her clothes so they'd fit most efficiently into her bag. Looking wrinkle-free had never been part of the lesson, but she was hoping to find new temporary digs that had a washer and dryer.

When she was finished torturing her clothing, she went into the kitchen in search of her laptop where she'd last sat while she used it to search for car rental places. Susan had put it aside in the pile of three or four other decrepit computers that James kept on his battered formica table. When Josie picked hers up, she found that the corner of its gray cover was cracked and a small piece of plastic had chipped off.

"Crap," she said to no one in particular. Her blog had just gone out and she was supposed to be fielding the comments as they came in—usually, there was a flurry of them from her more devoted readers who actually claimed they looked forward to post day, the day that the new blog entry was published.

Might as well see what the damage is, she thought, taking a breath and flipping open the laptop's cover. With a quick prayer to the tech gods, she pressed the power button.

And breathed a sigh of relief when she heard the familiar whirring sound of it booting up.

When it went right to a generic Microsoft image background image, bypassing the logon screen, she frowned. The background image on her laptop was supposed to be a closeup photo of an array of Chinese dim sum dumplings, glossy and tempting, nestled in their round bamboo baskets, curls of steam drifting heavenward above them. And where were all the icons that usually cluttered her computer's desktop?

Uh-oh. This wasn't her laptop. She had mistakenly picked up one of James's cast-offs. So, where the heck was her computer? Not immune to James's untidiness after all, Susan must have tidied up before she left.

Josie spied her own laptop on the bottom of the pile of books and the other laptop she'd already snooped her first night here. Her old battle-worn computer was of identical manufacturer, model, and outward appearance as James's, but not cracked, thank goodness. She checked to make sure the one she grabbed was hers this time. Yes, there was the slight stain in the corner from when permanent marker had transferred from the take-out container to her thumb to her laptop from some cheese blintzes. *Mmmm,* she had picked them up from that cute village deli in Waban about two years ago, back when she could still eat cheese without wondering whether her living will was up-to-date. Definitely DNR—do not resuscitate—on that point…

She looked back at the impostor machine whirring in front of her as she tucked her own recovered one under her arm. Once again, she pondered the ethics of the situation for about a half-second. *In for a penny, in for a pound,* she thought and shrugged. She double-clicked on a picture icon and had to suck in a gasp. The photo preview program had opened, displaying a photo of a desk at a workplace. She was looking at Ivan's desk, judging by the Star Wars figurines on the shelf above it. Yes, it was definitely Ivan's desk at PPS. Josie had stood in that exact spot at his desk not too long ago. She peered at the photo and leaned closer.

Ivan sat in his desk chair with a big smile on his rosy face, his eyes closed tightly, his blond hair neatly combed back except for an errant strand that curled across his forehead. A woman sat across his lap, her face turned away from the camera and buried in his neck. Her arms were wrapped tightly around Ivan, as tightly as his arms held her. They were locked in a tight embrace. The unquestionable warmth of their pose was enviable. Their clasp was soul-deep, whole-hearted, and honest in its intensity. The kind of devotion they displayed was rare—Josie knew that from experience.

Josie looked more closely. The woman's hair was long and jet-black. She wore black shoes, fishnet stockings, tight black short-shorts, and a jungle-print tank top with spaghetti straps. Her tattooed arms, full sleeves from collarbones to wrists, clearly identified her as Sasha Peters.

PART 3: THE PROOF

Poolish is a French baking term for the spongey bread batter you make with baker's yeast. If you're finished with your uncontrollable chuckling, now say *biga*, which is the Italian word for the same thing. In a disorganized kitchen, as in a disorganized mind, it's best to take out individual ingredients and inspect them one at a time for viability before you build your creation, knead your dough, or form your hypothesis. Make the yeast prove itself—hence, the term *proof*. Because if you want a golden brown loaf, perfectly risen and captured by heat, you cannot have a weak link or a dead ingredient in your theory.

Josie Tucker, *Will Blog for Food*

CHAPTER 23

The photo showed Ivan embracing Sasha, clasping her tightly.

Josie had proof now, *actual evidence* of a relationship between Ivan and Sasha. Now she needed to get the photo—actually, photos, because there were more than one—onto her own computer so she could get them to Detectives Lopez and Dicarlo.

After a forehead-slapping brainstorm, she got her navy blue flash drive from her room and plugged it into the port on the side of James's computer. When the drive's window popped up, she dragged all the photo icons into it and watched as they copied over, suddenly feeling the urgency to get it done quickly, as if James would suddenly walk in on her after having deserted Susan hours ago. Her heart thudded in her chest while she watched the progress bar slowly fill up as the files were copied to her tiny drive. But, no. It was all good. James was still a no-show. She wouldn't stay to boot up her computer to send the detectives the photos by email. Just logging in would take a good ten minutes or so while the ancient gerbil inside her computer—a.k.a. the hard drive—decided whether to give up the ghost. So, she shut everything down, finished packing up, and left, locking the door behind her and wobbling down those crazy metal steps one last time.

Twenty minutes later, Josie, with all her belongings in the backseat, arrived in her acid-green Kia Soul at a chain hotel in south San Jose that had free Wi-Fi and continental breakfast. Normally, she wasn't a franchise-type of person. She would have preferred a B&B in Los Gatos or even Santa Cruz, if she'd wanted to go that far south. But her new hotel offered a lot: a big, sprawling bed without a ditch in the middle like the futon at James's place and a dust-free generic desk and chest of drawers—because James's slovenliness had been bothering *even her*. Her new digs were located about halfway between the Pony Pagoda burlesque to the north and Sasha Peters's house to the south. And most of all, this particular room offered a locked door with plenty of personal space to do some serious ruminating.

But, later. That would have to come later, she thought as her stomach growled. Because the one thing the hotel didn't offer, was something to eat at 11:00 p.m. on a week night. Maybe a seared lamb chop or a grilled Portobello.

Where in San Jose can I find a place like that, hmmm?

Josie figured she might know somewhere like that, maybe one with dinner and a show.

⌘

The parking lot of the Pony Pagoda was full, and this time, Josie used the valet parking. It was close to midnight, and she wasn't a fan of walking around dark parking lots by herself. Especially since her Arizona experience—dark alleys now gave her the shivers—not that she was going to let one bad episode rule her life.

In fact, just the opposite. Some things about her were different since Arizona. Almost being killed could change a person. She still didn't suffer fools kindly, but she was more direct now, more willing to say what was on her mind, and damn the torpedoes. She was still the same old nosy person as ever, as evidenced by the fact that she pasted a broad smile on her face when she recognized the bartender as she bellied up to the bar. A saxophone was wailing, and a woman on stage was doing a number with white feathered fans to the approval of catcalls and whistles. Servers were working the tables, and the place smelled like roasted meat and vegetables. Josie's stomach, which had been pleasantly silent all day until a few minutes ago, growled.

"Hey, I remember you," the bartender said, his salt-and-pepper pompadour shining under the lights. "How's it going, girlie? Did you come back for the dinner special? You look like you could use a little sustenance." He put down a napkin, but then thought better of it. "Why don't you go on back to the kitchen? There are some girls back there. They said they enjoyed your company earlier. Something about wanting to teach you their moves and make you their mascot." He gave her a wink. This was news to Josie, but she thanked him and went around the bar to push through the kitchen door.

She entered the room exactly in the middle of a burst of raucous laughter. The kitchen side of the place was hopping. The grills were sizzling. Heat lamps were keeping the plates warm while servers hustled in and out at a crazy pace for nearly midnight on a weeknight. She would expect a flurry of activity in a town like Las Vegas, but this was San Jose, for crying out loud. Didn't these people have to get up for work tomorrow? Maybe they slugged breakfast Red Bulls as fast and furiously as James did.

"Hey! It's our little friend," Merrylin, the blonde Monroe lookalike, called out. "Come over here, hon. Have some dinner with us." Josie approached them, noticing both the picked over French fries congealing on their plates, and Merrylin's hugely dilated pupils—she was higher than a kite. So much for the claims that the dancers were squeaky clean. Either Marty and the bartender were both deluded about the healthy lifestyles of their staff or they were big liarheads. Josie was inclined to think it was the latter.

Merrylin came around the table and pulled Josie in a tight hug that was all cleavage and dried sweat. Josie was only about 5'3"—on a day when the wind was blowing upward—and Merrylin was a good half-foot taller. The embrace was like being engulfed in the arms of an octopus and being drawn slowly, inevitably toward the mouth on its belly. She fought the urge to struggle and was on the brink of an anxiety attack when the stripper gave her one last squeeze and released her.

"This is Shady, Bo-Peep, and Vivian," Merrylin said, pointing around the table. Josie received an array of grunts and waves from the other women. "Are you hungry, hun? Let me get you a dinner special. You're not a vegetarian, are you?" When Josie shook her head no, Merrylin said, "Good girl," and went over to the kitchen side of the room. She ordered Josie a steak, medium-rare, without asking her preference. Maybe Josie had medium-rare written on her face along with her slight amusement, but the steak worked for her.

Josie sat at the table listening to the women banter about the night, the customers, and the management—none of them in favorable light.

When a kitchen assistant plonked down a plate in front of Josie, her eyebrows shot up in surprise. Her head swiveled back toward the kitchen where she spied the chef over the grill, checking the temperature—clearly, his instincts were spot-on and the grill was perfect, probably around 600 degrees, exactly as hot as it needed to be. At that moment, he happened to glance up, and Josie gave him a thumbs up. He quirked a smile, saluted her with a knife, and got back to work.

On a warmed white bistro dish, her steak was uncomplicated and gorgeous, nicely-seasoned, with a slight crust on the outside. Glassy green beans and a mound of mashed potatoes rounded out the plate. She picked up her serrated knife and sliced into the meat, just the right amount of juice dotting her dish. When she took a bite, she may have moaned inadvertently.

Merrylin chuckled, "Good, huh?" When the dancer named Vivian got ready to leave because her set was coming up, Merrylin said, "Get the girl a house red on your way out, will ya?" She turned to Josie, "You're old enough, right?"

Old enough to drink? That was a funny one. "Yeah," she said, her cheek full of meat.

"You bet," Vivian said. "Hang around. Maybe we'll teach you some moves after my set. It'll be last call. Then the boys will shut down the front and we'll have the back all to ourselves. You ladies up for a little dress-up tonight, a little 'us' time?"

"Hell, yes," Shady said with a fist pump of her thin brown hand and dangerous looking manicure, but Bo-Peep begged off, saying she had to go home and let her babysitter off the hook. As an apology, she explained that she had two kids under the age of five waiting for her at home.

"It'll be you and me and Shady and Viv," Merrylin said, though Josie didn't exactly know what she was signing up for. "And maybe some Jack." Meaning Jack Daniels. Meaning Josie, the lightweight, was in trouble. *Uh-oh.*

"You bet," she said and toasted them with the green beans on her fork.

CHAPTER 24

"I'm not much of a drinker," Josie told the strippers. Her words may have been slightly slurred. The four of them were all on stage. The club was closed for the night now, and she was wearing…what the heck was she wearing? Four-inch heels, a hot-pink feather boa, a zebra-print leotard, and some kind of Pleather short-shorts that squeaked between her thighs when she walked. They had done her makeup and hair, which had been doubled in volume and height, thanks to some kind of temporary weave that made her offer up a prayer for whatever deceased animal it had come from. They gave her a look called "smoky eyes" that made her appear like a ninja wearing a mask, the whites of her eyes standing out like Sylvester Stallone's as he rose up out of the jungle water in *Rambo*. She was sporting false eyelashes for the first time in her life and she couldn't tell if her vision was blurry because she was drunk as a skunk or because her eyelashes were falling off.

Vivian, the red-headed instigator who kept calling Josie their mascot, had brought her iPod from her dressing room and had hooked it up to a sound system backstage. Unlike the sultry jazz the club played during their performances, Josie was now hearing some Rihanna, Pussycat Dolls, and Jason Derulo. She was seeing plenty of bump-and-grind moves up close from Vivian, her personal instructor, but she had hours ago given up her shock, awe, and dignity, so she was just laughing like a hyena along with the rest of them. Merrylin and Shady had dumped themselves, cross-legged, downstage where they were giving her helpful pointers.

"Strut, strut, turn slowly to your left. Lift the hip. Shimmy. Shimmy. Hands on the hips. Chin tip down annnnnd…wink." Vivian, like a gruesomely painted drill instructor, clapped and called out Josie's steps.

Josie wobbled at the end, and Vivian demanded, "Again. Do it this way." She quickly demonstrated, looking more athletic than Josie thought possible earlier. Now that she was up close and personal, she could see the muscle definition in her chest and thighs and smell the tangy sweat on the woman's skin.

Merrylin, still seated on the scratched and worn stage floor, kept turning to the side, hiding her hands in a furtive way that had her giggling. She was probably taking a hit of something, Josie figured, based on the woman's earlier dilated pupils and her maniacally jovial smiles. Shady, the dark-skinned woman, was more subtle in all things, including her criticism of Josie's moves, but she was still watching Josie like a hawk, contributing occasional comments. The women were somewhat ruthless, in a not-entirely mean-spirited way, but they definitely had an edge to them. Josie would not have wanted to be on the wrong side of an argument with any of them.

When Vivian started the song over, Josie ran through her sequence of steps again. "I don't know if you can tell this about me," she said, getting a handle on her wobble this time, "but I'm not really a girly-girl." She whipped her enhanced hair over her head just like they had showed her. *Look out, hair on hormones coming through.* Her weave's momentum almost took her balance with it.

From Merrylin came a burst of laughter. She had dug into the back pocket of Josie's jeans, which lay in a pile with her phone and the rest of her clothes. She was waving Josie's man styled wallet, a beat-up billfold that had been in her father's things after he died. The wallet was black leather with a grommet for a chain, which Josie had never put on. Yeah, it was kind of butch, but she liked it—and it made her think of him. She was a tomboy for sentimental reasons.

"I mean," Josie went on after a spin, which she totally nailed, despite her decreased sobriety, "I never went to prom or anything. I never had to wear a really frou-frou, fluffy dress until this massive wedding I was in last fall. But I'm not a dress-up kind of person. Although I'm kind of liking what these heels are doing for my butt." She rotated her knee outward and did the hip thing they had taught her, which was starting to feel more controlled and less like she was about to fall on her butt. Still, gravity was acting weird and unexpected this evening. Yeah, that was definitely the Jack. Mr. Daniels was a naughty evening companion. "No one ever taught me about all this stuff." That's what happened when a girl was raised mostly by her Army vet dad. She batted her eyes with their heavy makeup.

"You're a natural, baby," Shady yelled at her over the music. She was clapping and bopping her head in a loose, easy way that made Josie smile. She was feeling relaxed, too. In fact, she was thinking that a wee dram of alcohol in her life probably wasn't such a bad thing. After all, it wasn't good to live life so uptight about things, right? People who were uptight missed the fun things. Look at her new friends and her new dancing skills. She was a natural—they said so. And if she needed a drink now and then to loosen up, she shouldn't have to abstain completely. Didn't that sound reasonable?

When Josie ended with her chin tip and wink, they cheered and stomped their feet. And she ended up laughing so hard, she collapsed on the floor in a heap of feathers.

⌘

"You're more fun than Shasta," Merrylin told her later that night. Or maybe it was morning now.

They were watching Shady do an impressive routine to that old time Afro Caravan song—Josie hadn't known the name of it until they told her, but she thought she recognized the song from an old Betty Boop cartoon. Or maybe it was Looney Tunes with Bugs Bunny doing a drag routine—he had looked good in fake eyelashes, too. Maybe everyone did. As the music played, showcasing Shady's pure athleticism and sultry hand movements, Josie was temporarily mesmerized. The woman's lean limbs and dark skin tone made a beautiful display. Merrilyn had said earlier that Shady had an audition in a few days for a traveling burlesque troupe, so she had been practicing like a demon. She was in training. She had goals. The girl had places *to go.*

Merrylin was talking about Sasha, which made Josie perk up from her fumy stupor. "That girl has a stick up her butt. Goals and going places *much* better than here, if you know what I mean. Not the way Shady's getting ready for the big time, but how she made us feel we're not good enough for her, for Shasta. We tried to get her to hang with us, but she was always *too busy*, if you know what I mean." She made finger quotes to show they'd obviously been blown off by Sasha.

Red-headed Vivian cut in, "This lifestyle isn't for everyone, Mer—you know that's the truth. If you could get out of here and open that dance studio you're always talking about, you'd be gone in a heartbeat. Gone from taking under-the-table cash payments from Marty. Gone from the late hours and the busted knees and the sucky social life. Hell, you might even get a boyfriend." Josie's eyebrows shot up. She had read somewhere that roughly 60-80% of strippers were adult survivors of sexual abuse. Looking around, she could hazard a guess as to which ones of her companions were part of that statistic, and her jaw clenched for them. While this was a night of fun and games for her, this was their lives. This had been Sasha's life. Was she part of that statistic, too?

Merrylin snorted. "What do I need a boyfriend for? I got everything I need right here." She made a rude gesture with her hand near her crotch.

Vivian rolled her eyes. "Yeah, right. Whatever keeps you warm at night."

Merrylin turned back to Josie, "Anyway, about Sasha. She was still chasing the American dream. She was from another country. Russia or the Ukraine or somewhere. So she had this crazy work ethic. Perfecting her English, her website, her stock portfolio, or whatever," Merrylin said. "Got on my last nerve, if you know what I mean. Not that I have anything against immigrants. We're all from somewhere else—I get that. But, Lord, it was *exhausting* to watch her always try to better herself. I mean, give it a rest, girl. You're making all of us look bad." She rolled her eyes, and Josie realized she was only half-kidding, but Josie's foggy brain had picked up on something.

"Marty pays cash only?" Josie asked. Maybe that was why he'd been unable to come up with Sasha's employee records when Lopez and Dicarlo had asked for them. Maybe Sasha wasn't legally in this country.

"Yeah, for some of the girls, it's cash only. So don't call the IRS on him or we'll all be out on our asses. What, are you thinking of making some extra money while you're in town?" Merrilyn asked. "I'm sure he could hook you up with some hours since Shasta bailed on him. You're not so bad. You could audition during the early bird special hours."

Vivian laughed, though it was laced with scornful amusement. Josie just shook her head at them. Striptease artist, she was not. She was barely a food critic, for crying out loud. And whatever her opinions were on modesty and living in the shadows, the *dark underbelly of society,* she knew that taking her clothes off in public for money would do absolutely *nothing* for her lack of people skills and general misanthropy. Shady finished her number, so they clapped and catcalled her to show their support.

Josie gathered her clothes, making sure she had her phone, which beeped with a message, though she didn't want to look at it right now. She was ready to go back to her motel—it was way past her bedtime. Actually, she had no idea what time it was, and the club had no windows. All she knew was that the club had shut down at 1:00 a.m., and that had been hours ago. Luckily, they'd switched from whiskey to water some time ago, so she was feeling pretty normal now. Relatively speaking. For someone who was caked in eyelash glue and sweat.

"Marty said Shasta had a boyfriend who sometimes showed up," Josie said, off-handedly as she slipped off her borrowed shoes. "Maybe he didn't appreciate her working here. Was he as ambitious as she was?" She was trying to figure out Ivan's angle, his involvement with Sasha. Maybe the other women had noticed them together.

"Oh, yeah," Vivian said, plucking her iPod out of the cradle. Though her music player was a recent model, it looked a little worse for the wear. She smoothed a manicured finger over a crack in the screen. "Totally driven. I always got the feeling he was working every angle he could. They're going to pull themselves up by their bootstraps. I wish I had half that energy."

Josie frowned, trying to picture jovial, pink-cheeked Ivan as Vivian described him. "Weird that he had that rundown place in Chinatown though, right?" she prodded gently. "I guess getting a cheap place is the best way to save your money for something better?"

"Oh, his parents are from Chinatown. I mean, they live there. They have one of those nasty restaurants that serve dog meat or whatever. Some place that the health department ought to be shutting down. Not only flies in their soup, but roaches crawling all over the place. I never ate there, but one of the other girls did once."

"Sasha's boyfriend is *from* Chinatown?" Josie asked, to clarify, trying to cover her disbelief at what she was hearing. Her remaining buzz immediately dissipated.

"Yeah. Real cute for a Chinese guy," Vivian said. "Not really my type—he's not a big PDA guy and I crave a bit of hand holding and cheek grabbing—that's the stuff I love—but I could see the appeal."

Well hell, that puts a kink in my theory, Josie thought, suddenly exhausted.

CHAPTER 25

Back in her hotel room, Josie—face scrubbed clean and body happy to be released from restrictive Spandex—lay in bed wide awake. The bedside clock said 4:30 a.m. in angry, red numbers with a throbbing double-dot of a colon stacked between. She had guzzled about a gallon of water earlier, and strangely, hadn't heard a peep from her stomach since the full steak and potatoes dinner at the club. Her body was pleasantly exhausted. Her mind, however, was churning like Shady's athletic hips.

According to Josie's new burlesque buddies, *Sasha was dating James Yu*. If that tidbit of information were true, Susan was going to be doubly ticked off with her failed relationship with James, and Josie couldn't blame her in the least. *Geeze*. No wonder James wasn't any more demonstrative with Susan than some minor hand-holding...What was he even doing stringing her along if he already had a girlfriend to begin with? If he had been trying to hide from his parents the fact that he was dating a scary, tattooed stripper with an attitude akin to Natasha from *Rocky and Bullwinkle*, how was dating Susan—who was as Caucasian as Betty White—all that much better in their eyes? What was the immature weasel's hidden agenda other than taking measures half-assed if he was trying to hide the fact that he wasn't dating a Chinese woman? Josie was steamed, but she wasn't planning to tell Susan anything until she had more evidence. Or maybe never, because what good would it do? Learning that James had been cheating on Susan—making Susan into the so-called "other woman," even inadvertently—was infuriating, even to Josie. Susan would blow the top right off her Hermès head wrap scarf.

And what if James had been dating Sasha at the same time that Ivan also had been dating her, as the picture of her on his laptop showed?

Had Ivan been killed, not for money, but for love after all, as the result of a vicious love triangle? Josie groaned and tried to calm her spinning thoughts. The Pony Pagoda ladies had given her plenty of food for thought. She couldn't digest it all at once.

Her cell phone pinged, reminding her that she hadn't ever checked her messages. She rolled over and ran her hand over the night table until she located her phone.

She squinted at the too-bright screen in the dark. A text message from Drew, or as her screen said, *"Boyfriend."* She gave a soft chuckle as she saw that name, then frowned in slight confusion as she read the message.

"Loved the show. Drove me crazy. Can't wait to get my hands on you."

Loved the *what?* She scrolled back through their saved conversation history. In her darkened room, her face did a good impression of a cherries jubilee when she found that one of the ladies had taken a video of Josie while she had been doing her ridiculous routine on the stage. So that was what that sneaky harridan Merrylin had been doing covertly. She had been filming Josie's dance number on her own phone.

Josie's *private*, inebriated, for-no-one's-eyes routine.

She cringed.

Then she took a breath and then touched her finger to the screen to play the video.

A chipmunk-high voice was saying, "I don't know if you can tell this about me, but I'm not really a girly-girl." The woman on the screen whipped her hair over her head. *Oh gawd*, Josie hardly recognized herself. The fishnets and the drag queen lip liner...and the "work it like you own it" saunter. Merrylin's raucous laughter blared from the phone's speaker. Alone in her hotel room, Josie's face turned fifty shades of...red.

⌘

Not much of a drinker? Josie was a *horrible* drinker, which was why she swore time after time that she would never overdo it again. Bad things happened when she drank. Best friends got undeservedly insulted at weddings. Good judgment went into hiding, beat into submission by lousy decisions. Drinking had taken her places no person should go. To Las Vegas, for example, where she had years ago married her jerk of a boyfriend, Joe Armstrong.

Yes, she had married the social-climbing, brand-obsessed idiot. From whom she had never gotten a divorce. So, that was the annoying legal complication currently hanging over her head.

Lying in the dark in her hotel room, Josie groaned. Drew said he had something he wanted to ask her. What if Drew popped the question? As in, "The Question." What was she going to do?

Being married to Joe the Jerk was a technicality only. Josie had dated him only for a couple of months, and that was way in the past. Long, long over. Ancient history. In fact, she questioned the legality of the marriage itself. She didn't have a copy of the license. They'd been married by an Elton John impersonator—Elvis had been all booked up that night—for about 50 bucks. Which was a cut-rate deal because they had blown off the photos and the DVD although Elton had later serenaded them with an off-key version of *Tiny Dancer*. Honestly, Josie didn't remember the ceremony itself, but that may have been due to traumatic amnesia instead of the alcohol.

She did, however, remember zonking out after the ceremony, fully clothed, on her hotel bed next to a snoring Joe, only to wake up with the mother of all hangovers. *Duh.* A few over-the-counter painkillers later, she flew home to Boston, not speaking to him in her numbed-out apathy. Talk about regret. It was hitting the bottom of an empty ice cream sundae dish with her spoon—it had looked so, so good before she had eaten it, but now it was nothing but a mess wreaking havoc in her system. One final dinner date after returning from their ill-fated Nevada vacation and they were done.

Josie had been staring at Joe across a poorly executed chateaubriand that he was raving over—it had arrived at the table with steak sauce on it, which had nearly caused her to weep. "Do you play tennis?" he asked her in a voice that could have been heard in Manhattan, and not looking at her, but at a prominent plastic surgeon at the table next to theirs. At that moment, she realized that he wasn't Mr. Right. He wasn't even Mr. Right-Now. He'd been a poor substitute for Drew Cole, her decade-long Mr. Unattainable. So, she ended her thing with Joe then and there. He tried to cajole her into reconsidering. He was probably thinking that he could still make a perfectly socialized, professionally successful life partner out of her, but Josie was done. Staring across the pleasantly set table at Joe Armstrong, she realized that being alone was better than being with him. As soon as she found that kernel of truth inside of her which had probably been there the whole time, they were over.

Except for that irksome problem of being married to him.

Stupid legality.

Stupid piece of paper.

What kind of person got married in Las Vegas to a guy she'd been dating for only two months? Was she that kind of person? *Alcohol was the devil.* Granted, she and Joe Armstrong had been coworkers at *The Daily News* for a couple years before she'd finally consented to dating him, so, at least they weren't strangers. *But, still. You ought to be ashamed of yourself,* her inner Aunt Ruth chastised. In her mind's eye, Josie could see her aunt's mouth being pulled tighter than a drawstring purse. Josie wanted to blame alcohol consumption for the quickie Las Vegas wedding to Captain Outward Appearances, Sergeant Social Climber, but was there something else inside of her that had goaded her into doing it?

Maybe she wanted the fairy tale. Maybe she secretly longed for the *dim sum fantasy,* the tiny morsels of manna fed to her, bit by bit, from the chopsticks of a lover. She had really hoped she was more evolved than that. Women's rights and all. But still, thinking of spending a leisurely Sunday afternoon with the right person, with *Drew,* made something inside of her hum—her soul, her romantic heart, her lacy pink little princess heart...if she had one of those. That same something made her briefly consider recreating her saucy dance number for him when she got home. For about thirty seconds before she rolled over and punched the pillow with her fist. She had never learned how to be a *girl.*

Josie sat up and flipped on the light, giving up on sleep entirely.

The sky was lightening outside her window anyway, sneaking through the cracks where the blackout curtains didn't quite cover the window. Momentarily re-energized, she grabbed her laptop and started searching for a "quickie divorce." She would shoo this marriage monkey off her back, once and for all. How long could the dissolution of sacred, eternal vows take anyway? The whole ceremony had lasted maybe fifteen minutes. Undoing the stupid marriage had to be about the same, right? She clicked for a few minutes.

Crap.

According to the internet, in Massachusetts a divorce took six months from a trial date to be dissolved. She tried another tack and searched for quickie Nevada divorces. That was what all those songs about Reno were for, right? That was basic advertising. But when the search results came up, she groaned. Apparently, she had to live in Nevada for six weeks before she could get one. Maybe she could perfect her burlesque routine in Vegas while she was waiting. Right.

She was so screwed.

CHAPTER 26

A couple hours later, Josie sat poking one finger at a cellophane-wrapped pastry as she sipped too-hot tea in the hotel's mini-cafe. *Continental breakfast, her golden-yellow butt.* Any continent that claimed this as its breakfast should be ashamed of itself. But still, it was food — sort of — and she was hungry, so she took a bite, trying to avoid reading the ingredients listed on the back of the pack. And wasn't that the pitiful story of American nutrition right there in a pre-packaged nutshell?

After failing to fall back asleep, she'd spent the remaining early morning hours mulling over a possible Ivan-Sasha-James love triangle. Ivan's death had been particularly violent, very messy, and according to Lopez's Californian slang, very "stabberific." A crime such as that shouted it was a personal matter fueled by strong feelings, by violent passion. Slashing and stabbing with a blade meant the killer had gotten up close to Ivan. *Really close.* Multiple stabbings meant massive amounts of anger...blinding white-hot rage...An emotion that, well, Josie may have felt once or twice in her lifetime, though would never act out. Crazy came in 31 flavors, and that wasn't hers.

Also, there were the boot prints in Ivan's blood, which pointed to Sasha. The shoe impressions, with their size and type, were the strongest piece of evidence yet. And as Dicarlo had said more than once, hearsay and gut reactions were nice, but it was the job of police to collect scientific proof or a confession, for court. Only solid evidence could lock a bad guy away for life. Yet, Josie's gut told her she was probably right in booking a hotel so close to Sasha's house. After she found a breakfast better suited to humans, Josie figured she would drive back to Sasha's neighborhood to do some looking around.

However, running on fifteen minutes of sleep did not bode well for a productive day. She calculated she might have only about three hours of juice left in her before she would need to nap — and that nap would come where and when it wanted to, whether she was on her feet, in her car, or anywhere else. She wasn't a stupid college kid anymore. In a couple years, she was going to be 30, even if she didn't act it. She couldn't pull all-nighters and she couldn't run on an empty stomach. She sat at her table in the hotel's "cafe" area avoiding her pre-fab pastry by scanning the hotel's single copy of their complementary national newspaper. She noted with some interest a scandal involving a Boston businessman back home, something about embezzlement of campaign funds. She wondered idly if he was an associate of Greta Williams, and if there was some kind of inside scoop about it. Greta had many fingers in many different pies, possibly corrupt pies.

"Are you finished with that?" a hotel employee asked her. Josie looked up at the woman, whose name tag said, *Guadalupe*. She was pointing to Josie's unfinished pastry.

"Uh, yeah. I'm not sure it's meant to be eaten." Josie shrugged apologetically, as the woman cleared her table. As much as Josie didn't want to eat her factory pastry, she still felt guilty about the waste. Having a picky palate or temporary hunger from a stomach with a bad attitude was one thing—hunger from being broke was a whole different story. Wasting food of any kind rankled Josie, but she still couldn't bring herself to eat it.

The woman laughed. She was a slender, dark-skinned Latina in her forties maybe—though it was hard to tell with the salon-quality hair dye and smooth skin. She said in heavily accented English, "What you need is some eggs and bacon. Wrapped in a tortilla. That will keep you going all day."

Josie blinked, momentarily drooling from the description alone. She sat up hopefully. Then she said, "Aw, that's mean. You're teasing me when all I have is breakfast out of a plastic bag."

Guadalupe looked around and shrugged. "I could get you some. Breakfast burritos. Sometimes I sell tamales, but I have burritos today— you trust good old Lupe to help you out. I brought extra with me. I sell them to the construction workers across the street every morning, but I have some left over today."

"Oh yeah?" Josie wondered how much the street value of an authentic, pure-grade breakfast burrito was. She didn't care. Whatever it was, she would pay it. She was desperate for a fix at this point. Lupe might as well have offered her a free hit. "Do you have chorizo, Lupe?" Josie wanted to know.

"Are you kidding me?" she said. "Of course I do."

⌘

A half hour later, Josie parked her box-on-wheels, her Kool-Aid green Kia, across the street and a bit down from Sasha Peters's house. She planned to eat her breakfast in the car before she scouted the area. She had thought her rental car would stand out like a sore thumb—a bright green sore thumb—but there was a similar car, only white, three houses back. And another boxy, stunted thing that looked like a Scion xB, if she wasn't mistaken, one house ahead. Together, the three miniature vans made a funny collection of clown cars. They looked as if they were meant for delivering bread or transporting really short mimes.

In contrast, her "Green Giant" back home in Boston was a '75 Lincoln Continental, about a mile long and olive green, that coughed fumes more than actually ran. The Lincoln was almost the same color as her rental car, but a whole different kind of beast. It was currently wedged into her assigned parking space at her apartment building back home, having failed emissions testing again—something she needed to look into fixing. *I'm not two-timing you, Green Giant,* Josie thought silently. *But I'm glad you're not here because you'd be the sore thumb now.*

In Josie's lap were the still-warm, foil-wrapped spoils of her exchange with Lupe, her breakfast fairy godmother. Three rolls of tortilla-wrapped goodness—two bacon, egg, and potato breakfast burritos and one chorizo and egg special burrito. She had bought only one of the spicy kind, not sure how her stomach would react to it. Guadalupe wanted to charge her only a dollar each, but Josie had insisted on her taking a ten for the trio. She planned on tracking her breakfast dealer down every morning she remained in California. Because now, as she unwrapped the first one and bit into it, she sighed

183

with pleasure at the warm, fluffy filling and the homey scent of soft rolled tortilla. She ate the chorizo burrito second and was pleased to find that the spice didn't bother her. Her stomach seemed to be as much on vacation from its usual grind as she was.

Within fifteen minutes, Josie could now add the sensation of being pleasantly full to her sleepiness, and three small crumbled balls of foil littered the passenger seat next to her. She gazed at Sasha's house with heavily lidded eyes and realized she needed to stand up and move around or she'd be zero-to-asleep in less than sixty seconds. As in, *now*. As she stood next to her car, she felt slightly woozy, slightly dizzy for a second, but she shook it off and straightened up. Then, she felt a ticklish poke on her jeans right about shin-level. Looking down, she saw an Ewok. She blinked. *Okay, that was better—it was a dog.*

"Hello, Toto," she said to a little guy, who indeed, looked like the terrier from *The Wizard of Oz* movie. Kind of scruffy, kind of cute, kind of mixed breed—definitely a kindred spirit. He was sporting a red plaid collar and carrying a red leash in his mouth, one end dragging on the pavement behind him as if he were combing the neighborhood in search of someone to walk him. She looked at him, and then, torn, cast a glance at Sasha's house. She sighed, stooping down to take up the strap and her new Good Samaritan responsibility. Toto's stubby tail jacked up to hummingbird speed as Josie's face got within licking distance of his face. She gently scratched him behind one pointy ear and looped the end of the leash over her wrist while the other end was still in his mouth. Digging her fingers into the fur of his neck caused waggles of ecstasy and, at the same time, allowed her to read his tag, which said his name was Houdini.

"I beg your pardon," she said, well aware even in her sleep-deprived state that she was talking to a dog. "I had no idea I was addressing such a renowned gentleman as yourself." She checked the address on the dog tag and, squinting at the house numbers, discovered that he lived right next door to Sasha's house.

As the two of them started across the street to his owner's house, she told him conversationally, "I'm assuming you take after your namesake and that's why you're roaming the streets like a...well-mannered hooligan."

He wagged at her. When they stood together on the front stoop of his door waiting, after ringing the doorbell three separate times, Josie turned to him again.

"All right, Mr. Magician. Show me how you got out."

Despite his earnest expression, the dog was not very forthcoming about his means of escape. Similar to the historic master escapist, he was content to keep his trade secrets to himself. Josie looked around, hands on her jean-clad hips. The privacy fence to the backyard was a five-footer, so on her tiptoes, she was able to stretch her five-two-and-three-quarter inches, reach over, and unlatch it.

"It's not trespassing if you invite me in, right?" She looked to him for reassurance, and he gave her a wag. *Great, asking for ethical advice from a canine now—a rascal at that.*

While Josie waffled at the open gate, Houdini dashed into the yard, leaving her holding the useless leash. She was not eager to step inside, but she was still curious to know whether the dog would be all right in the yard until his owner got home from work. As a compromise, Josie stuck her neck farther into the yard, feeling somewhat like a chicken on the chopping block, stretching out those vertebrae more to make the axe blade slip between them with that much less resistance. She looked around at the messy, overgrown foliage, craning her neck to find where Houdini had gone.

She spotted him just in time to see him slip under the fence that led into Sasha Peters's backyard.

"Oh, crap. Dude. Houdini. Little doggie dude. *Harry.* Come back," Josie said, no longer dithering about whether to follow the dog. She glanced around as she walked lightly over the crunchy, drought-withered grass of Houdini's yard. Beyond a monster-sized lemon tree that had to have been over thirty years old, Josie peered over the fence into the next yard.

Houdini made a beeline for the backdoor to Sasha's, where there was an old dog door and, pushing it with his nose, slipped inside Sasha's house. The black rubber flap swung shut behind his furry tush.

CHAPTER 27

Standing in the backyard of Sasha's house, Josie crouched low, squatting outside the ancient dog door that led from the back directly into the kitchen. *How would I explain getting caught in this situation to Lopez and Dicarlo? Or to Drew or to Greta Williams? Would I have a snowball's chance in Tucson of convincing them that this is not breaking and entering. This is...canine intervention.*

The cracked rubber flap of the dog door had been screwed into a roughly sawed rectangular hole in the wooden door. She eyed the narrow opening and then looked down at her hips again. For probably the first time in her life, she wished she had boy hips. She took her wallet and phone out of her back pockets and visually measured again. Then she—queen of questionable decision-making, princess of poor choices— got down on her knees and went for it.

In for a penny, in for a...full misdemeanor?

Based on her previous visit to Sasha's home, when she'd been here with the detectives, Josie didn't think Sasha had a dog, so the door was probably a leftover from a previous owner. Clearly, it was an open invitation to uninvited guests like neighbor dogs and nosy amateur P.I.s. Judging from the weathering, the dog door was probably Reagan-era and made her wonder for the second time this trip about the state of her tetanus booster. A shot was pushing itself higher up on her to-do list— most people had a bucket list full of travel and personal milestones. Hers was prioritized by safeguards against sepsis. A rusty screw snagged Josie's favorite Ramones t-shirt and tore it, which caused her to mutter a canine-unfriendly curse. Luckily, Houdini wasn't within earshot.

Her shoulders went through with no problem. Her bust line was severely diminished by her recent weight loss from her stomach issue, so again, no problem there. She was able to shrug all the way through to her belt loops. Half in and half out, she set her wallet and phone on the kitchen floor—new and spotless linoleum, she was happy to note, because she was nose to nose with it. Getting this close to her own kitchen floor back home would not have been as pleasant an experience. Thank goodness for the OCD people of the world who turned a common B&E into a PineSol-fresh adventure.

She braced her sweaty palms on the floor now, as best as she could at this awkward angle, and heaved herself in. With a squeak, her hands slid back across the floor toward her, while she remained caught at the hips, snagged right at the belt loops. Another attempt yielded the same result—a giant squeak but no progress. She froze, wondering if the noise of her hands would draw attention to her, but no, the house was silent other than the click of Houdini's nails on the floor.

Speak of the furry pint-sized devil...the dog came trotting around the corner, delighted to find Josie at his own eye level. He attempted to kiss her. She shooed him away. She wasn't a mouth-kisser kind of girl on a first date, so she writhed and swatted at him until he finally retreated a few inches, sitting down daintily on his backside to watch her undoubtedly fascinating performance. While she squirmed, the back of her pants, which had been caught on another screw, unbeknownst to her, suddenly came free and she slithered the rest of the way into Sasha's house. With a happy bark, Houdini attacked her with his tongue, bathing her cheeks and forehead with a vigor that rivaled that of a mare welcoming her newborn foal. Josie lay gasping, and Houdini threw himself down on his back next to her. In capitulation, she gave him a few belly rubs.

She stood and looked around. Based on Sasha's on-stage Bettie Page persona, Josie had expected a retro black and red hotrod theme in her kitchenette, a 1950s diner with tons of Formica and a mini table-top jukebox. To her surprise, it was more Betty Crocker than *Greased Lightning*. Everything was updated—Corian countertops in neutral, flecked beige. Stainless steel appliances. Single-piece, high-end linoleum with which Josie had already been up-close-and-personal—but that she would bet had been some kind of high-end recycled, eco-friendly material. Why would a person spend so much money updating a kitchen without improving the layout of it?

As Josie thought about it more, along with what James had said about the real estate market, it started to make sense, especially if Sasha were only renting the place and the real owner...Josie froze, suddenly rocked by a brain flash. James had said he was saving up for a modest little San Jose house. Was he interested in buying *this house in particular?* Wouldn't that be a strange not-so-coincidence? Property ownership was public record. Even if Detectives Lopez and Dicarlo didn't have time to look into it, Josie could probably find out who owned the property and if she nosed around, she might be able to find out if there were any interested buyers for the scruffy, minuscule square of property, even if it weren't officially on the market.

She took a brief walk around the house, just trying to get a feel for whether or not the rest of the decor was by Murderers On a Dime. Unfortunately, she didn't find any *How to Kill and Maim* magazines lying around. The house didn't have much to it—just the front room, which was still sporting the black velvet drape and laptop with its webcam setup for Sasha's S&M & math tutoring. Other than that anomaly, the rest of the house had a generic, rental feel to it thanks to the neutral colors—beige, white, and more beige. The doors and the baseboards were all worn-down, scuffed oak. The windows were tiny and dated, not the glorious picture windows that newer houses had. Sasha's bedroom was boring as well—not the expected black satin sheets, just a navy blue poly-blend comforter. Standard medium-grade oak furniture. Lamps à la Target. On the bedside table was a family photo of a smiling, blond group in the snow, all of them bundled up to their red noses—Josie guessed it had been taken in Russia, or whichever country Sasha was originally from. *Interesting.* Apparently, Sasha was blonde under all that black hair dye. The whole room was fairly *blah*, other than a closet populated by leather and vinyl—costumes similar to the ones that Josie had seen at the Pony Pagoda.

As expected, Sasha owned a crap-ton of shoes. Josie went through them, careful not to disturb what was obviously a well-organized collection. She examined each pair, including the stacks of shoe boxes, in her search for work boots worn at the crime scene. She found a couple pairs of army boots and some calf-high purple Doc Martens, but no Danners brand of the type that Lopez and Dicarlo's shoe database had identified. Then again, actually finding the boots after Josie had illegally entered and searched the house would be of no help to the detectives unless they could manufacture some other reason for obtaining a search warrant. But still, Josie, in her bumbling Columbo heart-of-hearts, was disappointed not to find anything.

Houdini, who had been following her from room to room, sat on her foot and wagged, reminding her of her own dog Bert back home. "There's not even anything freaky here," she told him with a shrug. "I have to admit. I'm kind of disappointed." His tongue lolled at her, and he smiled. She narrowed her eyes and put her hands on her hips. "There's something you're not telling me, isn't there? If there is, mister, you'd better come clean. And stop smirking at me." She blinked a couple of times. Her nap time clock was ticking down. The more tired she was, the more likely she was to converse with this amiable canine. Hopefully, he was real and not a lucid dream.

Eventually, she returned to the kitchen, where she sidled over to the sink and eased the lower cabinet door open. She thought with exhausted desperation that maybe there'd be a pair of bloodied boots hidden inside—but, no. All she found were a garbage can that was mostly empty, a bottle of powder cleanser, and a fly swatter. She peered into the garbage, but didn't find any evidence of criminal activity other than an empty single-serving container of key lime pie flavored yogurt that had 26 grams of sugar. *Yuck. Just eat the real thing, sister. A little pie for breakfast never hurt anyone.*

Just as she shut the refrigerator door with Houdini wagging and peering up at her, a key rattled in the lock of the front door.

⌘

After three silently mouthed *Oh craps*, Josie was still rooted in place in the middle of Sasha Peters's kitchen, completely frozen with indecision. She'd always hoped that she would be the type of person who reacted with superhuman speed or strength under extreme duress. She wanted to be the girl who lifted a two-ton pickup truck off a loved one who had been pinned in an accident. Or the person who ducked for cover at just the right time to avoid a crazed shooter in a shopping mall—only to disarm him with a surprise jab to the nose. Standing here in Sasha's kitchen, Josie had no idea what to do. Duck down? No. Dive for the hallway? No. With blood rushing through her head and her time running out, she couldn't decide. However, Houdini had no such problem with his voluntary motor function—he trotted out, tail wagging and toenails clicking, to greet the new arrival. Josie knew the only part of her moving were her eyes, which were rolling wildly around the tiny kitchen, scanning for some nook or cranny in which to wedge her body.

Sasha's Russian-accented voice with her California-causal banter came from the entryway, "Hey, buddy. What are you doing in here? No girlfriend action today? Did you make yourself at home?" The jangling of Houdini's collar and happy puppy moaning meant he was getting a world-class neck scratching. Despite the distraction the dog was providing, there was no way Josie could sneak back out the way she had come—she'd barely made it through the dog door the first time without having to call the fire department for the Jaws of Life. Unlocking the back door and tiptoeing out to the backyard would take time—and she'd still be in full view of the kitchen window. She was stuck.

Then came James Yu's voice, slightly amused but impatient voice, more confident than Josie had ever heard it, "I don't know why you don't block off that old dog door. He's probably bringing fleas into the house. We're going to have to fumigate the place."

Frozen with indecision, one hundred percent sure she was about to be discovered by Ivan's murderers, Josie's heart pounded. They had to be in cahoots with each other. She would probably be hacked to pieces, her body tossed out the window of James's Nissan Leaf, her limbs scattered up and down the 101 to the manic beat of dubstep music.

"Look at his little face and his little bristly whiskers," Sasha was saying in a baby voice. *Little* sounded like *leedle*. "He's so cute. He couldn't have fleas. He wouldn't even hurt a fly. Would you? Would you, baby boy? You're not a murderer. You couldn't even kill a..."

There was a momentary silence, and Josie heard what might have been a sob. A keening moan. A loud sniffle. Sasha was weeping. Over Ivan. Josie frowned, suddenly more confused than frantic, suddenly more interested in listening than leaving.

James made some gentle shushing noises, and Sasha cried out, "How could he be dead? He can't be dead. They're wrong. It can't be him. Are they sure it's him? I just saw him a couple of days ago."

"Come here, sweetheart," James said.

Did he just call her his sweetheart in a super comforting, take-charge way? This was not the same James with whom Josie had been earlier acquainted. This was a whole new James. A masculine, mac-and-cheese-eating, Americanized dude who did not seem trapped under his parents' highly regimented thumb. Perhaps Josie needed to re-factor her whole impression of him and his ability to plan and carry out a gruesome, violent murder.

Sasha was full-on crying now. Josie tried to picture the scene going on in the other room, with its black velvet backdrop and webcam-ready setup. It should have been sleazy, but instead, it was just...sad. What was James's role? The comforting shoulder-to-cry-on? The strong, steady, manly boyfriend? Had Sasha been using Ivan for his money while secretly seeing James on the side? According to the ladies at the Pony Pagoda, James and Sasha had been open and obvious about their relationship, though it wasn't overly demonstrative. Josie couldn't bend her mind around an open arrangement involving the three of them. A threesome didn't fit the build here—she didn't get that kind of vibe from them at all, after having observed James's living arrangements and his relationship with his parents. Call it a gut instinct.

"Let me get you a drink, all right? I'll get you a glass of water, sweetheart. You just sit here on the couch." James said, treating Sasha as if she were a princess. Josie almost wanted to peek around the corner to make sure it was actually him. Maybe someone had changed places with him—not an evil twin, a more mature twin. Suddenly, her brain registered the rest of what he'd said. *He was coming to the kitchen to get Sasha something to drink.*

Josie twitched and snapped out of the trance that had held her frozen like a baby bunny in the path of a bulldozer. She hit the floor in a crouch and eyed the small space under the kitchen sink. Not big enough. Could she hide inside the fridge? The GE was a big and roomy, side-by-side, so there was no chance of her stuffing herself between the shelves. Not unless Houdini was a real magician and clever with chopping a lady in half. Josie thought her heart was about to pound out of her chest, right through torn up Joey Ramone.

"No," Sasha said. "I want to go lie down. Come with me. I need to be with you. I need you to hold me tight."

Josie heard some noises and murmurs, which she took to be kissing. The private nature of the interaction made her cringe—despite having been trapped into observing clandestine lovers more than once in her life, Josie was not a voyeur by choice. She always was finding herself caught in these awkward situations. Belatedly, she scowled on behalf of Susan, now safely home in Boston. Susan was now decidedly single.

More smoochy noises came from the other room, followed by a moan or two. Unsteady footsteps led toward the bedroom. A door closed. Josie was left alone.

Houdini trotted back to the kitchen, a grin on his whiskered face.

CHAPTER 28

Rather than risk getting wedged in the doggy door again, Josie slipped out the front door, banking on the idea that the rest of the neighborhood was either at work or apathetic. Josie joined legions of rednecks in thanking the gods of WD-40 because the hinges didn't squeak when she pulled the door open. For a minute, she debated whether to grant Houdini his freedom, but gently shoved him back inside with her foot, pointing a shaky index finger at him. No doubt he would be wandering the streets again in minutes, living the canine thug life—but not on her watch.

She reached the Kia with adrenaline still coursing through her system, causing a slight tremor in her hands. She was thankful the key fob worked remotely because there was no way she could have unlocked the car door the old school way. No sooner had she sat down in her rental car, her cell phone rang, causing her almost to fling it halfway across the car. *Holy heart attack.* If her ringtone had gone off just a few minutes earlier, she would have been discovered by one distrustful black belt nerd and his dominatrix math tutor. Her fate would have been sealed. She tried not to contemplate that too much before she pulled the door shut and pressed the answer button on her phone.

"So did you feel that earthquake about twenty minutes ago?" Lopez said without any greeting.

"Huh?" Josie said. She rolled back her memory, pushing it backwards through her most recent felony. Then she remembered feeling dizzy as she'd first stepped out of the car, thinking it was due to exhaustion.

"They're saying it was a 2.4. Not even big enough to get on the news," he said, referring to the earthquake's magnitude on the Richter scale. "Since you're visiting from the east coast, I figured you would enjoy it. We pulled out all the stops for you. Nothing but the whole experience for your trip."

"Well, thanks. I think," she said, peering at the street ahead of her. Kind of spooky to think that the ground under them all wasn't stable. The ground's ability to shake here in California served to remind her that just about everything in this state felt in flux. Unstable. Yeah, dynamic and amazing at times, but also a bit flaky and undependable. Like some of the natives she'd met so far. James, for one.

"Where are you, Josie?" Lopez wanted to know.

Josie looked across the street at Sasha's house, doubtful that Lopez would want to know where she had been and what she had been doing. *Illegally*. Instead, she stalled and said, "I moved out of James's apartment to a hotel. I'm staying down at the San Jose Suites on Bascom Avenue. Great breakfast, I have to say," she said, thinking of her burritos. She had no opinion about the firmness of the mattress because she hadn't been there long enough to thoroughly enjoy it, although she wished she were trying it out at this moment. The interior of her rental car had warmed up, and her eyelids were feeling heavy now. She could just lean her head back and... She turned the key in the ignition and lowered the window for some fresh air.

"Good, good," Lopez said, apparently appeased that she was out of harm's way. Clearly, he didn't know her well. She poked a finger through the new hole in her t-shirt. *Dang it.* It was right in the middle of Joey Ramone's bony chest like a rusty stab wound, his circular glasses making his face peer out owlishly at her, even upside down. "Let me tell you what we found out. It's looking good against Sasha Peters. I think we might even have enough to pick her up."

That meant he and Dicarlo would take her in for questioning—Josie knew that from TV. However, she doubted very much that the case against Sasha was building, based on what she had overheard. Sasha's reaction to the news of Ivan's death, her seemingly genuine disbelief and sorrow had convinced Josie that the detectives and she were barking up the wrong tree—entering the wrong dog door, as it were. Sasha's only audience for that private conversation had been James, so unless she had been pulling the wool over James's eyes, too, Sasha didn't seem to be the killer. But that wasn't proof—it was only a gut feeling that wouldn't help out the detectives.

Lopez was saying, "There's not much trace evidence that the lab has found so far, other than those boot prints, which were all over the scene, by the way. It was like the killer danced the foxtrot in the blood. Kind of like, *So You Think You Can Dance* on a murder scene. But other than the boots, there were no latents—no fingerprints—at least, none that match hers on file, so she probably wore gloves. USCIS had her fingerprints on record, just so you know." At Josie's silence, he explained, "That's Immigration. From when she applied for citizenship."

"Aha," Josie said. She didn't know anything at all about immigration and naturalization. Her own mother had applied for citizenship before Josie was born, but she'd also been a young Thai wife married to an American military man. Maybe the process had been easier back then. Of course, there was no one around for Josie to ask now.

Lopez continued, "If there's any blood other than Ivan's at the scene, it's going to be a long time until we know whose it is. The scene was a freaking mess. You should also know that Ivan didn't have any defensive wounds anywhere. Not on his hands. Nowhere. So, the lab is processing his blood for sedatives."

"James mentioned Ivan sometimes took a sleeping pill. Seroquel or something similar," Josie said. All those commercial drugs had goofy names, like Snoreesta or Zeeslux. If there were truth in advertising, they should have been called *Can't Sleep Without It Ever Again* or maybe *Sleep Like the Dead Even If Someone Kills You.* "Maybe that's why he didn't try to fight the killer off." Hopefully, it also meant that Ivan hadn't suffered during the attack. No pain. No fear or struggle. God willing, he'd slept through the whole thing. Until he wasn't alive anymore. An endless sleep in which the dreams simply stopped. Or maybe, if heaven existed, the dreams went on and on forever.

"Right. I'm guessing that's what we'll find. Other than that, there were a couple of hairs—dark black ones, like the color of Sasha's dyed hair. Witnesses saying she knew where the apartment was and had been there before. So because of that and the boot prints, we're pretty much looking at Sasha."

"What about a will?" Josie asked, wondering about motive. Lopez was sounding pretty gung-ho about Sasha right now, so Josie thought she'd gently prod in another direction. "Do Ivan's millions go to his wife?"

"So far, we're not finding a will. If he died intestate—meaning that he didn't have a will—that means everything goes to his wife. I mean, we're still trying to track down all the money and to see if he had a broker or a lawyer or someone who took care of the funds for him, pointed him toward making a portfolio or some kind of legal documentation. He's looking like a DIY type of guy."

"That's still a heck of a lot of motive for Olga, not Sasha. *Millions* of motives," Josie said, staring out the windshield of her car at Sasha's house. She wondered if it was enough impetus for the big woman to have crammed her enormous feet into boots half her foot size, put on a jet black wig, drive all the way into the city, and stab her sleeping husband multiple times. Just thinking about that sent a massive shiver down her spine.

"I can hear you pushing your own agenda there, Ms. Tucker," Lopez said after a pause. "You got something you want to tell me?"

She hemmed and hawed, delaying her answer. Any so-called evidence she gathered that Sasha was innocent had been illegally gathered and was questionable, at best. "It's a gut feeling," she said finally, downplaying it because she was unwilling to share. She had absolutely nothing concrete. Her theories were grains of beach sand that made a pattern but were easily swept away. Sandcastles that didn't hold up over time.

On top of it all, her sleep deprivation was making her even less prone to voicing her theories. When she felt vulnerable, her default behavior always was to withdraw, to protect herself, to rely only on herself, and go "lone coyote," so to speak, which had saved her bacon in the past.

"What's your 'gut feeling' telling you to do about it?" he said, pressing her in a quieter tone.

"Off the record?" she said, giving in. A small sign of compassion, a little sensitivity made her lone coyote roll over and expose its underbelly for scratching, just like any other dog. Houdini, for instance.

He was silent for a minute. "Yeah. Off the record."

"I'm going to head to Santa Cruz to see the widow."

⌘

Fatigued driving is dangerous driving. One of those illuminated overhead signs flashed orange letters at Josie, jolting her upright the instant her eyes were glazing over, her lids slumping downward.

"Jiminy Cricket, I need a nap," she said out loud, navigating highway 17 south to Santa Cruz. She was so tired, she was Disney-swearing. The four-lane road that stretched out ahead was kind of pretty compared to the rest of the Northern Californian roads she'd white-knuckled this trip. As the heavily-treed highway curved and sloped its way down the coast, Josie blinked rapidly, having an exhaustion-induced flashback to her teenaged self who'd driven herself here more than a decade ago.

As a teenager, she'd been as good as orphaned, with her dad dead and her mom institutionalized. Her great aunt and uncle who'd taken her in, though well-meaning, were from a different era. Her one cousin remotely close to her own age was...*special*. Red-headed Libby was sweet and awesome...and gigantic, but she wasn't a peer. As runaway Josie had sat on the Santa Cruz boardwalk that day so many years ago, she'd looked around, numb, not having very deep thoughts at all to begin with. She observed families, couples of all ages, dogs, surfers, flies gathering on discarded food wrappers. She'd sat there for a long time, hoping to glean some kind of sense from it all.

Josie had not been suicidal. She had run away because she had just wanted...to feel not so alone, ironically. She wanted someone to care about her. Sure, her aunt and uncle had taken her in when she had no one else. She knew a lot of kids weren't that lucky. She could have been shuffled into the foster system or sent to a group home. She could have ended up on the streets. But her Aunt Ruth and Uncle Jack didn't *know* her. They were willing to see about her basic needs, her food, shelter, and day-to-day stuff. She had a clean place to sleep where no one would get her. She wasn't being beaten or abused or traded as a commodity. She wasn't homeless, though she had a house to go to, not a home.

She had glanced ruefully behind her at Uncle Jack's Chevy parked across the street. On the street, but not on the streets. She'd rolled her eyes at her own joke.

She'd sat there until sundown.

Thinking.

Listening to her own breath.

From where do we derive our own sense of worth? What makes us—each of us—worthy of experiencing the world, the rising and setting of that giant ball of flame each and every day?

A church-going person probably would have had an immediate answer to that soul-searching query. But Josie Tucker, borderline juvenile delinquent, had come to a more roundabout theory. Sitting by the Santa Cruz pier that day with the seagulls squabbling over spilled french fries, she realized that though her mother and father were absent, they still traveled with her. And she extrapolated then, that she did have someone who cared for her. Deeply. She valued the memories of her father from when he was alive, and of her mother from when she was coherent—and these memories lived inside her. She fiercely loved these snippets of time, these immortal, encapsulated parts of her parents. They were a part of her. She loved them. Which meant that to honor them, she needed to love herself.

And underneath it all, she had realized that she did.

CHAPTER 29

Josie was more than ready for a nappy-poo, so much so that she was thinking to herself in toddler talk. *I just need my blankie and a ba-ba.*

Maybe it was her current loopy state of exhaustion, but Josie stood on Olga Sorokin's front step, having decided that a head-on approach was best for dealing with Ivan's wife. Mainly, Josie didn't want to risk a beatdown from the Amazonian *Ruskie* woman due to another stupid trespassing stunt. There was a good chance that Olga was a murderer. Physically, she looked capable of it. Pair that with millions of dollars at stake and it behooved Josie to be smart about this. So, sneaking up on a woman who had delivered multiple stab wounds to a man whom she'd supposedly *loved* wasn't an option in Josie's mind. Besides, Josie had already committed her misdemeanor for the day breaking into Sasha Peters's house. Quota met, she rang Olga's doorbell.

When Olga opened her door, she frowned in recognition. Yet she said, semi-civilly, "Can I help you?" to Josie, who appreciated it. Because frankly, she was too tired to run for her life at the moment. Maybe tomorrow. She could ask Olga to pencil her in.

"I was wondering if I could talk to you about your husband," Josie said, not at all expecting Olga to speak with her. Ivan's widow was in another eye-searing flowery top, this time paired with turquoise clam-digger capri pants. Eyes traveling warily from Olga's head to toes, Josie was once again struck by her height. She couldn't help but get another gander at the woman's giant feet. There was no way the woman could squeeze into size seven boots and then dance a jig in the blood of her dead husband—unless Olga were into foot-binding, which she definitely was not. Even now, her red painted toenails hung off the front edges of her man-sized flip flops. She probably had to buy shoes at a specialty store as it was. Though the motive was strong—millions of dollars strong—it just didn't fit. Josie's eyes traveled upward to Olga's smooth arms. The same gold bangles weighted down her wrists, maybe ten to twelve on each wrist. She was wearing a lot of makeup, but it still failed to conceal the puffiness of her eyes, nor the dark circles under them.

"Sure," Olga shrugged in a very Slavic manner. "Why not. Come on it." But then, unnervingly, she reached out and grabbed Josie by the forearm, pulling her into her beach-themed sitting room. The woman was more hands-on with Josie than she was comfortable with— particularly if these were the same hands that had just killed her husband—but then Olga propelled her into a padded rattan chair, and Josie was able to break free from the big woman's grip. Where the room had felt overcrowded and cloying before, it now struck Josie as sad and dismal, but maybe that was just Olga herself. Despite her gaudy attire, she appeared a little faded compared to last time, as if her light had been dimmed. She sank heavily into her shell-printed sofa opposite Josie.

Josie was silent, searching for words to say. Hallmark-card murmured condolences were inadequate and inappropriate for a woman who had thought her husband was cheating on her. Definitely inappropriate if she'd been the one to kill him. What the heck was Josie supposed to say? *Sorry about your dead husband, even if you offed him—and by the way, did you? And P.S. sorry about the stripper, but what are your plans for all of the money?*

Olga saved her from thinking of something. "I'm not sure why you don't go arrest that girl and be done with it. I don't understand all this waiting around. At least lock her up so she can't run away back to Russia. All this due process, I understand. I took my citizenship classes. I know there's legal procedure to follow, but *she did it*. She took that knife and stabbed Ivan. I don't see what the question is." Olga pushed her sleeves up and leaned forward, resting her arms on her knees.

On the previous visit with Olga, Josie had observed that there were no marks or scratches on Olga's arms. Although Lopez had said there were no defensive wounds on Ivan—no marks on his hands or arms from fighting off an assailant—that didn't mean the killer hadn't gotten wounded also. With the number of stab wounds and the slipperiness of all the blood, the knife would have become hard to grip...Josie could feel herself start to get queasy. Anyway, chances were that something would show up on Olga's hands or arms. Unless she had worn gloves. Big rubber industrial gloves. However, even gloves were slippery.

"The police were here again last night, late. They sent some kind of technician person who took my spit from inside my cheek with a long Q-tip. They took it for DNA. I guess they wanted to eliminate me as a suspect," Olga said. Josie couldn't tell if it was her natural Russian confidence, her strong accent, or what, but the woman was sure of herself, brimming with confidence. "I have never even been to his Chinatown apartment, so I'm not sure what they were expecting to find."

"You've truly never been there?" Josie asked.

Olga shook her head. "I don't even know where it is."

"It's above a liquor store on the corner of Clay and Stockton." Josie hadn't been there, of course, but the detectives had mentioned it, and she was trying to get some kind of sign of recognition from Olga. But, she got nothing.

Olga again denied knowing about the place. "Never been there. I don't care if they take my DNA sample. If it helps them nail that girl to the wall, I am willing to do it." She spoke with assurance and with anger, her face creasing with a frown. She pushed back her bottle-red hair with more clinking of her bangles. Josie didn't see how she'd be able to sneak up on anyone with those noisemakers.

"Why do you think it was her?" Josie said. Granted, the so-called "other woman" in an affair would be the first person Josie would have blamed, too—especially a young, sexually adventurous woman like Sasha. Josie definitely would have looked at her with suspicion—if Josie were an *innocent* woman in Olga's position. However, she wanted to hear it from Olga.

Olga looked astounded. She waved her hand full of painted fingernails, jangling her bracelets. "Who else could it be? James?" she scoffed. "He's a stupid kid. He thinks he is so smart, but what does he know? If not for Ivan, James would still be an intern. He doesn't have any self-discipline. None of that famous American work ethic. No sense of responsibility. He's still under the thumb of his parents. He wouldn't even sneeze without their permission."

So, Olga was about as impressed with James as Josie was—which was to say, not much at all. No need to explore that avenue further— James as a suspect—as far as Josie was concerned. She had witnessed James's lack of will personally when he failed to introduce Susan to his parents. Although…now that she was thinking about it, she'd witnessed a new kind of James at Sasha's house. Maybe his obedient son routine was all an act. It deserved more thought—when Josie was no longer seeing double from exhaustion. Even the seashell upholstery was taking on a wave movement at this point.

She'd been trying to puzzle it out, but the effort was making her brain cramp. Scarlett O'Tucker would have to save that thought for another day.

⌘

"Ivan and I met in Russia at university. For him, it was love at first sight. For me, I had to be convinced a little more before I decided to let him be my lover," Olga was saying with an arrogant chuckle. Josie had begun to slouch back against the cushioned padding of the rattan chair, but Olga didn't seem to mind. In fact, she was more relaxed as well, which also could have been effect of the white wine she had opened. She poured some into the wine glass with the shells painted around the rim. Josie waved her off when she offered a glass to Josie. Alcohol was a sedative, exactly what Josie didn't need right now. Or possibly ever again in her life.

I'm chatting with a murderer, Josie speculated, her eyelids feeling heavy. *Probably. Maybe.* Although she wondered why she didn't feel more fear. In a few more minutes, she might be napping with a murderer if she weren't more careful. With that in mind, she pulled herself up straighter and cleared her throat.

"When did you come to America? Did you both get accepted to M.I.T. at the same time?"

"Eh," Olga said with a slightly dismissive shake of her head, making her earrings shake. "Ivan worked for several years as a janitor in Boston. I was in housekeeping. "

"Seriously? Even though you had college degrees?" Although she made herself sound outraged, Josie wasn't all that surprised. She had heard of doctors from other countries who had opted not to get re-qualified after moving to the United States and had chosen far less academic jobs in the service sector. Like working in restaurants like Josie's own mother.

"My English wasn't too good. I needed time to get better before I applied for graduate school. Some people don't do that, I know. I heard of many people who hired English speakers to write their dissertations for them. I wanted to do it myself. I have the brains, so why should I cheat?"

Josie scratched her head, feeling like this morning's trek to Santa Cruz was a waste of time, a total bust. She was getting nothing from Olga except...lukewarm grief, anxiety about the future, and a blast of innate self-confidence—the woman could have been security for the Russian mob. She wasn't a woman-scorned-slash-psycho.

This whole day trip had been a waste of time. Josie could have used the morning to sleep in, for Pete's sake. When was the last time she'd taken a shower? Probably just a few hours ago, but time was standing still. Even her stomach was quiet—it was lunchtime, but her black-market breakfast burritos were tiding her over. She didn't know where she was going with this interview. Olga was subdued and grieving in possibly a normal way. Now all Josie needed to do was figure out a way to extricate herself from this fruitless tête-à-tête and go lie down where she could stare at the insides of her eyelids for several hours.

"Are you hungry?" Olga suddenly said, a line forming between her eyes. "I'm expecting my girlfriend to come stay with me starting tomorrow, but it feels so strange to be alone now. I actually...miss Ivan, the idiot. He could be such a sweet man sometimes. So funny. Why did he have to go and get himself killed?" The big woman looked vulnerable...despite her loud bangles, flouncy shirt, and calypso house.

Underneath her normal grouchiness, Josie was a sucker for someone in need. Even if Olga looked tough enough to benchpress a VW.

CHAPTER 30

Josie ended up eating a peanut butter and jelly sandwich—cut into quarters—on Olga's back patio. The sun-warmed bread melted the grape jelly, blending it with the creamy Jif. Choosy suspected murderers chose Jif, apparently.

Olga had made a plate of four sandwiches and piled them in a pyramid on a paisley-printed Melamine plate. She was eating two halves to Josie's one-half, but then again, their appetites were directly proportional to their sizes. Josie stared up at the woman, chewing her PB&J, who loomed over her despite the fact that they were both seated. Josie was never one to deny a person enjoyment of food of any type, quality, or quantity. She was no food snob. Not about everything, anyway.

"When did you and Ivan get married?" Josie asked, dislodging the peanut butter from her soft palate with a swig of sweet tea, which had enough sweet syrup to choke a southern debutante. Squinting in the sunshine, Josie could have been sitting anywhere in the United States south of the Mason-Dixon line. Except a seagull shrieked overhead, reminding her she was only a couple miles from the Pacific Ocean.

"Oh, that was later," Olga said with her trademark Russian nonchalance. "After graduation, we moved to Texas in the early 90s. It was the beginning of the technology explosion there in Austin and Houston. Sometimes we had to travel for work to Alabama, even. A lot of government contractors down there along with the...less educated people."

"Aha," said Josie, thinking about her Aunt Ruth, who was originally from one of the Carolinas. Josie appreciated Olga's effort not to insult down-home southerners. Aunt Ruth always said southerners were the only ones allowed to insult themselves—because they were the best at their own put-downs, even if it was unintentional. "That explains the sweet tea."

Olga shrugged and offered a smile. "I got addicted to sweet tea. Too much sugar, I know, but I *need* it now. I tried to stop drinking it, but I started to get big headaches." She shrugged, a what-can-you-do gesture that had her bracelets jangling again. Had Olga taken the bracelets off when she stabbed her husband?

Josie took another sip, examining her lunch companion with a sideways glance. Sweet tea wasn't her favorite, but it fit the afternoon and the bold sunshine. Besides, she knew all about needing certain foods. Food obsessions were nothing to sniff at. Her mind wandered in a sleep-deprived, fuzzed out kind of way, to thinking about cravings, like pregnancy cravings.

"Do you have any children?" Josie asked. She didn't intend to openly interrogate Olga. Luckily, the sleepy tone of her voice guaranteed that Olga didn't take the question that way.

"No, I was never interested in being a mother. When I was younger, I thought maybe someday I would change my mind, but I never did. I never got that biological clock urge that you always hear about. You know what I am talking about? My husband—with Ivan, it never came up as an issue. We were always both so busy with work. He was always going around with a thousand ideas. He had a good head for business. His projects were his babies. Now, I wouldn't even know what to do with one. I'm way past that age to start over. Besides, I'm not romantic like that. I never had dreams of big weddings, though sometimes I watch those shows on TV for the drama. Babies, eh. White picket fences. That's not me, you know." Olga pushed up her sleeves. Small beads of moisture had started to pop out on top of the makeup on her upper lip—but it was due to the afternoon sunshine, not nervousness.

Josie could relate to Olga's feelings about children. She'd never spent a lot of time around kids, so she didn't think about them much. But her boyfriend Drew was really great with kids—he had a million Italian-Catholic cousins running around Boston. Would he want a little Italian-Catholic-Thai kid to add to the pack? She pictured a small girl with crazy dark hair, a sassy mouth, and Drew's kind, caring eyes. With a blink, she wrenched her mind back to the conversation. "So, did you like Texas? I'm guessing you both were able to find jobs?"

"I don't know if it still is called Silicon Prairie, but parts of Texas used to be just as high tech as Silicon Valley. Maybe not as big, but just as advanced and growing at an even faster rate. You know what I'm talking about, with all the technological companies. There were so many companies out there. And it was cheap to find a place to live. I loved the weather after Russia and Boston. Snow—yuck. No more for me, if I can help it." Olga pursed her lips in an exaggerated frown of disgust.

"Really? Even the Texas humidity? I bet you didn't have an outdoor wedding." Josie was suddenly thinking about Drew again, wondering what she would say in the event that he actually planned to ask her to marry him. Was she ready for the next step on the relationship ladder? She toyed with the papery strip of bread crust left on her plate. Somehow, she couldn't picture herself ever saying no to him. Would they have a big wedding? One thing was for sure—she was never getting married in Vegas...again. *Ugh.*

"Yes, the weather was atrocious. So bad for the hair style. And the bugs? Terrible. We didn't have a traditional wedding ceremony. Nothing official, even though it's still considered a marriage. I changed my name and all that, but we had one of those understood, common law types of marriages. It was never one of my dreams, like those crazy bridezillas on TV. I've seen those reality shows about the weddings, but it wasn't really for me. So we lived in Texas only for about five years before we came here. And this..." She swept a bangled arm around. "This is perfect. I think it's heaven. I never want to leave. I could live my whole life here and be happy." Her expression suddenly sobered. And for the first time that Josie had observed, tears welled up in Olga's eyes.

Josie cleared her throat and reached for the empty serving plate, intending to clean up and make a hasty retreat. She had no right to be here poking at this woman's fresh sorrow. Yet, she couldn't stop herself from asking a couple more questions, now that they were both so relaxed and enjoying the afternoon ocean breeze.

"Are you going to be okay? Will you get to keep your house? I know real estate is so expensive here."

Olga shrugged, with a slightly poor-me expression that Josie found somewhat practiced. "I guess I will have to wait and see. I might be able to afford the mortgage after I get the life insurance money. I don't want to have to move. And maybe I could take in a boarder—a roommate—if I need to." She cast a glance back at the tiny house where her office took up the spare room. "You would think that two people in the software industry could afford to buy a small house. I mean, this is not a mansion. Three bedrooms and two bathrooms. It's not luxurious." She shrugged again. "But at least it's in California. There are so many other places that are worse to live in. I've been there. Most people would kill to live here."

Josie cringed. She wasn't sure that 75 grand worth of life insurance was going to cover it for Olga. And from what she'd just heard, that might be all Olga would get. And, most likely, it wouldn't be enough to keep the house. The heavyweight champion mermaid would be booted out of her under-the-sea palace, such as it was.

⌘

Back in her boxy rental car, about to make a beeline straight to her hotel bed, Josie dialed Lopez and put him on speaker—she didn't know if holding a cell phone to her ear was legal while driving in this state. She wasn't sure if she could even pass a sobriety test at this point under the influence of her current state of exhaustion, so she wasn't taking any chances.

"Whadya got?" he said, by way of answering, ever the smooth operator.

"Burning question for you."

Without missing a beat, he said, "Yes, I'm still single, cupcake. I can be at your place by 8:00 tonight. We can go dancing. I've got some sweet moves. I'll treat you right. I knew you'd see it my way sooner or later."

In the background was a huge snort, so Josie knew Dicarlo was listening in, too.

"Here's the thing," Josie said, ignoring him. "Is common law marriage recognized in the state of California? Because, if not, I don't think Olga and Ivan were ever officially married. They had a common-law marriage in Texas that was never officiated. So that would affect who gets Ivan's money, right?"

There was a long silence. Lopez swore a blue streak. The phone rattled, and Dicarlo's voice came on. "Thanks for that info," Dicarlo said. "I'm on it. I don't think a common-law marriage—especially if there's no certificate—would be recognized in terms of a will. Definitely not in California. Even if Ivan had a will leaving everything to his spouse, I'm not sure if she'd qualify as a common-law wife. If he doesn't have a will...then, we're looking for next of kin. That might mean contacting people at the Russian consulate to see what's going on back in the old country, in terms of cousins and whatnot. Who knows. I don't know the ins and outs of this legal stuff. We'd need to consult an estate lawyer."

"Okay, then," Josie said, leaning her head back against the driver's seat headrest, eyes closed. "I'm not sure if Olga herself realizes the ramifications of this, if it's true. She may be the beneficiary of whatever life insurance Ivan had through his workplace PPS or any other policy where he specifically named her as recipient—so she still may have killed him and just doesn't know it's not going to pay off. Frankly, I don't want to be the one to have to tell her. She's kind of scary. I mean, in a purely physical way." Not in a peanut butter and iced tea kind of way.

"Definitely don't you put your butt in harm's way. Don't even think of telling Olga any of this," Dicarlo admonished.

"Don't worry. Save yourself," Lopez shouted, now far away from the phone. "We'll get Dicarlo to do it—*owww*."

Josie heard more jostling on the other end of the line, and then Dicarlo said, "Listen. Definitely don't put yourself in danger. That's our job. I'm not just posturing here. We're the ones with the badges and the guns."

"My gun is bigger than hers," Lopez yelled.

"Fine," Dicarlo told him, her mouth sounding farther away from the phone. "Then you can wrestle with Olga. I'll get some popcorn and watch her twist you into knots."

Josie cleared her throat as she tried to erase that image from her mind. "Did you get any other results back from the crime scene or from the autopsy?"

"Oh yeah," Dicarlo said, coming back on the line, all business again. "Got another call right after Lopez hung up with you this morning. That black hair he mentioned, the one he thought might be Sasha's because her hair is dyed black? Well it turns out, the strand of hair is not dyed. The lab says it's consistent with a person of Chinese descent."

"Chinese like James Yu," Josie said, shivering despite the warmth of her car. Midday heat streamed through her windows, which she would have rolled down if she weren't a little freaked out by the new information.

"Could be," Dicarlo said. "The landlord is Chinese, too. We haven't tracked him down yet—his name's listed on the property record as Mok Yee-Chun. I think Mok is the surname. But you know, the hair could be left over from a previous tenant, seeing's how the apartment is in Chinatown. That wouldn't be out of the realm of possibility. Ivan had been renting that place for a couple years, so that's not really likely. Although by the state of the apartment, who knows. It definitely wouldn't pass the white glove test in there. Been gathering dust and whatnot for some time now."

"Sure," said Josie. "James or the landlord. In Sasha's alleged boots. Makes perfect sense." *Not.*

"Or someone who wanted to frame Sasha and make it look like she did it."

Josie was starting to get a headache. "But if that's the case, why are the boots missing? Wouldn't the killer want us to find the boots so we would immediately suspect her?"

"Eh. Who knows. You can't always use the words 'perpetrator' and 'logical' in the same sentence, if you know what I'm saying." Josie could almost hear Dicarlo shrugging her tiny frame in her utilitarian button-down shirt.

"Hey, do you wanna see the crime scene?" Lopez suddenly shouted from a distance. "We can take you there." Dicarlo didn't bother to repeat the question because it had been broadcast loudly enough for half the state to hear.

Josie blinked a couple of times. "Is he...flirting with me?"

CHAPTER 31

Josie tossed her car key with its rental company fob onto the bedside table in her room. She had made it back to her hotel without any major traffic incidents—and truthfully, the one tiff with an angry driver who flipped her the bird would have happened whether or not she was fully awake. The idiot was on his cell phone, fiddling with a second device in his lap, and driving with both feet—braking and accelerating at the same time. She was glad to have escaped the moron with just his one middle-finger digit, which was worlds better than three emergency digits: 9-1-1.

Mutt and Jeff—Lopez and Dicarlo—couldn't meet her until the next morning, so she planned to take advantage of her downtime while she could. Actually, *planning* was kind of an overstatement. She was running on pure primordial instinct to find shelter and to bed down for the present.

As in, *immediately.*

Her body was ready to tamp some grasses down in a tight circle like a wild dog making a bed out in the Serengeti. Or like her dog Bert getting ready to nap on her laundry pile back home. Josie pulled the blinds closed in the hotel room, barely took the time to kick off her shoes, and crashed face down on the bed.

⌘

She dreamed her phone was ringing, and then realized it *was* ringing. Picking her head off the bedspread, she wished she'd had the wherewithal to have pulled back the comforter before she'd fallen asleep, because *ewww.* She'd seen those exposé TV shows about bodily fluids trapped on these things. However, tired was tired, and she was grateful to have slept so deeply for—she reached for her ringing phone to check the time. She blinked. She'd been asleep for only fifteen minutes.

She pressed the green answer button when she saw Drew's face pop up, intending to say hello. It came out, "Huh."

"I like your new friends," Drew said. It sounded like he was outside. Maybe taking her dog, whatshisname, for a walk. Did Drew have the day off? What time was it back home in Boston? What time was it here again?

"Huh?" She aimed for comprehension again and missed the mark.

"The ones who taught you your new dance routine. That was something else. I think they're a good influence on you. I think I want to see your new skills in person, if you're up for it."

"Uh..." she said, trying to gather some thoughts, some words. Something.

"Did someone have a wee bit too much to drink last night?" he asked. She could hear the smile in in his voice.

"Uh-uh..." She denied it, trying to explain that she was just tired, but then remembered the large amounts of whiskey less than twelve hours ago. The massive bottle of Jack she'd shared with the dancers. So she nodded into the bedcovers. "Uh-huh."

"I woke you up, didn't I? You should go back to sleep, babe. It sounds like you're having a good time. I hope you're enjoying yourself, getting a little vacation time. Right? Not getting into trouble? I just...wanted to let you know I was missing you."

He sounded like he was going to hang up, but she had something she needed to tell him. What was it? Her mind was totally scrambled, even worse from the *napus interruptus* than having gone without sleep the previous night.

"Wait," she said, with her eyes closed, scanning back and forth on the inside of her lids, as if that would help her read an invisible script and jog her memory.

"Yeah?" he said. She could hear the clinking of Bert's leash, confirming that they were out for a stroll.

Dang it. What the heck did she need to tell him? Thoughts swirled in her mind. Seashell upholstery and peanut butter sandwiches—no. Broken record albums at the bottom of James's messy closet—no, again. The rip in her favorite Ramones t-shirt from Sasha's dog door—definitely not.

The correct thought swirled to the front of her mind and she said. "I gotta problem. I like you. What we have is special, but I'm already married. To some guy I can't stand."

There, she'd finally said it. Out loud. What a relief.

Her eyes popped open.

Oh crap, she'd said it out loud. Although it may have been slurred. It might have sounded like one long word: *Imareddymareed.*

And then Drew laughed. He said, "Go back to sleep, babe. You're dreaming. I'll talk to you later." He laughed again and hung up.

Josie was left staring at her phone. Now she was wide awake, and her stomach suddenly rolled and pitched like a canoe in the middle of a hurricane.

CHAPTER 32

No way could she go back to sleep after that.

Her stomach had twisted up into a fist in the center of her body. She got off the bed and plunked down heavily in the sole chair in her hotel room. What a mess. She had no idea how was she going to get out of this one. She'd confessed her betrayal—her secret and unresolved marriage—to Drew, *but he hadn't believed her.* Now when she got back home, she was going to have to argue her case that she had, in fact, actually participated in a quickie Vegas wedding with a moron. *Totally, utterly, mind-bogglingly ludicrous.*

What other options did she have?

She could track down Joe Armstrong and demand a divorce. Which would cost money. And time. Which would mean that she'd need to tell Drew exactly what was going on because he deserved to know—and to understand she wasn't joking around.

When he finally realized the truth, how would he react?

Here, her mind stuttered. Drew was Catholic, for Pete's sake. Technically, that meant he'd committed adultery every time he'd been with Josie. Sleeping with him was damning his eternal soul, according to his beliefs, which she—as his girlfriend—respected and should have been helping him to observe. She was going to Hell with a capital H. No doubt about it.

Never mind the fact that he would kill her if he found out that she was here in San Francisco investigating yet another murder. He'd nearly had a conniption after Arizona, when she'd gotten a few cracked ribs and an almost-busted head—even though her skull was decidedly too thick for the likes of that. He'd be *so pissed off* at her to learn she was doing it yet again.

She lay her head on the hotel desk, then thunked it a couple of times for good measure.

When she sat up, the tiny notepad with the hotel logo was stuck to her forehead. She peeled it off. The four or so sheets of paper held together by a strip of yellowish glue measured only about two by four inches. She picked up the cheap white pen next to it and started doing what she had always been so good at—ignoring the problem at hand.

⌘

Trying to compose her thoughts, she decided it would be good to make a list. A very nice man—Mr. Obregon—with his neat, mechanical handwriting—had once put Josie on the right track with his meticulous lists. Making lists gave her a modicum of power over people and events that were not under her control. That was the whole trick to organization: convincing herself that she had a plan, an agenda, and a goal. She'd follow Mr. Obregon's wise example and see where it led her.

In Ivan's murder, who were the suspects, the persons of interest? She decided to start with Ivan and work outward with the people in his innermost circle. She wrote:

OLGA, SASHA, JAMES

Olga was first, because statistically speaking, the spouse was usually the first in line to get stabby with a person, especially when millions of dollars were on the line. Olga was still a suspect despite her large feet and her lack of an official marriage license. What she didn't know about the legalities of their marriage still might have killed Ivan. Olga had shown enough motivation already, which was her jealousy over Ivan's attachment to the stripper-slash-dancer younger woman. And despite Josie's gut feeling that the big woman didn't do it, nothing cleared Olga, and Josie's gut had been wrong in the past. More than once—and not just about food.

Next came Sasha. So far, all arrows pointed toward her having two-timed Ivan with James. If, in fact, Sasha had been seeing James behind Ivan's back, she and James may have set up Ivan to die. Maybe James had access to Ivan's funds through their start-up company. The two younger people could have been scheming to dupe Ivan out of his money. If so, there should have been a more direct line of money from him to them. Sasha wasn't throwing a lot of extra cash around. James was still saving up for his modest San Jose hovel. Neither of them was flaunting that they had millions of dollars—or even the expectation of it.

Finally on Josie's short list came James, the tech golden boy. Without Ivan's business sense, James might not have a chance of success with their company. Ivan was the schmoozer, the suit, the palm-presser of the two guys, while James was the technical know-how, the boy genius. Together, they created a magical balance that might have blossomed into something big, something synergistic, if that was a word—something that might have made a lot of money. Now that Ivan was dead, would James go back to being a normal, entitled Northern California kid?

Working outward in the widening spiral of people around Ivan, Josie drew a line and continued:

SASHA'S COWORKERS AT PONY PAGODA (POSSIBLY JEALOUS?)

IVAN'S CHINESE SUBCONTRACTOR

SOMEONE ELSE AT IVAN'S WORKPLACE (PPS)

IVAN'S LANDLORD

She included the Chinatown landlord only because Lopez had mentioned the dark hair they'd found in the apartment was from someone of Chinese or Asian descent. *But gee, a Chinese person's hair in Chinatown?* Never mind locating the needle, this was trying to find a piece of hay in a haystack.

Again, she started at the top of her new list.

The ladies at The Pony Pagoda definitely had a hard edge to them. Maybe they'd developed their toughness over time from seeing a seedier cross-section of life than the average person. The night brought out a whole different cross-section of creepy-crawlies—there was a reason why cavemen were drawn to fire, and that instinct stuck with a person even now. Dark equaled scary because that was when nefarious goings-on happened. Too much drinking and loss of inhibition. Crime and deception. Murder.

Of the three dancers who had hung out with Josie the night before, Merrylin had been the ringleader. Vivian was a follower. Shady had her own agenda—with her competitive dancing, she was *going places.* Merrylin...probably deserved a follow-up visit, one in which Josie drank nothing but water—and kept all of her clothes on. If one of those ladies had wanted to frame Sasha for the murder of her wealthy lover, she would have had more details for Josie—and possibly a pair of bloody boots with Sasha's fingerprints all over them.

Josie perused the list again. Ivan's Chinese subcontractor had nothing to gain from Ivan's death. In fact, he probably profited more from keeping quiet. The revelation of his existence probably put him in danger of prosecution from more than one company—both PPS and PPS's intended client—and maybe even by several government entities. *Yikes for that guy. Hopefully, he wouldn't end up wishing he were dead like Ivan.* Also, there was the matter of physical distance. Again, how would the boot prints have fit into the equation? Unless there was a second person or witness at the scene...

Ugh. That was a whole separate complication that Josie hadn't put much thought into. What if the boot prints weren't even made by the killer, but rather by another person at the scene of the crime?

Josie shook her head and focused on her list. She felt comfortable crossing off the Chinese subcontractor, at least mentally even if she didn't actually cross him off. Because she was chicken. As soon as she swiped ink through his name, he would probably appear on Ivan's computer screen brandishing a cleaver.

Moving on. Josie thought about PPS, where Ivan and James worked. What the heck did PPS stand for anyway? *Pork, pie, and strudel. Peter, Paul, and Steve. Programmers, pitfalls, and strippers.* She rolled her eyes at herself. The only other coworker of theirs Josie had met was Colin, the petite English fellow. She couldn't see him interrupting his tea time to wave a knife at Ivan either. He struck her as more of an irate letter-to-the-editor type of person, a "pen is mightier than a sword" kind, although he might be willing to talk to her about Ivan and the general feel of the workplace. He had definitely been chattier than the average cubicle dweller. Maybe he had more to tell her.

Finally, there was Ivan's Chinatown landlord. Josie would have to ask Lopez and Dicarlo more about that in the morning...when they took her to the crime scene. *Gulp*. From the photos, there was a lot of blood. How long did it take for blood to dry anyway?

With that thought, she figured she'd be better off skipping her breakfast burritos tomorrow morning.

CHAPTER 33

After a change of clothes, with a briefly hung head to mourn the loss of her favorite Ramones t-shirt, Josie thought it might be a good idea to go back to PPS and nose around. Screw sleeping, she just needed to keep moving. She was chasing loose ends, she knew. None of the strands of information were tying together well, but they were all she could think of in the time she had left in California—she'd been here almost five full days. She had an open return airplane ticket, but how much longer could she stay if she weren't making progress? Greta Williams had been indulgent with her so far—Josie wasn't charging much on the credit card, but she hated racking up IOUs with anyone. Susan was gone already, so there wasn't any reason *socially* for Josie to stay and poke her nose in James's business. She needed to come up with some new information about Ivan soon. Or give up altogether.

When she got to the PPS campus again, she drove to the same spot that James had taken them the previous day. She parked behind the building and walked to the side door that had previously been propped open. To her disappointment—but not surprisingly really—the door was firmly shut and locked this time. *Maybe the discovery of having a Chinese national doing unapproved contract work at their company had caused PPS to ramp up their security measures, hmm?* Or at least, to start enforcing the ones they already had.

Her cell phone rang again as she was weighing her options, poking her toe at the scrappy periwinkle plant that was fighting its last gasp in the middle of a highly-trod path to the door.

Apropos of nothing, Lopez started the conversation by saying, "Hey, one more thing I forgot to tell you, Josie." Would the guy ever learn some phone etiquette? A simple *hello* would do. "We got an estimate on Ivan's time of death. These times are never exact, just so you know, but the lab is estimating he was killed early Saturday morning. Sometime between 12 and 6 a.m., maybe."

Josie shuffled out of the way of an employee leaving the building. The heavy door slammed too quickly for her to grab it, so she let it fall shut. She also wanted to keep her conversation semi-private, which would be next to impossible between those cloth-covered walls inside the building, or worse, in the open cubicle area. "So...he died in middle of the night or early morning. That means whoever did it was probably counting on him to be asleep."

"Yeah, pretty much. It also means that we don't have solid alibis for anyone. Sasha wasn't working that night. James was probably with your friend Susan for that window of time—although I'm guessing she wouldn't mind throwing him under the bus now that they've broken up." He gave a chuckle and continued. "Olga says she was at home. Her workplace says she was logged in overnight, but you told us already how easily that could be faked. She could have taken her laptop on a field trip with her to kill him for all we know." That was true. As long as Olga had internet access, she could have been working from anywhere, even the crime scene.

"What about forced entry? Did they break into the apartment?" Josie tucked her hair behind her ear, but she was in more of a mood to yank it out. Her frustration level was mounting.

"There's no sign of a break-in," Lopez said. "The lock on the door was a piece of crap though. We're waiting for prints to come back, if there are any. Or actually, if we can isolate any prints of interest out of the thousand or so smudges on the door. So, either they had a key, the door was unlocked, or a stiff breeze blew it open."

Josie sighed. "Well, dang. I guess we're kind of back to square one." She glanced up in time to lock eyes with Colin, James's English coworker, who was walking by. She gave him a tight smile and a wave. To her good luck, he held the door open for her and gestured for her to follow him in.

"Keep your chin up, Josie-girl," Lopez said, oddly calling her by the same nickname her Aunt Ruth often used, "These things take time. We'll figure it out. This one isn't going cold on us if I have any say in it." He hung up without saying goodbye.

⌘

"Hello again," Colin said, holding the door open for Josie. His plaid button-down shirt was neatly tucked into worn but spotless blue jeans. He came up to about Josie's forehead. "Piggy-backing your way in on my badge, I see. Forgot your own already? Security is buttoned up now. I can report you, you know." He gave a chuckle to show he was joking, and Josie tried to smile. "But never mind," Colin was saying. "Come have a chat with me. How has your week gone?"

She followed him to his office where he pulled out an ancient guest chair for her that had more of its fair share of coffee stains on the seat cushion. In her comfortable jeans, she didn't even flinch. She sat down, shaking her head. "It's been totally crazy," she said, not exaggerating in the least. Of course, she wasn't talking about working as a new hire for PPS, but he didn't need to know that.

As it turned out, he didn't care what she had to say—he was looking for a ready ear in which to pour his chatter. *Ah, office gossip.* Josie had forgotten what it was like to work in close quarters with other people. Her own job was now one hundred percent remote working from home. Her officemate was her dog Bert...and occasionally the pizza delivery man—back when she had still been eating dairy. She wondered briefly if Alfonso missed her, too; he was such a nice man. He liked to chat with her whenever he delivered her old favorite, a medium thin-crust sausage and olive pie. She knew he had three grandchildren and had been married to the same woman for thirty-nine years. Maybe she'd have to call him up and see if he could have them do a dairy-free pizza for her, using a cheese substitute. *Shudder.* The very thought of it made chills spider up her spine. An olive oil cracker dunked in tomato sauce would be less offensive...

"I'll say it's been nutso," Colin exclaimed, distaste thinning his lips. "I've been working here for nearly eighteen years, and it's never been this locked down. Security is locked down tighter than a drum—that's why I gave you such a hard time about your badge." He gave her a sharp nod, which caused her a pang of guilt. "Once we had an Anthrax scare back in the nineties, but it turned out just to be the CFO's wife sending him some ant poison in the interoffice mail. Nasty divorce. No one was hurt though. No harm done—although it did help them sort out their alimony in a flash. And then once we had an earthquake, but our building didn't suffer any damage. A tree almost fell on my car that time, but no harm done, again. Wouldn't have minded that much. I wanted to get a Mini. Cashed in some stock options the following year and got Minerva anyway—that's my car."

He swiveled in his chair to wake up his computer screen, for which Josie noted he entered a password. Then, seeing three new email messages, he quickly scanned through them, replied to one and ignored the other two.

"So anyway, darling," he said turning back toward her and then cringed. "Sorry. Not supposed to say 'darling' anymore. It's a hard habit to break—though I have been to sensitivity training once now. I honestly don't mean anything by it. My own mother called me darling, so it's not a pick-up because honestly, I loved my mum but not in that way. You look a bit done in, by the way. Not working too much, are you? Because the key to longevity around this place is to stick to business hours. No overtime. It's not good for the soul. Not like these infant geniuses, working around the clock, drinking their hideous energy monster drinks." He gave a delicate shiver of his narrow shoulders.

"Do you mean James Yu?" she offered. Colin's rapid-fire reminiscing was making her head spin, and she struggled to get him back on track. Well, *back on her track.*

Colin closed his mouth with a snap as if he weren't going to say anything, and then said anyway, "That's the one."

She waited for him to elaborate, hoping she wouldn't have to be too overt. And as it turned out, she didn't have to wait very long before he was off and running again.

His eyes sparkled in his neat hedgehog-like face as he told her,

228

"One evening, I had neglected to take my house keys home with me. I'd taken my car in for service, so I'd removed my house key from the keychain—just to make myself feel better, not that the guy changing my motor oil was going to break into my home. What's he going to do, drive to Los Gatos and steal my futon and infuriate my 17-year-old cat? But anyway, all joking aside, I'd had a busy day, going five directions at once, and I ended up leaving my house key here in the top drawer of my desk. So, back I came to work to get it. And when I got here, I noticed that James and Ivan's office was still lit up. So me being me, I strolled down there to say goodnight to them."

Josie could feel her eyebrows quirking upward.

"So around the door I peek and what do I see? James—not working. Absolutely not working. At all. Instead, he's got a *stripper in his office.* And she's doing some kind of dance for him. No music or anything. She was just humming some kind of song. It was that old song for strippers. I think it might actually have been called 'The Stripper.'" He hummed a few bars of it in a surprisingly on-tune and confident tenor, and Josie recognized the raucous, jazzy standard.

"A stripper?" Josie said with surprise—not so much about the actual stripping part, but about the poor choice of venue for adult entertainment.

"Yeah," Colin blustered, reliving the outrage. "You can imagine my shock. This frightening, tattooed Bettie Page lookalike doing a striptease. Fishnets and heels, legs up to her neck. I was gobsmacked, I tell you. I'm a fairly liberal fellow. As heterosexual as the next guy—well, maybe not in this part of the country, but you know what I mean. Anyone'll tell you I am. But to hire a stripper here, at the workplace? At night? It was just unbelievable. I mean, what kind of person would do that? Keep that stuff in your own home, I say. It doesn't belong here."

"Seriously," Josie agreed, looking around at the office ceiling. "What if there were security cameras in here or something." She eyed the sprinkler system above them, not doubting for a minute that they were being watched. Hopefully, her presence wasn't being tracked, but wow, it was an odd feeling to think they were being watched.

"That's the outrageous part of it," Colin said, leaning toward her, lowering his voice, his gray eyes widening. Her attention snapped back to his face as he whispered, "Ivan was there, too. And he had a camera. A video camera. He was filming the whole thing."

CHAPTER 34

"What?" Josie said, her jaw hanging open.

Ivan and James together, getting a private dance from Sasha? She shook her head, eyes squeezed shut. She could almost wrap her brain around the thought of James and Sasha going behind Ivan's back, but the three of them together? As in *together* together—in a lascivious, bobbing eyebrows kind of way? This was getting stranger and stranger. She had seen the photo of Sasha sitting on Ivan's lap at his workplace desk—that was the photo she'd stumbled across on one of James's old computers. From what Colin was telling her now, the three of them were all participating in this incident. "You actually saw this entire thing happen?"

Colin straightened his desk blotter and swiped some dust off his keyboard. Now that he'd obtained the desired reaction from her, he was drawing back his narrative, getting ready to ramp up the tension again. She knew his type—they hung out by the dozens in her Uncle Jack's garage—Colin was a born storyteller. He said the next words, drawing out his syllables, "Well, not exactly." She found herself leaning toward him. *Dang, he was good.*

"But you saw the girl in their office?"

"I certainly did. And as soon as I realized what exactly it was I was watching, I hightailed it out of there with my house key. I didn't want any part of it." He made a slashing gesture with his hand. "I haven't been here for eighteen years without keeping my nose clean. I have never had a single reprimand or write-up here. Well, other than that one issue with HR. But other than that, nothing. Straight level-two ratings for years—never want to be too good or they promote you right out of your skill set, if you know what I mean. Next thing you know, you're in management and on anti-anxiety tabs. So, yes, I certainly didn't stay to watch. They didn't see me, so I didn't see them."

"So...?" Josie encouraged him.

"How did I know about the video?" Colin cleared his throat, having the grace to look a little embarrassed. "I have a friend named Jeffery in IT. He's a good lad. From Sheffield, actually, not too far from my hometown. His mother actually knows my sister—went to school together. He's the one who's working on Ivan's computer right now, making sure the Chinese don't have all of our trade secrets, if you know what I mean, since they discovered that Jun fellow who was doing all of Ivan's coding. Really good code, actually. I think our best bet is to get the fellow over here, offer him a work visa, and make him sign a non-disclosure agreement ASAP. Lure him with our filthy lucre, so to speak. But anyway, that's neither here nor there, as far as my input on the matter is concerned. But when my mate Jeffery was recovering some erased files, he found this video. And he, well, sort of shared it with me." For the first time, Colin looked as if he thought he'd maybe said a little too much and suddenly clammed up.

"Unbelievable. You actually saw the video," Josie gasped. She covered her open mouth with her fingertips, egging him on. And it worked.

"I can prove it. I have a clip of it on my personal computer that I can show you." He spun in his chair and grabbed a shoulder bag from where it had been leaning against his desk on the floor. "I didn't even use a flash drive—didn't want any trace of it on the network because that would point straight to me and I can't have that. Not when I'm fully vested with my stock shares and 401(k). Absolutely not."

He kept his computer in his lap and turned it on, navigating through some folders with his finger on the touchpad. "Aha. Here it is. See for yourself. This is the kind of thing that gets a fellow murdered, I think," he added, with an apologetic tinge to his voice.

He spun the laptop toward Josie so she could see the video. In the upper left corner of the screen, a small movie was playing in color. Without a doubt, the stripper was Sasha, doing a little burlesque bump and shuffle. The video had begun in the middle of Sasha doing some of the very same basic but effective moves that Merrilyn and Vivian had taught Josie just a couple of nights before.

Now in Colin's coffee-spotted office chair, Josie sat stunned, watching Sasha saunter closer to James, who sat sprawled in his office chair, an expression on his face that could only be described as a proprietary smirk. He was looking at someone he clearly viewed as his. She drew closer and closer, leaned toward him, dragging her fingers through his inky black hair. He ducked his chin with a private smile, showing that same top of the head that Josie had seen so many times already, although this time, he was utterly focused on the person in front of him. No eye contact issues now.

Josie watched the camera zoom in and out awkwardly as the show went on for a few more minutes. The lens shook a little, as the cameraman shifted. Josie heard a voice—a deep, heavily accented voice—say, "All right, enough. Enough of this. Take the camera. It's my turn to be the audience."

⌘

Ivan's voice.

The recording captured the dead man's voice as clear as day—Josie heard him speak for the first time, and it gave her goosebumps. The past few days, Ivan had been like a character in a story to Josie, but hearing his voice now made him *real*. Less than a week ago, he'd been a living, breathing soul, a person who'd had dreams and desires, fears and flaws.

A pang of...*something* hit Josie right in the gut. She cleared her throat to try to get rid of the lump that had formed in it. Colin reached around the screen and hit the volume button on his laptop twice and the voices grew louder.

The camera was jostled around as Ivan handed it off to James. Judging by the steady picture, James was a better cameraman than Ivan. Now Ivan came into view sitting in his own desk chair—the same angle that Josie recalled seeing from the photo on James's laptop. And...yes, Ivan was wearing the same clothes from the photo, too. The stills on

James's computer had been captured from this very movie.

Sasha gave an uncharacteristic giggle—Josie had never heard the girl be anything but dour, upset, or dominating. Now her dance, which was focused on Ivan, turned slightly exaggerated and...almost silly. Her movements became a caricature of her sultry dance for James. Her previous slow steps morphed into a Shirley Temple soft-shoe tap dance ending with vigorous, overblown jazz hands as she dissolved into laughter. In her heels and fishnets, her dance was a little grotesque, her full-sleeved tattoos coloring her arms like a trendy off-both-shoulders hipster sweater.

She lunged closer to Ivan with a couple of awkward box steps. A kick-ball-change. She landed heavily in Ivan's lap, her arms twisting around his neck in a tight embrace. She whispered something in his ear—*and there*. This was the exact moment that matched the freeze-framed picture from James's computer, that same intimate moment that Josie had seen earlier when she'd been snooping in James's apartment— the one that had convinced Josie of an affair between Ivan and Sasha. The image was so very...private.

Why had James chosen to capture that exact, almost-sweet scene? Jealousy? Were he and Sasha planning to blackmail Ivan with the still photo of their embrace? Ivan's wife already suspected that he was having an affair. Maybe this photo had been the catalyst for the murder.

"Colin, can you tell what she said right there?" Josie asked, unable to disguise the urgency in her voice.

"Hmm? I dunno," he said, looking pleased that he'd stirred up Josie's level of interest high enough to match his own. "Let's see if we can find out, shall we?" Josie eyed him, thinking his fervor was a bit ghoulish and detached, as he peered at the freeze-frame of his dead coworker. Whatever Colin's personal motivation, he was also technologically skilled, way more so than Josie. As far as she was concerned, this particular office gossip had a future in computer forensics. He fiddled with his video settings, which she noticed were not like anything she'd ever seen before, although that wasn't saying much—she only knew it wasn't the same one-step video playback program as the one that came pre-loaded on her computer.

Colin dragged back the video play bar with his mouse and started the video up again from right where Sasha had put herself in Ivan's lap. They both leaned forward, straining to hear what she was saying in Ivan's ear. As it turned out, they didn't have to move closer—Sasha's voice was as clear as a bell.

"I love you, Daddy," she said as she snuggled in his arms.

Ivan, *her father*, pulled her closer.

PART 4: THE HEAT

Cooking is never more like chemistry than when you add heat. You've assembled the ingredients, measured them with precision—or with a practiced eye—and stirred them up. The fire, the control over a primordial flame that separated *homo erectus* from his furrier predecessors, however, is the catalyst, the spark that creates the magical transformation. Heat is the fairy dust sparkles that shower from the tip of a magic wand. *Pop, sizzle, poof.* A slab of meat turns into a juicy, encrusted ribeye. A pile of chopped veggies stir fries into a Buddha's Delight. A pan of batter turns into a wedding cake. A tank of inorganic powders turns into Oreos.

Josie Tucker, *Will Blog for Food*

CHAPTER 35

"Ivan Sorokin was Sasha's father, *not her lover*. Their relationship wasn't a dark and seedy secret. It was plain and simple paternal affection," Josie said into her phone, her excitement practically making her pant. She'd rocketed out of the PPS building to her car like her hair was on fire and had immediately dialed Lopez. He promptly put her on speaker to include Dicarlo.

Her hand shaking as she opened the door to her Kool-Aid car, Josie's body suddenly jacked straight up where she stood, keys forgotten in her hand. *Oh God, the picture of the blond family on Sasha's bedside table—* why hadn't Josie looked at it closer? Under all that Bettie Page black hair dye and tattoos, Sasha was as light-haired as Ivan. *Her father.*

Ivan wasn't a sugar daddy, a john, or a mark. And for some reason, that made an actual pain develop in Josie's chest. If she weren't mistaken, she would have said the ache was in the region vaguely where she was supposed to have a heart—she never knew for sure if she actually had one of those. Maybe having a boyfriend was making her soft. She was feeling things and it was making her uncomfortable. Before she knew it, she'd be eating bonbons and watching the women's TV channel. *Ugh. Shake it off, soldier.*

"Well, crap," Lopez said, adding in a few other curse words that had Dicarlo snatching the phone from him. His voice trailed off as the phone got farther away from him.

"—shouldn't be driving on the phone anyway, you idiot," Dicarlo said as she came on the line. "Josie? What did you say? I thought we weren't seeing you until morning. We got our big crime scene reveal with you, right? We have a running bet to see if you're going to puke, just so you know. I have my money on you having a stomach of steel, so you keep that tidbit in mind while you're choosing your breakfast in the morning, you hear?"

"Right," Josie said, and explained again what she'd told Lopez about Ivan and Sasha and their father-daughter relationship.

"Well, shi-oot," Dicarlo said. "I didn't see that coming. In fact, I didn't see any of that in the immigration papers for any of them. We'll have to dig a little deeper on that one, check out her social security number to see if it's a stolen. If I have to guess, there's probably something off about her immigration status. But if Sasha's the sole blood relative and Olga was never officially married to him, that means Sasha stands to inherit millions of dollars. Which means, she still could have done it. Now, it turns out, her motive is money, not love or sex. Or lust...Please, dear Lord, tell me they weren't having a sexual relationship anyway?"

Josie frowned, thinking back to the video she'd just seen in Colin's office. "Nah, I wouldn't characterize it as anything skeevy. Not even remotely. It was more....sweet. It was warm and affectionate. Genuine." She thought, with a pang, about overhearing Sasha's tears that afternoon while standing in her kitchen. Another *oh God* rolled through Josie's system, as she remembered the girl weeping, overheard after Josie had army-crawled through the dog door into Sasha's kitchen.

Inevitably—unbidden, and uncontrolled—Josie thought about the afternoon when she'd lost her own father. She'd been sixteen years old. Slamming open the kitchen door after a day at high school, she had found her father lying on the linoleum. Maybe that was why she had an undying hatred of that kind of flooring. The only time she saw it up close was when something terrible happened. For instance, when she was heaving up the contents of her stomach in the bathroom. Or when she was sixteen and her father had been dying of a heart attack in her arms on their kitchen floor. She pushed the memories back and sighed, unwilling to dredge up them up when she needed to be thinking about Ivan.

If Sasha were Ivan's daughter, had he made arrangements to take care of her in the event of his untimely passing? Unlike Josie's father. Without money or a designated guardian, Josie had nearly been shuffled into the foster system. If it hadn't been for the mercy of her Aunt Ruth...Josie didn't even want to think about where she might have ended up without the intervention of her strong-willed aunt, who had been willing to take on a surly, wounded teen. Though, apparently, the thoughts kept returning, unbidden.

At least Sasha was a legal adult who was able to take care of herself, but to what lengths was she willing to go to get what she wanted?

CHAPTER 36

It was only 6:00 p.m., but Josie had been running on fumes since her earlier aborted nap. She went back to her hotel on Bascom Avenue and headed straight for the shower, leaving a trail of clothes behind her. Her stomach should have been growling at this point—the last thing she'd eaten was a PB&J in the grieving widow Olga's backyard—but exhaustion won out. After turning off the shower, she dried herself off only enough so that she didn't soak the sheets, threw on a fresh t-shirt and undies, and crawled into bed.

She dreamed of eating dim sum with Drew, of them feeding each other glossy, pan-crisped dumplings from tiny china plates that had been garnished with orchids, sculpted carrots, and radish roses. They sat on silken red cushions in a garden full of waterfalls and ponds of gilded koi. He used his chopsticks like a pro.

She woke the next morning with a contented stretch, wishing for a certain someone next to her in bed. Her smile wilted when she remembered where she was headed next.

⌘

"Are you ready for this?" Dicarlo asked her. They'd met on the street level outside the liquor store, directly downstairs from the Chinatown apartment. From the murder scene.

"It's still pretty messy," Lopez warned her, putting a hand on Josie's shoulder—and not in a flirtatious way. "Did you eat breakfast?"

In fact, Josie had eaten, despite her best intentions. Because she'd barely eaten yesterday, her stomach had woken up clamoring for sustenance—breakfast burritos, in particular. Her dealer, Lupe, was as good as her word, so Josie had downed two soft and warm potato and sausage burritos about two hours ago. Josie was banking on the breakfast of the likes of Pancho Villa and Cesar Chavez to keep her stomach fiercely resistant and grounded through this upcoming ordeal. She did a quick stomach check and found that she was still all right. *Viva la resistance, right?* At least, she could hope. She gave the detectives a stoic thumbs up.

Dicarlo lead them inside the building through an open doorway to a set of dingy stairs. "Up until about a decade ago, the owners of the crime scene or the family was responsible for doing the actual cleanup. The owner is still responsible for paying for it. Sometimes insurance will cover it. But nowadays, there's companies you can hire that'll do the dirty work—we even have brochures we can hand out to the families or business owners. With this place, who knows when the landlord will get to it or if he'll do it himself, which is good news for us, because we can get back in and still see a lot of the scene as it was. Except for the parts that have been processed.'"

"Uh-huh," Josie said, bracing herself. She had that same feeling in the pit of her stomach that she'd had the last time Susan and Benjy had dragged her onto the Bizarro roller coaster at Six Flags outside of Springfield. On that spring day at the amusement park, she'd been clamped into the ride with this weird yellow block harness over her lap and while the car slowly climbed the initial ascent, she'd wondered, all of a sudden, what the heck she was doing. Did she have a death wish? As they passed over the top arc, with the view of the broad, gray-green Connecticut River wide open below them, that helpless feeling took over. As the cars plunged, she passed briefly into darkness before they began their second ascent. That was when fear and helplessness changed to hate. Next to her, Susan's arms waved in the air above them while Josie's hands clamped to the harness. People died on these rides—there was no way Josie was letting go. She gritted her teeth and shut down her mind, waiting for the ride to end, bearing out the painful G-forces on her body. After it was over, she walked steadily, pretending that the hatred of being helpless wasn't coursing through her body, flushing out with the excess adrenaline.

"You get ahold of the landlord yet?" Dicarlo asked Lopez as they climbed the stairs.

"No returned phone calls," he said. "I have an address though, so we can hit there next. You can tag along if you want," he told Josie, who realized that was a pretty big deal. She was glad to be included, but she couldn't muster up more than a nod at the moment.

"You said a neighbor found his body?" Josie asked, to keep her mind clear. She found she was taking deep, meditative breaths through her nose.

"Yeah," said Lopez. "The door was wide open, so the neighbor went in. Just between us, I think the guy was looking for something to steal."

"Here we are. This is it," Dicarlo said, stopping in front of a brown wooden door. The paint was peeling off in streaks. A tarnished brass pair of fours marked it. The number four signified death in Chinese because *shi*, meaning four, and *shi*, meaning death, were homonyms. The number 44 was very unlucky. Especially for Ivan.

Josie had been expecting yellow police tape across the apartment door, but instead, there was a piece of generic-looking copy paper taped up identifying the place as the scene of an unspecified crime.

Dicarlo set a black bag she'd been carrying on the floor. She pulled out booties, gloves, and masks for the three of them.

"I thought you guys already released the scene," Josie said with confusion. She certainly didn't want to be the one to screw up any uncollected evidence that would potentially lead to the killer getting away.

"BBPs, OPIMs," Dicarlo said gruffly, adjusting her mask as Josie examined hers and pulled it on, hopefully correctly.

"I have no idea what that means," Josie admitted.

"Bloodborne pathogens and other potentially infectious material," Lopez explained, sounding muffled behind his mask. Josie's eyebrows shot up. "Ivan leaked a lot of fluids. Even though his body is gone, there's still decomposition of the remaining blood. Until it gets cleaned up by professionals, there's a danger of getting sick. We got this whole

OSHA thing we have to comply with. You know, safety first. We're not wearing full suits, so try not to touch anything."

Josie felt ridiculous, like she was about to enter an Ebola zone, but she shut up and did what they told her. They were the experts here. This *was* her first rodeo, so to speak. After they all were outfitted, Dicarlo pushed the apartment door open.

"It's not locked?" Josie asked, surprised. After all that protection, the door wasn't even secured? Wouldn't looters or gawkers mess with the place? The story had been all over the local news.

"The scene's already been processed. The lock is the responsibility of the landlord," Dicarlo explained with a shrug. *Yikes. The poor neighbors, living with this right next door.* The two detectives went inside.

Josie took a deep breath and followed them.

⌘

She thought the smell would be the first thing she noticed, but she was wrong. The apartment smelled just as musty and stale as the hallway. The three of them stood in the main room of the place, looking toward a small, relatively tidy galley kitchen. A worn green and brown couch with an incongruous-looking knitted blanket across the back of it was pressed against the wall. The whole place was urban, grungy, and early modern *Death of a Salesman*, but otherwise unremarkable. Immediately to her right was a runt of a hallway with two doors—one opened to a bathroom, the other, a bedroom.

"This way," Lopez said, tipping his chin toward the bedroom. Dicarlo assessed Josie with a curious eye, as if to check her puke-o-meter, and then went ahead of her. Josie took another deep breath and stepped through the door.

That was when the smell hit her. Not a rotten smell—Ivan's body was long gone, transported to the M.E.'s office, and probably in the morgue by now. No, the smell was more...like iron and meat and rust. Still. Even now, a few days later.

The room contained a double bed, a night table, and a kitchen chair.

On the seat of the chair, neatly folded, were clothes in a somewhat tidy stack—a pair of pants and a button-down shirt, the kind that Ivan appeared to favor, based on many of the pictures Josie had seen of him. Her eyes had skimmed over the bed, but now she returned to it. A massive copper-colored stain pooled on the left side of the mattress. The sheets and covers were missing, probably having been taken into evidence to search for fibers or the hair that they had already found. The indentation of the mattress indicated that Ivan usually slept on the left side. She could picture him lying there in the dark, his back to her, as he slept a deep, medicated sleep. The room had a single, narrow window with a rubber roller shade pulled all the way down. If it had been down that night, with no light coming from the street, the room would have been pitch black.

Josie's line of sight behind her mask rose to the wall above the bed where there was a morbid, mortal array of Jackson Pollock style spatter marks. For some reason, she'd expected the blood to still be red like in the movies. Instead, it was brownish orange. The stains were completely identifiable—there was no mistaking that it was blood—and that they had splashed in more than one direction. She used to admire Jackson Pollock paintings for their energy, for their vitality. These splatters were, literally, Ivan's vitality as it had splashed out of him. She'd never think of those abstract paintings in the same light again, that was for sure.

"Eight stab wounds," Lopez said, watching where Josie's gaze fell. "Six in the upper back, one in the shoulder—probably as he rolled over or turned to defend himself—and then the killing one in the neck."

Josie looked down at the heavily stained carpet. Some pieces of the floor had been cut away, presumably to preserve the places with footprints on them and transport them to the lab. Someone had done this horrible thing. This person—he or she—had entered the apartment in the middle of the night and attacked the defenseless, sleeping man with an almost unimaginable violence. *One. Two. Three. Four. Five. Six. Seven. Eight.* Josie counted off the number of stab wounds, absorbing the thought of each blow.

"You doing all right?" Dicarlo asked her, and behind her mask Josie nodded. She listened to her own even breaths. Oddly, she was fine. For now.

The space was small, especially with the three of them in it. She turned in a tight circle and examined the remnants of black fingerprint powder on the door frame. On closer examination, she saw that dusty powder from print collection trailed all over the room.

"This is a nightmare for our latents guys in the lab," Lopez said again—he'd mentioned it earlier, but Josie was glad for the reminder. "There are just too many prints, too much data to process quickly. I don't think anyone has ever wiped down the door since this place was built." Josie figured the building was too new to have been part of the rebuild after the 1906 earthquake, but it could have dated back to the 60s or even the 40s.

"The whole place has been photographed and recorded though, right?" Josie asked.

"Yeah, all processed and released. That's why you're allowed in here," Dicarlo chimed in, her arms folded across her chest, obviously still affected by the sight. It was hard not to be, with the amount of blood in front of them. "The person who vouched for you told Lopez here that you might be able to help us out. I don't know what you're going to see that our team didn't, but it's worth a shot, right?"

Josie shot a sideways glance at Lopez, who gave a half-shrug. She wondered what ties Greta Williams had to the San Francisco PD, and how deep they went. If Greta's pockets ran that deep, why wasn't she living on a tropical island made of gold sand?

Josie stuffed her gloved hands in her own empty jeans pockets. She took a few steps out of the room to peer into the bathroom. Gray tile everywhere. A battered tub with a see-through vinyl curtain held up by metal rings that probably made a cringe-worthy screech when they were moved. Her gaze tracked to the floor and she froze.

"I think you guys might have missed something," she said. When Lopez and Dicarlo crowded behind her, they all stood staring like dummies at the pair of blood-splattered women's work boots neatly lined up against the bathroom wall.

"Where the hell did those come from?" Dicarlo finally said.

CHAPTER 37

After the detectives photographed and bagged the boots, they dropped them off at their SUV, intending to take them back to the lab on the way back to their desks. The boots had not been there during the initial sweep and examination of the apartment. Because the crime scene had been processed, it was no longer secure. The flimsy door may as well have been a welcome mat. Anyone could have left the boots there to be discovered. Any person walking by could have put them inside the apartment, any guilty person, that was. So, they were hoping against odds to get some prints from the boots.

Josie stood next to the Tahoe, taking deep breaths of fresh air. She rubbed her face where the mask had left a mark. Dicarlo had already collected all their safety equipment and stuffed it into a plastic bag for disposal.

"We still want to hit the landlord's address to see if he has anything to say. We can walk there. Now remember, you're only here to observe. You did good with the boots, but let us handle this part," Lopez said, leading the way up the street. They passed James Yu's family restaurant, which Josie eyed with interest, wondering if he were holed up in there now. She'd checked the message board a couple of times over the last 24 hours but hadn't seen any more posts from him, as his alter ego, Zenmaster.

They walked down Clay Street with the Transamerica Pyramid stabbing the clear blue sky ahead of them, turned a corner, and came to a clean-looking five-story residential building. The creamy, smooth exterior was a modern contrast to the older bricked parts of Chinatown, maybe redone during one of the many rebuilds after earthquakes. Nothing marked this building as being part of the Chinatown culture—

no green clay tiles, no gold-painted characters or color other than off-white. The three of them entered the building, went up a flight of steps, and stopped in front of a numbered door.

"Remember," Dicarlo said. "Let us do the talking." She rang the bell just as Lopez called her back a couple of steps to chat, probably to do a quick review on their strategy, their plan of attack, so to speak. Josie was left standing at the door, waiting for Ivan's landlord to answer it. *No big deal.* She stood there with a studiously polite look on her face, ready to "represent" the law, if need be. She could handle it. Maybe she'd even use her street smarts to bond with the landlord while the detectives were chatting in the hall. In other words, fake it. She could totally do this.

After a long silence, footsteps padded to the door and it swung open.

"I told you to come right in. You don't have to—" James Yu stood there wet, clearly having come straight from a shower. He was in just a towel, which was wrapped around his waist, beads of water dripping down his hairless, concave chest, his bare feet sinking into the plush, white carpet. He stared down at Josie, shock apparent on his face. "What the hell are you doing here?"

"You're Ivan's landlord?" Josie couldn't stop herself from blurting out. *What the ever-loving heck?*

At that point, Dicarlo and Lopez had finished their little pow-wow and caught up with them. "Mok Yee-Chun?" Dicarlo said, reading her little notebook.

"No," James said with a frown, "That's my mom."

⌘

"So, let me get this straight," Dicarlo said. James was fully clothed now in jeans with a polo shirt covering his thin chest, sitting on the couch in front of them. He was nonplussed and extremely ticked off to see Josie again. His expression said he probably could have lived the rest of his life happily without ever seeing her face-to-face again, limiting himself to calling her names in pixels and text. "Your family owns the building where Ivan Sorokin was renting an apartment."

"Yeah. I guess. I mean, my mom does. I never went over there. She hired someone to do all the maintenance and cleaning, the upkeep of the place. You guys had access to the property records. It was all public knowledge." Such that it was, Josie snorted inwardly. His mother's legal Chinese name, Mok Yee-Chun, wasn't as easy to equate with Cynthia Yu. Although, there was probably some esoteric link in the names' roots. They both could have meant Moon-something-or-other. Josie herself had a crazy Thai middle name, a gift from her mother that no other living human on earth, other than the Social Security Administration, knew. If anyone else knew it, Josie would have to commit bodily harm to protect her secret.

James was running a hand through his dark hair again, a gesture that Josie had seen before when he was upset or worried—the same gesture as when they'd first been unable to reach Ivan. Lopez and Dicarlo had now been questioning James in the sitting room of his parents' condo for a good twenty minutes, repeating the same things, hoping for different answers. Josie clenched her jaw.

Wasn't that a sign of insanity, repeating the same actions and expecting a different outcome? Like beating her head against the wall. Josie wasn't a major fidgeter, but she was having trouble refraining from jiggling her leg as she sat there in a spotless, beige, microfiber upholstered chair. They droned on and on, interrogating him right in his mother's living room. What did he know about the apartment? Had he ever done any repairs there? When was the last time he was there? Did he know how often Ivan stayed there? They backtracked and repeated questions until even Josie's head began to swirl. James could have stopped answering at any time, Josie thought, but he didn't seem to know it. He could have asked for a lawyer. Instead, he was being the James that Josie knew from before, the same entitled, weaselly guy, the nonconfrontationalist, the avoider. His face stayed placid, unreadable, taking a page from his silent father's book.

Lopez was pacing back and forth behind James, nudging the magazines and trinkets on the side tables with his finger. He stopped, "Oh yeah? You've never been to Ivan's apartment? So, we'd never find your fingerprints or hair or DNA over there?"

James backpedaled, after about the fifth time through the same pattern of questions. This was the first time they had mentioned DNA and it seemed to rattle him just a little. "Well, I mean. My mom's owned that place since I was a kid. I could have been over there when I was younger. Once or twice or something. Maybe now and then. I mean, not regularly."

Dicarlo said, "But you've never been inside Ivan's apartment itself? Never gone over to see him or had dinner or went over there to talk to him about work?"

They were back to tag-teaming him, yet neither was playing the role of the so-called good cop. They were trying to bully the truth out of him. No finesse. No artistry. Just pelting him with questions, hoping he didn't have the fortitude to withstand them. He would clamp down and give them nothing, she knew. He could be withdrawn—he would use it as his defense if need be. She watched him, knowing she was right. Personally, she was running out of patience with the irritating cheater.

"Why is *she* here?" James said, suddenly on the attack, pointing to Josie. She felt her eyes narrowing. The one time James got up in someone's face and he attacked her, as if she were the weakest link in the room? Their online squabble was about to leap from the world of pixels and message boards right into the real world. She would kick him in the shin if he thought he could intimidate her that easily.

Lopez ignored him. "Answer the question. Have you ever been inside Ivan's apartment?"

"I don't know," James said, his voice rising. "I guess so. Maybe."

Josie squinted at him. They were getting nowhere. Lopez was too lackadaisical. Dicarlo was too tightly wound. They were wasting time, playing their silly game, questioning and never approaching the real issues head-on. She wanted answers. And she wanted them now.

She met his eyes. "What about your girlfriend Sasha? Has she ever been inside her father's apartment?"

James stared at her open-mouthed. "Shit," he said. He pushed a couple of breaths noisily out through his nose and ran his hand through his hair again. Then he took a deep breath and addressed the detectives. "I don't know what you're talking about. I want a lawyer."

From over James's shoulder, Lopez glared at Josie, clenching his jaw, no hint of the easygoing flirt anymore.

Uh-oh.

She had screwed up. Badly. She'd been allowed to tag along with them this whole time, but she'd been treading on shaky ground. She'd fooled herself into thinking she knew a thing or two about investigations, about reading people and their ulterior motives. By opening her mouth, she had tripped the "I want a lawyer" IED and had abruptly ended the interview. What a joke. She was an amateur. A meddler. A nosy girl. She had gotten in the way of their jobs.

"You," Lopez said pointing at her. "In the hall. Now."

CHAPTER 38

Josie had been dismissed.

After a fierce, but succinct chewing out.

Lopez was irritated with her. Dicarlo wasn't speaking to her, and Josie had walked back to her ridiculous rental car and driven off, hands shaking.

"We're not playing around here," Lopez had angrily hissed at her in the hallway outside while Dicarlo had stayed with James. Technically, because he'd requested a lawyer, she couldn't continue questioning him. He wasn't under arrest. He hadn't been read his rights. They didn't have anything to pick him up on—no evidence to take him in as a person of interest, so to speak. "You've been a great help for us so far, so I'm not discounting that. But you need to let us do our jobs. We know what we're doing. I've cut you some leeway because of Greta Williams—and I know it sometimes looks like I'm not serious because I'm flirting or joking around. This is not a game."

Josie had nodded, humiliated and angrier with herself than anyone else could ever be. She muttered an apology, and headed for the stairs as fast as she could. She'd beat a hasty retreat from the building, fleeing from the site of her egregious error, her massive mistake.

She walked back down the street, back a few blocks to where she'd parked. They hadn't been gone that long, but she found a ticket fluttering in the breeze on the windshield of her rental car.

Just great. Pile it on, why don't you, she thought, glancing skyward.

Leaning against the side of her car, she pulled her cell phone out of the back pocket of her jeans and dialed Greta Williams to see what the best course of action was now that she was, for all intents and purposes, kicked off the case. *Utterly demoralizing.* She hadn't been able to keep her mouth shut. She'd interfered with the investigation. She'd thought she was better than the professionals whose jobs it was to find Ivan's killer.

When Greta answered the phone, she was as unruffled and unwavering as always. "I'm sure it's a temporary situation that you can repair," she told Josie. Easy words to say—Josie didn't agree with them, but Greta didn't seem to want to hear any more about it. If Josie had been hoping for reassurance, she was barking up the wrong tree.

She had an open-ended return ticket that she had a good mind to use. One click on her laptop and she could be on her way back to Boston. She could put the embarrassment and failure of this trip behind her. She could move on. Work on her other issues..."Speaking of repairs," she said, clearing her throat, "I have an issue that I need some advice about. What do you know about getting a divorce quickly?"

Greta's silence was heavy with condemnation. Her sigh was even more telling. "Am I to assume that your inquiry is not, in fact, for a hypothetical friend?"

"Correct," Josie said, her face heating up. She realized with a sinking feeling that this conversation was going to be even worse than she imagined it.

"Additionally, am I to assume that there was some kind of intoxication involved?"

Josie had never, ever spoken about her drinking habits to Greta. In fact, they'd never discussed anything personal about Josie's lifestyle or her friends. Still, she felt ashamed for the second time that afternoon. "It was a long time ago," she said, attempting to keep the childish tone out of her voice. Still, she suspected she sounded whiny.

"We all—every one of us—have to accept the consequences of our actions," Greta said with finality. Josie knew that Greta, of all people, lived by that tenet, probably more so than any other person she'd ever met. Accepting the consequences of her actions...that was the sum total of Greta's advice. Great. In theory.

"Right," Josie said. She had her phone tucked against her cheek, held there by her shoulder. She couldn't stop herself from crossing her arms over her chest and trying to huddle into a ball as she leaned against

DIM SUM, DEAD SOME

her car in the middle of Chinatown. Mental forehead slap. *Did I think she was going to offer some advice for a quick and easy solution to this mess?*

"As for staying in California," Greta said, clearly having finished speaking about Josie's marital status, "it's up to you to decide what to do next." She then said goodbye and ended the call. Greta was not the epitome of a nurturing mother figure. *Understatement of the century.*

Josie pinched the bridge of her nose.

Fat lot of help that was.

⌘

Maybe Josie was a masochist, but after that, she called Drew. In truth, she was hoping for some comfort. She missed the sound of his voice. She was hoping that maybe their last conversation was as much a blur to him as it had been for her. She was feeling useless, extraneous. Unskilled. Bumbling. Wallowing in self-pity. All of the above. She wanted some reassurance that maybe she still had people—or a single person—who cared for her, who valued her.

Drew was still at work, between patients, so it was automatically going to be a shorter chat than she thought it would be, but she had wanted to hear a familiar voice. Instead, she got a harried and harassed-sounding Drew, who was also breathless from running to the hospital cafeteria.

"I have five minutes to grab a coffee," he said. "I can't really talk right now, but I didn't want to send you straight to voicemail." That was a good thing, right? A heavy door slammed in the background, and then she could hear his footsteps pounding down the metal stairs at the hospital.

"I only wanted to—" she started to say, but the connection must not have been that good because he talked over her words.

"I have to tell you, Josie," he said sounding somber and maybe like he had his jaw clenched, "I thought you were joking the other night when you said you were married. I thought you were asleep or being silly. Pranking me. But you weren't. How could you really be married? I mean, what kind of person gets married and doesn't tell her best friend? And, by 'best friend,' I'm referring to myself. Because we were best friends at the time you were seeing him, weren't we?"

Josie cringed. "Yes," she said. Even to her ears, her voice sounded thin and wavering. Drew sounded like he'd been stewing about this, mulling it over nonstop since their last conversation. *This was bad. Really bad.*

"Never mind the fact that you're married, for fuck's sake." She flinched and wrapped her arms around herself as she leaned against her rental car again. Because he rarely swore. Maybe only once a year, and then he probably went to confession afterward. She probably should start thinking about going with him. Unless they didn't let her kind in. What was her kind? The horrible no-good kind.

"I—" She started to say she was sorry, that she was trying to figure out a way to take care of it, and that she had never meant to hurt him. That the sham marriage didn't mean anything to her. That Joe Armstrong didn't mean anything to her and never had.

"You've made a mockery out of a sacred institution, out of something that I hold dear. What is supposed to be important—maybe the most important vow you can take in your lifetime—and you made it into a quickie holiday weekend joke." He was definitely gritting his teeth. She could practically hear the enamel grinding off as he spoke.

She was going to say so many more things to him. She wanted to, but all she could say was, "I'm sorry."

"I can't even talk to you right now. For one thing, I don't have the time to say all the things I want to say to you. And I want to think about what I'm going to say more before I say it. But, believe me, I have things to say. I want you to think about this, though. If marriage means so little to you, when you finally find the right person who loves you, cares about you, *gets you,* how is that person going to believe anything you say if this is how you behave when you're just screwing around?" His implied, but unspoken meaning was that *he wasn't that person.* He huffed out a breath. "I can't talk about this right now."

He hung up without saying goodbye.

CHAPTER 39

Josie drove south, the blood rushing in her head. She drove until the roaring in her ears settled into a dull, throbbing headache. She didn't have a destination. She didn't have a stopping point. She just drove, gas pedal pushed to the floor. As if she were falling down, being pulled by gravity away from the mess behind her, she followed the map south on Highway 101. At Gilroy, where the fields were green and where the annual Garlic Festival would be held in the summer, she took a left and headed east, away from the coast, away from the craziness, the ups and downs of the Bay Area and of Silicon Valley. The landscape opened up into sloping hills covered with dry, drought-yellowed grass, cut back, either by nibbling animals or by farmers trying to keep the fire hazard down. She drove a while longer on a small, two-lane road that curved, and pulled onto a side road only when her empty gas tank and her empty stomach demanded that she stop.

Her chest, which was aching, proved that yes, she may have had a heart after all.

Out on the Pacheco Pass Highway, just off to the side of it, Josie parked at an open-air fruit stand surrounded by a cluster of shops, a full-service gas station, a restaurant, and, of all things, a kiddie train ride. She got out of her car to stretch her legs and reassess...things.

The fruit stand was hopping with business, crowded with people. Towers of melons, citrus, apricots, and berries caught her eye—jewel tones of orange, green, and red. As she approached, she smelled warm nectarines. Strand after strand of papery white garlic dangled overhead. Golden-green pineapples sprouted from the tops of each pyramid display, like tropical fountains.

A sign pleaded with customers not to sample the fruit, but next to it

259

stood a giant of a man in an apron with a paring knife and fruit juices on his thick brown fingers.

"Hey," he said to her, by way of a greeting.

When she walked by, staring at the mounds of fresh fruit, he popped a slice of apricot into her mouth. The flavor exploded, sweetness drenching her tongue, threatening to make her eyes tear up. She may have whimpered.

"Thanks," she said, turning back after she swallowed.

"You look like you're having a tough day."

She made a rueful face at the reminder of her transparent face. She thought about the myriad things that were weighing her down and went for the most understandable. "Had a fight with my boyfriend."

"Ah," the fruit man said. "Age-old story. Boy problems." He paused to hand a slice of apricot to a passing man, who took it with a wide smile. Josie watched the customer man walk away, then freeze in his tracks after two steps as the apricot hit his taste buds. He swiveled on his feet, came back to the display, and began loading apricots into his hand basket.

"It sells itself, doesn't it?" Josie said.

The fruit man just smiled as if he were her Apricot Fairy Godfather. He gestured, gently mocking, toward the parking lot. "Nice car."

Josie did a double-take from her green cube-shaped rental to the man and back. Then she saw from his twinkling eyes that he was laughing inside, obviously skilled at deadpanning. The car was ridiculous, and she knew it.

"It's a rental," Josie said in her defense. He merely raised his eyebrow. "Well, what do you drive?" she asked him.

He shrugged a shoulder. "Most days, a farm truck, but that's my ride over there." He cocked his chin toward the lot, and Josie followed the invisible line of his gesture to an insanely suped-up turquoise blue Chevy Impala, white wall tires glistening in the sunlight. It had the double row of front lights, a white cloth top, and shine to the body that would have brought a tear to her Uncle Jack's eye. Her uncle was a

Tucsonan who loved his cars, low-riders to Model-Ts and everything in between. She'd spent many afternoons in his garage hanging out with her cousin Libby, listening to them talk parts, ratchets and carburetors. Not that all of it stuck with Josie, but definitely an appreciation for, a recognition of the automotive passion.

"It's got a bubbly front, but not too bubbly, so what, a late 1950-something?" Josie guessed.

"1958. You got it," the fruit man smiled. "You know your cars, lady."

"Sometimes I make a lucky guess," she said, and he smiled at that. He fed her another slice of apricot as a reward. She took a few minutes to savor it while he talked with other customers. Sometimes she did luck out in the guessing department, but not lately. Her judgment was off, as if it were stirred up by being on shaky ground. What was it about the Bay Area that had her so off-kilter? She couldn't take a full breath. The land was trying to shake her off like a dog irritated by a tick.

Josie had never been one to believe in auras, spirits, and communing with nature. She'd spent her formative years in Tucson, so of course, she'd been to Sedona, where tourists gather to bang their drums and sing their chants. For her, Sedona meant sliding down the algae-slicked rocks into the waterfalls or falling on her butt. Of course, she'd been a kid at the time. Too dumb to feel anything outside of herself. Too self-absorbed to think about the bigger picture.

This trip to San Francisco...it was messing with her head. She couldn't think, didn't trust herself anymore, and didn't know what to do about it. She certainly wasn't doing well thinking about Ivan and trying to figure out what had happened to him. She hadn't been able to settle her mind until coming all the way out here to the south, to the farmland, where it was less populated, less confusing, and less...well, everything.

While she pondered this, she took up a basket and collected a half-dozen apricots. She added a pint of strawberries that nearly rivaled the apricots in their size. She collected a couple of nectarines because their tangy scent was calling to her. She made her way over to the fruit man.

"You made some good choices there," he said. "Sorry I don't have any romantic advice for you. I guess you have to go with your gut on that one, too."

She smiled. "No advice at all? Are you sure?"

"Well, any advice I give you would have to come with a surgeon general's warning," he said. "I've been married four times, so I'm definitely not the one to ask."

She gaped at him for a second, then burst out laughing, feeling marginally better. He gave her a parting wave when she went to pay at the register. Because he was right. In the end, she just needed to figure it out for herself. Who else would do it for her?

⌘

So Josie sat on a bench in the sun behind the fruit stand, eating a strawberry that she'd cleaned by wiping it on her shirt. She'd already filled up her car with gas and was thinking about her next approach — waiting for mental inspiration that would refuel her emotionally. Away from the city, her mind had cleared a bit, due in part to both the physical and metaphorical distance. She was best like this, at nearly rock bottom with things crumbling apart around her — but she needed her roots, her space, somewhere quiet with an open sky where she could think.

She knew she had all the pieces, all the components of Ivan's murder. She needed to put it together. She had all the dots and just needed to connect them in the right order.

If she drew a mental map, the dots fell in Santa Cruz, down south where Olga resided alone in her seashell bungalow; farther north in San Jose was Sasha's overpriced house; a sequin dot marked the Pony Pagoda; more northward into the city was James's ratty apartment; then, finally to Chinatown. The arrow pointed true north to Ivan's Chinatown apartment.

Everything focused around that apartment. It was the vortex, the crux. James said he hadn't spent much time there. Olga had denied knowing where it was. Sasha, also, supposedly knew about it — her boots had turned up there, clearly planted after the fact — and the women at the

Pony Pagoda, even, had mentioned it. It was the alpha and omega of this incident, the beginning of Ivan's journey as an entrepreneur, the end of his life.

Josie finished her strawberry. She wiped the juice off her fingers onto the thigh of her jeans. The rest of the fruit, she put on the seat of her car next to her. She climbed into her Kia and headed back into the fray, north once again.

CHAPTER 40

A few hours later, Josie stood on the street, once again outside the apartment in which Ivan had lost his life. On a Thursday night, getting close to 6:00 p.m., the traffic was lessening as people downshifted from work into dinner mode. Some, she could tell, were ready to celebrate pre-Friday with a vengeance—they had their drink-seeking faces on. *Does my face look that way?* If she got past this thing with Drew, maybe she would make sure she never had a thirsty look again.

She rubbed her chin and looked up at the building again. What would Ivan have been doing that day? Evidence in the kitchen of his grubby apartment had shown a take-out carton of rice and beef, some kind of stir fry with vegetables. Josie stood outside his apartment, picturing him walking up to its dusty, nondescript street-level door. He would have been wearing one of his favored cotton, plaid short-sleeved shirts, tucked into his pants over his rotund belly. His fair-skinned, rosy-cheeked face would have been serious, though ready to smile at anyone who met eyes with him, his white-blond hair falling across his forehead. His cheeks would have had the typical pink flush that was in every one of his photos. He would have been carrying his take-out food box in his hand—not a plastic bag because the city had recently outlawed them.

He'd pushed through the grimy front door, as Josie now did. Perhaps he'd arrived later in the evening, when it was full dark—Josie had the benefit of the last bit of sunlight. She stepped into the tiny entryway and was immediately assaulted by smells of cooking. Garlic, curry, onions, and frying oil. The clang of cooking utensils rang out as they hit metal pots and pans throughout the building. Dinner was being prepared in many of the apartments in the building. Maybe Ivan had heard the same sounds and smelled the same aromas while he climbed the stairs, as Josie did now. She glanced at the notices for local bands, performances, and things for sale posted in the stairwell as she ascended the steps. Would Ivan have been out of breath climbing these? Or was he hearty and heavy? James had said his partner was in poor shape. Ivan would have been sweating, then.

Why hadn't he picked a more upscale place to rent? Simple, Josie realized. Ivan had taken the place because James's mother owned it—he had a connection. And possibly Ivan had been thrifty. The man had tens of millions of dollars, after all, but hadn't spent it for whatever reason. He'd grown up poor and was in the habit of saving his money, believing that it was all ephemeral, that he would wake up one day and it would all be gone—not realizing, that one day, he would be gone and his wealth would remain.

Josie pushed open the door to the floor where Ivan's apartment was. Along with the sounds and smells of urban dinnertime in close quarters, she heard the voices of families—a baby crying, laughter, and a loud argument between two women. The doors to the apartments she passed were closed, but the walls were thin. The hallway light over the door to apartment forty-two was blinking. The door to Ivan's apartment, with its *double death* tarnished number forty-four, was open. Double death? Maybe there'd been another death in the apartment before Ivan's. The chances were good—the building was quite old.

Josie stopped in the hallway and stared into the apartment. Maybe James's mother had finally arrived with her cleaners to take care of the untimely mess her tenant had left behind. She saw two women, and neither of them were Cynthia Yu.

Standing just an arm's length apart in the middle of Ivan's sitting room, Olga Sorokin and Sasha Peters faced off. Olga was in her usual ocean-patterned clothes, but Sasha was in a simple black t-shirt and blue jeans, looking like a normal girl except for the dyed jet-black hair and the tattoo sleeves that covered her to her wrists.

Olga was yelling at Sasha with a face drawn tight with anger. "Why did you have to do it? You already stole him from me. Why did you have to kill him, too?"

Sasha bit back with her own venomous words, "If he hadn't been afraid of you, he would have been able to openly acknowledge me. Instead, I have to be the illegal one. I have to use a fake name, a fake passport, and get paid with cash everywhere I work."

Olga stuck a large, white finger in Sasha's face, "That's what you get for trying to steal him from me. He was mine, not yours. I stuck with him through all the hard years when we didn't have enough money, when no one in America would hire us even though we had university degrees. We barely had enough money to pay rent and buy noodle soup to eat. It was as bad as Russia."

"So, why didn't you give up and go back?" Sasha yelled, a snarl on her lips. She stepped forward and jutted her chin out at the big woman, getting right up into the larger woman's face, no fear in play.

"I don't give up," Olga yelled, her fury making her accent thicker. She tucked her red-painted nails into a sloppy fist and shook it at Sasha. "I worked hard for everything that I have. Ivan and I worked together to make it here. This is my dream, and you ruined it."

"Stop," Josie shouted. She stepped toward them, holding her hands up, trying to keep them apart, but neither woman paid any attention to her. As Josie reached them, Olga lunged at Sasha.

Josie was knocked back. She landed on her butt with an awkward bounce on the dirty carpet. For a woman with such an intimidating bearing, Olga fought like a wussy. She grabbed Sasha's pitch black hair and yanked hard, dragging the younger woman down. Sasha bent at the waist and shrieked, lashing out at Olga with her own dark painted fingernails. They grappled for a minute, slapping and clawing, while Josie regained her footing.

"Stop it," Josie shouted again. She hesitated, then went back in, arms spread in an attempt to separate the two, but Olga had an unbreakable grip on Sasha's hair. The younger woman went down on her knees, but not before she connected with a good hard slap on Olga's face.

Olga screamed with rage and tried to punch the back of Sasha's head, but her fist was too loose. The blow was weak and glanced off the back of Sasha's silky head, the stray ends of her dark hair fanning out around her shoulders. From her vantage point on the floor, Sasha grabbed one of Olga's knees and pulled the big woman off balance. Olga crashed down, and the two of them wrestled on the grimy carpet.

Josie stood, her hands on her hips now, as she shook her head. These two women were angry and willing to fight to the death, but they would die of exhaustion before either of them got in a decent punch. She put two fingers into her mouth, silently thanking her cousin Libby for teaching her the skill, and whistled shrilly enough to stun the squabbling women. And probably half the dogs in the neighborhood. She waded into the brawl and, this time, successfully yanked the two women apart, using the backs of their shirts. Glaring, she pointed to opposite sides of the room until they separated.

CHAPTER 41

"You ruined everything," Olga shouted across the room at Sasha from her spot on the floor against the wall. Tears began to streak down the big woman's cheeks. "You ruined everything," she said again and buried her face in her hands. Her large shoulders shook under her flowered blouse.

Sasha looked confused, and then unrepentant. "I ruined nothing," she said. "*You* killed him. You murdered my papa."

Olga's head shot up, and Josie watched the woman puzzle out Sasha's words. Olga's mouth fell open, but gradually, as understanding dawned, a new kind of anger took over her face. If Josie had been expecting some kind of miracle 9th inning reconciliation, she would have been sorely disappointed.

"He *did cheat on me* after all," Olga cried. Josie frowned in confusion, watching this Russian drama unfold. She was more befuddled than when she'd been assigned to read Tolstoy in college.

Sasha stared at Olga from where she was sprawled on the floor. She pushed back the black mess of her hair from her face and gestured her confusion with wide open colorful arms. "You stupid woman, I told you I'm his daughter, not his lover. He couldn't bring me into the United States the way he wanted to because he was afraid he would anger you. I have a fake passport, a fake identity."

Olga brushed her off with a shake of her head, a dismissive wave of her own hand. "I don't mean with you. He cheated on me with your mother. I remember her. She was that tramp at university. I'm not blind. You look exactly like her, other than your witch hair. I knew he was seeing her behind my back. And here you are, proof of their affair. I hate you. You're the evidence. Right in front of me."

Sasha growled and jumped to her feet. "How dare you insult my mother. She was twice the woman that you are. She raised me by herself with no help from anyone."

Olga, too, rose to her feet, which made Josie take a step back. Whatever had happened between the two women up until now was nothing compare to what was about to erupt. "And see how good you turned out," Olga taunted, pushing her sleeves up along with her gold bangles, which slid down again. "You're a stripper. With no future. You look like a whore with those tattoos. What kind of job can you get looking that way?"

"I'm a college-educated math instructor." Sasha howled and lunged at Olga, this time getting in the first strike.

⌘

In the back of her mind, Josie registered more footsteps coming down the hall toward them. A heavy pounding of shoes on the hallway floor grew closer and closer. Then James was behind her, shoving past her. She was once again knocked off her feet, landing on her hands and knees. The bruises were racking up. He rushed over to the women, and to his credit, held Sasha back instead of pinning down Olga for his girl to hit her harder. If faced with the same options, Josie might not have made the same choice.

With his arms tightly around Sasha, restraining her from behind, James glared at Josie as if it were her fault the women were going at each other like cats in a sack.

"What?" she said, gaping at him. "I didn't do anything." She stood and brushed the grit off her pants, patting down her pockets to make sure she hadn't dropped her phone. She could hear distant sirens—one of the neighbors had probably heard the women screaming and clawing at each other and had called the police. At least, Josie hoped so, because these women were too much for her to handle. The rapidly forming soreness on her bottom was proof of that.

James was still glaring at her. "So who told Olga how to find this place?"

"I didn't—" she started to say, but then realized that *she had* mentioned the location to Olga when trying to get some kind of reaction out of her. Josie had been attempting to see if Ivan's widow had recognized the address, but instead, Josie had given her directions. *Oops.*

"I would have found it anyway," Olga said with a smirk. She crossed her arms over her broad chest and looked at James with Eastern Block disdain. "I'm not stupid. I'm in Quality Assurance."

"Why are you even here?" Sasha snapped at Olga, massaging her head where Olga had been ripping her hair. Her face had angry red blotches. "If you're looking for money, there's nothing here."

They all stared at her.

"What money?" Josie said. *She* knew there was money—money all over the place, in fact—in off-shore accounts, investments, and other places Dicarlo had mentioned. But did *they* know there was money? Who exactly knew what?

"Shhhh. Don't say anything, sweetheart," James told Sasha. Again with the *sweetheart* endearment. It was enough to make Josie grind her teeth.

Olga repeated, "What money?" She narrowed her eyes, looking as if she were considering taking another swipe at her tattooed nemesis.

Sasha blustered poorly, flushing all the way down to her collarbone tattoos, "I don't know. Why are you so interested? There's no money that I know about, but if there was any money, it wouldn't be here."

Olga took a step toward the younger woman. "What. Money," she said again, her voice low and vibrating with menace, making even Josie shiver.

"Look," James said, obviously trying to diffuse the situation, "Ivan had a bit of money. He and I both did. We earned it from gambling. It was seed money that we were going to invest, but it didn't work out. We ended up having to get some investors for Applied Apps." He cast a glance at Sasha, and ran his hands up and down her arms, protectively, comfortingly.

Yuck, Josie thought. Now it was her turn to squint and she chose to aim her venomous glare at her best friend's ex.

She thought about what James was saying. Gambling explained their trips to Las Vegas, but if that was the extent of their plans to become millionaires, James had failed where Ivan had succeeded. Ivan had been sitting on millions of dollars while James had been living in a crappy apartment, saving up for a more expensive, equally crappy house.

"The money was for me, not you," Sasha suddenly blurted out, taunting Olga. "You thought you'd get your hands on it, but everything he did was for me because he loved me. He was my papa. He loved me, and I loved him. And you killed him." Sasha pulled free of James's grasp and lunged at Olga, clearly intending to attack her again.

Josie had meant to stay out of it this time. James was there—he was a black belt in karate, for Pete's sake. Surely he could control his rampaging girlfriend, the avenging Black Dahlia. As far as Josie was concerned, if the two women were hell-bent on slapping each other silly, he could break them apart. Josie was keeping out of it this time.

A hoarse scream came from behind Josie. She found herself being shoved from behind and pushed directly into the fray.

This was getting old.

CHAPTER 42

Josie felt a jab to her back followed by a strange cold sting in the muscle right over her right shoulder. Whoever had shoved her this time had scraped her, too. *Son of a...* Her t-shirt had snagged on something and she felt it rip in the back—another shirt ruined. This time, it was a Muse shirt, from their Absolution Tour. Benjy had seen the band perform at the 2004 Glastonbury Festival. She glowered down at the front of it because she couldn't twist her neck far enough to see the damage in the back. Josie squinted at the latest person to push her way in. Josie thought it might be one of the neighbors, alerted by the duet of shouting Russian harpies, but then Sasha was punched in the midsection. Olga clamped her hands on the new woman's arms, pinning them to her sides, and Josie saw that it was James's mother, Mrs. Yu.

"*Ma!*" James yelled, his face contorted with shock and horror. He supported Sasha, who was doubled over, clutching her stomach where she had been punched. James's mother, her face screwed up with anger, was yelling and swatting her hands at Sasha.

Mrs. Yu turned on her son, "You are always in this apartment with that girl. You are wasting your life. You should be running your own company by now. Your father and I work hard at the restaurant. We work hard every day so you could go to college. You got a good job. You and Ivan were following your dreams, making a good company that would make you rich. Then you get involved with this girl." She waved her fist at Sasha. "You're too good for her. She will drag you down with her bad ideas. She's horrible for you."

"Ma, what are you talking about?" James shouted. He let go of Sasha, who was still clutching her punched stomach, her dyed black hair standing out, sharply contrasting with the sick look on her pale face.

"You brought that white girl to the restaurant to fool us. You came with this one," his mother waved vaguely at Josie, "to try to fool us more. You think I am stupid? I know the truth. I know you are wasting your life with this one, this *chow fa hai.*" Josie didn't know what that meant, but she could make an educated guess it wasn't polite.

James's face turned hard. "*Ma.* Don't insult Sasha." While Josie was pleased to see him stand up to his mother, for once, she wasn't sure this was the best time for him to have suddenly developed a backbone. Two weeks ago would have been better—before he'd agreed for Susan to fly out and stay with him in his apartment. Josie, feeling oddly floaty and detached from all the shouting, wondered how Sasha felt about Star Wars décor.

"I don't care if she's insulted, if her feelings are hurt," Mrs. Yu proclaimed, shaking her fist at him. "I came here to stop her from ruining your life. I know you meet with her in this apartment all the time. You come here to see her late at night when I think you're at your apartment working on your company. I know you're sleeping with her in this apartment. That's why I came over here. I followed you and watched you come to meet her."

That explained today's parade, Josie thought, trying to massage the ache out of her shoulder. The discomfort had evolved from a twinge to a throbbing pain. Man, she'd really pulled something bad that last time she'd been shoved. Mrs. Yu had jabbed Josie hard, right in the shoulder blade, kind of where a wing would sprout if she were an angel, on her way into the room—it hurt like heck.

Mrs. Yu's accent was coming out thicker as she continued to harangue her son, "I follow you here all the time." She waved her angry fist in his face. Josie refocused on the woman's bandaged hand. "I watch you sneak in here. I come here to save you. I *save you* while she's sleeping in here waiting for you." She devolved into a barrage of Cantonese.

⌘

"What?" James looked at his mother, aghast. At about the same time, Sasha groaned and sank to her knees. In the dim, flickering florescent light of Ivan's sitting room, Josie became aware of the dark stain spreading from Sasha's clenched fist in the center of her abdomen. "Oh shit," James said, as he saw it, too. "You stabbed her, Ma? You stabbed Sasha?"

"I meant to get her before, too," Mrs. Yu said, sounding totally rational instead of batshit crazy. "But it was your friend instead. I didn't mean to stab Ivan—he was a nice man. He was very successful. He help you. It was supposed to be her, but I didn't know it was him until it was too late." She sounded weirdly apologetic though she was sweating, her dark curls sticking to her reddened face, her wire-rimmed glasses askew.

Josie stared at Mrs. Yu's bandaged hand, which was partly hidden in her sleeve. When she turned, Josie saw the thin knife that she held low and away from her body. Her precision chef's knife, so useful for filleting the meat from animal bones, was hidden by the dim light and the dark fluid covering it. It may as well have been invisible. Other than the fact that it was dripping.

Feeling detached and oddly not as surprised by the latest outburst as she should have been, Josie pondered the fact that the four of them had just witnessed Mrs. Yu's confessing to murdering Ivan. She had just admitted to stabbing him, having confused him for Sasha because it was dark. Mrs. Yu had meant to kill Sasha. Ivan had been in the wrong place at the wrong time.

So weird. Why am I not more shocked?

Josie pondered that, feeling light-headed.

Aha. I'm in shock. This whole thing is shocking. I was in a brawl. A cat fight. Would it be wrong to laugh?

More footsteps pounded down the hallway. Josie heard the crackle of a police two-way radio, the jangle of metal—keys or cuffs—and she didn't know what else. Authoritative voices told them to line up in the hallway. One-by-one, they were brought out of the apartment and pushed roughly against the grimy painted wall. Josie noticed that she'd be cuffed with Zip-ties, which was a new experience for her. She was patted down, too, which wasn't all that unpleasant. Kind of reassuring in an odd way, especially since she hadn't done anything wrong. This time.

Mrs. Yu's knife was held gingerly between two gloved fingers and put into a bag. Josie looked around for Mrs. Yu herself, but didn't see her—maybe they'd already cuffed her and taken her away first, since she was the bad guy. Capital B. Capital G.

An ambulance arrived for Sasha. There was more shouting from the police officers, something about keeping the pressure on the wound to her stomach. James was there, looking grim and upset, a bit pasty around the eyes.

When a cop started asking Josie for her I.D., he freaked out about how her shirt was ripped in the back.

"Are you a Muse fan, too?" she asked him, wondering why she wanted to pass out. He was really young, good-looking, with a head shaved so closely the light shined off his scalp. He was wearing latex gloves—all the cops were doing that for the pat-downs.

"We need someone to look at this," he yelled at one of the other cops, waving him over just as Josie started to tilt over to the side. The blinking overhead lights were confusing her about which way was straight. She felt like she was on a ship in the ocean. Maybe it was another earthquake, in which case she *did not* want to be inside of this old, crumbly building. She did not want to die in a heap of rubble in San Francisco Chinatown.

"I need to go outside," she said. She needed to see the sky. If they were all going to be buried under bricks, she wanted to see the stars one last time. She needed the open, endless ether above her.

"We'll get you out," he said, with a reassuring pat on her arm. "We need to get someone to look at this."

"It's my favorite shirt," she moaned. It was her favorite only because the Ramones shirt was trashed. Then, her eyes rolled back as she felt herself go down. And it was blissful.

PART 5: THE PLATE

In dining, you're allowed to act on your lust. You have license to be superficial, to judge a dish by its looks. I've said it before, but I'll tell you again, chefs: food is your message, but plating is your delivery. Color, texture, layers, levels, groups of odd numbers. Without that expansive white plate, the microscopic servings and multilayered slivers of color, the towers of plantain chips, turnip shavings, and endive, how would we ever know that our food was art?

Presentation above all else drove the fusion movement of the 1980s. Like high-waisted mom jeans and Aqua Net hairspray, it was all about looks. Are you smiling, making eye contact? Do you know exactly what you want to say before you begin? Presentation is *everything*. Why else do we drool when we look at frosted cakes in bakery windows even if there's no cake underneath, only cardboard and foam... oh, is that just me?

Josie Tucker, *Will Blog for Food*

CHAPTER 43

"Why do I always wake up in a hospital?" Josie mumbled, anger and frustration her overriding emotions. She hadn't opened her eyes yet, but she recognized the incessant beeping—which was good. Beeping meant she was alive. The slide of metal rings on the curtain rod meant she wasn't alone.

As she lay there weighing the pros and cons of opening her eyes, she heard Greta Williams's voice say to her, "I understand now, when you say you're interested in pursuing a matter, it means that you will insert yourself into the situation no matter the cost to your person."

Josie cracked open her eyes. A nurse had pushed aside the privacy curtain. Greta sat in the salmon-colored, vinyl recliner next to the bed. Josie tried to sit up, but pain zinged through her shoulder. She tried to twist her head to see behind her, but the skin pulled too tightly.

"Cut that out," the nurse said, placing a hand squarely in the center of Josie's chest and pressing her back into the pillows.

"That hurts," Josie said.

"Lie still and it won't." The nurse gave her the Nell Carter bug-eyed expression that Josie so often directed at her dog at home. She knew what it meant—a big ol' *duh*.

"I got stabbed," Josie said plaintively. It came out a question—she had figured it out by now, but still, a quick confirmation would be helpful.

"You sure did," the nurse said. "By that same crazy lady that killed the sleeping man in Chinatown that was all over the news. It was in the papers. You're famous now. Congratulations." She crossed her arms over her ample chest, and waited until Josie acknowledged her sarcasm. The nurse pursed her lips as if it were Josie's fault. *Which actually, it kind of was.*

Josie glanced out the window, which was letting in a pale kind of gray light. She frowned again at Greta, whose appearance didn't seem to be wavering at the edges...so, she was probably real. "How long have I been here?"

"Overnight," the nurse said, checking Josie's beeping machine, pressing a button to reset it. The blood pressure cuff on her arm inflated, squeezing her biceps like frosting was about to pipe out from her fingertips. "If Officer Awesome wouldn't have tied your hands behind your back, you might have been able to catch yourself before you passed out."

"Huh?" Josie said. Greta looked up from her lap where she was...knitting? What kind of alternate reality was this?

The nurse explained slowly and in plain English, "You got stabbed in the back. Then you passed out and hit your head on a wall. The doctor kept you here overnight because you had a concussion."

"Huh," Josie said again, this time in acceptance.

"Do you need to *yoorinate*?" the nurse said. Josie frowned at her, trying to figure out what she said. The nurse rephrased, "Do you need to tinkle in the toilet?"

"Uh. Yeah. No. I guess not yet," Josie said, feeling detached from her body. Other than her shoulder, which hurt. "If I have a concussion, how come my head doesn't hurt?"

The nurse grinned. "Those are the painkillers, lady. You're lucky you're in the hospital. We take good care of you here. I'll be back in a while to check on you. We'll probably take your IV out now that you're awake. Later, the doctor will come in to tell you all about your wound." The nurse gave her a gentle squeeze on the arm, which Josie appreciated. She'd gone four days now without any real human contact other than an apricot stuffed into her mouth and a knife in her back. The nurse continued, "For now, you're only job is to rest up. I'll get someone to bring you some juice.

"Great," Josie said. "I love juice."

Josie lay back gingerly and assessed her mental state. The truth was, she was angry at Mrs. Yu—Josie had *liked* the woman and had begun to consider her a role model. Mrs. Yu was a fierce Asian business woman. Successful. Straight-forward. Protective. Josie had wanted Mrs. Yu for a mom, for a minute there. Now, lying in the hospital bed, Josie was nothing but...pissed off. She felt betrayed. Stupid. Vulnerable. And maybe sort of weepy, though she forced that urge down.

She lay back and closed her eyes for a minute, listening to the elegant *clink-clink* of Greta's knitting needles. Probably whittled from human femurs, Josie thought wickedly, and had to hide her smirk.

"I saw that," Greta said, and Josie immediately cleared her mind. *Think of mac-n-cheese. Meatloaf. Salami—no don't go there, too phallic. Ham sandwiches. Tacos—no, not there either.* Josie had always suspected that Greta had supernatural powers. Mind-reading was probably the least of them.

Josie sighed and flopped her hand on the mattress, jostling her IV, which stung. The white tape holding it in place pinched her skin. "So, you're probably wondering how I screwed up so badly," she started, her eyes locking on the ceiling. The florescent lights above were grouped in rectangles, in blocks. Someone had covered the one above her head with a transparent vinyl image of blue sky and white puffy clouds. *You know, in case you might never see the real thing again, which was...morbid.* "I'm sorry I wasn't able to protect your investment better," she continued. After all, that was the reason she was in San Francisco in the first place, to investigate the startup company for Greta. "I'm sorry you won't be able to recover your losses. Twenty thousand dollars is not a nice hit to take even if—"

"Five hundred thousand dollars," Greta said.

Josie felt the blood drain from her head. She'd read descriptions of this phenomenon happening to people before, but she'd never experienced it herself, other than tingling in her cheeks she sometimes got when she was about to do something stupid. "Wh-what did you say?" Her voice came out in a thready whisper, and she was glad she was lying down.

"Five hundred thousand," Greta repeated, the *clink-clink* of her knitting needles not missing a beat. "The initial investment I put into Applied Apps was five hundred thousand. With two later infusions of cash in bundles of twenty thousand each. That's probably what you are remembering." She stopped to count her stitches under her breath, moving those thin pinched lips that reminded Josie so much of a natural land formation, a crevice in the dry cracked desert ground. The click of her needles resumed, presumably because she had done it perfectly the first time. During this time, Josie was quietly forcing the bile back down into her stomach and quietly calculating how many years it would take to work off a debt like that. Technically it wasn't Josie's loss, but she certainly felt responsible.

"At least I saved you the last twenty," she croaked finally, running a hand with her scrubby nails across the faded hospital johnny. The roughness of her fingers snagged the thin cotton.

"On the contrary," Greta said, putting down her yarn. She reached for an envelope on the table beside her. She held it up between two strong, bony fingers for Josie to see the printed return address that showed through the cellophane window. "I've received a return of the full amount beginning from day one. When James Yu stopped by your room last night—incidentally, his fiancée is a patient at this same hospital and she's recovering well, I hear—he was quite alarmed to see me, naturally, since he was unaware of our association. He brought me this reimbursement within twelve hours. I'm not sure exactly how he has access to these funds, but now that my interest in him has reached its end, I'm no longer concerned."

⌘

Josie let that information rattle around her brain for a minute— honestly, it was probably echoing inside her skull at the moment, with not much else sinking in. The last bit registered, and she said, "Waitaminute, fiancée?"

Greta said nothing more about that, which left Josie to wonder how long James and Sasha had been engaged. Or was it just so that he could come see her in the hospital? Too many questions left unanswered. It was driving Josie crazy.

"And how did you get here so quickly?" she suddenly asked Greta. She was half-expecting her to say that she had been in California the whole time, monitoring Josie's movements. *It wasn't paranoia if people actually were out to get you, right?*

Greta looked unperturbed as she said, "I have a plane."

Of course she did. Josie stared at the fake clouds on the ceiling and flopped her arm on the bed. Like a fish out of water—her flopping hand, and her entire being as well. She was out of her element, ready to tuck her tail between her legs and run home. She flopped her hand one more time before giving up. "Well, at least we caught her—Cynthia Yu. With four witnesses to her confession, she should be locked up for a long time." Josie sighed at that and let her eyes slowly close.

Greta cleared her throat. "Well," she said, and nothing else.

Josie opened her eyes. She turned her head to look at her gray-faced benefactor with her pursed mouth. "What do you mean, 'well'?"

"It seems the San Francisco Police Department was unable to apprehend Mok Yee-Chun, whom you know as Cynthia Yu. She is, at this moment, *at large.*" Greta didn't look up from her knitting. She simply cast off and continued moving her needles.

What little was left of Josie's spirit plummeted to somewhere down near the base of her spine in the droopy hospital bed mattress. "She's getting away with it," she said aloud, although she didn't want to believe it.

Greta didn't respond to that either, which made Josie wonder if the other woman was already working on the problem. From her past encounters with Greta, Josie had learned that wealth and privilege allowed the older woman to take matters into her own hands and to serve justice however it suited her. Come to think of it, Josie was just like that, minus the wealth. And well, minus the privilege, too.

But, damn it all, wasn't Ivan Sorokin going to get justice for the loss of his life?

CHAPTER 44

Josie didn't even try to resist when Greta informed her that they would be flying home on Greta's privately chartered plane. The hospital was going to release her into the care of "her personal physician," which was Drew. Greta had somehow worked it all out without ever having met Drew. Josie had a sheaf of papers with her "wound care instructions." Which she would need because—wonder of wonders—she didn't even have stitches. What did that even mean? She didn't know. She couldn't even see her own shoulder.

The doctor at the hospital, an intelligent but devious-looking man named Dr. Rajagopal—Josie quietly rolled his name around her mouth a couple of times while she stared at her motionless cloud light—said that she was "extremely lucky indeed" that she had not needed surgery. Cynthia Yu's professional-grade kitchen knife had speared Josie above the right shoulder, missing anything vital, the knife going in and out cleanly. "It was lucky to be stabbed by a chef!" he added, his dark eyes sparkling with disturbing enthusiasm.

Sitting quiet as a wraith in her chair in a darkened corner of the hospital room, Greta Williams quirked a single thin, gray eyebrow, clearly not on board with the doctor's sense of humor.

"And chefs love their knives, so I'm sure it was clean and sharp," Josie agreed.

"And it is lucky that you were stabbed first and not Miss Petrovich, not the other way around," he continued. "For reasons which I cannot disclose due to the Privacy Act, this is another lucky happenstance. Let us simply say that one who has so much body ink is more likely to have blood that is not as clean as yours. If you know what I mean. Not that I have disclosed anything that might incur a lawsuit or any such breach of personal private information." Josie's eyes bugged out at that, which was something she definitely had not considered. Hopefully, James would get his blood tested *a-sap*, since she assumed he was intimate with Sasha, *his sweetheart.*

Dr. Rajagopal continued, "Your wound was inflicted cleanly with superior precision. In and out." He demonstrated with a cheerful face and a sharp hand motion. "The perpetrator could have been a surgeon. The blade went in about three inches just above your shoulder blade. For someone with your small frame, that is not insignificant. We're lucky again that nothing of importance was ripped or torn. A modicum more *oomph*, a couple inches deeper, and the blade would have emerged *right out the front of your torso.*" He clapped, as if that would have a been a fascinating sight to see.

Meanwhile, tiny dark spots floated in front of Josie's eyes, and her fingers uncontrollably grasped at the flimsy hospital blanket. Lucky? She was lucky she was already sitting down. For the amount of blood that she'd seen on this trip, she should have been more used to it. *But, no.* Still a wussy. For some reason, thinking about her own blood pouring out of her made it even worse.

"You do not even have any stitches," he continued. "Bonus! Very easy wound care, if you can get someone to help you reach it. Just keep it clean, and it should kind of suck back together." He made a slurping noise with his lips that got Josie again, right in the quease box.

"Great," she said weakly.

"Anyway," Dr. Rajagopal said, "It has been a pleasure being your physician, Miss Tucker. You were the perfect patient." He shook her hand.

"But I was unconscious most of the time," Josie said with a frown. She probably had a crease in the center of her forehead, as her dog did when she asked him philosophical questions about love, life, and the universe.

"Exactly," the doctor agreed with a white-toothed grin. "You remind me of my younger sister. Excessively feisty. Unconscious is preferable in some cases. Best of luck. Goodbye, madam," he said to Greta as he backed out of the room. Greta, it seemed, commanded respect even from the shadowy corners.

⌘

Once again—similar to the circumstances of her Arizona adventure—the incidental details of Josie's trip were tidied up without her participation. Her boxy green rental Kia was returned, the fruit on the front seat pitched out because it had spoiled in the warmth of the closed car. Which was a shame. Josie would have given her eyetooth for another perfectly ripened apricot like the one she had tasted that day. Her hotel room was paid for and closed out, her things packed up—she regretted that she would not get a chance to say goodbye to her black-market breakfast burrito dealer.

Detectives Lopez and Dicarlo stopped by as Josie was getting ready to leave the hospital, lowering herself into a wheelchair—which was ridiculous, but hospital policy. She'd been stabbed in the upper back, not in her legs. She was perfectly fine walking, but she had to ride out like a granny with a hip replacement. It was bad enough that she wasn't used to having people wait on her—it was even worse that she'd been injured enough lately that it had been happening more and more often.

"I'm real sorry we didn't get the bi—eeyotch," Dicarlo said, shaking her head, her small face puckered in a grimace, as they stood outside the limo that would take Josie and Greta to the airport. She smoothed a hand over her tight, blonde ponytail. "We have a warrant out, and we will get her. There's no way she's leaving the country without a thousand cops tackling her a—hindquarters."

Lopez wasn't saying much, just looking at Greta warily. Josie had never seen him so solemn, so straight-laced. His normally elastic face that bounced from one expression to the next was shuttered and placid—that freaky, inscrutable Charlie Chan thing again. She almost missed his flirting. Almost. He was hunched over, his lanky form bent, with his hands in his front pockets. However, Greta didn't say a word to him. She merely nodded, which Josie took to mean the two of them would speak together later, privately.

"Don't blame Lopez," Josie blurted out. "It's totally my fault. He tried to tell me to let them do their jobs. I couldn't mind my own business… kind of like right now."

He gave her an amused half-smile and gently squeezed her good shoulder with his big hand. He leaned down to give her a kiss on the cheek, unable to stop himself from whispering in her ear, "Call me, cupcake. I know you have my digits."

She rolled her eyes, but felt better as they helped her settle herself in the car. She watched the dirty roads go by on the way to SFO airport. The sky had finally turned into what everyone here called a typical gray Bay Area day. There was that quote attributed to Mark Twain about the "coldest winter he ever spent was a summer in San Francisco" although no one really knew if he was the one who said it. Josie understood what it meant now. With no sun, a true chill swept through her body, even as the leather seat under her began to warm up. As when she first arrived, standing with her back to the bay, shivering in her jeans jacket, the weather had nothing to do with the atmosphere of her mind. Which was…also cloudy.

Greta, who sat next to Josie on the bench in the backseat of the limo, had at last put away her knitting in her Chanel shoulder bag, the black quilted one with the gold chain straps that Josie had seen before. Her spine as ramrod straight as ever, her hose-covered legs crossed beneath her gray suit skirt, Greta was now fiddling with an outsized, shiny new smartphone playing, of all things, a Scrabble game. Josie wondered who her opponent was. She eyed Greta again. Though they'd had several face-to-face meetings, they'd never spent this much time together, and now they were travel companions. *Awkward.* Josie thought about it for a few more minutes. Actually, it wasn't awkward at all. It was surprisingly comforting.

Greta dug around in her massive bag. "Gum?" she said to Josie, who took a piece of the proffered Doublemint from its classic light green pack. She folded the long strip of gum into her mouth and gingerly leaned back on her good shoulder, her head facing the window. She may have heaved a big, self-condemning sigh.

"Here," Greta said with a business-like calmness, thrusting a large yellow envelope into Josie's lap. "This may make you feel better. Open it later when you're done feeling sorry for yourself."

CHAPTER 45

They had yet another wheelchair waiting for Josie, curbside at the airport. She protested, but Greta pointed out that they'd get to their private gate faster, which turned out to be true with an escort-slash-wheelchair-driver who power-walked as if he were trying out for an Olympic event. Before she knew it, they were in the correct place and ready to embark. Her wheelchair attendant, Mario Andretti, pushed her all the way down the bridge. They finally let her stand at the plane's door, at that weird gap between the plane and the retractable tunnel where she could see down to the ground—way, way down to the ground. Daylight was never a natural thing to see through a crack below her feet.

As she hauled her butt out of the hammock of the wheelchair, the jet bridge started shaking. She grabbed the arms of her wheelchair and fell back into it, pressing her bandaged shoulder against the vinyl back of the chair. Ahead of her, Greta inhaled sharply and stepped onto the plane, her two-inch high pumps moving with surprising speed. To Josie's dismay, the plane also trembled. The jet bridge rattled as if it were origami, a delicate folded paper. A piece of carry-on luggage tipped to its side. After a minute or two, the quake was over.

The pilot stood in the galley behind Greta, looking calm and competent. In his uniform, he was one of those square-jawed men that other people wrote books about. He would have looked at home with bullwhips and cargo planes and long-lost treasure. "Well, ladies," he said. "Looks like we had a minor shakeup. Everyone all right?"

Josie lurched out of the chair and pretty much jumped onto the plane. If the path to the aisle had been clear, she might have attempted to ninja-roll in, but Greta and the pilot blocked the way. She didn't use actual words, but she knew her face was hollering for him to get his butt back into the cockpit and take off as soon as humanly possible. Her heart was pounding as though she were in a Bruce Willis movie. Without the necessary survival skills.

"This whole place is out to get me," she mumbled as she was shown to her seat. She clicked her belt low and around her hips, shifting to the side so she didn't rub her hurt shoulder too much. While she waited for the tremor to leave her hands, the flight attendants made light jokes, *as if the ground shaking were an everyday occurrence.* Maybe it was for these people, but not for Josie. Eventually, she stopped gripping her armrest so hard that her fingers were falling asleep. Greta sat across the aisle from her. The plane wasn't all that fancy or new, and some other passengers were flying with them— but Josie was grateful to be on her way home.

By the time they took off and the city disappeared behind the clouds below them, her heart rate had returned to normal, so she focused on the thick envelope she still gripped in one hand. She flipped it over and undid the metal brad keeping the flap down. When she slid the packet out, it was upside down, so she turned it over. Across the top, the title on the first page said *Complaint for Annulment,* which made her brow wrinkle with confusion.

"What the—?" she flipped through the documents. One clause in particular caught her eye and throbbed on the page like a neon light. The check box next to it had been selected.

Voidable marriages

Your marriage is voidable if: One of the spouses did not have the mental capacity to consent to the marriage at the time. For example, a spouse may have been drunk or mentally ill.

Drunk. Yeah, that part stuck out like a particularly sore thumb to her. So that was why Greta had been asking about Josie's level of intoxication when she had gotten hitched in Vegas. Instead of making a moral judgment, Greta had been fishing for reasons to void Josie's quickie mistake marriage. But that didn't make the confession of drunkenness sit any better on Josie's conscience. She was still a world-class idiot.

Scanning farther down the page, Josie caught Joe Armstrong's hastily scrawled signature, the bold and loopy, yet oddly back-slanted, letters across the bottom of the page. She recognized it from the autographed headshot he used to keep of himself inside the top drawer of his desk at *The Daily News* back when they all had desks in an actual building. He said he kept the photos handy in case a fan happened to be passing through their grubby offices and requested it. Even thinking about that made her want to snort. But his signature on these papers? She'd mentioned a divorce to Greta... what...less than 48 hours ago?

"Is this even real?" she said running a finger over the signature before realizing she had spoken out loud accidentally. *Oops*. Greta gave her a look, but Josie wouldn't have been surprised to turn the page and find her own signature already in place where she was required to sign—her presence not even necessary. Greta was the Woman Who Got Crap Done.

Scanning the papers, Josie didn't recognize the official signatures, but she made a mental note to do internet searches on them as soon as she could—it would be helpful to know who Greta was...*acquainted* with. Judge William Tate. Father Michael Sanborn at St. Ann's Parish in Needham, that suburb of Boston that Josie thought was populated largely by doctors, college presidents, and retired Nobel Prize winners. She committed Judge Tate's and Father Michael's names to memory for future reference. In case she ever needed either an exorcism or a lenient sentence. File those names under *Good to Know*.

From across the aisle, Greta handed her an uncapped fountain pen—one of those pens with actual ink in them.

Josie signed on at the marked line and handed the whole sheaf back to Greta, who signaled the flight attendant over. She requested copies, which apparently, they could make on board. The plane probably had a full service Kinko's reproduction store in back. With a notary clerk in an apron.

"Do you know if there's a phone I can use on board?" Josie asked Greta.

"Do you have your cell phone?" Greta said.

"Can I use my phone during the flight?"

"Of course," Greta said, further proving to Josie that there existed an entirely different set of rules than the one that most people knew. She was beginning to get a better sense of them.

⌘

Josie wasn't sure what she was going to say to Drew. Improvisation rarely worked out for her. Having a plan, a scripted conversation from which she didn't deviate, was probably a better idea. She desperately needed to work on *how to plate it,* how to present it. But she needed to talk to him, to hear his voice. Yes, she was going to have to admit that she was once again the walking wounded due to her own carelessness, if a person could call getting stabbed in the back careless. That was neither here nor there. The fact was, she was hurt, and he was going to be pissed off about it.

He answered the phone with a sigh, which she heard loudly and clearly despite the hum of the plane's engines around her. *Not good.* "I already know what you're going to say," he said.

She dove into the conversation before he could shut her out, or even worse, hang up on her without having heard what she wanted to tell him. "I'm so, so sorry," she said. That had to be a good way to start, right? Especially since she didn't know which of the myriad things she'd done wrong he meant.

He sighed again—it wasn't an eye-rolling, passive-aggressive sigh *because she knew him,* and he didn't do that kind of thing. He was direct and get-to-the-point, what her dad would have called a straight-shooter, whatever that meant. *How could a person shoot on a curve?* Drew was the type of guy who followed the rules and didn't expect, but *hoped* other people would eventually discover that the only way to exist is to follow the rules. He strongly believed in the "lead by example" paradigm, in a non-pedantic kind of way. When he picked a candy wrapper up off the ground, he didn't *tsk-tsk* the person who missed the trashcan. He simply did it. When he told a patient to start exercising and stop eating so much junk food, he did it kindly, but sternly. Not with condescension—was it his fault that she never listened? *No, it was not.*

He was the white knight here in this scenario. Straight, strong, true, and admirable. Attractive. And she missed him.

"I can't do this anymore," he said.

CHAPTER 46

Before Josie hung up, she and Drew agreed that they had more hashing out to do that couldn't be done over a phone. At least it wasn't completely done. However, the rest of the flight was as long and as uncomfortable as a person who had an open wound on her back and a lump in her stomach could expect. Never mind her heart.

When the plane landed at Logan Airport—at a small private gate Josie had never known existed—she figured that Greta Williams would be good enough to spring for a ride to Josie's apartment. They had about a 20-minute ride on 28 going around Beacon Hill, following the Charles River toward Fenway. Storrow Drive, people called it. Greta's driver, Mr. Peepers—not his real name, which was Henry, but what Josie secretly called him—avoided the Mass Turnpike, which was just fine with Josie. She liked the roundabout curves they took around the downtown area. Besides, it gave her a little more time to think about how she was going to manage a one-armed, left-handed shower when she got home. She still had a bottle of pain pills from Dr. Rajagopal. She might actually have to use one just to get herself cleaned up.

To Josie's surprise, however, when they pulled up in front of her building, a walkup not too far from the Big Green Monster, Greta instructed Mr. Peepers to double-park and wait for her. Not in the slightest perturbed by the illegality of the situation, the little man put the hazard lights on, then leaped out of the limo to retrieve Josie's Army duffel from the trunk. He escorted them up the stairs to Josie's door, where he took the key from her. There was another awkward moment in which Josie had to force down the hysterical laughter while Greta stood with her sturdy black pumps on Josie's doormat, which read *Go away*. Then, he led them inside.

Josie's dog Bert lurched up awkwardly from his spot on the couch—where he knew he wasn't supposed to be—at their entrance. He lumbered across the room toward them, his whipcord tail knocking papers to the floor as well as bits of drywall off the battered walls. Josie greeted him in her normal silly voice reserved just for him, asking him if he missed her and if he knew who a good boy was. After a proper greeting, he turned to Greta. Josie was about to pull him back, but suddenly, Greta's thin, blue-veined hand came down tentatively on Bert's broad, bony head. She gave him a couple of smooth strokes, and to Josie's relief, the dog didn't snot on her stately benefactor's suit skirt.

"Well, thanks for seeing me up here," Josie said. Mr. Peepers had lugged Josie's bag all the way to the kitchen, where there was a stacked set of mini clothes washer and dryer. He looked like he was about to unlatch her bag and start a load of her dirties, so she said hastily, "I'll get that from here. Thank you, though." True, she had considerably fewer clothes than she'd left with, thanks to the loss of two of her favorite shirts, but she still didn't want a virtual stranger going through her undies.

"Do you want something to eat?" Greta asked. Her steely gray eyes flicked toward the kitchen. Josie seriously doubted there was anything edible left in there. She thought there might be a stale bag of tea in an improperly closed box, the store cellophane wrap haphazardly torn off from her last bout with her stomach. Otherwise, she suspected her refrigerator and shelves were as bare as she'd left them, unless the food fairy godmother had visited while Josie had been out of town.

"Uh, no. I'm fine, thanks," Josie said. She gazed at Greta while the other woman looked around the apartment—it probably appeared landfill-ready to a woman who was used to Aubussons and Louis XVI limited editions. Josie's tables were Target, circa 2007.

"Why don't you sit on the couch. I'll get you a pillow." Which was the last thing in the world Josie expected to hear Greta say. Wait on Josie, hand and foot? Fluff her pillows? This was too weird. Yet, she agreed to sit down and let Greta plump up a dingy couch cushion and set it behind her back, simply because she couldn't think of a faster way to get the woman out of her apartment...as grateful as Josie was.

Mr. Peepers had left the apartment to wait with the limo. No doubt, to flash some kind of Illuminati membership badge if any police officer tried to ticket him for double-parking. Josie was left eyeing Greta Williams, who stood in the center of Josie's small sitting room—dead plant still on the window sill—with her hands folded in front of her, looking a bit...out of place. Josie marveled at the sight, the likes of which she'd never witnessed before. Greta Williams stood as stiffly as a mannequin in a designer suit that had somehow found itself parked in a second-hand store or thrift shop.

Five minutes passed. Then ten. Josie had a couple of false starts. She nearly asked Greta if she had enjoyed her short stay on the West Coast. Josie certainly hadn't, other than a fun encounter with a new four-legged friend-slash-escape artist. Yes, she'd enjoyed Lupe, the burrito lady. And the Palacia de Fruta man who'd stuffed an apricot in her pie-hole. And, well, even her Pony Pagoda frenemies, though they'd taken an incriminating video of her dance.

And, yes, she had been stabbed, but she would be fine, right?

Right.

She would take a couple of days to get her bearings again. Rest up. Heal up more. Try to let go of her ticked-offedness at Mrs. Yu, who'd made the whole trip a mess, an epic fail, and killed a man in a psychotic rage. Josie figured it was time to pay a visit her real mother in the nursing home. Then, she'd call up Drew so they could have that talk he wanted.

She and Greta were saved from the torture of trying to make small talk by the apartment door swinging violently open. Bert yodeled his approval as Drew entered.

"Excellent," Greta said to him, collecting her handbag. "You've arrived. I'll be leaving now."

Just great.

⌘

Greta departed faster than a witch out of Oz, though it was

debatable which witch Greta was. Drew quickly rubbed Bert's head and then kneed him away gently before sinking onto the lumpy couch next to Josie.

Josie sighed, bracing herself to face the break-up speech head on, though avoidance was more her style.

"Let me see it," Drew said first, gazing at her with those dark eyes of which she was so fond.

She frowned. "See what?"

He shook his head with a rueful smile and leaned down so they were eye-to-eye. "Your shoulder, babe. I am your attending physician this evening."

"Oh," she said, and twisted around a tad trying not to re-injure herself. So that was why he'd come. Greta had released Josie into his care. Well, this was uncomfortable.

He peeled back the bandage with more care than the nurse who had put it on. The groan that came from his throat made her stomach squeeze, but also brought a frown to her face.

"What?" she said. "I'm sure you've seen worse."

He smoothed the bandage back on. He moved close to her ear until she felt his breath on her hair. "Yeah, but none of those other people were you." His fingers lingered on her shoulder.

She almost leaned into him then, but first she had to ask, to clear things up. "You said you couldn't do this anymore. I thought that meant you were done with us."

He groaned again, his fingers suddenly tightening on her skin. "Shit. I didn't mean *that*. I just meant that every time you go off on one of these trips, you say you're going to be careful and follow the rules and take care of yourself. I know now that's impossible for you. So, I don't want to make you promise stuff that isn't realistic. I worry about you when you're out there causing trouble, and I have to find some other way to deal with it."

"Oh," she said, with the blood rushing around her head, in her ears and in her cheeks. "That's a relief." *Understatement of the century.*

"I don't know what I'd do if I lost you, but I have to face it, to make some kind of peace with it. You stir up bad shit all the time. *It's what you do.* I don't like it—because you're mine—but at some point I'm going to have to realize this is you. This is what you do, and I want you to know that I'm here to put you back together again." His doctor side was battling his boyfriend side—she appreciated that about him. She liked it that he cursed when he was upset. She liked pretty much everything about him.

Josie's vision may have blurred a bit. "Does that mean you're going to be my nurse, too, for a while?" She cleared her throat, retreating from the emotional overload, hiding behind humor.

"You want a bath?" he said, stroking her neck, pushing her crazy hair to one side. Her eyelids started a slow descent, too heavy to remain open.

"A...what?"

"To get clean," he said, one dark eyebrow raised. Very *GQ*. Very *Men's Health.*

⌘

Drew wasn't in a kidding mood about the bath. Nor was he in a mood for playing around either, which was kind of a shame. But her tub was too small for more than one runty-sized adult, so she had a soak alone, propped up so that her shoulder was not submerged. She almost fell asleep, but he wouldn't let her, coming in with a fluffy clean towel a while later. He wound one towel around her chest, low enough to avoid her wound. A second towel went over her head, gently wrapping the wet strands she had managed to wash one-handed, and held them to the side. The towels smelled fresh, not stale from her cabinet.

"You...did laundry?" she said, tilting her head to look back at him.

"You had a deplorable lack of fabric softener and dryer sheets."

She rubbed her cheek in the towel that covered his hand. "It smells good." She could detect his fresh, clean scent as well, and that was even better.

He took the towel from her hair and used it to gently pat her neck, her shoulders, and upper back, showing extra care with her hurt places. His hands lingered on her skin, and she knew he would take it further if she let him. They needed to clear the air about a few things first, so she reached for her clothes, which were neatly folded in a stack on the bathroom counter.

His fingers hesitated, and then he left the room to let her dress.

CHAPTER 47

A bit later, she found Drew sitting on the couch. He was watching TV, but it was muted. When she sat next to him, she realized he was taking a call, talking about dosages and drug interactions with a pharmacist. She waited silently until he finished, and then she handed him the envelope that Greta had prepared for her. Josie had taken the time to dress it up with a self-stick purple bow.

"What's this?" he said.

She didn't say anything, just gave a little shrug. She'd already apologized—more than once now—and it felt like the more she said she was sorry, the more her sincerity would seem diluted to him.

He slid the annulment papers out, first reading the heading as Josie had done, then slowly flipping through each one, reading them carefully. Then he set them on his lap and said, very softly, "Thank you."

"It's probably not enough," she said, staring at her chewed-up nails.

"It's good," he said. "We're good."

She looked at him then—really looked at him—at his dark eyes, which were looking right back at her. They were *good*. He'd been interrupted on the phone a couple days earlier when he said he had a question to ask her—would they ever be that good again?

"I read on the plane to San Francisco that opposites don't attract as often as people think they do. That something like 40% of men look for a mate who's similar to them, both in looks and personality. I haven't been able to stop thinking about that. I mean, I can't stop looking at every couple I see walking down the street. Some of them look like siblings." She stopped to clear her throat because she had gotten off track as she often did when she was nervous. "Anyway. I want to say how lucky I know I am that it's not that way for you. That you chose me anyway." She looked at him, his broad jaw that was so different from her rounder face, and his dark coloring that was still lighter than hers. "I'm so lucky—"

His mouth came down on hers. The papers fluttered to the floor as his arms went around her waist, lifting her onto his lap. Their tongues met, slid against each other, pulled away, and then went back together again. This was what she had missed so much being away from him, both the physical and emotional closeness.

Soft noises came from her throat, and they both lost their breath. His fingers worked at the buttons on her pajama top. She tried to lift off his t-shirt working from the front, and their hands tangled together. They separated, like-minded, and removed their own tops. His eyes darkened as he looked at her, the corner of his mouth lifting. His appreciation lit her up, and she ran her hands down his shoulders, down his arms. He leaned toward her, pressing his lips to her breast, and she put her arms around his neck, holding him closer, letting him drive her slowly crazy with his mouth.

"You are so soft, so beautiful," he said, and at that minute, she believed him.

She smiled, then gasped as he stood up. She nearly slid down the front of him before he caught her, but not before she felt him between her legs. "I want you so much," she said, putting her mouth to that silky patch of skin behind his ear. She'd been thinking about this for days.

He groaned and took them into her bedroom. She braced for the impact of landing on her back, but he never wavered in his consideration for her hurt shoulder—he sat down, keeping her balanced across his thighs. When he lay back, and she braced her hands on either side of his head on...soft, washed new fabric that she didn't recognize.

"New sheets?" she said on a throaty moan of pleasure that would have embarrassed her under any other circumstances.

He broke away, panting. "Yeah...uh. Yeah, I wanted to ask you about that."

Ask? As in *question*? *The* question? She pulled away from his neck, where she'd been tasting his skin. *She'd been worrying about sheets for the past few days?* She wanted to slap herself upside the head. Could she have blown the whole thing more out of proportion?

She swallowed. "I...uh...think they are nice?"

"Well, good," he said with that side smile she liked so much. "Because they're ours." He watched her face for a reaction. But he also bumped his hips into hers accidentally, which took away her ability to think for a minute or two longer. Suddenly, she understood what he'd said.

"You're...moving in?" She couldn't stop the smile that had started to spread across her face.

His hips pushed against hers again, showing her it hadn't been an accident the first time. "Exactly what I've always wanted," he said. "A half-naked woman in *my* bed."

He reached for the nightstand drawer, opening it to pull a condom from a box that hadn't been there before. "I figured the hospital stay messed up your chance to take your pill," he said when she looked confused. She was amazed he'd thought of it. Then they were pushing down his waistband. She lifted up just enough to let him shove his pants to his knees, but she stood up anyway to slither out of her pajama pants. Then she climbed back on him, and they slid together.

"Wait," she said, reveling in the first sensation of it.

"That's my line," he said, his breathing shallow. He grasped the back of her neck, his other hand on her lower back, and he started to move.

⌘

"You should walk around naked all the time, babe," he said the next morning. They were standing in the kitchen, each of them wearing only lounge pants. She was twisting her neck, trying to see the wound on her shoulder, to which he was about to apply a fresh bandage.

"What does it look like?" She wanted to know.

"You'd be disappointed. It's a two-inch cut that probably won't even leave a decent battle scar. I know it hurts more than it looks like it should. I saw the scans of how deep it goes." She wasn't surprised to hear that he'd already looked at her medical records. He probably had them memorized. She actually didn't mind—it made her feel like they were on a team, in a weird, twisted way. "By the way, Susan dropped off a dress for you that won't touch your cut. She said it was strapless, which sounds pretty awesome to me."

"A dress for...?" Josie wasn't in the habit of wearing girly clothes. The last time she'd worn a dress had been for a wedding that had ended badly. However, Drew was looking at her with amusement, so she slowly leaned to the side—subtly, she thought—until she could see the calendar hanging on her fridge. Today's date showed an entry for just two hours from now, she realized with a glance at the clock on the microwave, which said *Giovanna's Christening*. Baby GiGi was Drew's newest niece. "...The christening. I mean, *of course* for it," she fudged. Badly.

He chuckled and smacked her lightly on the tush as she hurried out of the kitchen to find the dress her BFF, Susan—who didn't hate her, *yay*—had left for her. The dress was cut above the knee, strapless with a built-in bra thingy, which was good because Josie didn't have a strapless bra anywhere. Susan must have known that. Josie dialed her thoughtful friend while she pulled on the dress.

"How's the color?" Susan said immediately. The color of the dress, in fact, was a lovely orange-red color, like a fiery tulip, and looked amazing with Josie's golden skin tone. "You've performed a miracle," Josie said, and she should practically hear Susan preening on the other end of the line.

"I also left you my ecru cashmere sweater in case the church is cold. Do you have shoes to match? I should have brought you some shoes, too, shouldn't I have? Drat."

"No, no. I have shoes."

"Not the teal ones from the wedding, right?" Susan said, carefully. Josie had, in fact, been eyeing the teal ones from Leann's wedding. However, there was a drool stain on the right toe that made Josie narrow her eyes at Bert, who lay in the corner of the room on a…new dog bed, clearly purchased in her absence. He sighed heavily as if his new cushion could in no way replace his favorite mountain of her dirty laundry, even though his bed looked like it was made from NASA-developed memory foam and covered with lush sheepskin.

"Don't look at me," Josie told him. "Your new daddy is a doctor. You're living the high life now. Suck it up and pretend to like it."

"Wear the brown leather Mary Janes with the embroidered toe," Susan directed. "They have enough heel to look awesome with the length of that dress. It's perfect, right?"

Josie dug the shoes out of her closet, as commanded, "Really perfect," she assured her friend. She meant it. "I owe you. In more ways than one. I'm sorry I let you down—"

"Shut. Up," Susan said, saving them both before Josie got maudlin. Stupid pain pills. "You saved me from a bad relationship. Can you imagine if I had that woman for a mother-in-law?"

They were both silent for a minute, contemplating the horror.

"All right," Josie said. "Also, I got stabbed, so we're even."

"Totally even," Susan said.

CHAPTER 48

As a special treat, Drew commandeered Josie after the christening. He took her to Boston Chinatown for lunch, to a dim sum parlor near Beach Street that was famous for its black bean sauce snails. She'd already explained about dim sum meaning "heart's delight" and being a gift between two ancient lovers. He'd been a trooper to try slurping the snails and had even insisted he liked them. For some reason, she was feeling off today, unsettled about the whole meal. She definitely wasn't up to her usual form, not ribbing him as much as she normally would have. Today, as they waited in line for a table out in the sunshine, he put a hand on her lower back while they leaned against the iron rail of the restaurant steps.

He said in her ear, "I love this part of you. This part right here. When you're lying on top of me and I put my hand right on it, your skin feels like velvet." He stood up straight, but kept his hand there, gently stroking her, back and forth.

She knew her cheeks were flushed as she looked up at him, trying to keep the dazed expression off her face. She took his big hand, rough from frequent washing with harsh soap from the hospital, and held it tightly, blinking at the ground for a second or two. She often didn't do well with *feelings*, but even she knew they were having a special time right now that she would want to remember for the rest of her life. She unlocked her smartphone because someone might as well take their picture and make it a real moment. Here she was, on a dim sum date with her boyfriend. She was even wearing a dress, for crying out loud.

When she turned back to look at him again, she inadvertently locked eyes with a woman waiting outside the rival dim sum restaurant across the street. Her hands uncontrollably gripped tighter, squeezing both Drew's hand and her phone. Something clicked. The woman had bright red, dyed hair. Thick black-rimmed designer glasses—those were new—because, as God was Josie's witness, the woman staring back at her was Cynthia Yu.

⌘

"It couldn't have been her," Josie said later, still breathing erratically, when they were back at her apartment—*at their apartment*. Now that Drew had a key, it was his place, too. They would start moving his stuff in little by little over the next couple of weeks while the lease on his place ran out. Her apartment was smaller, but the location was prime. "Why would she be in Boston?" Cynthia Yu had no reason to be in Josie's city, even if she were in hiding. The woman had turned away and had been lost on the crowded street. But then—*oh, no*—Josie remembered her mentioning a younger sister here. Maybe her mind wasn't playing tricks on her, conjuring up the very woman who had stabbed her in the back…

Josie got out her phone, turning it over and over between her hands, unsure who to call.

She was having second and third doubts. *It couldn't have been her, could it have been?*

"Not all Chinese people look alike," Drew said solemnly, but with a slight tease to his voice. He knew she was upset, and he was trying to ease her discomfort as they often did for each other, with humor. She cocked an eyebrow at him.

"Very funny. Don't go confusing me with any other Asian girl," she said. But she was doubting herself.

As she ducked her head to look at her phone, she had the sudden realization that she was showing him the top of her head, just as James Yu had often done to her. She hated having a phone, but it was becoming more and more of a necessary evil. Even for her, the self-proclaimed technophobe.

With a sigh, she started to scroll through her contacts, looking for someone to call, hoping to find someone before she came to Greta's name. She unlocked her phone and found herself staring at the camera app, at the picture she had inadvertently taken of the red-haired woman, the woman Josie had sworn was Cynthia Yu. "Crap," Josie said.

Since owning her phone, she'd never—not once—successfully taken a non-blurry photo despite all of the camera's built-in auto-focus features. However, this particular photo was crisp as a high def widescreen movie. Without a doubt, it was Cynthia Yu.

Josie thought about her options, what to do about the woman she had admired who had severely disappointed her. Josie had been duped. She had nearly adopted the woman as a role model, a surrogate mother more or less. She had been swindled into respecting her, if only for a few afternoons.

Unless you subscribe to the idea of reincarnation, you are given only one life. How you chose to use it is a measure of your character.

Josie thought about her own mother, who lived not only within the four walls of a nursing home, but within the confines of a ruthless disease. Dementia made those boundaries move relentlessly closer together every week. Yet the early days that Josie had spent with her crazy, laughing mother with her silky, dark hair still remained precious. She hoped that they had made the most of them.

In the bedroom, she sat heavily on the edge of the bed with its new, soft sheets. She had kicked off her sandals and was probably wrinkling her new dress that she actually might wear again someday, even after her shoulder wound healed. She touched the picture on her phone again before the screen could go dark. She sat for some time, contemplating the nature of duty, the weight of neglected responsibility, and the right of the injured to seek justice. After a while, she sent the photo in a text message to Greta Williams with a brief explanation, including the time and location.

She sat for a minute or two longer, but there was no response.

With great deliberation, Josie removed her dress and hung it up in the closet, where she had, one-by-one, been weeding through her clothes, taking care to hang up the ones she still wanted, even if they were simple t-shirts and old jeans. She pulled on a pair of exercise pants and a soft shirt that didn't rub her bandage. After that, she gently pushed all of her hangers to the right, so that they took up exactly half of the small closet leaving a big bare space for Drew's clothes. Probably, he would need more space than that. His professional clothes for work—his doctor costume—couldn't be wrinkled and needed to be dry-cleaned. She'd figure out how to deal with that later.

Fifteen minutes later, there was still no response from Greta, and Josie was wondering if she had done the right thing. She typed another message to Greta: "Should I contact police?" but didn't send it. Her finger hovered over the green button.

What would Greta do?

Twice now, Josie had suffered bodily harm while running errands for the woman. By Josie's calculations, Greta had paid both debts in full, with money, more, and now, with the annulment. And yet, Josie knew full well that Greta would continue to pay, no matter what Josie asked. She knew the depth of this commitment by the way the woman had sat by her side at the hospital. They had an arrangement, a bond that defied description, a *familial* relationship that Josie had never in her life experienced before.

Greta had proven time and time again that she didn't play by the rules, especially the minor, insignificant ones *like laws*. Though she might have government officials in her Louis Vuitton pocket, including police, Greta might not make use of them in this case. Or would Greta employ the unofficial people on her payroll to take care of this particular matter? In other words, would she send men to kill Cynthia Yu?

The question was, did Josie care? Deep inside, did she already know this answer to this before she sent Greta the photo this afternoon? Were Josie's hands as soiled as a murderer's for sending that message?

⌘

That evening, Drew ordered Thai food delivered—it wasn't officially delivery, but the restaurant was right down the street. They were fans of Josie's column, so they didn't mind sending their busboy

Priyun, also called Brian, up the block with Josie's order. Drew called it a perk of being the boyfriend of a food critic-slash-blogger.

They sat on the sofa flipping through TV channels, looking for something decent while they ate out of the delivery boxes—one fork stuck in each box, trading the boxes with each other but leaving the forks in them so the sauces didn't get mixed. They finally settled on a superhero show about a rich guy who turned into a green-hooded vigilante at night.

Perfect.

The exact moment the hero punched the living daylights out of this week's bad guy and delivered his patented motto in growly sotto voce, Josie's phone buzzed with a new message.

She wiped her hand on her pants, not that they were messy from dinner, but rather from sweating with anxiety. She glanced at Drew, but he was chewing and staring raptly at the television. She surreptitiously keyed in her screen code and touched the new message symbol. Holding her phone by the side of her leg, she read the words and swallowed the mouthful of food that had suddenly turned tasteless in her mouth. Her stomach churned.

The message from Greta said, simply, "It's taken care of."

⌘

Woman, 54, victim of fatal pedestrian accident in Chinatown

BOSTON, Ma. — Police are investigating a deadly accident involving a pedestrian in Chinatown. The coroner says the victim, 54-year-old Mok Yee-Chun, a tourist from California, was hit as she crossed the street on Saturday night near the intersection of Washington and Lagrange Streets in Chinatown. Police say the woman was not in a crosswalk and the area was poorly lit at the time.

In the past two years, nearly 5,000 people have been injured or killed by cars while walking in Massachusetts, according to MassDOT.

ABOUT THE AUTHOR

EM Kaplan's first real job was as a technical writer in Cupertino, California, but she's been writing fiction since fifth grade. Other awesome jobs she's held have included brain study lab rat, exam proctor for a course on human sexuality, and exotic bird feeder. She now lives in Illinois with her husband, author JD Kaplan, their two kids, and their dog Max, a.k.a. the officemate.

Visit www.JustTheEmWords.com to discover Em's other online hangouts and blog, sign up for a non-spammy newsletter, and see upcoming events.

OTHER BOOKS BY EM KAPLAN

Mystery
The Bride Wore Dead, A Josie Tucker Mystery

Fantasy
Unmasked